Hands shaking, Mia sprayed the water vigorously, but there was simply not enough flow to combat the hungry fire.

She retreated to the front porch, skin stinging from the poisonous air.

Dallas appeared at the upstairs window. He shouted something to Mia, but she could not understand. The fire was nearly upon her, heat scalding her face and hands, smoke filling her lungs. She backed farther away, praying the fire engine would arrive soon to douse the flames.

Finally, Dallas came out carrying Cora and led her away from the burning house.

Mia put her cheek to the woman's mouth, praying for a reassuring puff of air. Panic swirled through her veins as she felt nothing at all. Starting CPR, she pressed her hands to Cora's chest.

"Come on, Cora," she said. "You're not going to leave me now."

Dallas dropped to his knees and performed the rescue breaths at the end of her compression cycles. After a full minute, Dallas checked Cora's pulse.

He shook his head.

Tears trickled down Mia's cheeks as she began the next cycle.

Dana Mentink
and

USA TODAY Bestselling Author

Margaret Daley

Deadly Risk

Previously published as *Flood Zone* and *To Save Her Child*

LOVE INSPIRED
INSPIRATIONAL ROMANCE

LOVE INSPIRED®

INSPIRATIONAL ROMANCE

ISBN-13: 978-1-335-42460-0

Deadly Risk

Copyright © 2021 by Harlequin Books S.A.

Flood Zone
First published in 2014. This edition published in 2021.
Copyright © 2014 by Dana Mentink

To Save Her Child
First published in 2015. This edition published in 2021.
Copyright © 2015 by Margaret Daley

Love Inspired
22 Adelaide St. West, 40th Floor
Toronto, Ontario M5H 4E3, Canada
www.Harlequin.com

Printed in U.S.A.

CONTENTS

Dana Mentink is a nationally bestselling author. She has been honored to win two Carol Awards, a HOLT Medallion and an RT Reviewers' Choice Best Book Award. She's authored more than thirty novels to date for Love Inspired Suspense and Harlequin Heartwarming. Dana loves feedback from her readers. Contact her at danamentink.com.

FLOOD ZONE

Dana Mentink

Trust in the Lord with all your heart;
do not depend on your own understanding.
Seek his will in all you do,
and he will show you which path to take.
—*Proverbs 3:5*

To my Mike, who is always there through the floods.

ONE

Forget meeting tonight. Must speak to you and Dallas now. URGENT.

Mia risked another peek at the cell phone screen as she guided her battered Toyota up the steep mountain grade to Cora's country house just after six in the evening. She'd thought Cora's proposed after-hours meeting at the medical clinic where they both worked was odd in the first place. Now the message to cancel. Stranger still. But Cora had been acting oddly, excusing herself to take phone calls, peeping into file folders squirreled away in her desk for weeks. On this particular day, Cora had left at lunch time. Strange.

Her gaze darted to the rearview mirror. Dallas Black drove his truck behind her. Something about the tall, tousle-headed rebel made her stomach flip, no matter how sternly she chided herself.

Look what the last dark-eyed charmer did to you, Mia.

Stuffing that uncomfortable thought back down into the secret place where she kept all her worries, Mia focused on navigating the winding, wet road, finally pulling onto Cora's graveled drive. Dallas got out, long and lean in jeans and a T-shirt, a couple of months overdue for a haircut. Somehow, the hair spidering across his face suited him, refusing to play nicely.

She knew he'd finished patching Cora's roof only the day before, while on break from teaching Search and Rescue classes. He'd been there every weekend for the past month or two working when the rain let up. While Dallas banged on the roof, Mia and her young daughter, Gracie, helped Cora organize closets. Cora insisted the little group take a long dinner break together every evening during which even Juno, Dallas's German Shepherd, got his share of fragrant stew. What Dallas got out of the deal, besides some pocket change and women chatter, she had no clue. Surely, he didn't need the money that badly. *Maybe he's just a nice guy, Mia. Maybe,* her suspicious heart echoed mockingly. *Yeah, and maybe you were happy to see him every weekend just to admire his roofing skills.* Never mind. They were almost done organizing closets, and then she could put Dallas safely out of her thoughts.

The residence was at the back of a large property, a good acre of shrubland screened it from the road. It was cool, the May rain puddling the already saturated ground. It was to be a bad storm season in Colorado, talk of floods coming. It made her long for Florida's mild climate, but she'd never return there. *Ever.*

Juno hopped out, nose twitching.

"Stay out of the mud, dog," Dallas advised.

Mia joined him.

"Ideas regarding what Cora needs to talk about?" he asked.

"No." Mia shook her head. "She's been secretive

lately, spending extra hours at the clinic. I almost got the feeling she might be lying to me about something."

They looked at Juno who had busied himself snuffling through the underbrush until he froze. Mia thought at first that he'd caught the scent of a bird or groundhog. Then she got it, too. The acrid tang of smoke as she took a few steps toward the house.

Dallas sprinted up the drive with Mia right behind him. They cleared the thickly clustered cottonwood trees in time to hear the whoosh of breaking glass when the lower story window exploded. Mia nearly skidded into him as the shards rained down on the muddy ground.

Her mind struggled to process what was happening. He gripped her arms, and she saw the tiny reflected flames burning in his chocolate irises. "Call for help. Keep Juno out."

Mia's hands shook so badly she could barely manage to hold on to both the phone and Juno's collar. The dog was barking furiously, yanking against her restraining arm in an effort to get to his owner. Nearly eighty pounds of muscle, Juno was determined, and he definitely did not see her as the boss.

Frantically, she dialed the emergency number. Tears started in her eyes as she realized she was not getting a signal. The tall Colorado mountain peaks in the distance interfered. She would have to move and see if she could find another spot that would work. Dragging Juno with one hand, she made her way back toward the car. They'd only gotten about ten feet when Juno broke loose from her grasp and ran straight for the burning house.

"Juno, stop!" she yelled. The smoke was now roiling through the downstairs, and she'd lost sight of Dallas. There was no choice but to keep trying to find a place to make the call. Three times she tried before she got a signal.

"Please help," she rasped. "Cora Graham's house on Stick Pine Road is on fire."

The dispatcher gave her a fifteen minute ETA.

Her heart sank. They could both be dead in fifteen minutes. She stowed the phone in her pocket and ran to the front porch where she remembered there was a hose Cora used to water her patches of brilliant snapdragons. The wood of the old house crackled violently, letting loose with a spark every now and then that burned little holes through the fabric of her jacket. One started to smolder, and she slapped a hand to snuff it out. Flames flashed out the first-floor windows. Juno barked furiously, dashing in helpless fits and starts, unsure how to get to his master.

She cranked the hose and squirted the water at the open front door. *Where are you, Dallas?* Inside, the flames had spread through the sitting room, enveloping the oak furniture in crackling orange and yellow. She climbed up the porch steps, dousing the wood with water and forcing her way into the entry, past the spurts of flame.

She sprayed the water vigorously, but there was simply not enough flow to combat the hungry fire. She retreated to the front porch, skin stinging from the poisonous air.

Dallas appeared at the upstairs window. He shouted something to Mia, but she could not understand. The fire was nearly upon her, heat scalded her face and hands, smoke filling her lungs. She backed farther away, praying the fire engine would arrive soon to douse the flames.

There was no welcoming wail of sirens.

She scanned the upper story and once again caught sight of Dallas. He was batting at the flaming curtains with a blanket. She saw a way she could help. Climbing a few feet up an ivy-covered trellis allowed her to stretch the hose far enough that she could train the water on the burning fabric. Dallas jerked in surprise and then disappeared back inside, returning a moment later with Cora in his arms and stepping onto the roof. Mia's heart lodged in her throat as she watched Dallas walking on the precariously pitched shingles with his precious burden.

His feet skidded, and he fell on his back, somehow stopping his slide before he fell over the edge. Mia jumped off the trellis and cast the hose aside. "Here, lower her down to me."

It was an awkward process, but Dallas managed to ease Cora low enough that Mia could grab her around the waist. Staggering under the weight, she tottered backwards until Dallas jumped down and they both carried Cora away from the burning house. Juno raced behind them to a flat spot of grass where they laid the old woman. Dallas ordered the dog to stay.

Mia brushed sooty hair away from Cora's forehead. Her sparkling blue eyes were closed, her mouth, slack. She put her cheek to Cora's mouth, praying for a reassuring puff of air. Panic swirled through her veins as she felt nothing at all. Starting CPR, she pressed her hands to Cora's chest.

"Come on, Cora," she said. "You're not going to leave me now."

Dallas dropped to his knees and performed the rescue breaths at the end of her compression cycles. After a full minute, Dallas checked her pulse.

He shook his head.

Tears trickled down Mia's cheeks as she began the next cycle. "You haven't finished learning Italian," she said to Cora. "You're only on lesson three, and that's not going to be enough if you want to go to Rome." Another set of compressions and rescue breaths.

This time she didn't allow herself to look at Dallas. Cora was going to live. Shoulders aching she pressed with renewed vigor. "And your nephew is happily married in Seattle. He's not going to want to come and take care of this sprawling old place, isn't that what you always said, Cora?"

Sirens pierced the air and a fire truck appeared through the smoke, rumbling up the grade, followed by an ambulance. Mia did not slow her efforts.

"You wake up right now, do you hear me? I mean it. I told you over and over not to keep those silly scented candles in your bedroom. They did not keep away the mosquitos, no matter what you say. You wake up so I can chew you out properly." Tears dripped from her face and cleared spots of black from Cora's forehead.

The medics ran over, but stopped short when Juno barked at them until Dallas quieted him. They pushed forward, eyeing the big dog suspiciously, and edged Mia out of the way.

"I have to stay with her," she pleaded.

Dallas drew her back, his voice oddly soft. "They've got it, Mia. Let them work."

"But…"

He gently, but firmly, took her arm and moved her several yards distant from the paramedics.

She breathed in and out, forcing herself to stop crying. "I'm okay, I'm okay," she repeated, waving him away when he came close.

Dallas stood there, long muscled arms black with soot, the edges of his hair singed at the tips, looking at her until she couldn't stand it anymore. "What is it? What are you thinking?"

Dallas didn't answer.

"Please tell me." She moved closer, the dark pools of his eyes not giving away anything.

Dallas considered. "I wasn't sure what type of service dog Juno would be. Before I trained him in Search and Rescue, a buddy of mine had a go at making him a drug-sniffing dog, but Juno doesn't obey anyone but me, so he flunked out. Mastered only the first lesson."

"What are you saying?"

He pulled a plastic pill bottle from his pocket. "These were on the bedside table. Do you know what she takes them for?"

Mia took the bottle and held it up to the light from the engines. "It's her blood pressure medication. I pick up her prescriptions myself."

Dallas frowned.

Mia felt the seeds of dread take hold deep down. She put her hands on Dallas's unyielding chest. "Dallas, please tell me what you're thinking."

"The first lesson, the only one that Juno mastered…"

She found she was holding her breath as he finished.

"Was alerting on drugs…like cocaine."

Dallas mentally berated himself for mentioning Juno's behavior at that moment. Mia was already trembling as the shock of what had happened settled in.

Should've waited. How many times had he said that to himself?

This time he did not allow her to pull away when he

folded her in a smoky embrace. She was so small, so slight in his arms, and he resisted the urge to run his hands along her shoulders. He thought of all the things he should say, the comforts he could whisper in her ear, but everything fled, driven away by the feel of her. She stiffened suddenly, and he wondered if she'd been hurt in the fire.

"There," Mia gasped, pointing behind the house.

He turned in time to see a woman with a wild tangle of red hair framed by the trees that backed the property. She stood frozen for a moment, eyes wide and face soot-stained and then she bolted into the woods.

"Stop," Dallas called, and he and Juno took off into the trees, Mia stumbling along behind.

"Who was that?" she asked, panting.

He didn't know.

"I thought I saw her outside the clinic one time, talking to Cora, but I'm not sure," Mia said.

A cursory search yielded nothing, though the falling rain and smoke didn't help. After a short time, they left off looking to follow the ambulance to the hospital.

In the waiting room, Mia sat on a hard-backed chair, and Dallas paced as much as the narrow hallway would allow until the doctor delivered his news. "I'm sorry. She didn't make it."

Dallas watched the spirit leak out of Mia as she put her head in her hands. Something cut at him, something deeper than the grief at Cora's death. He swallowed hard and stepped aside with the doctor. "Do you have a cause of death?"

The physician, whose name tag read Dr. Carp, hesitated. "She was dead upon arrival, but we called the police immediately after you told us about the pills.

They took possession of them. Autopsy will be later this week." That much Dallas already knew as he and Mia had told their story to a young uniformed cop named Brownley.

The doctor left and Dallas sat next to Mia. He didn't speak. There was nothing to say anyway. Best to wait until she could articulate the thoughts that rolled across her face like wind sweeping through grass. Finally, he took her hand, hoping she would not yank it away. She didn't.

"Cora wanted to tell us something, something important," Mia said, her voice wobbling as she clutched his fingers. "Can you guess anything at all about what it was?"

Dallas shook his head. "No."

"I'm sure Juno was wrong about the pills," she said, a tiny pleading note to her voice. "Those were for her blood pressure. I delivered them to her myself. They couldn't have hurt her. Could they?"

He covered her hand with his palm. "Whatever this is, however it went down, was not your fault."

"That woman… Who was she?" Her brown eyes were haunted. "Dallas…" she whispered. "I'm scared."

He pulled her to her feet then and embraced her because he did not know the words to say. He never did, probably never would. "I'm taking you home."

A short, balding man with a thick, silvered mustache came close. "In a minute. I'm Detective Stiving, Ms. Verde, and I need to ask you some questions."

Dallas felt his gut tighten. Stiving. Perfect.

He and Stiving had been oil and water since Dallas had butted in on a missing-person's case and found a

teen lost near Rockglen Creek whom Stiving had insisted was a runaway.

"Kid's a loose cannon," Stiving had insisted. "Drinks
and parties like his father."

Runaway or lost, Dallas and Juno found the kid
named Farley who'd fallen into a ravine, and the press
was there to catch it. Since then, Dallas had gotten a
bogus speeding ticket and been stopped twice by Stiving for no particular reason. Not good, but in a small
town like Spanish Canyon, Stiving was it.

"Doc says you're making allegations about drugs,"
Stiving said, holding up the bottle of pills nestled in
an evidence bag. "Looking to get some more publicity
for yourself?"

"Juno alerted on that pill bottle."

"Juno is a drug-sniffing flunk-out, from what I've
heard. I thought his forte was tracking down idiots who
get lost in the woods."

Mia wiped her sleeve across her cheeks. "What kind
of talk is that for a law enforcement officer?" she said
indignantly. "Cora is…was a long-time resident of this
town. I should think you'd want to be thorough investigating her death."

His blue eyes narrowed, face blotching with color.
"Yes, Ms. Verde, I will. I started by running a check
on you. It made for interesting reading. Since you've
had such a long and storied history with law enforcement, I guess you'd know that I'll be contacting you for
follow up information as soon as I get this to the lab."

Mia went white and then red.

Dallas clenched his jaw. *Don't mouth off to the cops,
Dallas.* "We saw a woman with red hair running away
from the house."

Stiving blinked. "Really? Did you recognize her?"

Mia shook her head. "She might have come to the clinic to talk to Cora, but I'm not sure. I only saw her for a moment."

"And you?"

Dallas shrugged.

"Right. Well, we'll investigate that while we're checking into things." The detective's phone rang, and he walked away to answer it and then left abruptly.

Mia put a hand on Dallas's wrist, her fingers ice cold. "I have to go. Tina needs to get home, and I want to read Gracie a story before bed." She looked at her soiled clothes. "It will take some explaining about why I look like this." Her lip trembled. "I'll need to tell Gracie about Cora."

He wondered how a woman with filthy hair, torn clothes and a grief-stained face could look so beautiful, like Whistler's painting of the woman in white he'd seen in his mother's art books decades ago. Would she be so trusting if she knew the truth about what brought him to town? Dallas had been many things in his life, a gang member, a wanderer and a drinker. He'd never been a liar, not until now, with her. It tightened something deep in his gut. He had to remind himself he had good reasons for the subterfuge.

He'd been hired by Antonia, Mia's sister, to keep watch over her due to the prevalence of Mia's ex-husband Hector Sandoval's many enemies. Cora, a friend of Antonia's new husband, was in on the whole thing. An accomplice, he thought ruefully, who'd arranged for Dallas to hang out on her property just as often as the stubborn and ferociously independent Mia did.

He returned to the truck where Juno was sound

asleep and waited until Mia got into her car. Following her home, he ran things over in his mind. Cora was obviously disturbed when she messaged both Dallas and Mia. How coincidental was it that her house burned down and she lost her life on the very same night Mia spotted some mystery woman fleeing the scene? Very coincidental, and Dallas Black did not believe in coincidence any more than he believed that Elvis still strolled planet Earth.

He walked Mia to her front door and waited while she stepped into the tiny front room.

Four-year-old Gracie came flying down the hall, short bob of hair bouncing around her, eyes alight with pleasure at the sight of him. They'd encountered each other many times at Cora's house while he was on the roof and she was digging holes around the property. When rain interrupted the roofing, they built card houses together, impressed with their creations until Juno knocked them over with a jerk of his tail.

"Did you come to play?" She took in his appearance and laughed. "You need a shower, Mr. Dallas."

He laughed, too, and Mia tried to draw Gracie away.

"Can he come in for a snack?" the child asked. "I've got Goldfish."

Dallas got down on one knee. "You eat goldfish? Don't the fins get stuck in your teeth?"

She giggled. "They're cracker fish. Juno will like them."

"Juno can't have Goldfish tonight, but we'll come another time."

She frowned. "Okay, but what if I don't have Goldfish then? Mommy eats them sometimes when I'm asleep and she's off her diet."

Mia's face flushed, and Dallas hid a grin.

"Tell you what, Goldfish girl. Next time I come with Juno, I'll bring some Goldfish along. How's that?"

She nodded, finally trotting off into the kitchen.

"You don't have to make good on that promise," Mia whispered as she let Dallas out. "As a matter of fact, I'd rather you didn't promise her things at all. I know you'd never mean to disappoint, but Gracie's been let down in a big way by her father."

"No sweat," he said. Something flickered in her face, something thoughtful. "You're not planning to go to the clinic, right?"

Mia jerked. "How did you know I was thinking about that?"

"Call it a knack. Don't go there by yourself, just in case whatever she was looking into has something to do with the fire."

She stayed silent.

"If you do have to go, I'll go with you."

She offered a courteous smile. "Thanks, Dallas. I appreciate it."

But you'll never allow it. He understood. He recognized the shadows that danced in her eyes for what they were. Fear. A desperate, ponderous weight of fear that she did not want to expose to anyone. Who would? He'd known that, tasted that when he was being beaten within an inch of his life during his gang days. That fear was hideous and bred on itself, multiplying exponentially the longer it was kept in the dark, like a poisonous fungus. He wished he could tell her. There is only one antidote, One who could defeat that fear. Instead, he remained silent until he heard the sound of the lock turning.

Juno and Dallas made one more stop on the way home, purchasing a bone for Juno and a handful of hot peppers for himself. With some help from the store clerk, he also secured five bags of Goldfish crackers, which he stowed in the back of his truck. Who knew Goldfish came in so many flavors? Dallas smiled to himself. Gracie knew, and that was enough.

TWO

The parking lot was empty, quiet, save for the patter of a cold rain and the scuff of Mia's shoes as she made her way to the darkened clinic hours later. She was grateful that Tina offered to stay late. It was almost eight by the time Mia embarked on her mission. She knew she should have called Dallas, but the only thing that scared her more than what had happened to Cora was the thought of losing herself to another man who would betray her and Gracie. She realized her hands were in her pockets, hidden away, a habit she'd developed after she'd stabbed her husband.

The horror lapped at her afresh. Her own hands had lashed out with that knife, powered by terror that Hector would kill her and take Gracie away into his corrupt world. She would never have done it, but she believed, heart and soul, that Hector meant to end her life. After Mia's arrest, she'd endured six months of jail time, knowing Gracie was with Hector, near people both ruthless and greed-driven, the worst being her own husband. After her release, she'd fled with Gracie, unaware that Hector would soon concoct a plot to outwit his enemies that involved kidnapping her sister, Antonia. While her sister fought for her life on a hurricane-ravaged island, Mia hid out like a frightened rabbit.

Sometimes her mind told her it was a dream, a nightmare, but she still remembered the feel of that knife in her hand and how her life had almost ended because she trusted the wrong man in spite of her father's warnings, Antonia's pleadings. In spite of her own troubled intuition.

Never again. Better to go it alone. A quick stop at the clinic. See if by chance Cora had left anything there that might be of help. In and out. Something wheeled along by her feet, and she gasped. Just a leaf, torn loose by the storm.

She bit back a wave of self-disgust at finding herself scuttling along, cringing at every leaf. She was an office clerk at the Spanish Canyon Clinic after all, and Cora was, had been, a volunteer. All perfectly aboveboard. But why had Cora originally insisted they wait until long after closing time to meet?

Her throat ached when she thought of her friend. Had she suffered? Had she known her house was burning around her?

Quickening her pace she sought shelter from the spring rain under the awning, keys ready in her hand, heart beating a little too hard, too erratically. Cora's nightmarish death came on a date that already held terrible memories, her wedding anniversary.

An annual reminder of the worst mistake of her life. But Hector had been so gentle when they'd first met, even professing to be a Christian, until he'd begun to worship another kind of God, the god of money, power and excitement, when he'd gotten involved in the drug trade. It was long over. Hector was jailed on new charges, the divorce finalized two years before, but

Hector did not want to accept his losses, so she lived as anonymous a life as she could manage.

With teeth gritted, she wondered—Had Hector found her again?

His reach hadn't extended to Spanish Canyon, Colorado. Not this time.

Wind carried a cold spray of rain onto her face that trickled down the back of her neck. She wished there was someone else around, the janitor, a late working nurse, anyone. They might be parked in the underground garage, she thought hopefully. With a surge of relief she saw the lights on in the back of the building where she and Cora shared a desk.

Jamming her key in the lock, she left the rain behind and headed down the silent corridor to the rear of the building. She did not know what she hoped to accomplish. Maybe it was all just a way to keep busy.

Cora's desk was bare, save for a paperweight rock engraved with the words *Be Still*. An impossible task, it seemed, for the nearly eighty-year-old woman who had recently decided to learn Italian and tour Europe. Her eyes were drawn to her own desk. Shadows must be deceiving. Silhouetted in the lamplight was a vase full of long-stemmed roses. Trancelike, she moved closer and turned on her own work light. Yellow roses, which had once been her favorite. A gilt-edged card.

I'm sorry. I love you and we can be a family again. Hector.

Sweat beaded on her forehead. It was as if he was there, right there, standing in the shadows. Fear turned into hatred for the man who had stripped away her belief in herself.

Hector didn't strip it away. You handed it over, wrapped in a bow.

The floor creaked, and she spun around with a scream.

"I'm sorry," Dr. Elias said with an apologetic smile. "I didn't mean to scare you. I was working late and noticed the florist had been here. Nice roses. Curiosity won out, and I checked the card." He raised an apologetic eyebrow, the fiftysomething face calm and serene. "My wife says I'm incurably nosey, and I hate to admit that she's got me pegged."

Mia forced out a calming breath. "I'm surprised to see you here so late."

"Insomnia. It usually sends me to the computer to play solitaire, but I get tired of beating myself, so I come here sometimes."

"Did you…did you hear about Cora?"

He nodded, mournfully. "Tragic. Cora was an excellent lady and a noble spirit." He shook his head. "Why do the good die before their time?"

It was a question she'd asked many times to a God who'd never given her a straight answer.

Dr. Elias cleared his throat. "Anyway, I'm glad you came so you could get your flowers, but why so late? Insomnia trouble for you also?"

She was about to tell him about the prearranged meeting with Cora, but something stopped her. "I just wanted to clean up Cora's desk."

"Looks clean already." Something in his inflection made her wonder if he'd been looking through Cora's belongings. Ridiculous. Crazy suspicion.

He surveyed the ceiling for a long moment. "It's good, actually, that we have a private moment so we can talk. I feel as though I have treated you well, hired you on in spite of your criminal record."

She winced. "Yes, you have. I appreciate that."

"It was Cora who went to bat for you, you know. She felt passionately that you would be an asset to this clinic. I was reluctant, I'll admit."

Mia started. She hadn't even known Cora when she moved to Spanish Canyon. She'd been following a lead on a job that her sister had dug up. Close to nursing school. Quiet town where nobody knew her.

"So I'm loathe to ask it, Mia, but when were you going to mention the truth about your criminal husband?"

She kept her chin high, even though at five three she barely reached his shoulder. Her phone vibrated in her pocket. "Ex-husband."

He blinked, his smooth complexion bordered by a distinguished head of gray hair that went well with his stature as head of the town's largest general medicine clinic. "I knew he was abusive, you were arrested for stabbing him I realize, but you didn't quite tell me the whole story. The flowers got me curious and I did a little checking. Nosey, just like my wife says. He wasn't just an abusive spouse. He's a Miami drug kingpin with powerful friends." His pale gray eyes locked on hers. "You didn't feel like you should mention that?"

Mention it? She was too busy trying to forget it.

"Is that why you don't use your married name? Sandoval?"

"It's not my name because I'm not married anymore. I haven't been for years. Simple as that."

He looked at the ceiling again while he talked. "Not really so simple. I've tried to support you here, to give you the hours you need to get you through nursing school and help you earn some money to keep food on the table for Gracie."

She didn't like it when he said Gracie's name, for some reason that she could not articulate. Did she feel the swell of distrust when she looked at him because he had the same self-assured manner as Hector? The doctor had been nothing but gracious.

"I would do anything for my own kids, as you know. It hasn't always been easy to afford everything times two, but that's the price of having twins. Jake and Renee are both in private high school now, so I understand wanting the best for your kids. But why lie? Especially to me."

"I never lied. You asked about my ex-husband, and I told you the reason I was sent to jail."

"You neglected to mention your husband is a Miami drug lord. You thought you'd pulled the wool over my eyes, didn't you? Simple country doctor. Easy to do, you figured?"

"No, nothing like that, really," she said.

The phone buzzed again.

Something sparked in his eyes. "Omissions are lies, and I'm afraid I'm going to have to ask you to leave." His brow furrowed. "It pains me to do it, it really does, but I have a professional obligation, no matter what my personal feelings are. My patients have to have absolute trust in me and my staff, and if you're still getting flowers from a drug kingpin, I can't risk having you here."

Mia would not let him see her cry. Head high, she nodded. "I'll be out of here in fifteen minutes." She went to the desk in the corner of the Spanish Canyon Clinic and shoved the picture of Gracie into a bag along with a collection of notepads. Cora's *Learn Italian Today* book was on her desk, under a box of tissue, and she scooped it up as well. She'd never dropped a phone call, never misplaced a file or been anything but pleasant to everyone and even that wasn't enough to overshadow her disastrous marriage.

Blinking to keep the tears at bay, her mind ran wild. No job. How would she finish school? Would it be the end of her dreams to finally give Gracie a stable, normal life? Her phone demanded her attention again and this time she yanked it from her pocket. It was a text from Dallas.

Ok?

Was she?

Dr. Elias still stood there, filling the doorway with his blocky shoulders, a look of indecision on his face. "This husband, Hector. He's tracked you everywhere, hasn't he?"

One of the notepads sliced into her finger giving her a paper cut. She shook off the sting angrily.

"Hector must be jealous." The lamplight etched Dr. Elias in tight shadow. "Have you given him reason?"

She froze. "What?"

"The tough guy with the dog. I've seen him talking to you. Hector can't be happy about this."

Seen Dallas? Something cold trickled through her. Why had Dr. Elias noticed whom she'd been talking to?

He flicked a glance into her bag. "You're not taking any clinic information, are you?"

She burned. "No, Doctor. I would not behave unethically, even after I've been wrongly terminated."

A glimmer of a smile lit his face. "I always liked your spunk, Mia Verde Sandoval. Too bad."

Mia grabbed her bag and purse and went to the door, but he barred her path.

He didn't move, just watched her as if he was weighing something in his mind. He reached out a hand to touch her forearm, but she recoiled.

"Hold on. I can see the truth now. You didn't lie to deceive, you lied because you're afraid."

Her breath caught and she shook her head.

"Yes, that's it, isn't it? You're afraid that Hector will find you." He stared closely at her. "No, you're afraid that you can't trust yourself, your choices, your judgments." He took her arm.

The fingers felt cold there against her skin, her own feet rooted to the floor. It was as if he'd stepped inside her, peered into the cold dark place in her heart where she herself dared not go.

"I know what it's like to be lied to. I'm so sorry, Mia," he said, pupils glittering in the dimly lit office. He leaned toward her and lowered his voice to a whisper. "I'm dense, sometimes. I didn't realize. I can help you."

Standing this close she realized how strong he looked. Her fingers clutched her car keys, and she raised them in front of her.

"I want to leave. Now."

He laughed and moved a step closer. She was acutely aware of how empty the clinic was, how dark the outer corridors. "You're a beautiful woman, you know that?" His gaze flickered up and down her body. "You deserve more. I can help you get your life back."

She pressed back until she bumped into the file cabinets, a metal handle digging into her spine. He put his hands out, kneading her shoulders.

She jerked away from his grasp. "I want to go," she whispered, gripping the keys. "I will scream the place down if you touch me again."

He chuckled. "You came here after hours, almost as if you were looking for me."

The implication was clear. *Who do you think they'll believe?*

She gripped the keys, palms clammy, readying herself to gouge and bite and kick. Unsure.

"You're not seeing things clearly, Mia. You don't know what's right and wrong anymore, do you?" The words were almost a whisper, his mouth curved in a soft smile. "You need help."

Help? Was that what he offered? Her gut told her to run. Should she trust that instinct?

From somewhere far away, she heard herself say, "I want to go. Now."

"Maybe you don't know what you want," he said, eyes glittering.

"Yes, she does," said a low voice. The doctor was jerked back and dumped in an unceremonious pile on the floor. Dallas Black looked down at Elias, his dark eyes blending with the shadows.

She realized Dallas must have been expecting her to act stupidly and visit the clinic and her cheeks burned, but relief overrode any other sensation.

"I was just fired," Mia announced. "And now I'm going to leave."

Dallas didn't move. "Good. Doesn't pay to work for dirtbags."

"Trespassing and assault," Dr. Elias snapped at Dallas, scrambling to his feet. "I will have you arrested."

Dallas ignored the comment completely. "Ready to go?" he said to her.

"Get off my property," Dr. Elias snarled. Gone was the genial smile, any vestiges of warmth, fire blazed in his eyes.

Mia gripped her bag and walked to the door on shaky legs, grateful to have Dallas looking over her shoulder at the doctor. She was desperate to end the situation. Dallas had a complete disregard for rules and she wanted to finish the whole confrontation before anything worse happened.

"You are turning away from someone who wants to help you, Mia," Dr. Elias said, nostrils flared. "And look what you're walking into."

"Goodbye, Dr. Elias," Mia said.

"Don't forget your flowers," he yelled.

"Keep them," she said.

Dallas's truck was parked at the curb, and Juno sat next to it. When he saw her his tail went into overtime, and he whined until she gave him a cursory pat. He licked her face.

"If a man approached my ride, Juno would bark up a storm, but with you he'd hand over the keys," Dallas said. *Smart dog.*

Juno was once an aggressive shelter resident after having been beaten and starved by a cruel owner. Dallas had spent six months tracking down that negligent owner on his own dime, until the man was charged with animal cruelty and subjected to hefty fines. It wasn't enough in Dallas's view.

Mia straightened in spite of Juno's disappointment and gave him a tight smile. "He must know I'm a cat person and he's trying to help me see the light." She paused. "I would have handled the situation, you know. No one will keep me from Gracie."

"No doubt. I'm just glad I was in the neighborhood." In truth he'd been driving around town, too restless to stay home, checking the clinic lot every so often in case Mia showed up like he suspected she'd do. "I'm not sure…" She bit her lip. "I don't know if Dr. Elias was going to hurt me. He said he wanted to help."

Help? That wasn't what Dallas had heard in the good doctor's tone when he put his hands on Mia. "What did your gut tell you?"

"To leave."

"Then you did the right thing." Dallas clamped down on the anger that ticked at his insides. His own instincts told him Dr. Elias was interested in much more than Mia's well-being. He despised the thought of Elias being anywhere near Mia. Or touching her. Or looking in her general direction.

Overprotective, Black.

Overprotective? How could that be when she kept him at arm's length and he wasn't interested in a relationship anyway? Whatever the reason, something about her, her strength perhaps, stayed in his mind like a lingering fragrance.

It made him pretty sure that if she knew the real reason he'd come to Spanish Canyon, to protect her without her consent, she'd let him have it with both barrels, but the roses on her desk indicated there was ample cause for him to keep an eye on her.

He'd met Mia at the wedding of her sister, Antonia, to Hector's brother Reuben Sandoval after the two barely survived a hurricane. Oddly, he'd befriended Antonia three years prior in the wake of a massive earthquake that struck San Francisco where he assisted his brother, Trey, in rescuing Antonia and Sage Harrington, now Trey's wife. At least Antonia and Trey had both found love matches in the midst of disaster. A memory from that wedding stayed sharp in his mind. Mia's face torn with sorrow, or was it guilt, cradling Gracie in her arms. Hemingway said people healed stronger where they were broken. Mia, though she didn't ever discuss her past, was like that, he figured. *Sometimes it takes more strength to ask for help than to go it alone, Mia.*

He snapped out of his reverie when she sighed heavily. "Go ahead and say it. I was dumb to come here, after hours, in light of all that's happened."

He considered. "Yeah."

"I have good reasons for doing things my own way."

"Don't we all." He tried to catch her eye, but she avoided his gaze. "You okay?"

"Yes."

"Sure?"

"I'm perfectly fine," she said with a little too much bravado. He caught the tremble of her lips in spite of the dim light. It made his stomach tighten.

"I'll follow you home again."

"I'm fine. There's no reason."

"It's dark, weather's bad and you were harassed. That's three reasons." He opened the door for her.

She rolled her eyes and started to get into the car when the bag slipped from her hands. She snatched it up but not before Cora's Italian book plopped out. It fell open, and she saw something stuck inside. Picking it up hastily, she said, "What's this?"

From between the pages she pulled out a four-by-six photo, and Dallas shone his penlight on it.

"We've seen this woman before," she said grimly.

Dallas felt a stir of foreboding flow through his belly. "Running away from Cora's burning house."

THREE

Sleep eluded Mia. Though she felt like throwing herself on the floor and sobbing at the loss of her dear friend, she would not allow Gracie to witness such an outburst. The best thing she could offer now was a heavy dose of mothering in between scouring the want ads and internet sites for employment opportunities. A breakfast of scrambled eggs, toast cut into a heart shape, and a half dozen stories later, and Gracie was content to go into the soggy backyard and hunt for snails. Unless the snails had teeny scuba suits, Mia didn't think she'd have much luck.

She sat on the couch and considered the facts.

The little house they now occupied was rented. Cora had helped her find the place, and though she received a settlement when she divorced Hector, she steadfastly refused to take any child-support money. Dr. Elias was right. Hector Sandoval was involved in the drug trade, and she did not want a single penny of tainted money to find its way to Gracie.

Hector claimed in every letter that he'd repented, but she did not believe him or any other man for that matter. The most important person in her life was Gracie, and Mia would not fail her. So how could she tell her daughter about Cora? Images of the fire raced through her memory, especially the moment when the red-haired woman had appeared through the smoke. Whoever she was, she had answers. Hopefully, the police chief could help ferret out the truth, though he'd not been able to grant her an audience until the following day. Dallas had advised her to bypass Stiving, and she'd agreed. It was best to talk to the chief. For now, the picture was tucked safely in an envelope in the back of the top desk drawer.

The doorbell rang.

Tina stepped inside, chewing madly on a piece of pink gum with a stack of books under her arm to be perused during Gracie's nap time. Mia greeted her warmly. The stick-thin college sophomore babysat for Mia during the day and took community classes at night. Since Mia's nursing school was off due to a semester break, she'd been logging as many hours at Dr. Elias's clinic as she could and Tina had been invaluable. The two exchanged a quiet talk about Cora's death, news of which had already spread all over the quiet mountain community.

"Have you told her yet?" Tina asked, discarding her gum into a wrapper and snatching a leftover piece of toast.

"No." Mia sighed, eyes misting. "I haven't had the courage."

Tina gave her a hug which almost loosed the flood gates of emotion until Mia stepped back. "I'm glad you could come today. I've got to find another job."

"Yeah? What happened to the gig at the clinic?"

"I was…let go last night."

Tina swallowed the last bit of toast. "Oh, bummer. What are you going to do now?"

"Go into town and beat the bushes if I have to. Anything to make the rent."

"That's the spirit."

Mia nodded. "There's got to be somebody looking for a hard-working gal like me."

"We are women, hear us roar," Tina cried, pumping a fist. "Go get 'em!"

Wishing she could share some of Tina's enthusiasm, she grabbed her bag. After they'd made arrangements for Tina to deliver Gracie to Mia in the late afternoon, she headed for the car.

"Time to hit it," she murmured to herself. "Hear me roar."

Fearing that her roar was more like a pitiful mew at the moment, she headed to town.

After a full day of walking the main streets of Spanish Canyon, Mia had nothing to show for it but sore feet and a rumbling belly. She'd already gobbled her peanut butter and marshmallow fluff sandwich, and at a little past three, her stomach was demanding attention, as it seemed to do no matter what diet she was doing her best to adhere to. Besides, a sign on Sam's Sammies advertised for "help wanted."

I'm a master of the peanut butter and fluff, she reminded herself as she entered and introduced herself to the owner.

Sam Shepherd, a massive man with sprigs of white hair sprouting from the top of his head met her inquiry with enthusiasm. "Sure thing. Why don't you fill out an application?" He pushed over a greasy piece of paper affixed to a clipboard. "Say, I was sure sorry to hear about Cora."

She nodded. "Me, too."

"You know her well?"

Mia only managed a quick yes.

He raised a bristly eyebrow. "Heard talk that it wasn't an accident."

She hadn't noticed Detective Stiving sitting in the corner booth until he spoke up. "Looking more and more like that's the case," he said.

A moment later, Dallas strolled in, surveying the group with quiet amusement and causing Mia to wonder about the timing.

"Well, Sam, seems like business is picking up," Dallas said.

Stiving chewed a pickle spear. "What do you want?"

Dallas arched an eyebrow. "A sandwich. Isn't that why you're here?" He smiled at Sam. "The usual, my good man."

"Vegetarian with extra mustard and no eggplant, heavy on the jalapenos," Sam rattled off.

Dallas slouched into a chair, long legs extended. "Don't let me interrupt."

Mia felt the twin pangs of affection and irritation at seeing Dallas there. She wanted the man out of her life, yet why did something inside her warm up whenever he appeared? Was he keeping tabs on her? The thought both infuriated and tantalized her.

Focus, would you? "I'll just fill this out," she said to Sam, making her way to a chair well away from Dallas.

Stiving followed her. "You might not want to take a new job, just yet."

Something about the gleam in his eye worried her. "Why?"

"Because it seems you're an heiress."

She blinked. "What are you talking about?"

"Just got word that Cora left her house and property to you. Of course, the house is pretty messed up, but the twenty acres of property, well that's worth a nice tidy sum, I'll bet."

Mia realized her mouth was hanging open. "Cora left her property to me?"

"Does that surprise you?"

"Of course it does. I had no idea."

"That right?" He wiped his thick fingers on a paper napkin. Graying chest hair puffed out at the top of his uniform shirt. "No idea at all?"

"None. What are you implying?"

"Cops, you know, look at these things called motives. Inheriting a nice chunk of land is motive."

"For what?" Mia managed to squeak out.

"For murder," he said with a smile.

Dallas moved closer when it seemed as though Mia was unable to marshal a response. "What do you have that points in that direction?"

Stiving leveled a derisive look at him. "Not that it's your business, but the coroner's initial take is that Cora didn't die from the fire."

Mia let out a little cry, her face gone deadly pale.

Dallas tensed. "Cause?"

Stiving stretched against the upholstered booth. "That's as much as I'm going to say right now. You all have a great day. I'll be in touch. Soon."

He left. Dallas realized that Sam had been standing

just behind them holding a sandwich on a plastic plate. "Uh, well, I'm real sorry and all that, Mia, but maybe Stiving is right. With everything going on, it doesn't seem like a good time to have you start working here."

He shoved the plate at Dallas and waddled back to the kitchen.

Dallas dropped money on the counter, no tip, and left the sandwich on the table. By the time he'd finished, Mia had made her way outside, sinking onto a brick planter, oblivious to Juno, who had been watching through the window the whole time, swabbing an eager tongue over her hand.

Dallas sat next to her. Dark clouds overhead promised more rain and dulled the soft brown of her eyes. Or maybe it was the shock that did it. What to say to comfort her in the present situation eluded him, so he went with his gut.

"They don't have any proof. He's trying to rattle you."

The words seemed to startle her. "He thinks she was poisoned with the pills I got for her."

"Speculation and proof are two different things."

"Juno knew there was something in those pills."

"Doesn't mean you put it there."

She pressed shaking hands to her mouth. "I can't believe it. He wants to put me in jail. I can't go to jail, Dallas."

Her voice broke and it killed him. "You won't."

"But my past…isn't lily white."

"Whose is?" He wanted to smooth away the furrow between her brows, the agony in her expression. "It was self-defense before. Totally different. Your ex admits that now."

Her eyes rounded. "Have you been studying my past?"

Smooth, Dallas. Why don't you explain how you know every detail of her life? He went for casual. "Heard it somewhere."

She was too upset to think more about it. "Maybe I should leave here," she whispered. "Go back to Florida."

His pulse accelerated the tiniest bit. He said as gently as he could, "Thought you wanted a fresh start."

"Away from the Sandoval name," she finished. "I do, but my past seems to have followed me here."

And did her husband's past have anything to do with her current situation? He did not see how it could, but it was his job to find out. He'd made a promise. "There was someone else at Cora's house who could have tampered with the pills. We just have to figure out who the woman in the photo is."

Mia chewed her lip. "This is a nightmare."

"We'll fix it."

Her eyes flickered at the pronoun.

We? When had loner Dallas Black begun to think of them as partners? The only partner he'd ever really trusted was the kind covered with fur and with a tendency to slobber. "Look who's just hit town," he said as Gracie broke away from Tina and ran to them, splashing through the puddles on the sidewalk.

"Hi, Mr. Dallas. Hi, Mommy. I'm here," she announced, heading straight for Juno to give him an ear rub. "Tina said we could get ice cream."

Mia recovered herself to give Tina a stern look.

The girl shrugged. "Sorry. I can't say no to those dimples."

"I can," Mia said, her mouth twisting in sadness. "But I won't. I think I could use a scoop, too."

"Mr. Dallas, come on," Gracie said, tugging on his hand. "We can get some for Juno."

Mia's look was enough to discourage him. "I've got to go right now, Gracie. Maybe another time."

Mia's slight nod affirmed he'd made the right choice, so why did his heart tell him otherwise? He moved close to Mia, talking low in her ear and trying not to breathe in a lungful of her shampoo-scented hair. "I've got a friend who works at the police department. I'll go see what I can find out."

She put a hand on his biceps. "I don't want to ask you to do that for me."

"You didn't ask."

He heard her sigh, sad as the sound of a blues song, as she led Gracie away without looking back, her shoulders hunched against the storm-washed sky.

Mia tried to keep Gracie occupied with the ice cream parlor and the park, but all the while her mind was racing. The police thought she'd killed her dearest friend. How could it be happening? And to inherit when Cora had blood relatives to whom she could pass her estate? The only spot of comfort was Dallas, and she had to steel herself against any connection, no matter how much she craved it. Still, she thought she could remember the feel of his hard muscled arm under her fingers—strong, solid, the steady warmth in his eyes.

You've seen eyes like those before, remember, Mia?

Rain began to fall a little after five, and she zipped Gracie's jacket and insisted they return to the car where a nasty surprise awaited her. Her rear tire was flat all the way to the rim.

"Great. I must have driven over a screw or something." With a heavy sigh, she gave her purse to Gracie to hold and got the jack and lug wrench from the trunk. Two gentlemen and a young couple out walking their dog stopped and offered help, but Mia waved with a cheer she did not feel and finished the job herself. The effort took much longer than it should have and it was nearly sundown when she cleansed her grease-stained hands with one of her endless supply of disinfectant wipes and took the road toward home.

Gracie sang "Where Does the Ladybug Live?" as the miles went by and Mia even joined in for a while, but, as darkness fell, her stress returned. No job, no way to pay the rent and now a replacement tire needed to be purchased.

Gritting her teeth, she forced the worry down deep.

"I'm hungry," Gracie announced as they pulled into the garage.

"How can you be hungry when you ate two scoops of ice cream?"

Gracie twisted a strand of hair while she thought about it. "Dunno, but I am."

"Mac and cheese?"

The little girl nodded as she helped Mia unbuckle her car seat straps.

Mia mentally inventoried the pantry cupboard, hard to keep stocked with a voracious babysitter and child. Fortunately, there was one box left of nature's most perfect food. She helped Gracie from the car and hit the button to close the garage door.

Mia noted the interior door was unlocked, probably

because Tina simply could not be induced to lock it. Mia sighed. Oh, to be an innocent eighteen-year-old again. Gracie pulled out her step stool and disappeared into the pantry.

Suddenly, the burdens of the day crashed in on Mia and she felt much older than her twenty-eight years. And why shouldn't she as the ex-wife of a drug runner and now the object of suspicion for her friend's death? *Murder, murder,* the word crawled through her mind. Tears threatened, but she would not allow them, not for a moment. Mothers did not have the luxury of folding up like tents. A shower. A quick five minute shower would wash off the grime from the day.

Hanging her purse on the kitchen hook and plugging in her cell phone to charge, she headed for the bedroom, removing her jacket. Finger poised on the light switch, she froze. A shadow was silhouetted in front of the window, just for a second before it slithered behind the cover of the drapes. Someone was in her bedroom.

Fear rushed hot into her gut, firing her nerves as she ran down the hallway. Behind her she could hear the swish of fabric as the intruder detached from the curtains. Feet thudded across the carpeted floor, her own clattering madly on the wood planked hallway as she raced for the kitchen, sweeping up her purse and grabbing Gracie who was shaking the box of macaroni and singing.

She seized her daughter with such force she heard the breath whoosh out of her, but Mia paid no heed. The man was in the hallway now, only a few feet behind her. Mia burst into the garage, hit the button and dove into the driver's side, shoving Gracie over onto the passenger seat and cranking the ignition.

The interior garage door opened, and the man appeared—thin, white, crew cut. She saw him reach for the button to stop the door from opening. She would be trapped, she and Gracie, at the mercy of this stranger.

No, she thought savagely, flipping the brights on. He flinched, throwing a hand over his eyes. The door was nearly half open now. Only a few more inches and she could get out.

Terror squeezed her insides as she saw him recover and reach for the button again.

Hurry, hurry, she commanded the groaning metal gears.

This time when he reached for the button, he succeeded and the door stopped its upward progress.

He pressed it again and it began to slide down, sealing off their escape.

FOUR

Dallas listened to the rain pounding down on the metal roof of the twenty-nine-foot trailer he rented. It was a gem of a unit as far as he was concerned, far enough away from the other trailer park residents that he enjoyed the illusion of solitude. That and the fact that the river just at the edge of the property had already persuaded many folks to temporarily relocate to another trailer park on higher ground. He wasn't completely familiar with Colorado weather patterns, but he'd give it a good couple of days before he needed to grab his pack and head for another spot.

Dallas sprawled on his back on the narrow bunk, Juno snoring on his mat on the floor. His thoughts wandered back to Mia and the fire. His police contact hadn't been able to tell him much, but he knew that circumstantial evidence could convict a person in the eyes of the law and the community.

Motive and means. Mia had both.

He got to his feet and took up his guitar from the closet. Juno burrowed deeper into his mat as Dallas strummed out a few chords on the instrument that was a gift from his brother, Trey. So, indirectly, was Dallas's damaged spleen and knee, but he did not hold that against his brother anymore. Dallas got into gang life to emulate Trey, but no one had forced him.

He'd gone in willingly and come out so damaged he would never realize his dream of being a Marine like their father.

He tried to remember his sixteen-year-old self, armed and patrolling the ten-block territory as a sentinel of sorts, a lookout for Uncle, the older leader of the gang who pedaled dope, which kept the wheels rolling. He'd admired Uncle, feared him even, yet watched him hand out new shoes and Fourth of July fireworks to the kids who couldn't afford either. They were the same kids who would be members one day, looking for that combination of belonging and protection that Uncle provided. Sixteen years old, carrying a gun, drinking and protecting a hoodlum's drug business. He cringed at the memory. What an idiot. What a coward.

How many trailers had he stayed in over the years? How many apartments or cabins had he called home until people got to know him a little too well and he felt that restless urge to move on? Was he still looking for that place to belong?

Or was it more cowardice? Probably, God forgive him. It was safer not to get to know people and to prevent them from knowing him. Safe…with a helping of sin mixed in. His grandfather's favorite baseball player, Mickey Mantle, said gangs were where cowards went to hide. Maybe they sometimes went to trailer parks, too. He fought the rising tide of self-recrimination with a muttered prayer.

The clock reminded him he hadn't eaten dinner. The fridge didn't offer much so he grabbed a rainbow of hot peppers and an onion. Armed with a perfectly balanced knife, he allowed himself to be soothed by the precision of the slices as they fell away onto the cutting board.

Juno surged to his feet, ears cocked.

Company.

So late? And in the throes of a pounding rain? He put down the knife and sidled to the window, peering through the blinds. Nothing. No cars visible, but then his windows faced the tree-lined creek so he wouldn't see one anyway. Juno was standing in front of the door, staring with laser-like precision, ears swiveling, as if he could see beyond the metal if he just worked hard enough at it. With hearing four times greater than a human's, Juno was not often wrong about what he heard.

Dallas tried to peer through the blinds again, but the angle was wrong. Still no one knocked. Juno maintained his ferocious intensity, which told Dallas someone was out there. The slightest sound or scent telegraphed to a dog just as strongly as a stiff-knuckled rap on the door.

Okay. Let's play. Dallas gripped the door handle. Juno's whiskers quivered, body trembling, sensing a game in the offing. Juno, like every great SAR dog, had an intense play drive that never wound down.

Dallas did a slow count to three and yanked the handle.

Wind barreled in along with a gust of rain, and Juno charged down the metal stairs onto the wooden porch. He turned in circles looking for something that wasn't there.

Dallas kept his fists ready and gave the dog the moment he needed to get his bearings. Moisture-laden air confused Juno's senses, but not for long.

The dog shoved his head in the gap under the trailer and began to bark for all he was worth, tail whirling.

A woman's scream cut through the storm.

"Sit," Dallas yelled to Juno, who complied with a reluctant whine.

"Whoever you are under the trailer, come out."

No answer.

"If you don't come out, the dog is coming in."

Now there was movement, a raspy breathing, a set of slender fingers wrapping around the edge of the trailer, the impression of a face.

"He'll bite me."

Dallas called Juno to him and held the dog by the collar, more to assure the woman than out of fear that Juno would disobey. Juno didn't bite people. He was more interested in getting them to throw a ball for him to fetch. "Come out."

She emerged, soggy and mud streaked, her hair plastered in coils against her face. Red hair.

"You were there at the fire."

She didn't answer, trembling in the falling rain.

"Come inside. We'll talk."

She didn't move. "Are you a friend of Cora's?"

"Are you?" He could see the thoughts racing through her mind as she chewed her lip without answering. "All I can tell you is I won't hurt you."

"How do I know I can trust you?" she said through chattering teeth.

"Guess you can't. You came here to find me and here I am. If you want to talk, we do it inside. Don't want the dog to catch cold."

After another long look at Juno, the woman ran up the steps.

He tossed her a towel, which she wrapped around her shoulders before she sank onto the kitchen chair. Juno did his thing, sniffing her muddy shoes and the hem of her sodden linen pants.

Dallas studied her while he heated water in the microwave and flung in a tea bag which had come with the trailer. Some sort of fruity herbal stuff. Her clothes had been nice at one point, ruined now. A light jacket was not up to the task of keeping her dry from the pummeling rain. No purse.

"Who are you?" he asked as he handed her the tea.

She clutched it between her shaking hands, her knuckles white.

"Susan." She swallowed. "I was going to meet Cora, and I saw the house burning. I tried to get inside to help her."

Nice story. "Why were you meeting her?"

"She was…looking into something for me." She locked eyes on his, hers a pale gray. "Is she all right?"

Dallas considered. Time to find out if Susan really was a friend to Cora. "Dead." He gauged her reaction.

The woman did not move, as if the words were lost in the steam from the mug she held to her lips. "Dead."

"So why were you going to see her?"

She gazed into the tea. "How did the fire start?"

"Maybe I should be asking you that."

She jerked. "You think I set it?"

"So far I've seen you running away from a fire and sneaking outside my trailer. Puts your character in question."

A glimmer of a smile lifted her lips, but there was something under the trailing wet hair, behind the gaunt lines of her mouth that revealed a hardness he hadn't seen at first. "So you're wondering if you can trust me?" she said.

"Not wondering. I'm not going to trust you, not until you give me the truth."

"You're a hard man."

He sat opposite her. "I've got peppers to sauté. What are you here for?"

She held his eyes with hers, a slight lift to her chin. "Justice."

"Not easy to find."

"I know. But I'm going to have it. I'm going to get back what belongs to me." The last words came out as a hiss.

"What were you doing at Cora's?"

"Meeting her there. She was trying to help me unmask a villain, so to speak."

"Who?"

"It's private."

He rapped a hand on the table. "We're wasting time. Cora was likely murdered and you were there at the scene."

"If I was going to kill someone, or burn a house in this town," she said, after drinking deeply of the tea, "that's not the one I would have picked. And by the way, you were there, too, at the scene. Did you have something to do with Cora's death?"

Dallas resisted the urge to raise his voice. "If you thought I did, a quick phone call to the police would take care of it. You came here for another reason."

"I wanted to know about Cora, and I'm not asking the police for personal reasons."

Very personal, judging from the flicker of emotion that pinched the corners of her mouth. Impasse. They'd gotten there, he could tell. Whatever her motives, he wasn't going to pry them out of her. Women didn't work that way, he'd learned. Instead he sat back in the chair and waited.

Mia's mouth went dry as the garage door stopped with a groan, halfway up. The man hopped off the step and ran to the car. He was coming to drag her out. The old car had no automatic locks so she slammed the button down and realized in a hot wave of panic that he was not headed to her side, but Gracie's.

"Lock the door, Gracie," Mia shouted.

Gracie sat frozen, staring at her mother.

Mia dove across her and hammered the lock, the back door, as well. The man banged his palms against the glass.

Gracie screamed. "Stop, stop!"

Mia nearly screamed too until the man stepped away suddenly. He picked up a metal bucket and swung it hard at the passenger window with a deafening crash until the glass was etched through with cracks.

"Get down onto the floor," Mia yelled to Gracie, "and cover your head with your hands."

She yanked the car into Reverse. After one quick breath, she stomped on the gas. The car shot backwards into the garage door. There was a terrible moment when the roof met the unyielding mass and she thought she had made a fatal error. Groaning metal, the sound of breaking glass and then quite without warning the car punched through, shearing the garage door into a crumpled mess, exploding onto the rain-slicked driveway.

Mia was oblivious to the damage. Only two facts remained, her car was still functioning and they were free from the garage. She reversed down the slope, cranked the car into Drive and sped off down the road, putting as much distance between the man and Gracie as she possibly could. One mile, two, her stomach remained in a tight knot, fingers clenched around the steering wheel.

She forced several breaths in and out before she could coax her voice into action. "Gracie Louise, are you hurt?"

Gracie's tiny voice floated up from the floor. "Scary."

"You're right," she said, relief making her voice thick. "But it's okay now. You can climb back on the seat. Be careful of the glass."

Gracie emerged like a hare having narrowly escaped the fox. Her lips were parted, eyes wide and wet. "Mommy, that was a bad man."

Mia gave a shaky laugh and took her daughter's hand. "Yes, he was."

"Why was he in our house?"

She swallowed. "I don't know, but we'll go someplace safe until we find out, okay?"

"Where?"

The million dollar question. The nearest hotel was an hour away, and they didn't have the money to stay in one for long anyway. Rain splattered through the side window that had broken when it impacted the garage door. She felt the bitter tide of anger rise as she contemplated her own helplessness. Mia risked a quick stop, engine running, to move Gracie to the backseat and buckle her into her booster. She kissed her and caressed her daughter's plump cheeks. "I'm going to figure out something, okay?"

Gracie nodded, shaking the box of macaroni she still clung to. "But I'm hungry."

Mia smiled as she climbed back into the driver's seat, but worry soon overwhelmed her. She didn't even have a cell phone to call the police. The storm intensified as she drove along, rattling the sides of the car. If she could call her sister for advice…

Your sister who is busy with her new husband and her new life. They were tight now, together again after all the anguish Mia had caused, but still there remained in the shadows between them, a heavy weight of guilt. It stemmed from the fact that her sister had been right about Hector when Mia refused to hear a bad word about him, a feeling that burgeoned during her time in jail with all its horrors. Because of Hector, Antonia was almost killed and there was nobody to blame for bringing him into their lives but Mia. No, she would not call Antonia.

"Why not call Hector?" her derisive thoughts chided her. He was sitting around in prison with nothing much to do and a reach that seemed to exceed the metal walls that caged him. She could grovel even more and throw herself on Dr. Elias's mercy. Was there any pride left to salvage? Self-pity gave way to a hot flood of determination.

Stand on your own two feet, for once in your life.

Mile after mile gave her no clarity, no better sense of what to do. Only the instinct to keep going, to get away from whoever had violated their home, kept her pressing the car forward. She'd made up her mind to stop at the next town she came to and call the police when she realized where she was, at the entrance to the trailer park where Dallas lived. She'd given him a lift there once when his truck had engine trouble.

She saw the silhouette of his vehicle, and she pulled her car next to it, motor still running.

"Where are we?" Gracie said, unbuckling her strap.

"Nowhere, I was just stopping to rest my eyes for a minute." What was she doing? She would not go to Dallas for help, the man who already seemed to have a strange influence over her pulse. An image of long-stemmed yellow roses floated into her mind. It was followed by a vision of Hector, the man whom she'd loved desperately, blindly, the husband who lied to her from the first kiss and right on until his arrest for drug dealing and later for the attempted abduction of her sister. *Fool, fool, fool.* Tears brimmed, captive in her eyes.

She swallowed hard. "Put your seat belt back on, we're not stopping here."

"But there's Juno," Gracie gabbled, shoving open the door and hopping out.

"Get back in the car right now, Gracie Louise," Mia said, noting the spill of light from Dallas's door as he emerged onto the trailer steps, peering into the darkness.

"Hi, Dallas," Gracie called. "Can you make me some mac and cheese?"

Mia sighed. God could not lead her to another dark-haired man who would prove her a fool again. If that was His plan, Mia was going to make one of her own. Jaw tense, she stepped out of the car and went to retrieve her daughter.

FIVE

"Sorry to bother you," Mia said, forcing a light tone, as Dallas bent to talk to Gracie, Juno dancing on eager paws beside him.

"Someone broke into our house," Gracie said. "I think it was the Boogeyman. He wanted this." She thrust the box of mac and cheese up in the rain.

Dallas's face was a picture of confusion. "Huh?" he finally managed.

Mia squished up to him, feet sinking into the grass. "We had a break-in. We're going to the next town to call the cops."

It was hard to read his expression through the sheeting rain. "Come inside."

Gracie hooted her approval and headed for the trailer.

"No," Mia said too quickly. "I mean, we don't want to involve you. I can handle it." She wished her teeth had not begun to chatter madly at that moment.

"You can handle it inside, out of the rain."

"I appreciate the offer."

"Inside then." And that was that. Dallas turned his back and ushered Gracie and Juno up the steps, politely holding the door for Mia, his muscled forearm gleaming wetly. And what was a woman on the edge of desperation supposed to do about that?

Just a phone call. A quick stop to rest and then out. She squelched up the trailer steps and inside, stopping abruptly in the doorway until he came up behind and pushed her gently through.

"I'll leave puddles."

His gaze flickered around the tidy interior. "You won't be the first one." He sighed. "Gone."

"Who?"

"The redhead from the fire. Name's Susan. She came here."

Mia gasped. "What did she want? Who is she?"

He shrugged. "Not the chatty type. Only got that she was meeting Cora and she has some big trust issues. She was sitting at the table when I heard you pull up. She must have snuck out." He leveled a look at Juno. "Aren't you supposed to alert me to people sneaking around, dog?"

Juno shook water from his thick coat and hurled himself on the floor to offer his belly to Gracie for scratching.

Mia giggled.

Dallas did not, but she thought there was a slight quirk on his lips. Mia made one more trip into the rain to fetch the bag of spare clothes she kept in the car. In a few moments, Gracie was wearing faded jeans and a T-shirt, one size too small but dry.

"Can you make this?" Gracie said, shaking the box of macaroni at Dallas.

"What is it?"

The child blinked. "It's mac and cheese. Don'tcha eat that?"

"No," Dallas said.

"Well, what do you eat?" she demanded.

"Spicy food that makes you sweat. But I can probably manage mac and cheese."

"No need," Mia said.

Dallas pointed to the tiny bathroom. "There's a sweatshirt hanging on a hook in there. It's ugly, but dry."

"We're not staying."

"I got that. Go put on something dry anyway. I don't think I can enjoy eating this mac stuff while you're dripping all over the floor." He turned to Gracie. "How do you cook it? The label's blurry from the rain."

"Dump the stuff in bubbling water," Gracie sang out as Mia headed to the bathroom.

"Don't get too close to Juno," she warned Gracie. "He'll get mad if you pester him."

Dallas quirked an eyebrow. "He's never mad at kids, but I'll watch them anyway."

Mia walked into the bathroom and leaned her head against the door. *Safe. You're safe for the moment, and so is Gracie.* She wanted to whisper a prayer, but something hardened the words in her throat. *You got yourself out of that jam, Mia, and you can handle whatever comes next. All by yourself.*

She squeezed the water out of her hair and slicked it down straight as best she could. Rolling up her sodden shirt, she pulled on the soft gray sweatshirt that went down past her knees. It felt warm against her skin.

She emerged to find Dallas in deep discussion with Gracie as she stared at the pile of jigsaw puzzle pieces set out on a piece of plywood that served as a table.

"I don't know what it's going to be," Dallas said.

Gracie blinked. "But what's the picture on the box?"

"A mouse chewed the box, so I put the pieces in a plastic bag. Can't remember what the picture is."

She touched a piece with one soft fingertip. "You haven't gotten many pieces together."

He nodded, staring ruefully at the corner where a half dozen pieces were connected. "I move a lot. Gotta put it away each time."

"How long have you been working on it?" Mia asked.

He squinted. "Going on twelve years now."

She wasn't sure whether to gasp or laugh. "Really?"

"Well, I think it's going to be a dog puzzle," Gracie said.

"Could be. My mother gave it to me for my fifteenth birthday. She can't remember what the picture was, either." He sniffed. "Is mac and cheese supposed to smell like that?"

They looked at the pot which was bubbling madly on the stove. Mia grabbed a potholder and took it off the heat. There were bits of packaging swirling through the noodles and grainy orange tinted water. "Uh-oh. You dumped in the cheese envelope."

"The what?"

"I forgot to tell him," Gracie wailed. "You're not 'posed to put the cheese envelope in the water."

Mia put the mess into the sink. "I'm afraid it's ruined."

Dallas sighed. "I should have paid better attention while I was dumping. Who puts cheese in an envelope anyway?"

Gracie sat forlornly next to Juno. "Awww, rats."

"Hang on," Dallas said, wrenching open the cupboard. "I just remembered something." He held a bag of Goldfish triumphantly in the air. "How about some of these?"

Gracie cheered, and Mia had to laugh as he handed Gracie the crackers with all the solemnity of a professor awarding a diploma. "Just don't feed too many to the dog," he said.

After a moment of hesitation, he said to Mia, "I'm making tofu and peppers. Share them with me?" She had not shared a private meal with a man since her disastrous marriage. Sweat popped out on her forehead.

"Oh, I couldn't."

"There's no meat, but I've got plenty." His black eyes fastened on her.

Mia was a committed carnivore, but how could she say no to the man whose sweatshirt she was wearing and who had massacred a box of mac and cheese in an effort to feed her child?

"Yes," she said humbly. "That would be very nice."

"Here's a phone to call the cops. Then you can tell me about what happened."

She sank down at the table. "You're not going to believe me."

"Try…" His words trailed off as he scanned the kitchen counter.

"What's wrong?"

"Before she took off, Susan helped herself."

"To your dinner?"

"No," he said, voice low and deep. "To my knife."

Dallas kept the words low so Gracie wouldn't hear, but he needn't have worried. She was deep in conversation with Juno about the merits of some or other Goldfish flavor over the rest.

He selected another knife from the block and began slicing peppers, while Mia phoned the police. There was no way to avoid listening in and that was fine since he was itching to know the details of what sent Mia and Gracie out into the night. To him.

Was she really there in his trailer, rolling her damp hair into a ponytail? He nearly nicked his finger trying to take a sideways glance at her.

Mia explained the break-in to the dispatcher and gave Dallas's cell number as a contact before hanging up.

"They'll send a unit when they can, but the levee is failing just north of town." She laughed, a bitter sound. "They may need to evacuate my neighborhood anyway. It's true what they say, when it rains, it pours."

He dumped the peppers into sizzling olive oil and applied himself to neatly cubing the silken tofu. "It's not a coincidence. Guy was looking for something, maybe."

"Or looking to…" Her voice trailed away.

He stirred the pan with a wooden spoon. "I think he was searching and you surprised him. You said you had a flat. My guess is he made that happen to buy some time so he could search."

"For what? Why?" Her lips parted in exasperation, dark eyes flashing. He found his own mouth had gone dry.

"Could it be connected to the fire?" Mia pressed her hands to her forehead. "I don't even know what Cora was looking into. She didn't give me the slightest clue."

"Yes, she did," he said, sliding a plate in front of her.

Mia gasped. "The photo. It's in a file drawer. I have to go back and get it."

"In the morning. Sleep here. Juno and I will find an empty unit, and you can have this one."

"No, we couldn't displace you."

He sat on a chair across from her. "You're tired, and Gracie needs a safe place to sleep."

He could see the struggle unfold across her face in magnificent waves. "Mia, I'm not pressuring you to do anything. I'm just offering a safe place to sleep until morning. That's all."

She bit her lip.

He took her hand, the delicate fingers cool in his own. "Let's pray." He closed his eyes and thanked the Lord for keeping Gracie and Mia safe and for the provision of food and shelter. When he straightened, he thought he could see a million thoughts, a cascading river of emotions rolling through her eyes.

"I wouldn't guess you to be the kind to pray."

"Yeah? Because I'm a troublemaker?"

"No, no, of course not." She laughed. "Well, maybe a little."

"Troublemakers need God more than most." He picked up his fork and started to eat.

She did the same. "Wow, hot." She panted, reaching for a glass of water.

"Sorry." He handed her a piece of bread. "Water doesn't really help much. I've done a lot of backpacking. Spicy adds flavor to camping food." He considered the contents of the fridge. "I have some eggs. I'll scramble you some."

He started to rise, but she stopped him with a touch on his arm that seemed to ignite an odd flicker of nerves all the way up to his shoulder.

"This is fine." She swallowed. "Hector…loved spicy food, too, I just haven't had it in a while. Thank you for cooking it for me."

He should have gone with the eggs. "Do you worry about what he'll do when he's out?"

She swallowed and wiped her mouth with a paper

napkin. "He already knows too much about my life, even from prison."

And Hector's enemies did, too. He had squirreled away money, so the rumor went, a hefty sum extorted or swindled from his competitors, including the ferocious Garza family. Garza wanted it back and he'd sent out feelers to discover if Mia knew the whereabouts of the jackpot. Could be the guy who broke into her house wasn't searching for the photo, but the money.

A friendly DEA agent had alerted Reuben and Antonia to Garza's interest. And Antonia had hired Dallas to keep tabs on Mia. Dallas was good at watching people, finding the lost—fighting—if necessary, and skirting rules when they did not serve. He had no home, no ties. He was the perfect man for the job.

And Mia would despise him when she found out. He speared another slice of pepper.

For now, he would allow himself to savor the relative closeness between them, a feeling he had not experienced in a very long time. It was a shame that staring was bad manners, because all he really wanted to do was sit motionless and drink her in.

Her gaze was soft as she watched Gracie play with Juno, feeding him way more Goldfish than any dog should consume. When a gust of rain hammered on the metal roof with such force that it boomed through the trailer, Gracie ran to her mother's arms.

"It's okay, baby," Mia crooned. "Just the rain."

"Where's the bad man?"

Mia exchanged a quick look with Dallas.

"Bad man isn't going to come here," Dallas said.

"Why?"

"Because Juno is big and scary, and so am I."

Gracie smiled and hopped in his lap. He was so startled he didn't know what to do, sitting there as if he had a live grenade on his knees. Should he stand up? Give her a pat? Instead he sat rigid, hands raised, like a complete dork.

She grabbed him around the neck and pasted a cheesy kiss on his cheek. "I'm glad we came here."

So am I, his heart supplied, much to the surprise of his mind, but he was still relieved when she vacated his lap.

He saw to the details as best he could, thinking his mother would have played the job of host much better than he. Extra blankets for Mia and Gracie, heater turned on to a low hum to ward off the chill. Couple of clean towels in case anybody needed showering. Was there something else? Antacids, to cure any hot pepper damage. And magazines? *Wilderness Survival*. Did women like that sort of thing? He stood awkwardly in the doorway.

"Keep my phone here." He pulled out a spare he always had handy and programmed his cell into the one he gave Mia. "Call if you need anything. Use the laptop if you want. You can sign on as a guest."

Gracie crimped her lips. "What if the bad man comes while you're gone?" she whispered.

He considered telling her about the trailer he would sleep in across the way which gave him a direct line of sight that he intended to monitor on a regular basis. There were other things he could share, but he did not. "You want Juno to stay with you?"

"Yes." Gracie nodded, hopping from foot to foot. "Juno will watch me sleep."

"Actually, he'll sleep, too."

Mia shot him a look that indicated he probably should have kept that fact to himself. How was someone supposed to know what to divulge to a kid and what not to? Was there some kind of instruction manual?

"Juno will sleep, but he hears things that you can't."

"Like bad men?"

Dallas nodded.

"If he hears me, how will he know I'm not bad?"

"He just knows."

"Like God?"

Dallas took in the little bow of a mouth, the sweet innocence in that sober gaze and something moved inside him. "Yes, Gracie. God made dogs smart that way."

"My daddy's bad," Gracie whispered, so low he almost didn't hear it.

He heard Mia gasp, her lips pressed together. He swallowed and sent up a little prayer that he wouldn't say something stupid and took a knee. "Your daddy made mistakes. If he's sorry, God will help him be a good man again."

"God can do that?" she said, eyebrow raised.

"Yes, He can."

"How do you know?"

Dallas blew out a breath. "Because I was a bad man, and God helped me to be good again." Gracie gave him a long, serious look, then hugged him.

Mia wrapped her arms around herself. Had he made things better? Or worse? He could not tell from the expression on her face. Without another word that might tip the balance to one side or the other, he let himself out into the rain.

SIX

The night droned on. Rain hammered down and thoughts thundered through Mia's mind, three words pinching uncomfortably at her heart.

My daddy's bad.

Hector had done terrible things. He was bad, in some ways, but he had nearly died trying to save her sister from the trap he'd set for her on the island. He'd gone to prison, professing he would come out a better man. They had no future together, nothing that should stir her toward forgiveness. She would never love him again. The rage and hatred inside her would stay forever, she feared, blackening and staining her whole life. If Hector was bad, unforgivable, unredeemable, what did that mean for the child he had fathered? Or the wife who'd made so many mistakes herself?

And what of Dallas? She knew only a small bit about his troubled youth, but without question she was also certain Dallas Black was a good man. Then again, she'd thought Hector was, too.

Mia felt the soft rise and fall of Gracie's breathing, her back curled against Mia's stomach on the narrow bunk bed. How small she was, this little girl who looked to Mia to show her who God was, a god of forgiveness. It was something Mia could say with her mouth, but not embrace in her soul.

If he's sorry, God will help him be a good man again.

She wondered afresh about the strange and straight-forward Dallas Black. The troublemaker with a certainty about himself and God that she could no longer deny attracted her. She itched to soothe her restlessness with movement. Careful not to wake Gracie, Mia crept from the bed, earning an intense look from Juno who was stationed on the floor.

He stared at her, pupils two glimmers in the dimness. Dogs were strange to her, galumphing creatures who made messes and were prone to biting. The big lumbering animal scared her a bit, but he undeniably enchanted Gracie for some reason. Slobbery tongue, muddy paws, sharp teeth.

And a friend, to a child who had no others.

She crouched down next to the animal. "Thank you, Juno," she whispered.

The dog swiveled his ears, considering, and then laid his head back on his paws and assumed his watchful rest.

She clicked on the small light above the kitchen table and powered up Dallas's laptop, navigating to her inbox. While the computer booted up, she peered out the blinds into the unceasing rain. Across the way, a dim yellow light gleamed from the window of Dallas's trailer. It made her feel better to know he was there and at the same time grateful there was a safe distance between them.

The previous day played back in her mind like a bad movie. Cora gone and so was her job. Dr. Elias's face flashed in her memory. Had she misread the whole situation? Had he really been offering help? Trust your instincts, Dallas told her. But she trusted nothing about herself anymore, especially where men were concerned.

Pulling her attention back to the laptop, she opened her inbox. A message from her sister.

How are you? Hurricane cleanup continues here. Reuben is confident that he can start replanting the orchard soon. The man lives, eats and breathes oranges. How did I get fixed up with a guy who loves oranges more than me?

Mia smiled. Reuben loved his orchard, but they both knew that the man was desperately in love with Antonia. She felt the pang of envy. Hector had loved her, too, in his own way, but he'd loved power and money more.

I hear there is flooding in your area. Come to visit us in Florida. Aside from the odd hurricane, we've got perfect weather. We'll put you to work, but you'll be above water. I'd feel better if I could keep my eyes on you.

Antonia knew that Hector tracked Mia everywhere. And Hector's enemies? The people he'd cheated and double-crossed? Did they track her everywhere, too? A shiver rippled up her spine and she read the remainder of the message.

I know you don't want me to do the protective big sister thing. I'll try to be good, I promise. Reuben wants you here, too. He misses Gracie, and he wants to see her climb a tree. Waiting for your reply. A

Mia's fingers stiffened over the keyboard. See Gracie climb a tree? How did her sister know Gracie had managed to clamber up the old cottonwood tree in the backyard of their rented house a few days prior? The child was bursting with pride, even though Dallas had to get a ladder to fetch her down, and reported the accomplishment to everyone who crossed their path in the small town. Was Antonia having someone spy on her? Teeth gritted, she forced out several measured breaths.

She was turning into a nutcase. Reuben's life was trees. Of course he'd want to see Gracie climb one. She read the email again. The tree-climbing reference was purely coincidental, and her paranoia was turning her against the one person she knew was completely on her side. Hitting Reply, she contemplated how to put into words all that had happened the past two days.

Cora is dead. I am under suspicion for the murder. An intruder broke into our house. I'm staying in Dallas's trailer. I'm scared, worried, alone.

She perused the words that would send her sister into a panic. The sister who had been right all along. The woman who deserved above everyone else to enjoy the start of a marriage to the man she'd loved and lost and found again.

Backspace. Delete.

Blinking back tears she typed instead:

Gracie's growing like mad. She checks her teeth every day to see if they are loose, so desperate to use the special tooth box you sent. So busy here with work and school. Will write soon. Love you and Reuben. M

The inbox was cluttered with ads and offers from every company she'd ordered from recently using a credit card with her maiden name. It was a very tiny victory, but she took comfort in the fact that she had been able to provide the bare bones necessities with her very own hard-earned cash. Thanks to a secondhand store in town, she'd even managed a plastic wading pool that had gotten them through the hot months. It was light-years from the expensive toys and top-of-the-line clothes Gracie had when she was a baby in Hector's home, but it was bought with honest money. Gracie didn't seem to realize they were living perilously close to the poverty line. Not yet, anyway.

Clearing out the junk brought her to the last email. Her heart hammered. It could not be. The sender's name, *c.graham,* did not change no matter how hard she blinked. Cora Graham had sent her an email at four-thirty on the day she'd died, shortly after she'd sent the text summoning them to her house.

Panic squeezed Mia's stomach, and for a moment, she was too terrified to click open the email. Finally, with fingers gone cold, she did.

Find P. Finnigan. He knows the truth. I can't...

The message ended abruptly. Mia's heart pounded. Cora had sent the message when? As the smoke overcame her? As the poison paralyzed her body and she realized she could not escape?

Sobs wrenched through Mia. She clapped a hand over her mouth to keep from waking Gracie and staggered to the porch, stepping outside, grateful that the rain had momentarily slowed to a trickle. Sucking in deep breaths, she tried to rein in her stampeding emotions. It should not have surprised her to hear Dallas's door open. In a moment, he was next to her, peering into her face.

"Tell me," he said softly.

She couldn't answer over the grief that welled up inside.

With arms both strong and gentle, he pulled her close, not offering any more words, but the warmth and solace of his body pressed to hers.

With her head tucked under his chin, he let the mist dance lightly against his face, finding himself oddly relaxed with her in his arms. It was as if she molded naturally into his embrace, a perfect fit with a man who never fit in anywhere. He pressed his cheek against her hair and wondered if there was something he should be saying.

He went with silence. She would tell him what made her cry, or not. He would do everything in his power to help. That was all there was to it. So instead he relished the feel of her there, until the mist turned to drizzle and he guided her back into the trailer.

She wiped her face and sat at the kitchen table. He slid in across from her.

"I'm sorry," she said. "I slipped into hysteria there for a minute."

"No sweat."

"It was because of this." She turned the laptop to face him. "It's from Cora."

He read it. "Do you know a P. Finnigan?"

She shook her head, eyes huge in the near darkness. "Should we tell the police?"

"Yes. When you meet with them tomorrow. I'll work on it."

"How?"

"Let me worry about it. Get some sleep."

She offered an exasperated look. "Easy for you to say. You don't seem to need any sleep. Were you keeping watch on us all this time?"

I haven't been able to take my eyes off you since the day I met you, his fickle heart supplied. Fortunately, his mouth was still in charge. "Don't need much sleep."

"Or much furniture?"

He shrugged.

"Or a TV?"

"Too noisy." He won a smile with that one.

She rested her chin on her hand. "What do you need?"

The question surprised him. "Simple stuff. Backpack. Hot shower. Dog kibble."

That got a giggle that faded rapidly. "I mean, you move around all the time, like you're looking for something. What is it?"

How did he get himself into this sticky conversation? The silence stretched into awkward so he broke down and told her. "Ever hear that verse from Proverbs? Starts with 'trust in the Lord' and ends with 'Seek his will in all you do, and he will show you which path to take?'"

She nodded solemnly.

"Well, I tried to take my own path plenty of times, and it got me in jail and beaten badly and deep into gang life." He watched carefully to see if she would recoil. Most women did when he got around to his sorry life history. Those brown eyes stayed riveted to his face.

"Why a gang?"

"My dad died when I was a teen, and I went nuts.

Joined a gang, figured it made me a man, cool, like my brother."

"But he got out, didn't he?"

"Yeah. He's smarter than me. Military straightened him out. He tried to get me out, too, but I'm hardheaded. Took the beating to do that. I woke up handcuffed to the bed, and the first thing I thought of was, had I killed someone?"

She stayed quiet.

"I hadn't. God spared me from that, but I could have." His voice hitched a little. "Oh, how easily I could have done it."

"You wanted to go into the military, didn't you? Your brother told me, I think." Her voice was soft and soothing, like water over river stones.

He sighed. "My whole life I wanted to be a Marine like my father. My choices ruined that for me. They don't take people with damaged legs and gang histories." It still hurt to say it, but somehow, telling it to her, it was more of a dull ache than a ripping pain.

"I'm sorry."

"I'm not. Oh, I wish I could have done it some other way, but destroying my life brought me to the edge of ruin and that's where I finally found God. From then on, I figured I'd let Him show me where to go and I guess He brought me here for a while."

"Until it's time to go again?"

"Dunno. He'll thump me on the head when He wants me to put down some roots." He paused. "What about you? What do you need?"

She laughed, but there was no joy in the sound. "I need a place to call home, where I can put down roots so deep Gracie and I will never be uprooted again, but I'm never going to get that."

"No?"

"No, because Hector will never leave us alone, and everywhere we go his bad choices follow us." She closed her eyes for a moment and breathed out a sigh. "No, our bad choices. I've…" She swallowed. "I've been to jail, too, and now it looks as if I might be going there again." Her face paled. "What have we done to Gracie? Two people who were supposed to love and protect her? What have we done?"

Tears sparkled there in her eyes, but she would not let them fall. *Good girl, Mia.*

He took her hands and squeezed hard. "Gracie is happy and loved. Even I can tell that, and kids are like space aliens to me."

Small smile.

"Not one person on this Earth has no regrets."

Juno thrashed in his sleep.

"Except dogs."

"That's probably true." He fell into the warmth of those eyes. "I'll help you find a place to put down roots." Dumb. The moment he said it she pulled away. Way to go, Dallas Foot-in-Mouth Black.

Her tone became careful, formal. "Thank you, but I'm going to take care of us. That's a lesson I learned the hard way. I can only count on myself."

Wrong lesson. No bigger disappointment than one-self. "Sure. I didn't mean anything by it." He looked outside. "Sun's almost up. I'll follow you into town so you can talk to the cops."

He headed for the door, not at a run but close to it.

"There are some eggs, like I said, and maybe cheese somewhere. Will Gracie eat that?"

She nodded, face still tight. "Yes, thank you. I'll replace it all when I can."

He let her have that, if it was what she needed to feel in control.

"Good night, Mia."

Two hours later he followed her bashed up car toward town. Ominous signs of disaster preparation were visible as they drove along the main street. Shop owners were filling burlap bags with sand to be piled along the embankment that would optimistically stem the flood. Mia decided to stop and retrieve the photo before meeting with the police chief, so they drove along rain-drenched streets toward the lower lying valley where she rented a home. His gut tightened as a dark-colored SUV trailed behind them along the main drag and onto the narrow two-lane road. Not cause for alarm, per se, but he thought it just might be the same SUV he'd noticed parked on the side of the road several miles back. Colorado plates. Might be a rental.

Dallas slowed and so did the SUV. Not good. Keeping a distance. Nothing to be done to lose the guy at this point. Besides, in one of his stay-up-all-night reading frenzies, hadn't he read some sage advice from a Chinese general in 400 BC about keeping your friends close and your enemies closer?

"All right," he whispered, earning an interested look from Juno in the passenger seat. He maintained a steady pace, and the car dropped back just enough to preserve the gap between them.

He braked hard when Mia stopped abruptly. In a moment, he understood. The road dipped down, following the slope of the valley, only now the asphalt had disappeared under several feet of water. The surface was muddy and rippled, speckled with leaves and broken branches. She got out, hands on hips turning to give him an exasperated look that almost made him smile.

He joined her, noting that the SUV had pulled over a half mile behind them.

"Can your truck make it across?"

"Might, but I'm not going to risk anyone's safety. There's a bridge back a ways. We'll double back."

She groaned. "That will take us another half hour."

"Better late than drowned."

She looked as though she didn't appreciate his pearls of wisdom, but she acquiesced.

Juno sniffed disinterestedly at the water, stopping a moment to eye the car behind them on the road.

A look of fear flashed across her face. "Who is that?"

"Dunno, but I'll find out in a minute. Let's head for the bridge."

Mia gave the SUV a second look. He knew she wanted to ask more questions, but instead she got behind the wheel and turned around. Dallas fell in behind her and by the time they were rolling, the SUV had disappeared. Not for long. As he predicted, it picked them up again some five miles in, once again hanging back just enough.

The bridge was of sturdy steel construction, spanning the river that was normally well below its concrete piers. Now the water lapped considerably above that mark, but not enough to leave the structure impassable.

Yet.

Dallas decided it was time to get a better handle on the situation.

Mia drove over the bridge, and when she was safely across, he followed suit. A couple of feet in, he stomped on the brakes, bringing his vehicle to a dead stop.

"Time to come clean," he muttered, looking into the rearview as the SUV made the approach to the bridge. He stopped abruptly, too.

If their shadow was there for purely innocent reasons, he'd wait patiently, figuring there was some obstruction, maybe even honk after a bit, or try to pass. Certainly he'd get out of the car to investigate why Dallas was stopped, blocking the road.

Instead, the driver backed rapidly off the bridge, did a jerky three-point turn and took off in the other direction.

Dallas almost smiled for the second time that morning. He rolled down the window and called to Mia who had stopped and stuck her head out the window to question him.

"Go on. I'll be there soon."

Her eyes widened, quarter-size. "What are you doing?"

"Just making friends," he called out the window.

SEVEN

Dallas let the SUV outdistance him until it sped around a sharp bend in the shrub-lined road. He slowed and turned up a rough stretch which was probably more a trail than a road, but a way Dallas and Juno had explored many times in their backpacking travels. He stopped for only a moment to call a friend and give him the plate number.

"You know I got things to do 'sides hack info for you, right?" Farley said.

Dallas laughed. "Gonna help me or not?"

Farley snorted. "If you and Fido hadn't saved my life, I'd be in the bottom of a ravine with vultures using my bones for toothpicks."

"Vultures don't have teeth. Staying sober?"

"Yeah, man. Prayed myself through the last real bad stretch."

Dallas had prayed right along with him. And picked Farley up when he hadn't made it through, cleaned him up, filled him with coffee and nearly hog-tied the kid to get him to a meeting. "Gotta win, every day."

"I know, Mother, I know. Stop nagging and let me get to work."

"While you're at it, can you see if there's a P. Finnigan living in the area?"

"All right. See ya." Farley clicked off.

Dallas pushed the truck along, rocks pinging into the bottom, irritating Juno who barked just once.

"Half a mile more." Dallas squeezed the truck by a narrow section of path, branches scraping the sides, until he'd looped back out to the main road. A recent rock slide took out a bend of the highway, leaving the section blocked with a mess of boulders and only one lane passable. It was marked with cones and caution signs. Handy. He rolled down the window and listened to learn if he'd guessed correctly.

The sound of the SUV's approach told him he had. He edged past the rockfall and pulled the truck across the road. SUV guy would pass the blockage, encounter the truck and have to stop and back, which would slow him down enough for Dallas to get a good look. Risky, but with Mia's situation worsening by the minute, he needed some intel. Keep your enemies close…

The SUV was taking an unhurried pace. Dallas got out of the truck and he and Juno took a position behind a pile of rocks. Juno gave him the "you're probably crazy but I'm happy to participate in your insanity" look. They waited less than five minutes.

The SUV made the turn, stopped so fast the tires skidded a few inches. Dallas crouched low, peering over a granite lip of rock to identify the driver. To his surprise, the man shoved open the door and got out. Dallas took a picture with his cell phone.

Not much to him, but strength had nothing to do with size. Fair skin, buzz-cut hair. Tight skinny jeans and a shiny jacket that was probably fashionable somewhere in the world where Dallas hoped he never found himself.

The guy looked slowly around, hands loose at his sides. "We gonna talk?" he called out, voice higher pitched than Dallas guessed.

Dallas climbed out from behind the rock, and Juno scampered over to the man. He gave him a careful circling before he settled on sniffing his sneakers. "You're following Mia. Why? Who are you?"

The kid had to be no more than twenty. "Archie. How do you know I'm not following you?"

Dallas considered. "I'm not worth following. Did you break into her house?"

Archie crouched slowly and offered an outstretched hand to Juno. "I love dogs. Miss mine. He's some sort of lab and husky mix. Chews my shoes when I don't walk him enough and leaves them on the bed for me to find."

Dallas waited, watching to make sure Archie didn't reach for any kind of weapon in his ridiculous excuse for a jacket. "I asked you a question."

"My boss sent me here. I do what I'm told."

"Who's your boss?"

Archie straightened. "Guy who wants his property back."

Dallas's pulse sped up a fraction. "Do you work for Hector?"

Archie laughed. "Good one. I like to be on the winning team." He checked his watch. "You're a roadblock, in more ways than one. You need to step aside."

"Not if you're after Mia."

"She has something that belongs to my boss. He wants it back. No need for any pain. Just a simple negotiation."

"She doesn't have anything, and if you hurt her, it will be the last thing you ever do." He had not raised his voice, but the intensity made Juno return to his side and sit, rigid with expectation.

"All right," Archie said, pulling out a switchblade and flicking it open. "This is as good a place to kill you as any, but I don't want to hurt the dog. Tell him not to attack."

Juno wasn't an attack dog. In fact, he was the perfect Search and Rescue dog because he was passionately interested in people, but they also had a bond that surpassed owner and worker.

"All right," Dallas said calmly. "I'll send him to fetch and then you and I can get down to business. May I?" He gestured to a stick on the ground a few feet away and Archie nodded.

Dallas bent over to get the stick and while he was at it, grabbed a palm full of gravel loosed from the earlier slide.

"Okay, Juno. Ready to fetch?"

Juno shot to his feet as Dallas tossed the stick into the trees and then turned to fire the handful of gravel at Archie who instinctively raised an arm to cover his face. It was enough. Dallas aimed for Archie's arm and threw himself on top of the man, bringing him to the ground.

Juno returned and danced in crazy circles around the two, barking at a deafening volume.

Dallas used all his strength to slam Archie's knife hand into the ground, but the kid held fast. He dealt Dallas a blow with his free fist that got him in the back of the head, sending stars shooting across his vision. A flash of fire across his forearm rocked Dallas back as

Archie rolled away. Dallas scrambled to his feet, a line of red dripping from the wound on his arm.

Archie was already standing, eyeing the dog who continued to bark, uncertain, taking darting hops toward Archie and Dallas. "What happened to fetch?"

"He fetches people, not sticks, and he's not an attack dog, so don't hurt him."

"No," Archie said. "I guess I won't. Nice moves. Heard you were in a gang back in the day."

Dallas did not react to Archie's knowledge. Kid had done some research. "Not anymore."

"You can never get out of that world."

"Yes, you can. I did."

"You're gonna be in my face if I let you leave."

"If you're after Mia, then you're right. I will."

"Why? You into her or something?"

"Just a friend."

Archie gave him a look. "Uh-huh. Sure." He straightened. "Short on time, so I'm gonna end it here, but I'll take care of the dog for you."

"Appreciate that." Dallas went into a ready stance, learned not in a karate studio or a self-defense class, but from adrenaline-fueled fights with other lost young men bent on self-destruction. To defend their brotherhood, what had been his brotherhood, his family, or so he'd fooled himself into believing. All for Uncle, for the territory. He did not want to fight, but if it would free Mia, then he would do it. Juno whined, big torso heaving with confusion. A finder, not a fighter. Dallas wished he had spent his life doing the same.

Self-recrimination later, he told himself. There was no effective way to defend against a knife attack and he had the scars to prove it. Only one alternative that wouldn't get him killed and he took it. When Archie lunged forward, Dallas jerked aside and aimed a crushing kick at Archie's knee.

Archie's grunt of pain told Dallas he'd hit the target. He stumbled and Dallas aimed another kick at the knife hand which sent the switchblade spiraling into the bushes as Archie fell stomach-first onto the wet ground.

Dallas immediately knelt on his back, knee between the shoulder blades, shushing the furiously barking Juno.

Dallas's heart was pounding, the pulse hammering so loudly in his ears he did not at first hear the chug of a heavy vehicle approaching from the other side of the rock slide.

"Someone's coming. Moving fast," Archie puffed. "What are you gonna do? You don't move your truck, whoever that is could slam right into it and go over the cliff."

He was right, but the second he released Archie, the guy would bolt or find his switchblade and have another go at Dallas. The pop of gravel sounded louder now.

No choice. He couldn't risk causing an accident.

He leaned closer to Archie. "Stay away from Mia."

Archie answered with a laugh. Dallas released his hold and ran to the truck, cranked the engine as Juno leapt in and got the truck out of the way with a screech of tires. He made it just far enough to pull off onto the narrow shoulder when Archie flashed by in his SUV, snapping off a salute to Dallas. A moment more passed before an emergency vehicle swept by, no sirens going, but lights flashing.

They, too, had to take the roundabout way to Mia's neighborhood since the main road was underwater. The driver gave Dallas a wave, thanking him for pulling off the road.

He settled in behind, trying not to crowd the responders. Should he worry more that the situation ahead had turned into an emergency? Or that he'd let Archie, the guy with a switchblade, get that much closer to Mia and Gracie?

Hands gripping the wheel, Mia answered Gracie's myriad questions mechanically, not realizing what she was agreeing to.

"I can have ice cream for breakfast? Super duper," Gracie said. "You never let me have that before. Not even Tina lets me have ice cream for breakfast, only cookies."

Mia blinked. "What? No of course you can't have ice cream for breakfast. I was thinking about something else, and Tina should not give you cookies for breakfast, either."

In truth, she was trying to squash down the concern that washed through her belly. Dallas had taken off after a stranger to do what? Confront him? Follow the car? She hit the brakes as a roadblock appeared. A police volunteer in an orange vest approached her open window.

"What is it? What's going on?"

"Levee failed. Town's flooded. We're evacuating now."

"But I've got to get to my house. I need to…" Retrieve a picture of a woman who was at the scene of a murder? That seemed too fantastic a tale to drop on the harried-looking volunteer who was already wet to the skin, though it had stopped raining. "I have to get something. It's important."

"Sorry, ma'am. It's not safe to drive in. You can see from the road there, where everyone is gathered. No farther than that."

She dutifully pulled the car off the road, turned off the engine and helped Gracie out. They skirted giant puddles and slogged through patches of grass until they came to a gathering of a half dozen people wearing emergency vests who were peering at clipboards along with the volunteer firefighters. It was a sort of makeshift emergency center with a pop-up canopy to keep off the rain. With Gracie bundled close, Mia drew to the edge of the bluff, gazing down at what had been her home.

The house she rented was one of only a half dozen, scattered in between with thickly clustered trees. Now the quiet, country road was a river, water lapping the middle of the doorways. At first she couldn't locate her house, until she saw the weathervane turning lazily in the breeze.

Gracie pulled at her mother's hand. "Where's our house?"

Mia breathed out a long sigh. She had not yet even managed to tell Gracie the hard truth about Cora, but there was no way to shield her child from this. "The levee couldn't hold all the water. It spilled over and flooded our house."

They stood for a moment in silence.

"When will the water go away?"

Great question, and she'd give her eye teeth to know the answer. "I'm not sure."

And when the water did recede, what would be left behind? Sodden clothes, ruined furniture acquired a bit at a time on her meager salary. And the rocking chair, oh that precious wooden chair snatched up at a garage sale when she shouldn't have spent the money. How many hours had she spent in that chair after Gracie went to sleep, studying her nursing coursework, dreaming about the future she imagined she was providing for her daughter.

A lump formed in her throat.

"Where are we gonna sleep, Mommy?"

The question danced away, unanswered on the wind. They watched an inflatable Zodiac boat, guided by two firefighters, as it approached the bluff carrying an elderly couple swaddled in life jackets, their sparse white hair pasted in wet clumps to their foreheads. She searched the area for Dallas. What had happened to him?

Mia felt a hand on her shoulder.

She turned to find Dr. Elias wearing an orange vest over a long-sleeved denim shirt and jeans. Her mind was still dealing with the shock of seeing her whole life submerged and she wasn't sure what feeling floated to the top at the sight of her former employer.

"I'm sorry," he said, eyes somber. "The Army Corps of Engineers couldn't save the levee. They tried their best."

Mia nodded. "I'm sure they did."

"Hiya, Dr. Elias," Gracie said.

He smiled and knelt in front of her. "Well, hello there. I'm glad to see you."

"Our house is all watery now."

"Don't worry, honey. We'll find you a place to live."

Mia took Gracie's hand. "The doctor is here to help people who are hurt. Let him do his job now."

Dr. Elias straightened and put an arm around Mia's shoulders. "Really, I can help you find a place."

She didn't move, torn between shock and uncertainty. Was this the man whom she'd thought meant to harm her only days before? There was no longer a clear answer to any issue crowding her mind and heart.

Where would they go? She had maybe twenty dollars in her purse and a credit card on which she'd already charged a semester's tuition. "Why would you want to do that after you fired me?"

He sighed. "I told you I would help you, even if you couldn't work at the clinic. You lied to protect your child, not to hurt me. I'm sensitive about lying. A foible of mine."

How had the talk become about him?

He squeezed her shoulders. "I can fix you up in…"

A woman approached, dark hair cut into a stylish bob that remained neatly coiffed in spite of the elements. The fragrance of a floral perfume clung to her, odd and out of place at a disaster scene. Green eyes flashed under delicate brows. "Thomas, you're needed at the launch point. They're going out on a rescue for a possible heart attack in progress."

"Of course." He patted Gracie on the head and jogged toward the Zodiac that was being readied to embark on the rescue mission.

The woman gave Mia a tight smile. Her face was carefully made up to show her fortysomething years to full advantage, jewelry small and tasteful. "I'm Catherine Elias, the good doctor's wife."

The slight sarcasm left Mia off balance. "I'm Mia Verde and this is Gracie, my daughter. I work… I worked for your husband until just recently. We met at a party you were kind enough to host for the staff."

Mia's eyes were drawn again toward the water. "That was my house down there."

Catherine's face softened, giving her a more youthful look. "I'm sorry. This must be hard for you. No job, no house and a daughter to care for." She seemed to consider for a moment. "I heard Thomas telling you he could help you find a place and I guess…" She shrugged. "Never mind. I'm tired, that's all. Our kids are almost finished with high school, but I remember how difficult it is when they're young. But sweet, too, those little ones." She looked wistfully at Gracie.

"Yes," Mia murmured, uncertain how to respond to the sudden change in mood.

"We have a small cabin up in the mountains here. It's remote, but you are welcome to stay there until you get another place."

"Thank you. That is incredibly kind of you, but we'll find something." Mia was amazed that her tone was calm and controlled. Inside, her gut churned like the gray water splashing against the bluff.

When? Where? And most of all how? She felt like dropping to her knees and praying, but she would not crumble. Not now. Not ever again. She would make a way, where there was none. "Where are the townspeople being evacuated to?"

Catherine pulled her gaze from Gracie. "The college gym just up the hill. It will work for a night or two anyway. You can walk up, or there's a van arriving in a minute to carry people."

"Great." Mia scooped Gracie up. "Mommy always wanted you to go to college. You'll be the first four-year-old attendee ever. We'll just wait with the gang until the van arrives."

Feeling Catherine's eyes following them, she hastened toward the wet neighbors gathered in a forlorn group under a sodden canopy. She texted Tina, relieved when the girl answered back.

College classes canceled. Gone home to folks until flood's past. Kiss Gracie for me and try to stay dry.

"Hiya, Dallas," Gracie called over her shoulder.

Mia whirled, her spirit rising at the sight of Dallas loping toward her with Juno at his heels.

He gave Gracie a tight smile and she immediately crouched to administer an ear rub to Juno. Mud streaked his shirt, and Mia's eyes traveled downward, caught by the circle of bloody gauze tied around his forearm.

Her stomach clenched. "The man in the car."

"I'm okay, but he got away." Dallas seemed to weigh something in his mind before he leaned close and spoke in a low murmur. "He's keeping tabs on you for his boss."

She forced out the question. "Who is his boss? Never mind. It's Hector, isn't it?" Bitterness rose in her throat like a bubbling acid. "He's got people watching my every move. He'll never let us build a life without him."

"I don't think that's it."

Wind slapped her hair into her face. "Who then? Who would bother?"

"People who think Hector passed something on to you."

"Passed what?"

He didn't answer. Instead he showed her the picture on his cell phone. "Recognize him?"

Everything went fuzzy. She inhaled deeply, trying to stem the whirling in her head. "It's the man who broke into my house. I can't understand this. What is happening to my life?"

He embraced her then, and she let him. His arms pressed away the panic, the fear that grew with every passing day. The heat of his skin melted some of the numbing cold that gripped her.

"I'm checking into it. I'll have more answers soon."

"I've been in Spanish Canyon for months. Why would he come here now? What am I going to do?"

His embrace tightened. "Come back to the trailer. I'll keep watch. He won't get close."

Protection. Strength. Safety. And a delicious sliver of fascination. Dallas Black made all those things erupt in her belly. She turned so her lips touched the smooth skin of his jaw. His dark hair cocooned her face against the warm hollow of his neck. How her body craved the comfort of his touch, her soul cried out to have a partner to help her through the flood that she knew was far from over.

But she'd had that perfect union before. A God-blessed marriage, or so she'd thought, until she finally saw Hector for what he was. Now "until death do us part" sounded more like a sentence than a comfort. Never again. Never.

She stepped back, sucking in a breath. "I'm going to the college. They've got an evacuation shelter set up there."

He frowned. "You want to go sleep on the gym floor where anyone can get at you and Gracie?"

She took Gracie's hand. "We'll be safe there."

"Safe?" His face was incredulous. "This guy Archie was ready to kill me to get to you."

"There are lots of people going. We'll never be alone."

The muscles of his jaw jumped. "Absolutely not."

She stiffened. "We'll be in a group all the time. Never alone. Besides, you don't make decisions for me."

"Somebody should, because you're letting what happened to you with Hector color your judgment."

Cheeks burning, her stomach tightened into an angry ball. "I'm doing what's best for Gracie."

"Are you?" He fisted his hands on his hips, and she saw fresh blood welling through the white gauze when his muscles flexed.

Am I? Suddenly she wondered, but she couldn't reverse course now. Right or wrong she had to call the shots for Gracie. Just her and no one else. "I'll return your phone as soon as I can."

She pulled Gracie along to the van that had just wheezed up the slope, not allowing herself to look back. She knew what was behind her anyway. A disappointed German shepherd.

And one very angry Dallas Black.

EIGHT

"What?" Dallas barked into the phone.

Farley whistled. "Bite my head off, why don't you? Got a burr under your backpack?"

"Sorry. Bad day." Too bad to try to explain to Farley. He molded his tone into something that might pass for civil. "Do you have anything for me?"

"Seven P. Finnigans in the vicinity. Sending you those addresses."

"Thanks."

"And the car was rented to an Archie Gonzales, from Miami."

Miami. Not a surprise. "Okay."

"One more thing, man. Norm, over at the rental car place. I know him, and he's a crusty old codger. He's got trackers on the rentals."

Dallas's nerves quickened. "Illegal, of course,"

"Of course, but he's in favor of slapping a nice hefty fee on the cars if they're taken out of state. Anyway, it was easy to hack into his tracking system."

"Do I want to know how you did that?"

"Probably not."

"What did you find out?"

"Most of his routes were routine, except one I found interesting. Guess who he's been to see recently?"

"Not in the mood for guessing games."

"Dr. Elias."

"That's not news. I think he's been at the clinic shadowing Mia."

"Not the clinic. Archie's been to the doctor's house."

His house? Dallas struggled to put it together and almost missed the finish.

"At 3:13 a.m."

Not the usual time for social calls. "Thanks, Farley. I owe you lunch."

"Yeah, and a vacation in Maui."

"We'll start with lunch."

"All right, cheapskate."

Dallas disconnected. The next call would be to Reuben and Antonia. There was no more room to keep secrets. Mia needed to know everything. He swallowed, picturing her maddeningly stubborn brown eyes, the need for independence burning as bright as the hurt. When she knew, she would hate him.

But at least she'd still be alive.

Dallas's arm throbbed. He strolled as casually as he could through the collection of hastily parked cars on the grassy shoulder of the road, leaving Juno in the truck to catch a nap. He realized he was grinding his teeth when he passed Mia's battered car. If she'd listen to reason…if she'd consider the smart choice.

Like you did? His conscience flipped through the myriad prideful mistakes he'd made. Rival gang members he'd fought, threatened. Store owners he'd intimidated. Petty theft he'd committed to prove himself to his ersatz family. His damaged body would always be a reminder of that disastrous past.

Most of his shame came when he remembered the way he'd coveted the looks he'd gotten from people, the respect he'd imagined in their eyes. Turns out it was not respect, but fear. He'd been too blinded to turn from the smothering blanket of gang life.

In spite of his brother Trey's tough love born of experience.

With no regard for his mother's pleading requests and avalanche of prayers.

It had taken waking up in the hospital with part of his spleen missing and his knee on fire, shaking from alcohol withdrawal and his boyhood dream to become a Marine ruined, for him to fall on his face in front of the Lord. Maybe it was the humiliation of being handcuffed to the hospital bed, knowing he deserved to go to jail for many things, including possession of an illegal firearm and simple assault. Possibly it was the realization that he had shamed his mother, his brother and his father's memory. Undoubtedly, it was God shouting his name.

At rock bottom, there's no more room for pride.

Only God.

Once he'd let go, God had shown him the goodness in people, the desperate love of his family, his own potential to be a man who lifted others, rather than striking them down. Somewhere along the way, he'd found there was goodness inside him, as well.

The fall had hurt, and he wished he could help Mia learn what he had without the dramatic descent. He sighed. *God's job, Dallas. Yours is to keep her safe.* It was a good reminder. No matter what the oddball storm of feelings brewing inside, Mia was his job, his mission. In spite of the pain from Archie's knife, and Mia's ridiculous desire to stay at the college shelter, he moved on through the sea of parked cars.

He saw no sign of Archie's rental, a small mark in their favor.

Sunset was not due for another hour, but the clouds succeeded in sealing the light away behind a wall of gray. Bad sign. The levees were similarly stressed all over Spanish Canyon and the rivers and catchments swollen to capacity. On an up note, the last weather report he'd heard called for only a mild rainfall in the next forty-eight hours. With that weather break, they might be able to stave off any more serious flooding and evacuations.

The flood lent strange odors to the air—the scent of wet stone, sodden foliage and trees uprooted from centuries of packed earth. Mia's house was underwater to the eaves, and so was the picture that might shed some light on Cora's death. He guessed Archie had not been there in Mia's house looking for the photo, but searching for Garza's money. However the meeting between Elias and Archie still puzzled him.

He was about to return to his truck, parked well away from the others when a stealthy movement caught his attention. Trick of the cascading shadows? No, there was another pulse of motion near a well-appointed blue BMW.

He drew back, crouching behind Mia's car to watch as a slight figure stealthily opened the passenger door. Whoever it was wore a hat and a dark windbreaker. Pretty low for someone to take advantage of a disaster situation to rifle through someone's car. But it was true that disasters brought out both the best and worst in people. He was about to demand an explanation, when he realized this wasn't a stranger, not a total stranger anyway.

Easing closer, he could see Susan's profile well enough to be sure it was her, the red-haired woman who'd shown up at his trailer.

And snuck out with your knife, he reminded himself.

Still keeping low between vehicles, he crept nearer.

She sat in the passenger seat of the car, examining the pile of papers in her lap that she'd taken out of the glove box. So intent was she on her mission, she didn't look up until he wrenched open the door.

With a scream she bolted out, spilling the papers on the muddy ground. For a moment, she stood frozen, staring, chest heaving with panic.

"Breaking-and-entering a specialty of yours?"

She let out a gust of air. "The door was open. That's not breaking in."

"Whose car?"

Still no response. Keeping her in his peripheral vision he picked up one of the papers. Catherine Elias. "Why are you interested in Dr. Elias's wife?"

"She's a fake."

"A fake what?"

"She's living a lie, and I'm going to prove it."

"I thought you were interested in finding out who killed Cora."

She nodded, lips tight, eyes flat and hard as wet stones. "That's right."

"Do you think Catherine killed Cora?"

"Leave me alone, Dallas. This doesn't concern you right now."

He took a step toward her. "You're coming with me

to the police. No more sneaking around breaking into cars. I'm out of patience with these guessing games."

She shook her head. "I'm not going with you anywhere."

He did not want to force a woman to do anything against her wishes, but this particular woman was dangerous. He took her wrist, the tendons standing out against the skin, pulse slamming violently through her veins. "You need to come with me, Susan."

He'd prepared himself for her to pull away. Instead she surged close, her clawed fingers pinching his biceps, face so close her sour breath bathed his face. "Listen to me," she hissed. "There are dangerous people in this town, people who are not who they appear to be." Her mouth twitched at the corners, and he fought the urge to recoil.

"Like Mrs. Elias?"

She did not seem to hear him. "Dangerous people who will kill Mia Verde and her little girl, just like they killed Cora. If you try to go to the police, or anyone else, they'll just kill her quicker."

His stomach flipped. "Who? Tell me, and I'll help you."

She moved back slightly to search his eyes. "Ah, sweet boy. Are you going to protect me from a killer?"

"If I can."

"I'm not afraid to die," she said, releasing his shoulders. "It's the living part that's scary."

He felt as though he was stuck in a strange horror film. Was she crazy? Was he, for letting go of her wrist?

The sound of voices made them both turn. Susan quickly returned the papers to the glove box and ducked down, yanking him to a crouch next to her. Through the window they saw Catherine Elias and an orange-vested volunteer consulting a clipboard as they walked toward the car. Catherine pointed to something on the first page and the two stopped to talk.

"Remember," Susan whispered, "if you tell anyone, Mia and Gracie will die. I'll contact you when I can." She sprinted off through the cars and ducked into a screen of trees. He scooted far enough away from Catherine's car that he would not be taken for a stalker, and then walked back to his truck where he sat on the front seat, brooding.

The obvious course of action was to go to the police, but they already suspected Mia of being involved in Cora's death. What would they make of his wild story about some mystery woman poking through Catherine's car?

Her words circled in his gut, cold and heavy. *"Dangerous people who will kill Mia Verde and her little girl, just like they killed Cora."*

Now his head pounded right along with the throbbing in his forearm. He should go home, back to the trailer to think it through, but he didn't want to be that far away from Mia and Gracie with Archie on the loose. If he checked himself in to the college evacuation center, Mia would be furious and possibly try to go find yet another unsuitable place to house herself and Gracie.

Juno poked his nose at Dallas, bringing him back. "What next?" his eyes inquired. The dog was eager to do just about anything Dallas requested except get his nails trimmed. That required several dozen treat bribes and some strong-arming from his owner. "Looks like we sleep in the truck again, boy, but I've got some kibble for you, don't worry."

He opened the door for the dog.

"Don't suppose you've got any notions on how to handle a stubborn woman, do you, Juno?"

Juno huffed out a breath and laid his head on his paws.

"Yeah, that's what I thought," Dallas said, giving his friend a pat.

Mia took the blankets offered to her and found her way to the side of the gym designated for women. She chose two cots together, but at a bit of a distance from the nearby family consisting of a wife and three teenage girls and a few older women who had already set up their makeshift beds. The two older women sat together, hands clasped, praying softly, one with wispy white hair. Perhaps they were sisters. Longing surged through her and she wished Antonia was there.

Gracie stared. "Is that Miss Cora? I want to go see her."

A pain stabbed deep inside. "No, honey. Just looks like her. The hair is the same color."

"Oh." Gracie said, looking up at the ceiling lights. "I don't like it here. Maybe we can go stay with Miss Cora. She prays nice, with songs and everything."

Tears collected in Mia's eyes, and she blinked hard. It hadn't dawned on her until just then that she had never prayed with Gracie, that she'd funneled her own anger into a deluge that kept her daughter far from the Lord, too. Her choice had bled down to Gracie, staining her with Mia's own sin.

"Gracie, I'm sorry. Do…do you want to pray with me?"

Gracie nodded, grabbing Mia's hands. "Okay. I'll say it. I know how." Gracie thanked God for Mia and

Cora and the cheese sandwich and cookies she'd gotten from the volunteer who'd included an extra sweet for the little girl and the blue blanket and Auntie Nia and Uncle BooBen. "And thanks for Dallas 'cuz he says Daddy can be good again and thanks for Juno 'cuz he plays with me. Ayyyyyy men!" The last word came out in such an unexpected volume that the others shot amused glances their way.

Mia raised an eyebrow. "That was a big amen."

"Cora says you should always fill up the amen with joy," Gracie said. "So can we go see her?"

That innocent heart had never confronted death before. Certainly Mia would never have chosen to tell Gracie in the wake of losing every possession to the cruel water that engulfed their house. This time, she did send up a prayer of her own, a halting, awkward, stumbling effort.

Help me tell her.

Help her cope.

Mia forced out the words. "Honey, I have something sad to tell you."

Gracie regarded her soberly, bouncing a bit on the cot beside her.

"Miss Cora died. I'm so sorry. Her house caught on fire and the smoke got inside her lungs." Mia watched in fear as Gracie's brow puckered. "She's in Heaven now."

"Oh." Gracie considered the news as a full fifteen seconds ticked away. "Can we stay at her house until she comes back?"

It was as if her heart shrank smaller and smaller, concentrating the pain until it nearly choked her. "She's not coming back, baby," Mia whispered.

"Never?"

Mia took Gracie's small fingers in her own. "No, honey. Never."

"Mommy, I think that's not right. She's gonna come soon. Can I keep the blanket?" Gracie held up the blue blanket neatly folded at the foot of the cot.

"Yes," Mia said weakly. "The volunteers said you could if you want to."

Gracie wrapped herself up and laid down on the cot, singing softly to herself.

Mia watched her, filled with a river of tenderness that almost overwhelmed her. It would sink in, in time, that Cora was gone. Maybe that was a gift God gave his little children, a gradual realization that was kinder, somehow than the swift bolt of knowledge. Shadows crept along the edges of the gym, and quiet conversations gave way to silence. Mia found she could not sleep, though the cot was not at all uncomfortable.

She tossed and turned on the prickly choices she had made, ignoring Dallas's advice. His words floated back through her memory.

"Ever hear that verse from Proverbs? Starts with 'trust in the Lord' and ends with 'Seek His will in all you do, and He will show you which path to take.'"

She yanked the covers up around her chin. He could afford to believe such things; he had no one depending on him except for a dog. Dallas would not wake up tomorrow to a hungry child with not a single spare pair of socks, no place to live and nowhere to go. That was going to be Mia's scenario in the morning and she'd have to figure out how to deal with it.

A gleam of light crept across the gym floor. Someone entered carrying an enormous pile of towels, heading after a moment of hesitation, toward the locker room.

She sighed. At least there was the possibility of a hot shower in the morning. Again she tried to force her body to relax on the cot. This time her wandering attention was caught by whispered conversation as two people talked by the light of a battery-powered lantern.

Giving up the attempt at sleep, she got up in search of a drink of water and caught a sentence of the conversation going on near the doors.

"She's practically a stranger," a familiar voice growled.

"No, she's not," Catherine Elias hissed. "That red-headed wacko is stalking me."

Dr. Elias reached for his wife's hand, but she jerked it away, nearly upsetting the lantern. "She lost her husband. I treated her some time later. She attached herself to me and Peter."

"Peter Finnigan? You never mentioned that."

Peter Finnigan? Mia's heart beat faster at the name from Cora's email. She wanted to ask, to step forward into the lamplight, but she decided to retreat from the private conversation instead. As she did so, she heard Dr. Elias continue.

"I didn't want to upset you, honey."

"What's her fixation with me?"

He sighed. "She wants to be with me, ever since I treated her all those years back. I've tried to keep her away because she's…unhinged."

Unhinged. Mia crept back toward her cot, but not until she heard Mrs. Elias's reply.

"She's dangerous."

Dangerous. They had to be talking about Susan, the woman from the fire, who'd showed up at Dallas's trailer.

She was in such a state of confusion, at first she

thought she'd gone to the wrong cot. "Gracie?" she called softy, turning in a quick circle.

Gracie's blanket lay on the floor, but the girl was nowhere to be found. She'd gone to the bathroom. That was it.

Mia made her way quickly to the ladies' room. Empty. Jogging now back out into the main gym, she raced through the rows of cots, peering intently to see if Gracie had mistakenly crawled into the wrong bed.

There she was—at the end of the row, curled into a ball under the blanket. Mia felt the weight of the world rise off her shoulders and she heaved out a gusty sigh.

"You scared me, Gracie," she whispered, laying a hand on the girl's shoulder. "You're in the wrong bed."

The child sat up, blinking dark eyes. The woman on the cot reached out a protective hand. "This is my daughter, Evelyn. Can I help you?"

Shock rippled through Mia. Gracie was gone.

NINE

Gracie's here somewhere. She's not gone. Mia began to run now, around the perimeter of the gym to the men's area, in case her daughter had gotten confused. She rechecked Gracie's cot, snatching up the blue blanket to prove to her hands what her eyes could not accept.

Gracie was not there.

"Gracie?" What started out as a whisper, grew in volume until people began to sit up on their cots.

Dr. Elias and his wife materialized, lantern in hand. "What's wrong?" the doctor asked.

"Gracie's gone."

Catherine scanned the room. "I'm sure she's here somewhere."

Fear clawed at Mia's insides, prickling her in cold waves of goose bumps. "What if she wandered outside?" Down the hill, to the edge of the bluff where there was six feet of floodwater to fall into?

"We'll look right now," Dr. Elias said, heading for the door. "Catherine, keep searching inside." He put a hand on Mia's shoulder. "We'll find her."

At the moment, all her anger at the doctor dissipated in a cloud of hope.

We'll find her.

They ran outside, sprinting along the path to the edge of the bluff, looking down into the swirling, moonlit water. Mia's stomach was twisted into a knot. Would she see her little girl floating there, facedown in the merciless waves? Shaking all over she forced herself to look.

"No sign of her. I'll look downstream," Dr. Elias said, handing her a flashlight. "Would she have gone to the woods back up by the gym?"

"I don't know," Mia answered. "I'll check there." She turned toward the patch of trees, dark silhouettes against the sky. Why would she head out of the gym on her own? Gracie was not afraid of the dark, but she did sleepwalk sometimes. Mia looked for signs that Gracie had passed by, but the ground was littered with bushels of fallen leaves and downed branches. The darkness wasn't helping, either.

"Gracie?" Mia called, her voice tremulous.

She walked under the dripping canopy. Droplets landed on her face like tears. "Gracie?" she called again. There was no answer but the rustle of pine needles, the movement caught by her flashlight the result of debris blowing along the ground. Gracie wasn't here, Mia could feel it.

She had to be inside the gym, she'd fallen asleep somewhere or gone to look for a snack. Mia was beaming the flashlight ahead to find her way out, when a man grabbed her from behind. A hand, smelling of nicotine, covered her mouth, as a strong pair of arms held her in a tight clinch.

"Mrs. Sandoval, listen carefully because I'm not the patient type and I want to go back to Florida. We know Hector has sent you a stash of money and it belongs to my boss. He wants it back. I've already searched your home and followed you around like a tracking dog, and I'm sick of it so I decided we should have a little meeting. Now, I'm going to move my hand so you can tell me what I want to know. If you scream, I'll hurt you. Understand?"

Blood rushing in her ears, she managed a nod. He peeled away his fingers and she turned to face him. It was the same man who had tried to trap them in her garage. She didn't care. There was only one thing her mind screamed out to know.

"Did you take my daughter?"

Archie's expression was hard to read. "I asked you a question. Answer."

"I don't have any money from Hector, and I don't know where it is."

"Mr. Garza thinks otherwise."

Garza. Powerful. Ruthless. A man who ran the Miami drug trade. "I don't have it. If I did, would I be renting a house here? Driving a secondhand car?"

Archie shrugged. "Not my job to figure you out, just to return the money. Got a tip that you've hidden it somewhere."

"A tip from whom?"

He didn't answer.

"Please," she whispered. "Did you do something to Gracie?"

Flashlights played over the grass outside the gym. Archie stepped back into the shadows. "Think about what's important and what you will lose if you don't give me what I want."

He melted away into the wet trees.

She ran blindly, branches slapping at her face, back toward the gym.

Gracie, Gracie, her heart chanted as she sprinted straight into Dallas, rocking back off his hard chest.

"Gracie's gone. Archie got hold of me."

His fingers dug into her shoulders. "Did he hurt you?"

"No."

His eyes dropped to her hands. "Is it hers?"

"What?" She realized through her fog that she was still holding the blue blanket. "This? Yes, it's Gracie's."

He called Juno and held out the blanket to the dog. "Find."

Juno bounded over the grass, startling those doing the flashlight search.

"Can he smell her?" she whispered.

"He's air scenting, following her smell." They watched the dog jog up to the gym entrance, scratching to be let in.

Dallas eased the doors open and Juno disappeared inside. Mia and Dallas followed her in. The dog followed the scent to the girl's bathroom, but stopped before he made it to the threshold. Juno circled a few times and stood, nose twitching.

Mia pressed shaking fingers to her mouth. "He doesn't know where she is."

"Give him a minute. There are a lot of scents in here. He's an older dog, so he's better at thinking it out and taking his time."

"Are you sure?"

"Trust the dog."

Trust a dog? With her baby's life? She wanted to yell, to scream at the top of her lungs as she watched Juno make a slow perusal of the room. Most of the occupants were awake now, helping look under cots and in corners, while others stood on the sides of the gym, giving Mia looks of abject pity.

She felt Dallas's hand take her hand and he squeezed hard. She clung to that touch as if it were the only thing that could keep her alive. Maybe it was. If Juno didn't find Gracie… She could not breathe, her ears rang.

She felt the room spinning, and Dallas forced her into a chair. "Deep breaths."

Waves of nausea and panic alternated through her body as she struggled not to black out.

Juno scratched at a darkened door in the back of the gym that Mia had not noticed.

"Stay here," Dallas said. "I'll check it out."

No way. Mia struggled to her feet, shoving down the dizziness by sheer willpower and staggered after him.

The exit opened onto a chilly hallway with metal doors at even intervals. Juno charged into the inky darkness.

Dr. Elias trotted behind them. "All the doors along this corridor are locked except the far exit door, for safety's sake. I saw to it myself."

"And the exit door? Where does it open?"

"Onto the parking lot," Elias said.

Mia ran to the end, ignoring the men. She was about to plunge through.

"Wait," Dallas said. He nodded at Juno who was pacing the corridor in regular arcs, nose quivering.

"You stay with your dog. I'm going to find my kid," Mia snapped.

"We might be wasting time," Dallas said. "Let the dog work, just for a minute longer."

"I don't have a minute," she shrieked. "Gracie might be out there in the water."

"This is why we train rescue dogs, Mia," Dallas

barked. "They save time and effort and find a victim faster than a person ever could. You've got to trust the dog. Trust me."

For a long moment she stared at him. Seconds passed into excruciating minutes. Trust. She could not give it to him, not now, not with Gracie's life at stake. She pressed on the panic bar, just as Juno scratched furiously at one of the doors. Dallas opened it.

"So much for locked. It's a door to the stairwell." He held it for Juno who raced away. In a matter of moments, the dog returned, sat rigidly at Dallas's feet and barked exactly two times.

"It leads to the roof, I think," Dr. Elias said, voice low and hushed. "How did she unlock the door? Could a little girl climb three stories all by herself in a darkened stairwell?"

Gracie could. Hope and fear clawed together in her throat and she pushed forward, but Dallas had already plunged through the door, long legs churning up the stairs leaving Mia racing to catch up.

Dallas reminded himself as he ran that Mia did not know Juno like he did. Trust a dog? With his life. If Juno alerted, he'd found Gracie all right. The question was, in what condition? He knew she hadn't unlocked the door that led to the stairwell by herself. Dallas did not allow himself to dwell further on the thought. Three flights at top speed, following the sound of Juno's nails clicking on the concrete until he got too far ahead for them to hear. When they reached the door to the roof, Juno was sitting, nose shoved to the gap under the threshold, tail wagging for all he was worth.

I know, buddy. You found her.

With adrenaline surging his gut, he threw open the door and half fell onto the rooftop, Mia and Elias right behind him.

"Gracie," Mia screamed. "Where are you?"

Juno had already disappeared around a utility enclosure. When they rounded the corner, he was licking the tears off Gracie's face. The girl was sitting in a little ball, sobbing and hiccupping all at the same time.

His own sigh of relief was drowned out by the wail that came from Mia as she threw herself on her daughter, adding her tears to the mix.

Dallas called Juno and gave him a thorough pet and scratch. "Good boy, Juno."

"That's an excellent dog," Dr. Elias said with a winded laugh.

"Yes, he's the best air scenter I've ever worked with."

"And to think he does it all for kibble." Dr. Elias stared at Gracie and Mia.

Dallas caught something in the doctor's tone. "He does it for the joy of the find."

"How do you know he'll come back to you?"

"He's trained that way."

Dr. Elias nodded thoughtfully. "Good investment. You make a nice wage for that kind of work?"

Dallas tried to keep the disgust out of his voice. "We're all volunteer."

He nodded as if he'd just figured out why Dallas wore beat-up jeans and drove a ten-year-old truck. "My son, Jake, always wanted a dog, but we never caved in to that desire. We bought him lacrosse gear instead. Now he's the best on his team."

Dallas figured a lacrosse stick was a pretty poor substitute for a dog, but he refrained from saying so. He waited for a few more moments while Mia held Gracie so tight the girl squirmed for breath.

"Why did you come up here?" Mia said, at last pulling Gracie to arm's length. "You could have fallen. Why did you do such a dangerous thing?"

"It was dark and I was going to find the bathroom. A man told me they were closed and I had to go upstairs. He opened the door for me with a funny stick thing that he stuck in the lock."

"What man?" Dallas said.

Gracie shrugged. "I don't know. It was dark and he had a hat on."

Mia let out an exasperated sigh. "Why didn't you come back to ask me to go to the bathroom with you?"

"You weren't there."

Mia's face whirled through a storm of emotions before she settled on grabbing Gracie again and hugging her close. Over Gracie's shoulder she shot Dallas a look.

Dr. Elias reached for his phone. "I'm glad that's over."

"It's not over," Dallas snapped. "Someone sent Gracie up to the roof on purpose."

"For what purpose? To steal something while we were all busy searching? Mia and Gracie have nothing worth stealing." He looked thoughtfully at Mia. "Do you?"

Mia tightened her grip on Gracie. "No, we don't."

"I don't suppose it's…" He shot a look at Gracie and lowered his voice. "Someone who is reaching out from prison, for some reason?"

"Why would it be?" Dallas said.

The doctor shrugged. "True, I guess that's letting the past color the present. The door must not have been latched properly. Probably her imagination about the man." He chuckled. "My son was convinced for months that there was a bear living in our attic." He looked at Gracie, bending to look her in the eye. "I'm very happy that you are okay, Miss Gracie. I would be quite sad if anything happened to you." Dr. Elias dialed his cell phone to report that Gracie had been found. "I'll head downstairs and get everyone settled again."

He wiggled his fingers at Gracie and departed.

Dallas knelt next to the child, while Juno rolled over so Gracie could scratch the dog's belly. "Gracie, the man who told you to come up here. Do you think it could have been Dr. Elias?"

"No." She babbled to Juno. "You're a good doggie for finding me. I'm going to get you some Goldfish and we can share my blanket."

"How do you know?" Dallas continued. "How do you know it wasn't Dr. Elias?"

"'Cuz Dr. Elias smells nice."

"And the man who sent you up here didn't?"

"Nope," Gracie said. "He smelled like cigarettes."

Horror filtered past Mia's eyes as she squeezed her daughter closer. "Oh, Gracie."

"I told him cigarettes are bad." Gracie patted her mother's back. "He said to tell you something."

Mia tried to speak, but no sound emerged.

"What did he say?" Dallas used the calm tone he employed whenever Juno located a traumatized victim, the "everything is going to be absolutely fine now" tone.

"He said he was going to see us again real soon," she said.

TEN

Mia would not stay another second. Heedless of anything but the need to get Gracie out of that awful gym, she waved away the well-meaning urgings from Dr. Elias and Catherine to stay until morning.

"It's dark and the roads are treacherous," Dr. Elias said.

"Not as treacherous as staying here," she snapped.

"Someone phoned the police. They're sending someone, but it's not high on their list since Gracie's been located," Dallas said, grabbing the stuffed animal someone had given Gracie as Mia plopped her on the nearest empty cot to wrap her in a jacket.

"They can come find me if and when they send anyone." She pulled up the zipper. "We're not staying here."

Dallas did not ask where she was going. Honestly, she didn't have the foggiest notion, but Archie would not touch Gracie ever again and if he showed up, he'd wish he hadn't. Fury had replaced the fear. Anger was good, much better than helplessness.

Dr. Elias started to follow her as she led Gracie out the gym doors, but his wife stopped him with a whispered comment and a hand on his arm.

"Do you have my number at least?" the doctor said. "In case you decide you can't go it alone?"

Mia whirled to face him. "Thank you for everything, but that's exactly what I'm going to do."

Dallas followed her out. She hoisted Gracie on her hip and charged toward the makeshift parking lot, stopping short when she peered into the sodden interior of her damaged car. The rain had sheeted through the broken window and the seats were now sopping, bits of glass she had not seen before sparkling on the tattered vinyl.

One more thing. Another small obstacle, but it felt like the last tiny nudge toward complete desperation. She tried to keep her breathing steady as Gracie launched into a round of sleepy questions, rubbing her eyes with a fist. "Where will we sleep? I'm tired."

"Just a minute. Let mommy think." Could she get a ride? Borrow a car? Wait for the police and ask them to take her somewhere, anywhere?

An unusual detail caught her attention through the tension rippling her insides. Gracie's booster, still buckled in the backseat, had been covered up in a plastic garbage bag. She stared for a long moment before she turned around to face Dallas.

"Didn't want it to get wet," he said simply, hands in his jeans pockets. "Would have sealed the window, too, but I only had one bag."

The man had thought about something as menial and foreign to his world as a child's booster seat. "Dallas," she said, but a thickening in her throat kept her mute. She reached out very slowly and pressed her palm to the side of his face. He gazed at her in silence. She searched for signs of pity or disgust in his expression. There was nothing there but compassion and worry. "I am pretty sure that was the nicest thing anybody has done for me in a very long time."

"You deserve nice things, and so does Gracie." He stroked the back of her hand, tentatively, as if it were a bird that might fly away at any moment.

She reached up to press a kiss to his cheek, but his greater height caused it to land just below his jawline. The stubble on his chin tickled her lips. The pulse that revved up in his throat seemed to pass into her body, until her heart matched pace with his. "Thank you," she whispered.

He cleared his throat as she stepped away. "I know you don't want to come back to the trailer. I'll help you find another place in the morning, but we can't right now. It's all there is. It's all I have to offer."

He left the question unspoken. *Will you come with me?*

"Why," she whispered, giving words to the question she hadn't known boiled and bubbled in her broken soul, "is it so hard to do it on my own?"

A beam of moonlight caught his face, highlighting the strong chin, wide cheekbones and a boy-like vulnerability under the tough guy mask. "Maybe because you weren't meant to. No one is."

Mia sagged under the weight of the words and her daughter's limp form. Dallas stepped forward, taking Gracie from her. She fetched the booster and they made a quiet procession back to Dallas's truck.

She squeezed the booster into the backseat of the double cab, and Dallas put her in and secured the buckle.

Juno hopped in next to Gracie whose eyes were at half-mast, licking her when he thought Dallas was not looking. After what Juno had done, Mia would never discourage him from being near Gracie again.

Dallas opened the passenger door for Mia, his body close to hers, and she pressed herself into his arms. "I don't want this," she said into his chest, dizzy with the nearness of him and the relief that Gracie was safe. "I don't want to...need someone."

"I know," he said as he bent his head and kissed her. Electric warmth circled through her and pushed back a tiny corner of fear as her lips touched his. Breathless, she pulled away. "I should have said it sooner, but thank you for finding my daughter."

Eyes wide, he offered a tentative smile. "Juno found her."

"I'll pay him in Goldfish," she said, her own voice tremulous as she chided herself mentally. "But I don't know how to repay you."

"There's no debt."

The softness in his eyes brought her back to the heady emotion of that kiss. She almost lost herself in the feeling again before she snapped herself back to reality. His kiss was just a physical expression of what they'd just been through. *Don't feel for him. Don't love him.* Deep breaths helped her stop the wild firing of her nerves as he shut the door and went around to the driver's side.

The first ten miles passed in silence until Dallas told her about Susan.

Mia gaped. "Is she crazy? Making it all up?"

"I don't know."

"I heard Catherine say she was basically stalking him. She couldn't get over her husband's death and she became fixated on the doctor after he treated her. They mentioned Finnigan's name, too."

They mulled over the situation for the next half hour. Dallas edged the truck past a monster puddle that nearly swallowed the road. "I don't know who is telling the truth, but maybe this Finnigan is the place to start since his name has come up a few times now."

"Should we tell the police?"

"That's the million dollar question." He shot her a glance, dark eyes unreadable. "Your call." They made the final turn into the trailer park. "But you'd better decide now," he said as Detective Stiving emerged from the police car parked in front of Dallas's unit.

Dallas tried to hide his dismay that it was Stiving and not Chief Holder who greeted them. He lifted the sleeping Gracie from the back and handed her to Mia. Stiving let Mia get Gracie settled inside, Juno flopped down on the floor next to her. He stood on the front porch with Dallas until Mia joined them, a blanket wrapped around her shoulders.

"Folks told me you left the college gym. Said something unpleasant happened. How about filling me in?" Stiving took careful notes about Gracie's disappearance and the encounter with Archie in the woods. Dallas waited to see if she would reveal what Susan said, but she did not, nor did she mention Peter Finnigan's name.

Stiving arched an eyebrow. "So the Archie guy from Miami. He thinks you've got money from your husband squirreled away somewhere?"

Mia nodded wearily.

"Is he right?"

"No," Mia snapped, "as I explained to him. I'm a single mother with next to nothing in my wallet, no house, a ruined car and only the clothes on my back. I don't even have a change of clothes for Gracie. That's it. And even if I got Hector's money, I'd send it back express mail because I don't want anything to do with my ex-husband, thank you very much." The last few words came out a near shout.

Dallas could not have been more proud. After all she'd been through, she would not be steamrolled.

To Dallas's surprise, Stiving smiled. "Got it. Archie from Miami is a misguided individual. Targeting you for no reason."

Mia let out a squeak. "Does it matter the reason? He sent my child up onto the roof. He could have... hurt her."

"And no one else saw the guy?"

"I did, earlier," Dallas said.

"You don't count," Stiving said without looking at Dallas. "But adding a menacing stranger isn't going to throw me off the trail of who killed Cora."

"Incredible," Mia huffed. "What kind of woman would I be to use my daughter to deflect suspicion from myself?"

"The kind of woman that married a drug dealer and lived in the lap of luxury until hubby went to prison."

Mia's face blanched and she took a step back. "You don't know anything about me."

"I know more than you think. Fire Marshal says the house burned due to a candle fire, so that we have to rule as accidental, but the toxicology reports are what I'm eagerly awaiting. That's going to make for some interesting reading."

"I would never poison anyone, especially Cora," Mia said, arms folded tight across her chest.

"You stabbed a man before. Poison, knife." He shrugged. "Both can be lethal."

Dallas stiffened. "Knock it off. She doesn't deserve that."

Stiving looked close at Mia. "How do you know what she deserves?"

Mia sucked in a breath, then without another word she slammed back inside the trailer, leaving Dallas and Stiving alone on the porch.

"That was low. She's a good mother, the best," Dallas snarled.

"Really? You sound so protective. Good friend?" He quirked an eyebrow. "Or more?"

He burned inside. "None of your business."

"Let's lay it out here, Mr. Black. You and I don't get along."

"No kidding. Because I made you look bad by doing your job for you? Finding the kid when you didn't think it was worth your time?"

The smile vanished. "No, because you're a hotshot who makes trouble in my town. Whatever you think of me, I'm a good cop. Thorough."

"So do your job and investigate. You'll see she's telling the truth."

"Could be, but I think it's more likely that your friend Mia Sandoval murdered Cora and when the lab tests come back and prove that the pills were doctored with poison, I'm going to arrest her. As far as this Archie from Miami thing goes, if he really is threatening her, it's just deserts."

"Just?" Dallas spoke through gritted teeth.

"Sure. She's experiencing the fallout of being married to a mobster. She probably had full knowledge of Hector's activities the whole time."

"You're wrong."

"Maybe, but I'm right about the murder and you'd better believe I'm going to look real carefully at you, too, since you're so tight with Miss Sandoval and everything." He grinned. "Gang boy like you? Arrest record and the whole nine yards? Real stand-up guy."

Dallas bit back his response. It wouldn't help Mia to shoot off his mouth. It probably hadn't helped her that her supposed protector was an enemy of the town's police detective.

"I'll be seeing you around soon," Stiving said as he walked down the steps.

Dallas felt a desperate need to act, to take some small step that would help shed some light. He took a shot. "Do you know a Peter Finnigan?"

Stiving stopped. "Finnigan? Why?"

"Do you know him?"

Eyebrows drawn together, Stiving chewed his lip before answering. "Guy of that name lives about an hour from here in Mountain Grove. Used to live in California until he bought a real nice cabin here in Colorado."

"Know him personally?"

"Read about him." He shook his head. "Witness in a case a colleague of mine worked on in California decades ago. Surprised I remembered it."

"What kind of case?"

"Why do you want to know?"

"Why did it stick in your memory? A case that wasn't even in your state?"

His eyes narrowed to slits. "This colleague talked it over with me. He thought something smelled funny about the story. Just like something smells funny about this one. So you're not going to tell me why you're interested in Peter Finnigan?"

Dallas remained silent. He was not going to get anything more and he wondered if he'd blown it by bringing Peter's name into the mess. Besides, he needed to check on Mia. Now.

Stiving started up the engine, still smiling, and Dallas tapped on the trailer door before letting himself in. Mia sat at the little table, elbows propped on the surface. He tried to read her expression. Angry? Wounded?

"Sit down and quit staring at me," she said.

Angry. Good. "Stiving has no sense. Ignore him. He did give me a tip on Peter Finnigan in spite of himself. I've got a town name to research."

She drummed fingers on the table. "He truly believes I am a murderer."

"Cops are like that. Don't trust anyone. Don't take it to heart."

"Easy for you to say. He doesn't think you killed Cora." She shot a hasty look at Gracie who slept peacefully. She stared at the little girl, face softening until it was so tender he had to look away.

"Dallas, you…you don't think I would ever put Gracie in danger on purpose, do you?" She turned those luminous eyes on him, and suddenly breathing was difficult.

"No."

"But what if I do it unintentionally? Trying to make a life here has only gotten us in trouble."

"Not your fault."

"I'm not so sure. My number-one priority is to give her a good life, you know?"

He nodded.

"But I look back over my life, and I can't believe

some of the things I've done." She looked at her hands. "I stabbed my husband. I actually did that."

"You thought he was going to kill you and take Gracie, didn't you?"

Her sigh was miserable. "But I never imagined I could do such a thing—that I was capable."

It cut at him to see the self-doubt. "You were protecting yourself and your daughter. Don't let guilt twist it around."

She beamed a smile at him that lit up even the farthest corners of the trailer. He could have been sitting in a glorious cathedral and there would be nothing to rival the beauty he experienced at that moment, sitting in a trailer parked on the edge of a flood-threatened town.

"I appreciate your friendship," she said, "I really do, even if I haven't shown it. It's been a long time since I could trust someone."

Trust. The word fell hard on his heart. *But I haven't told you the truth, Mia. Not all of it.* He opened his mouth to let it spill. Tomorrow, everything would change because of the phone call he'd made outside that rain-soaked gym. He remembered the cascade of emotions she'd triggered in him with their kiss that seemed to live inside him long after her mouth was no longer pressed tight to his. Would it all be gone in the morning? Perhaps it was for the best. She needed a friend, not anything more. He would be lucky if she still counted him in that circle after tomorrow.

"What is it?" Mia said, squeezing his fingers. She looked so tired, circles smudging her eyes. He could give her one night of rest, of peace, before her world turned upside down and his did, too.

"Nothing. Get some sleep. We'll talk later."

She laughed softly. "'Oh, I've got miles to go before I sleep.'"

He found himself smiling back. "Robert Frost. You listened in poetry class, too."

"Yes, I did." She pressed the laptop to life. "And I'm going to dig up some dirt on a certain P. Finnigan before I turn in."

He understood. She needed to do something, to manage one small element in a life that was spiraling out of control. "How about if I help?"

She slid over on the bench seat, and he settled next to her, his big shoulder pressed against her soft one, admiring her slender wrists as her fingers danced across the keyboard.

It took them two hours of following cyber bunny trails before they had the pertinent details.

Mia gathered her long hair to the side, eyes darting in thought. "So this Peter Finnigan was a dishwasher at a greasy spoon in Southern California. He's out walking one day and sees a man boating. The boater falls overboard and is caught up by a rip current and shouts for help. Finnigan tries to get to him, but is unable and fearing for his own safety he leaves the water and calls the authorities. By the time they show up, the man is swept away, body never recovered."

Dallas consulted the screen. "The drowned man is Asa Norton, a thirty-year-old small-business owner. He's presumed dead after the appropriate length of time. Survived by his wife—" Dallas leaned closer "—Susan Norton. There's a picture."

Mia crowded close, her cheek nearly touching his. It took everything in his possession not to turn his head and find those lips again. *Knock it off, Black.*

"Does she look familiar?" Mia breathed quicker. "Could that possibly be the red-haired Susan we know?"

"Could be, but it's a bad picture." He leaned away a little, to quiet the pulse rushing in his veins. He read on. "Susan received the ten million dollar insurance settlement for her husband's death." He scrolled down. "Nothing further about it."

Mia chewed her lip. "Something Cora knew about Finnigan troubled her. It has to be a clue as to who killed her, doesn't it?"

Dallas saw the kindling of hope in her eyes as if a light had been turned on inside, somewhere down deep. *Help me keep that hope alive, Lord.* "We'll find out." But would there still be a *we* tomorrow?

They were silent for a moment. Pine needles scuttled quietly along the trailer roof.

"Do you think Peter Finnigan has answers?" she said finally.

"Possibly, but it could also be dangerous to go track him down."

"Dangerous, how?"

"Take your pick. Floodwaters, Archie on the loose and Cora's murderer."

"Could Archie have done it? Poisoned Cora's pills?"

Dallas thought it over. "I don't see why he'd go to trouble. Let's say he suspected you'd left this treasure from Hector with her. He might have searched her house, but he could have done that while she was out. No need to bring attention to himself or the property by causing her death. He's here on Garza's behalf to retrieve Hector's stash, that's his priority."

Mia's breath caught. "But what if he was there

searching for all this money he believes I have, and she stumbled across him?"

He saw where she was going. "Cora did not die because of you. Period."

"I wish I could be sure."

"I'll be sure for both of us." He got up from the table, put a hand on her shoulder, trapping some of her silken hair under his palm. Without stopping to think it out, he pressed a kiss to her temple.

She curled a hand up around his neck and held him there. He was certain at the moment, as the nerves tingled through his body, how blessed he was to know Mia Verde Sandoval. But there was a secret between them, a secret that would hurt her. Though it took every bit of will power he possessed, he pulled away. "You've got to get some sleep. Tomorrow will be a bear." *And I want to leave now, while you're still looking at me with that half smile on your lips and eyes that make my heart pound.*

"Okay," she said, a puzzled smile on her face. "Tomorrow has to be better than today."

He wished with everything inside him that it could be, but his brain knew differently.

"Good night, Mia. Sleep well."

He said good-night to Juno, made sure Mia locked the trailer door and settled into the old chair in his own unit, positioned to keep watch, the feel of that kiss still dancing on his lips. It was the last time he'd share a kiss with Mia. He pushed away the sadness and rustled up some grit. *Do the job, Dallas.*

If Archie came, he'd know it.

Protection was all he could give Mia.

And he'd give it with his dying breath.

ELEVEN

Mia awoke to the sound of sneezing sometime after eight o'clock. It took her a few moments of blurry-eyed confusion to figure out it was Gracie who lay in a tight ball on the bed. Juno poked his nose at her, tail wagging.

Mia padded over on bare feet across the sunlit linoleum. "Hey, baby. The rain stopped."

Gracie sniffed. "I gotta sore throat."

Pulling the covers back, she found Gracie pink-cheeked and nose running. "Uh-oh."

"I got germans?"

Mia laughed. "Germs. Yes, I think you're coming down with something." Her forehead felt warm under Mia's palm. She fetched a glass of water and encouraged Gracie to drink it. Fishing through her bedraggled purse, she was thrilled to find the slightly sticky bottle of grape flavored medicine purchased after Gracie's last go around with the "germans." Cora had tended to her through that illness, offering homemade chicken soup and plenty of read-aloud stories. Mia's throat thickened at the thought. In spite of the groans, Mia managed to get Gracie to swallow a dose of the medicine.

"I want my turtle slippers. Can we get 'em?"

"I'm sorry, sweetie. Your slippers are all wet at the house. I'll get you some more soon." Anxiety cramped her stomach as the worries attacked in full force. And how exactly would she get slippers, or Gracie's pajamas, let alone a house? Especially while evading a murder rap and a mobster who'd threatened a return visit?

We'll find Peter Finnigan, and he will have some answers, she told herself firmly.

She grabbed a pair of neatly folded socks that Dallas had left, along with a clean T-shirt. The socks went nearly to Gracie's thighs and they both laughed as she rolled them onto the child's skinny legs. Mia let her mind stray back to the kiss. Why had she allowed herself to be kissed, let alone to respond? She had no clue, other than it was the most amazing kiss she'd experienced in her whole life.

Juno shot to his feet and ran to the door. Mia froze, heart hammering, until there was a quiet knock followed by a familiar voice.

"It's Dallas. I've got some things for you."

Mia found that her spirits ticked up a notch as she went to the door, pulling fingers through her messy hair and straightening the big sweatshirt he'd loaned her before letting him in.

His dark brows rose at the sight of her. "I didn't know that sweatshirt could look so nice."

She blushed.

He held up a brown bag. "Trailer park manager gave me some clothes for you and some that might work for Gracie left over from her granddaughter's last visit. And guess what—" He shook a pink pastry box. "Anybody want doughnuts for breakfast instead of Goldfish?"

Gracie coughed. "Can't. I'm sick."

Dallas shot her a panicked look. "Sick? How sick?"

"Terrible sick," Gracie piped up, adding a cough on the end for good measure.

"Should we take her to the doctor? I'll get my keys." He turned to leave, but Mia grabbed his arm.

"Not that sick. Kids come down with things all the time. It's okay. I gave her some medicine. She'll be okay. I promise." Mia hid a smile at the uncertain look on his face. "Really, it's fine. Kids are tough."

"They are?" His lips quirked. "They're just so… small."

She took the pink box from his hands. "Gracie won't eat them, but I wouldn't want these doughnuts to go to waste."

Soon he'd brewed a pot of coffee and she'd devoured two sugar-glazed doughnuts down to the last crumb. Dallas sipped out of his mug, a look of amusement on his face.

She wiped her sticky fingers. "Don't you eat doughnuts?"

"No sweet tooth."

"You're missing out," she said with a sigh. "Doughnuts are nature's second most perfect food next to mac and cheese. I think they're even on the food pyramid."

"It was worth it to watch you enjoy them." He added in a low voice. "To see you smile."

She returned the grin. "You know, for a tough guy who lives with a dog, you've got a sweet side."

"Don't let it get around."

"Why? Are you afraid you might have girls pounding at your door? Surely there must be some woman who wants a chance to get to know the softer side of Dallas Black."

He flicked a glance out the window before he answered. "I don't usually let them get close."

"Why not?" She shouldn't pry, but for some reason it felt so natural to talk to him and she wanted to understand what made him tick, and why she could not get him out of her mind.

"Don't want to disappoint them, I guess."

"When the mistakes of your past come out?"

He sighed. "Something like that."

"It's funny. You're trying hard to keep moving, and I'm going crazy trying to put down roots."

Yet here they were, sitting in the same banged-up trailer while a storm of trouble whirled around them. She watched the steam from the coffee drift past the waves in his hair. God had sent her a friend in Dallas Black, she realized. A friend when she most desperately needed one. But why did her feelings for him seem like something else?

He fidgeted with his coffee cup. "Mia, listen. I've got to tell you something and it won't wait anymore."

She felt a tremor inside. "Okay. I've had two doughnuts to shore up my spirit, and I don't see how things could get any worse than they were yesterday. Go for it."

Juno barked, and a second later they heard a car approach. Dallas peeked out the blinds.

Archie? The police? Her mind ran wild.

His expression was inexplicably sad as he went to open the door.

Mia blinked incredulously when her sister stepped inside.

"Antonia," she cried, wrapping her older sister in a massive hug. "Why are you here? How did you know where to find me?" She pulled her sister to arm's length. "Is everything okay? Is Reuben all right?"

Antonia chuckled. "I think I should be asking those kinds of questions." She looked over Mia's shoulder at Gracie. "Hey, Gracie girl. How's my niece?"

Gracie waggled her fingers and squealed. "Hiya, Auntie Nia. You're here. Where's Uncle BooBen?"

Gracie was perfectly capable of pronouncing Reuben's name, but her toddler nickname for him had stuck fast and it always made Reuben grin. Antonia kissed her. "I'll tell you in a minute. Let me talk to Mommy first, 'kay?"

"'Kay."

During the exchange, the flutter of unease in Mia's belly grew as she put some of the facts together. Dallas had not been at all surprised to see Antonia arrive. What's more, they seemed to be at ease with each other, as though they'd been in frequent contact.

The three moved away from Gracie. "What's going on?" Mia demanded.

Antonia squared her shoulders and kept her voice quiet. "First off, I'm here because Reuben and I love you and we're worried about you. We know Cora is dead and the police think it's foul play. We also know Archie is in town because Garza believes you've got Hector's jackpot somewhere. Reuben has gone to the prison to talk to Hector and tell him if there is such a prize, he has to fess up, because he's put you and Gracie in danger."

Mia held up a hand. "Antonia, how do you know all this?"

Antonia exchanged a worried look with Dallas. "Because Dallas has kept us informed. We hired him."

She could not believe she had heard correctly. "Hired?"

Dallas sighed. "They asked me to come to Spanish Canyon and keep an eye on you."

It took several tries before she managed a response. "What?"

"There were rumors that Garza's men were looking for something Hector had stashed," Antonia said. "Reuben and I feared they would come after you and Gracie."

The information landed like a bomb in her gut. "That's how you knew about Gracie climbing the tree. Your informant kept you apprised."

Dallas flushed.

"My fault," Antonia said. "I hounded him for details about Gracie. I shouldn't have, but I missed her so much."

Mia folded her arms, trying to steady her pounding pulse. There was more. She could see it in their faces. "What else?"

"Cora was an old friend of Reuben's mother," Antonia continued. "When we heard you were thinking of settling near here to go to school, we contacted her and she offered to help."

Help? Cora? The truth started to worm its way through Mia. "So Cora helped me get a job, find a house to rent. She made sure Dallas had work fixing her roof so he could spy on me. What an amazing network to put together a life for one helpless woman and her kid."

Antonia touched her arm, but she shook it off. "Mia, we knew you wouldn't accept any help because you're stubborn and desperate to prove you don't need anybody. I'm sorry. I didn't want to tell you like this, but that's the truth."

"You knew I wouldn't accept it, but you arranged it all anyway, didn't you? Totally against my wishes." Anger hummed through her veins. "All this, everything I thought I accomplished here, was just charity, set up by people I thought were my friends."

"I'd like to think I am your friend," Dallas said quietly, "no matter how it came to be."

Mia turned her eyes on him. "You don't *hire* friends." Each word fell out of her mouth, cutting like glass. She saw him flinch and she was glad.

Antonia's chin went up, as it had for every head-butting argument they engaged in over the years, from which breakfast cereal to eat to the dire consequence of dating Hector Sandoval. "Listen, Mia. I know you're mad at me and that's okay. I knew that was a price for trying to protect you, but Dallas isn't doing this for pay. As a matter of fact, he refused any compensation at all. He cares about you, like we do."

Cares about you. And lied just like Hector and her sister. She found it hard to breathe. "So, why exactly are you here now, Antonia? Dallas hasn't been feeding you enough information? You had to check up on me personally?"

"Dallas called us after Garza's man showed up at the college. I came to try and convince you to come back to Florida with me, until the thing with Archie is resolved."

"Didn't your informant tell you I'm shortly to be accused of murder? I don't think I'll be able to leave even if I wanted to."

"We'll get a lawyer if it comes to that. Let's try to get you out while we can. It's safest for Gracie."

Mia exploded. "Don't tell me how to be a mother

to Gracie, Antonia," she snarled. "That little girl is the only thing I've done right in my whole life. Please don't imply I've messed that up, too. I can't take it." Dismayed to find tears on her face, she dashed them away.

"I never would," Antonia said, eyes anguished. "Honey, you're a wonderful mother. You just need help right now. That's all."

The emotion on her sister's face, the moisture that shone in her eyes, was too much for Mia. The fire ebbed out of her body, leaving only a dark despair in its place. She sank down on the bench seat. Antonia was right. She could not make a life for herself and Gracie. She did not even realize that her whole world in Spanish Canyon was a setup, neatly arranged for a woman who could not manage on her own.

But Dallas… She could not even look at him. Everything she imagined he'd done for her out of kindness, or, she hardly dared admit it, love? It was a job. She was a job to him.

"I guess I'd better do what you say. I can't trust myself."

Dallas sat across from her. "Mia, you're stronger than anyone I know. What we did… It was only because you have too many powerful people working against you."

"No," she said, her own voice sounding strange and dull in her ears. "You did it because you and Antonia and Reuben all believe I could not manage my life on my own."

"No…" he started, reaching for her hands.

She would not touch him, not look at him. "I said 'All right.'" She fought the thickness in her throat. "You're both right, and I'm not going to argue. When do we leave?"

"I'll get us a flight tonight," Antonia said.

"Tomorrow." Mia glanced toward the bed. "Gracie's sick, and there's something I need to do first."

Antonia quirked an eyebrow. "What? There's talk that the weather might turn bad again. I really think tonight is better."

Dallas stood, hands on his slim hips, eyebrows drawn together.

Mia stared at the pink doughnut box, incredulous that only moments before she'd wondered if her feelings for Dallas could be more than friendly. *They're right. You can't trust yourself.* Dr. Elias's words came back to her.

"*...you're afraid that you can't trust yourself, your choices, your judgments.*" Even her former employer had been able to see her deepest fear that had now been proven true. But she would not walk away, not from the murder of an old woman who had been trying to help her purely out of kindness. She was not a coward, not yet. "I'm going to find Peter Finnigan. He may be able to shed some light on Cora's death."

"No way..." Antonia said.

Mia whacked her hand on the table, startling Juno. "No matter how it came to be, Cora was my friend and Gracie and I loved her. I have to at least try to find out if Finnigan knows something. Please allow me to do that. Will you stay with Gracie?"

Antonia chewed her lip. "Of course, but I don't think..."

"I'll go with Mia," Dallas said.

"You don't need to do that," Mia told him. "Your spy identity has been compromised."

He flinched as her arrow hit the mark. "I'll go."

She didn't argue. If she said no he would follow her

anyway. It was his job, after all, she thought bitterly, and he would do it until she and Gracie boarded that plane to Florida the following day.

She knelt next to Gracie and smoothed her hair. "I'll be back soon."

"Mommy, are you mad at Auntie Nia?"

"No, honey. We just had a disagreement. Auntie's going to stay with you while I run an errand. Is that okay?"

"Yes. Will Juno stay?"

Dallas nodded. "I think that's best."

"When you come back are we going to Florida?"

Mia exhaled. "I think so, baby."

"Is that gonna be our home?"

Mia thought there was never such a perfect little face as that of her sweet girl, staring at her expectantly, trusting that no matter what, her mother would provide a home. Was Florida going to be that home? Would any place ever be?

"I'm not sure if we'll stay in Florida."

She sneezed. "Will Juno and Dallas come, too?"

She could not answer above the sudden wave of sadness.

"Hey, Goldfish girl," Dallas said. "You just work on getting better. We'll talk about it later."

"'Kay."

Dallas offered a hand to help Mia get to her feet. She pretended she didn't see. *I'm a job to you, Dallas. Let's keep it that way*, she thought over the grief washing through her body.

Dallas tried to open the door of the truck for Mia but she scooted around and got in herself before he had the chance. What had he expected? She believed he'd betrayed her—and maybe to a woman who so desperately craved independence, he had. He'd crossed many people in his life, disappointed dozens, notably himself, but what he'd done to Mia hurt her worse than any other offense he'd dished out. It had been wrong to deceive her, even though the reasons were right.

I'm sorry, Mia.

The distance between them seemed like miles instead of inches. She stared out the window as his tension grew.

Should he try small talk? Apologize again? Mention the haze of clouds that had started to gather along the sunlit horizon?

Talk about the weather? Stupid, Dallas.

He settled on silence, trying to ignore the leaden feeling in his limbs. He'd hoped in that idiot macho way of his the truth might blow over as the miles went by and he could start again, trying to show her how much she meant to him. Judging from the hard line of her mouth, he'd thought wrong. If only women were as forgiving as dogs.

"Why did you do it?"

He jerked a look at her, startled, praying he would not make it any worse with more idiotic conversation. "To protect you. At least that's what I thought I was trying to do."

"No, I mean why did you do it for nothing? Agree to take the job without pay."

Because to me, it's not a job. "Antonia asked me. I respect her and Reuben."

"You didn't move to a strange town because you respect my sister and brother-in-law."

He shifted, setting the seat springs squeaking. "I never care much where I am. One town is as good as another. Spanish Canyon offered a decent place to teach Search and Rescue classes. Why not?"

She turned gleaming brown eyes on him, skewering him to the seat back. "That's not it. You moved to this town, spent hours working on an old roof and living in a trailer, for no pay, to protect a woman you barely knew. Why did you do that? I think I deserve to hear the truth."

She did, but he knew it meant sharing messy, unformed feelings, incoherent ramblings of his heart that he himself did not understand. He flipped through the memories that had swirled through his mind almost daily since he'd seen her in Florida following the hurricane. "At Antonia and Reuben's wedding. I saw you talking to Gracie before the ceremony."

She waited.

He sighed. "I dunno, something about what you said to her got inside me and stayed there."

"What did I say?"

He tried to repeat the words exactly. "Gracie was little then, just a toddler. Is that what you call that age?"

She nodded.

"Anyway, she asked you where her daddy was and you knelt down, right next to her and told her Daddy was in jail because he made mistakes."

He heard her sniff. "Yes. I remember now."

"And she started to cry so you said, 'We're going to be a family, you and me, and Mommy's going to make it all right.'"

Mia lowered her head. "I haven't made it anywhere near all right."

He went very still, the sound of the tires creating a soothing cadence. *Lord, help me to put words to the feelings, words she can understand.* "You were strong then, and gentle, too, just like you are now. I knew how hard it was going to be, with your past, and starting all over with a daughter and Hector's legacy. I understood because I have wreckage in my past, too." He reached out slowly, praying she would not jerk away from his touch, and covered her hand with his. "I wanted to help you and Gracie have a better shot at making a way for your family. That's why I told Antonia I'd do it."

She looked at their joined hands and one tear splashed onto their twined fingers.

"My whole life has been about where. Where will I go next. This time…" He struggled to find the words. "This time it was about the who, about you and Gracie. I wanted you to have a life." He swallowed hard. "And I guess maybe I wanted to be a part of that in some way."

It was too much. She pulled from him. "I didn't ask you. You invited yourself into our lives and you deceived me."

It cut at his heart. "I'm sorry."

She fished for a tissue in her pocket. "I understand your motives were sincere. Hector was sincere, too, but he did not trust me with the truth, either."

Her words stung like acid. He'd been put on the same shelf as Hector, a manipulator, a disappointment. Had he permanently severed that delicate strand between them? He could think of nothing to say to repair the break, not one word of comfort to bring the warmth back to her eyes.

The miles droned by in miserable silence until he turned on the weather station just to break the terrible quiet. It was not good news.

"More rain is on the way from an unexpected grouping of storms rolling in. A series of flash-flood warnings and advisories have been issued. Mudslides are already being reported near Mountain Grove and Coal Flats where rainfall on burn areas is causing ground failure. Residents are advised to be ready to evacuate."

Dallas took comfort in the fact that at least the trailer park was high enough to keep Antonia and Gracie safe. For a while.

"We should…"

She shook her head. "I'm going to see Finnigan. If you want to head back, just let me out."

Right. As if he would even consider leaving her on the side of a mountain road. Women. He wisely kept his thoughts to himself and pressed on at as quick a pace as he could manage. The steeper the grade, the more he began to worry about the possibility of mudslides. Slopes already sodden with moisture needed only a tiny push from nature and gravity to loosen tons of debris on the road below.

Finally, they turned off on an uneven path that took them through acreage so densely crowded with lodgepole pines that he thought Farley might have ferreted out the wrong address, until they came to the edge of a swollen river with a striking house set beside it. The dark wood tones and forest green roofing material made it appear as if the house was a part of the mountainside behind it.

They got out in time to receive the first drops of rainfall.

"Peter Finnigan has a nice little piece of real estate," Dallas said, perusing the boathouse that perched at the waterline and the modern shingled siding on the house above. "And he doesn't like being too close to the neighbors."

"He must have found something better paying than being a dishwasher." Mia started up the graveled path toward the house. As he followed, Dallas noted a green car parked behind the shrubbery, and the muscles in his stomach tightened. He put a hand on the hood. Still warm.

"Mia," he said.

There was the sudden sound of breaking glass followed by a shout.

Dallas took off for the house at a dead sprint.

TWELVE

Mia was gasping for breath by the time she made it to the house, pulling up next to Dallas who had just about reached the front door when it was flung open. A short, balding man stopped short, mouth wide. His arm was half raised, as if to shield himself from a blow.

"Peter Finnigan?" Dallas said.

The man glared, the fleshy pouches under his eyes bunching. "Who wants to know?"

"We heard a scream," Mia panted, by way of explanation. "Glass breaking."

"There's nothing wrong," he said. "Everything's fine. Go away."

"Not quite, Peter" came a singsong voice.

Mia gaped as Susan stepped up behind Peter. She wore clean clothes, her hair in a neat twist, a placid smile on her lips. Dallas seemed equally at a loss for words until he managed, "Are you hurt?"

Susan laughed. "Such a gentleman." She gave Mia a coy look. "You should keep him."

Mia's cheeks burned. "Susan, what's going on?"

She waved them in with an airy gesture. "Come in, why don't you? I just came to see Peter. We're acquainted. He's the man who tried to save my drowning husband, so he says."

Peter scanned the porch quickly, as if he was assessing the likelihood of an escape. Then he mumbled something, stepped aside and allowed them to enter.

"I'm glad you're here. She's some loony who busted in. When I wouldn't give her what she wanted, she started throwing things. I'm leaving just as soon as I can get her out."

Mia noticed a floral fragrance in the air and there was something familiar in the smell. Peter pulled keys and a wallet from a small bowl. While his back was turned, Mia spotted an old photo on the floor, partially hidden by shards of glass that littered the hardwood floor.

The snapshot was old and grainy, but it showed Peter with a taller man, heavily bearded, standing in a small boat. A third man was seated, holding a net. Peter stood to the left of them, dangling a fish for the camera, grinning.

She saw Susan looking at her. Quickly Mia tucked the picture into her pocket.

"What got smashed?" Mia asked.

Susan waved an impatient hand. "I startled Peter and he dropped his drinking glass. I was asking him what he knew about my husband's death."

He flashed a sullen look. "I dunno what you're talking about. She's crazy, like I said."

Susan sighed. "All right, I'll get the ball rolling. Let's stroll down memory lane. Fifteen years ago, you saw my husband, Asa, drown, didn't you? What a story you told the police about how you tried in vain to save him, battling the waves at your own peril. Made yourself look like a real hero."

Peter folded his arms, then unfolded them and shoved

his hands in the pockets of his faded jeans. "You already know what happened, Susan."

"So," Susan said, her tone cheerful as if she was reciting a bit of poetry. "You lied. You and Thomas." She looked at Mia and Dallas. "Dr. Elias, as you know him. To me he'll always be Thomas. Peter arranged with Thomas to make it look like an accidental death. Thomas was hoping to get his hands on the life insurance money. He pays you to keep quiet. That's how you afford this lovely home, isn't it?"

Peter grimaced. "You're nuts, and you're not telling the whole story."

"I probably am nuts. I've had a hard life after all. It took me a long time, years and years, to find Thomas and you. I tracked him down to Spanish Canyon. What a surprise to find out he'd started a whole new life here as a well-respected doctor. And you, too. Cora overheard Thomas threaten me at the clinic after I confronted him. She wanted to go to the police, but I told her they were on his side. She promised to help me find proof to take to the authorities."

"Cora?" Mia gasped. "Susan, tell us what happened."

Peter cut Mia off. "This is nuts. I'm not talking to any of you anymore. Get out, all of you."

Susan's face whitened and filled with hatred. "Thomas killed Cora because he knew she was looking into his past, and the truth was coming out. Now Thomas's going to have to eliminate anyone who can incriminate him and that means you."

"Are you insane? I've never caused him any trouble. I've kept my mouth shut about everything for all these years. He trusts me."

"Not anymore," she said quietly. "Not after he's had

to murder again. This time he's going to button up all the loose ends."

Including Susan. Mia shuddered.

"Crazy, but I'm not gonna take the time to sort it out," Peter snapped, turning away. The back of his neck was red.

Mia's mind was still spinning, trying to put it all together. When Peter whirled back around, he held a gun snatched from his pocket.

Dallas stepped in front of Mia. "You don't need to do that, Peter. We're not here to cause trouble for you. We just wanted the truth."

"I'm getting out of this whole business. I was going to leave because of the flooding anyway, so I'll just make it permanent. If any of you tries to come at me, I'll kill you. I don't want to, but I will."

Susan chortled. "You can't get out. You'll never get out."

"Shut up," Peter barked. "Move away from the door."

Dallas and Mia edged aside. Mia took Susan's skinny wrist. "Let him go, Susan." Surprisingly, she did not resist.

"He won't get away," she said softly. "You'll never, ever get away."

Susan allowed Mia to guide her to the corner. When Peter fled out the door and down the path, Dallas ran to the window.

"He's got a boat ready." Dallas was dialing 911 as he watched. After a minute, he disconnected with an exasperated groan. "No signal."

Peter thundered down to the edge of the dock where a motorboat was moored. He cast off the lines and began to putter out into the swiftly moving water. A duffel bag in the back indicated his departure had been planned out.

Keeping low, Dallas sprinted toward the boathouse. He was going to see if there was another boat.

"Stay in the house," he yelled.

Mia watched as Peter piloted through the rough waters.

She and Susan edged out onto the porch. Mia could not stand it a moment longer.

"You have to tell us everything, Susan. We have to know who killed Cora."

Dallas vanished into the darkened interior of the boathouse, emerging a moment later with hands on hips. There was no other boat. Peter would get away and take his answers with him.

Dallas began to jog back to the dock. Mia started down the steps, leaving Susan behind. Thirty seconds passed. A flash of light and an earsplitting bang shook the boards under their feet. Mia's ears rang. Following Dallas's horrified gaze she realized the explosion had come from the boat.

Peter's duffel bag was burning, along with the interior of the vessel. Peter lay facedown in the water, his shirt on fire.

Susan stared, hands jammed into her pockets.

Dallas finished his sprint to the dock and jumped in the water, arms chopping through the waves. Bits of flaming debris sprinkled down around his head as he pressed on. It was a futile effort. By the time he'd cleaved through the swirling river to the spot where the boat had exploded, Peter's body had been sucked away by the current. The swollen river jerked and pulled at Peter, tumbling him along like a discarded doll. Dallas swam after Peter, and Mia found herself shouting, stomach twisted in fear.

"Dallas, come back. The water's too strong." *You'll drown,* her heart finished for her. She doubted he'd heard over the swirling cacophony, but he must have come to the same conclusion. She watched with her heart hammering at her ribs as he fought the water back toward the bank and Mia grasped his forearms to pull him from the river.

He stood, head bowed, water running from his hair and clothes. His broad shoulders drooped and quite suddenly, she wanted to comfort this man who had betrayed her. She raised her arms to embrace him. *Strength, not emotion, you ninny.*

Instead, she snatched up a towel that lay drying on the wooden rail and draped it around his shoulders. His eyes were shocked, horrified, drawn to the river where Peter Finnigan had just lost his life. In spite of herself, she pressed her hand to his biceps for a moment.

He imprisoned her palm there, his own fingers cold. "I couldn't get him."

She allowed the touch to linger before she pulled away. "No one could."

He heaved in a breath. "I'm guessing there was an explosive device in his duffel bag. It was motion triggered." He paused. "Or someone set it off by cell phone."

Mia glanced into the acres of dark trees and shivered. Were there eyes watching from the shadows? Eyes glowing with satisfaction at the death they had just witnessed? As they moved back toward the house, she realized Susan was still staring out at the burning boat, spinning in helpless circles as it moved downriver.

"I told you, Peter," she whispered.

Dallas left a trail of water along the floor as the three of them searched for a phone with a landline. Nothing.

His own cell was now waterlogged thanks to his instinctive plunge into the river and there was no chance of getting a signal anyway. In the course of their hunting, thunderclouds began to roll in along the river canyon, obscuring the mountaintops under a blanket of grey.

"We need to get out of here," Dallas said. "We'll keep trying to call on your cell as we drive."

Mia patted the photo still tucked in her pocket. "Come on, Susan. You can fill us in on the way."

"My car is here," she said. "In the bushes."

"We'll bring you back for it later." Dallas was not about to let the woman slip out of their grasp again. Especially not after what had just happened to Finnigan. He still burned inside with the knowledge that he had not been strong enough or fast enough to pull the man from the monster river. An epic failure and a life lost. Trying to keep watch for any sign of movement from the tree line, they returned to the truck. He fought the urge to bundle both women back into the house and barricade them safely inside, but with floodwater rising all around them, it was not an option. "Let's move a little faster," he said, putting an encouraging palm on Susan's bony shoulders.

Back in the truck with Susan in the backseat, Mia didn't waste a moment.

"How did you know about Peter?"

Susan sighed. "I'm very tired." She leaned her head back on the seat.

"I'm sorry, Susan," Mia snapped. "But we just saw a man murdered back there. You need to start talking."

Dallas felt the tingle in his stomach at the strength in her tone, the fire in her words.

Susan sighed and tears welled up in her eyes. "I killed him."

Mia gasped.

Dallas gripped the wheel as Mia blinked in shock. "Who?" she managed.

"My husband, because I got involved with Thomas. He was a medical student, deep in school loans and credit card debt, but charming, and he seduced me. Made friends with Asa, or pretended to. He knew how unhappy I was in my marriage, but I never dreamed… How could I know Thomas would murder Asa? Actually murder him? I blame myself for Asa's death. I always will for bringing Thomas into our lives."

"You had no idea what kind of man he was?"

"None," she sniffed. "Thomas knew Asa had planned a fishing trip. Asa had a high-stress job running his own business, so fishing was his escape. I think Thomas drugged his bottle of tea so he became unconscious. Peter was waiting nearby, and he made sure Asa tumbled out of his boat and drowned and then he told the story of trying to save Asa so the police wouldn't look into it too closely."

"Dr. Elias did it, why? Out of jealousy? So you two could have a life together?"

Her voice hardened. "Nothing so romantic. Thomas knew Asa had a life insurance policy, and he figured after he killed Asa I would give him the money because we were, um, in love. At least I thought we were. Completely stupid of me, of course. Maybe Thomas figured once I received the payment he could kill me then, too."

What was one more murder for the guy? Dallas thought.

"When the insurance company signed off, I collected the money and ran as far and as fast as I could, but I always knew I'd make Thomas pay." An edge crept into her voice. "Thomas wanted to make a fresh start with a new identity, the good doctor beloved by all, but I found him. And Peter, too."

Dallas hit the brakes as a small pile of rocks showered down onto the road. He guided the truck around it, trying to process Susan's revelation.

"I confronted him, and Cora overheard and started checking into things. She told me she found a photo that she could use against Thomas, but before she could show me, she died. Thomas killed her, I'm sure of it." Dallas saw tears slide down her face. "He got himself a new life. And a pretty new woman."

He remembered finding Susan breaking into the BMW outside the makeshift evacuation center. "It's Catherine Elias, you've been following, isn't it?"

Mia jerked. "The floral perfume fragrance. I thought it was familiar. It's Catherine's. You followed her to Peter's?"

"I've been watching her house. I was curious to see if she knew what kind of man she was married to." Susan laughed. "She's scared of me. Anyway, she brought him the photo of Peter and Thomas. Don't know how she got her hands on it unless she was in on Cora's murder the whole time."

Mia took the photo from her pocket. "Who is the seated man in the boat?"

"Asa." She chewed her lip. "You see? Shows the three were acquainted, though Peter claimed to be a random stranger who saw Asa drowning. The photo proves a connection between them, and the police would connect the dots, I have no doubt."

"And why would Catherine take the photo to Peter? Blackmail? To set him up to be murdered?" Mia wondered aloud.

"Or she's innocent," Dallas said. "Could be she found

the photo after Elias took it from Cora and she became suspicious, wanted to check up on her husband."

Mia slid the photo in the visor, staring at it as they drove.

Rain slammed into the windshield. Susan turned her face to the glass and watched the water sheeting along the window. Her eyes drooped. "I'm too tired to talk anymore."

He did not think Mia was even breathing until she heaved a long shaky breath. "It's true. Dr. Elias killed Cora."

"And Asa, and Peter," Dallas said.

"And he'll do the same to me, if he gets hold of me," Susan said.

"But now we have proof." Mia's voice held a tone of wonder. "We can go to the police and expose him. I can have my life back."

The hope shone on her face and his pulse trip hammered. Where would that life take her? Back to Florida? To some other faraway place? Didn't matter. Wherever it was, it wasn't going to include him. He cleared his throat. "Try the police again."

She did, with no better result.

They made it over the top of the mountain and began the descent. Half a mile later, he pulled the truck to a stop behind another truck and an SUV. A gnarled ponderosa pine had clawed free of the earth and fallen, blocking the road in both directions. The road was hemmed in by a steep drop on one side and the mountain on the other.

Dallas got out to talk to the bearded man from the truck just ahead of them. The guy was fetching a chain saw from the covered cab of his vehicle. He introduced himself as Mack.

"Gonna have to chop it up and haul it off as best we can," Mack shouted to Dallas over the roar of the chain saw. "Folks are gonna be packing this road to get out of here if the rain don't stop."

"How much time you figure before they order evacuations?" Dallas called.

"If the storm don't turn ASAP, they'll be evacuating before nightfall. Rivers are full."

Recalling Peter's body whirling away on the swollen river, Dallas fought a pang of horror. He started in, hauling away the branches as the bearded man cleaved them from the trunk. The two from the other stopped vehicle, a father and his strapping teen son, set to work helping also.

"Got some orange cones in my truck," Mack hollered. "Put 'em out on the road so we don't have a pileup."

Dallas nodded and retrieved the markers. He walked past Mia who was still trying to get a signal on her phone. Susan appeared to be sleeping, her forehead pressed against the glass. He had thought she was deranged and he still wondered about her sanity, but he could not deny what she said made sense. Dr. Elias was a killer. And he had to be stopped.

Splashing through puddles, he set the cones down a few yards from the back of his truck to signal oncoming drivers. One more set around the turn in the road would be sufficient, he thought, as he slogged onward. Just in time as a dump truck eased to a stop. He got a glimpse of the driver's face, older, scruff of a beard.

But it was the passenger that made his blood run cold.

Archie Gonzales gave him a startled look as he leapt from the cab.

Dallas was at the passenger door before Archie had shoved it fully open. There was no time for Archie to reach for a weapon. Dallas grabbed him by the collar and slammed him against the side of the truck.

"Funny how you always turn up," Dallas snarled.

The truck driver appeared around the front fender. "What's going on?"

"Private business," Dallas grunted. His tone must have convinced the driver.

"I'm going to help clear the road," he mumbled, ambling away over the muck.

Archie tried to move Dallas's hands away, but he did not loosen his grip. "Wasted effort, man. I'm leaving town. My piece of junk rental got stuck in the mud, and I hitched a ride. Going to the airport."

"Leaving? Why?" It occurred to Dallas that he might have been wrong about what had happened at the river. "Did you arrange to have Peter Finnigan killed?"

"Guy who bought it in the river? No. But I have to say, I didn't see that coming. Nice piece of work. Cell phone trigger?"

"Yeah, and I'm sure you've got a cell phone handy."

"Who doesn't? It wasn't me, though. As I said, I'm out of here."

"Explain," Dallas said, applying pressure to Archie's windpipe.

He squirmed. "I was following you and Mia, like I'm paid to do. Don't know who blew up this Peter guy, but I'm thinking it's probably the doctor. He's the one who looped me in. Or maybe his wife."

Mia ran up in time to overhear, cheeks pink, rain rolling down her long hair. "Dr. Elias contacted you in Miami?"

"He contacted Mr. Garza. Tipped him off that you were in Spanish Canyon, and that's why I got sent here." Archie shot her a look. "What did you do to cross that doctor? He's more ruthless than my boss."

"Oh, no," Mia said. "He knew Cora was going to tell me, warn me about what she'd learned. He must have been tracking her emails."

He shrugged. "Don't care. Not my business. I was sent to find the stash."

Mia let out a cry. "But I don't have any money. How many times can I say it? Hector didn't leave me a thing. How can I convince you?"

"Already done. Seems brother Reuben went to see Hector and explained that you and tiny tot were in trouble. Hector came clean. His stash was in Miami all along. Mr. Garza has his money, and my job here is done."

Mia shook her head and let out a sigh.

"Not done," Dallas growled. "You led Gracie up to the roof. She could have been hurt. You have to pay for that."

Archie managed a choked laugh. "Lying to a kid isn't against the law. People do it all the time."

"We'll see if the police agree. You broke into Mia's house, too. Better get a lawyer."

Archie struggled under Dallas's grip. "Don't have time for that. This whole county's gonna be underwater and I want to go home."

"Well," Dallas said, anger at the fear Archie had caused Mia still bubbling in his veins, "this just isn't your day."

Rain stung his face as he turned Archie around. "Mia, there's some rope in the back of the truck."

She dashed through the rain back up the road.

A trickle of mud ran down from the mountainside and past Dallas's feet.

"I hate Colorado," Archie spat.

"Should have stayed in Miami." Dallas could not prevent a feeling of satisfaction from sweeping through him. Maybe the cops wouldn't charge Archie with anything, but upsetting his easy escape was a small triumph. At this point, he'd take what he could get. Archie first, Dr. Elias next.

Another wave of muck flowed under the truck and across the road. Dallas looked through the sheeting rain. The mountainside was black, denuded a few years back, he estimated, by a wildfire.

The ground trembled under his feet.

Archie's eyes rolled as he tried to process what was happening.

There wasn't time.

With a roar the mountainside fell away into a river of mud that swept toward the truck.

He thought he detected a scream, Mia's scream, but it was lost in the rumble of movement as the mud carried Archie, Dallas and the truck over the cliff.

THIRTEEN

The river of black engulfed Dallas and Archie, the cacophony swallowing up Mia's scream as she struggled to keep her footing on the trembling road. For a moment, she thought the entire stretch would be sucked up by the massive flow, like a monstrous inverse volcano. There was nowhere to run.

As the movement of the earth slowed, the mighty roar ebbed to a murmur. The flow softened into a trickle and then, eerie silence. Her heart cried out for Dallas. She half stumbled, half crawled, along the edge of the road, wiping the rain from her face. Down below was a sea of mud, coating the steep slope, blanketing the trees, blotting out everything it touched. The upended truck had caught on a trunk, wheels spinning lazily above the black ooze that imprisoned it.

"Dallas," she screamed.

The truck driver and the man with the chain saw raced up.

"Two men are down there," Mia screamed, trying to discern a path she could take to reach them.

"Make that one," the truck driver said, pointing.

A mud-caked figure detached itself from the mess, struggling upright.

The men tied a rope to a tree at the edge of the road and lowered it down. The man grabbed it and hoisted himself up, hand over hand.

Was it Dallas or Archie? Mia found she was holding her breath as the victim fought to pull himself up from the pit. When he was within a few feet of the top, the men reached over and grabbed his arms.

With one synchronized heave, he was pulled over the edge. On hands and knees, he crouched, sucking in a breath. Mia pressed close, unable to force out the question.

"Man," Archie said, wiping a layer of mud from his face. "I really hate this state."

Mia's breath choked off as she ran to the edge again. There was no movement from below, no sign of Dallas.

No, Lord. Please, no.

"I'll try the radio," the truck driver said gently. "We'll call for help."

The other man helped Archie to his feet and moved him away from the slide. Mia stared down into the muck. *Think, Mia.* She spotted the place where Archie had emerged, just behind a stand of three trees that had caught the truck. The thick trunks would have deflected some of the force of the earth flow. If Dallas was there...

"Hey, lady," she heard someone call, as she climbed over the roadbed, clinging to the rope as her feet sank in the mud.

What am I doing? What if I drown in this smothering blanket?

What if she did?

What would she have to show for her life? A perfect daughter, yes, and a heart choked with so much anger, hurt and distrust that it was nearly drowned already. *I've wasted time being afraid. I'm sorry. So sorry.* Her soul offered up the words and it was as if they rose up to the clean, storm-washed air above, even as her body sank into the filth below. A sense of calm ate away at the panic. Mud oozed and sloshed around her, her legs sinking in up to her thighs and then her waist until she was more swimming through it than climbing down. When she came level with the truck, she pulled up the rest of the rope and tied it around herself, transferring her grip from the rope to the sturdy truck fender.

"Dallas," she called. The rain drilled tiny craters into the mud surrounding her. Everything was so monochromatic, a sea of black. She would have to edge around the front of the truck to be able to see beyond. Fingers cold and caked with slippery mud, she groped her way along. A metal shard on the fender nicked her palm.

A few more feet to go, sodden soil sucking against her every inch of the journey, she made her way around the fender.

As she'd suspected, beyond the stand of tightly clustered trees was a space relatively unscathed by the flow. He was not there. Body tingling with despair she scanned frantically.

"Dallas," she yelled again.

A small movement caught her eye. She'd been mistaken. Among the roots of one of the massive trees, she saw him, lying on his side, covered with mud, as black as the shadows that cloaked him.

She scrambled along, fitting between the trees, and made it to his side.

Breathing, let him be breathing. With a shaking hand, she brushed some of the cloying mud from his face.

His eyes blinked open, and it seemed at that exact moment, something inside her opened up, too. She leaned her cheek on his forehead. "Oh, Dallas" was all she could manage.

His eyes widened, the whites brilliant against his mud-streaked face. The breath caught in her throat, and she realized she'd never seen such a truly spectacular sight as those black irises, regarding her soberly, flaming to life as his senses returned. She reached out and stroked his face, running her fingertips along his forehead, his cheeks, again and again, until she began to believe he was really and truly alive.

Was it relief she saw in his eyes? She might have thought it joy, but why would it be so? Her brain reminded her what her heart did not want to acknowledge: she was a job, and she had every right to be angry at this deceiver whose hand she now clung to, their filthy fingers twined together. He had tricked her and withheld the truth from her.

Yet it was definitely not anger she felt, nor anything close to it. And that scared her more than the mudslide. She let go.

His lips moved, but she couldn't detect any sound until she leaned close.

"That was a wild ride," he muttered.

She laughed. It was absurd. Nestled in the mud up to her knees with a man who'd nearly been buried under tons of mountain, rain sheeting down on them both, she could not hold in the relieved giggle that bubbled from her mouth.

"I thought you were dead," she said, biting her lip to steady her frayed nerves.

"So did I, for a while there," he said, struggling to

pull himself to a sitting position, letting loose a shower of broken twigs and debris.

"Are you hurt?"

"Dunno yet." Clods of dirt fell away as he moved, the rain washing some of the grime from his face. He stared at her, his gaze so intense it made her look away. "I'm just glad you didn't get sucked down here with me."

"No, I got here under my own steam."

Eyeing the slope he shook his head. "Incredible. Why didn't you wait for help?"

She gave him a casual shrug. The truth was, she did not fully understand why she had done something so rash, for him, when the hurt still echoed inside. "Seemed like the thing to do after only one of you made it out."

He stiffened, as if remembering. "Archie?"

"He climbed up, unharmed, of course."

"Of course." Dallas tried to get to his feet. "We've got to get back up there. Go to the police."

He stood too quickly, staggering backwards. She quickly shoved her shoulder under his. "Slow. I can't carry you out of here, so don't push too hard."

He considered the slope and groaned. "That's a long way back up."

She showed him the rope tied around her waist, ridiculously pleased at the respect on his face.

"Smart thinking to tie the rope."

"I'm not as good at rescue as Juno, but I do my best."

He laughed, winced, and put a hand to his ribs.

"Broken?"

"Probably bruised, but I'll make it."

She unknotted the rope from her body so they could both grab hold. They began the arduous ascent, first climbing around the ruined truck and then struggling up

the slope, stopping every few feet to rest, sinking sometimes to their knees, sometimes to their waists in the
sticky mud. When he stumbled back, she would grab his
arm, holding him steady until he regained his balance.
When she slowed, mired down by the cloying mass, he
pulled her through the worst of it. Though she did not want
his help, she was grateful. Now that the adrenaline from
the rescue was depleted, every muscle in her body seemed
to resent the effort it took to climb back to the road.

Mack met them halfway down, lowered on another
rope fed to him by the truck driver. Mia could have
cried in relief when the big man grasped her around
the waist and they were hauled to the top by the men,
and, to Mia's surprise, Susan.

Susan helped her to sit on the fender of Dallas's truck
while Mack went back down the slope to assist Dallas.
From somewhere Susan produced a handkerchief and
wiped the grit from Mia's face as best she could.

The rain continued to thunder all around them, and
now she found herself pleased with the downpour that
washed some of the clinging film of mud off her clothes.
She felt light and lifted inside, as if she'd somehow left
some of her anger at the bottom of the cliff. She was
not ready to forgive, not yet, but it did not stop her from
enjoying the relief that came from putting down some
of her burden. Quietly, she thanked the Lord for blessing her and Dallas with another day of life. How odd to
feel thankful. How very strange and foreign.

Dallas was helped over the top, and he walked gin-
gerly over to join her. "Archie's gone," he said morosely.
"He got away again."

Mia shook away her strange ponderings, and rubbed
at a scrape on her arm. "Good riddance. I never want

to see him again. I hope he's right that Mr. Garza is finally satisfied."

"He's got no reason to go after you anymore," Dallas said. "Hector gave him what he wanted."

"Only when he had to."

"Because he heard you were in danger."

She felt shamed. "Yes, I guess so. He loves us, in his own fashion."

"That's one thing he has right." He held her gaze and she found she could not look away. Had the rain become warmer as it fell? The wind melodious as it swept along the road? Had Dallas become even more attractive, filthiness aside? Could be it was all colored by relief, she concluded.

Mack called out from the spot where the tree had fallen.

"I'm going to help clear the road," Dallas said.

"I'll help, too," Mia insisted.

He started to protest and then sighed. "It won't do any good to tell you to wait in the truck, will it?"

"Not one bit," she replied, walking straight to Mack and the truck driver. "Thank you for helping us out of that mess. We're ready to pitch in and clear the road."

Mack chuckled. "And I had you pegged for a city girl."

Mia shot him a sassy smile. "A city girl who's ready to get home to her daughter. Are you going to fire up that chain saw or am I?"

Mack and Dallas exchanged amused looks. In a matter of thirty minutes, Mack sliced off enough of the fallen tree to allow vehicles to squeeze by. Mia, Dallas and the truck driver hauled the branches out of the way while Susan continued to try to get a cell phone signal.

After a shaking of hands all around, Mack and the

driver loaded up in his vehicle and the others in Dallas's truck. Mia could not hold back a sigh as she slid onto the passenger seat and Dallas got behind the wheel. The old, cracked vinyl felt like a cloud of comfort compared to the scraping she'd enduring traversing down the cliffside and back up again. It was sheer bliss to be out of the hammering rain. The mud clinging to her skin coated her with an earthy funk.

What she wouldn't give for her favorite lavender lemon bath scrub that Gracie said smelled like candy. She sat up, a current of memory stinging everything inside.

"What?" Dallas said. "Are you hurt?"

"I just thought of something." Mia turned to Susan in the backseat. "You followed Catherine to Peter's house. How long was she there?"

Susan considered. "Only a few minutes. She pounded on the door, but he didn't answer at first. Finally he opened up, they exchanged a few words, and Peter grabbed the photo out of her hand and slammed the door closed. She went around the back and looked through the windows but he refused to let her in. After she left, he came outside and that's when I caught up with him."

"It occurred to me that if Catherine lingered awhile, she also could have put something in Peter's duffel bag while Susan and Peter were inside."

Dallas let out a low whistle. "Is Catherine in on the whole business?"

Mia gave voice to the question that was burning inside her. Peter's duffel bag was already in the boat when they arrived. "Did you see Catherine put anything in Peter's duffel bag?"

"I couldn't see down to the water from where I was in the house," Susan said.

Mia bit back a frustrated sigh.

Was Catherine Elias an unwitting cog in Elias's schemes? Or did she have her own part in Peter Finnigan's death?

Though Dallas had the wipers set at full speed, they hardly kept up with the water sheeting across the glass. His head was pounding a rhythm that matched the throbbing in his ribs. There was no option to drive fast, though he had to fight the urge to ram the gas pedal down. Dr. Elias was a murderer. And his wife, Catherine, might be his partner in crime. Most likely, Elias had taken care of Finnigan, who could prove his guilt. But Mia and Susan could still expose him, and there was the photo tucked under the visor in his truck. The miles passed excruciatingly slowly back to Spanish Canyon.

They headed straight for the police station, against Susan's wishes.

"That detective, Stiving, he won't hear anything bad about the precious Dr. Elias. He's protecting him. Could be the doctor has him on the payroll, even. We can't go to the police here."

"There isn't much choice, Susan," Dallas said. "We'll talk to the chief."

"And you trust him?" she demanded.

"He's given me no reason not to." But Stiving had.

Mia straightened, clutching her phone. "Got a signal. There's a message from Antonia. She got word to evacuate a half hour ago. She packed up Gracie and Juno. They're heading for the airport. She said she'll wait in the parking terminal until we get there." She groaned. "I feel like I should go meet them right now."

"As soon as we report what you…" He broke off as

they took the main road into town. The paved surface was covered by inches of water. Shop owners and police officers worked side by side in the rain, filling sandbags. They were fighting a losing battle, as the water was already lapping the sidewalks. Soon it would be spilling through doorways and flooding the businesses all along the block. The police station was obviously evacuating, officers and volunteers carrying boxes and equipment to a waiting van.

Dallas tried to park nearby, but he was waved at by a drenched police volunteer. "Can't stop here. Cantcha' see we're flooding?"

"It's an emergency."

He eyed Dallas and Mia skeptically. "Wet and dirty, but y'all look fine to me. Nobody's getting into the station right now."

Dallas kept his temper with serious effort. "We have to speak to the chief. It's urgent."

"Chief's already gone to our mobile station in Pine Grove. Stiving's out on a call, and every available officer is assisting the fire department. Sorry, can't help you unless you want to drive to Pine Grove and see if they have time for you."

Dallas was about to fire off an angry reply when Mia took his arm. "We'll go to Pine Grove. It's on the way to the airport, anyway."

A pang of grief stabbed at his insides. The airport would be their goodbye, the last time he would ever see her and Gracie. He rolled up the window and drove through the water. Pine Grove and the airport. End of the line. There was no way to stop it. He knew it was better, anyway. Mia and Gracie needed to be safely away from the floods and Dr. Elias. Once they were away, securely settled in Florida, Elias would pay for what he did to Cora, Susan and Finnigan.

Dallas would see to it.

They took the road to Pine Grove, which would provide a higher elevation for the police to regroup. The locals told of floods that had occurred some twenty years before, but nothing like this, and the town was simply not prepared for such a magnitude of disaster.

"Where will you go, Dallas?" Mia said, breaking into his thoughts. "Will you wait until the water recedes and live in the trailers still?"

Why would he? The only thing that meant something was his Search and Rescue classes and he was only filling in for a temporary vacancy. The job would be gone soon, too.

"Dunno. I'll have to ask Juno what he thinks."

Mia smiled and closed her eyes as they drove. She looked very young with her wet hair framing her face, smudged with both dirt and fatigue.

His thoughts wandered. If things had been different and they'd met under other circumstances. Would he have risked a relationship with her? Would she have allowed him past the protective wall she'd built? Might he have stuck around long enough to chip away at it?

Maybe he wouldn't have been brave enough to attempt it. He would have packed up his unfinished puzzle and his uncomplaining dog and left town rather than face his own vulnerability. He would never know if he would have let the most amazing woman he'd ever known walk out of his life because now it was too late. She was flying away, and it felt like she was taking his heart with her. Despair felt as weighty as the oppressive storm.

He almost didn't have time to slam on the brakes. A car he didn't at first recognize, was stopped in the road, doors open, hazard lights on. Juno stood next to the car.

"It's Antonia," Mia cried, leaping from the truck. He was behind her in a flash. Juno raced up to him, electric with some kind of excitement.

Antonia stood in the rain, body shaking, mouth tight with terror. "Oh, Mia. She's gone. She's gone." Tears rolled down her cheeks as Mia gripped her forearms.

"What happened, Antonia?" Mia demanded, voice hard as glass. "Where's Gracie?"

Antonia tried to answer, but no sound came out. Mia's hands tightened, viselike, around her sister's wrists. "Where is my daughter?"

Sucking in a breath, she tried again. "He took her."

"Who?" Mia's words rang with anguish.

"There was a chair overturned in the road. I got out to remove it. When I turned back, a man was there at the passenger-side door. He…he took Gracie and ran up the road. I heard him get into a car and then he was gone." She heaved in a breath. "Juno barked, but I had him leashed in the back and he couldn't get out. I called the police. They're coming."

"No." Mia's hands flew to her mouth. "No, no. This can't be happening."

"He always wins," Susan said, her own eyes round.

"I'm sorry, I'm so sorry," Antonia kept repeating.

"Who?" Dallas said. "Who was the man? Did you recognize him?"

The look she gave him was pure agony. "I know his face because I looked him up online when you told me he fired Mia." She swallowed. "It was Dr. Elias."

FOURTEEN

Mia saw the ground rush up to meet her as her legs failed. Dallas caught her before she hit the asphalt and carried her back into the passenger seat of his truck. She did not feel him lift her, she could not feel anything except a cold river of terror that seemed out to numb her limbs, her mind, her soul. He had Gracie. Dr. Elias had taken her baby.

"Sit for a minute," Dallas's soothing voice urged.

She felt pressure and realized that Antonia was gripping her hand, squeezing hard enough that her sister's nails bit into the tender skin of her palm. She was speaking, and Mia tried to follow. Antonia told the story in halting bursts. "After I called the police, I checked back with the trailer park. They haven't been ordered to evacuate, yet. It was a hoax."

Dallas said. "He probably pretended to be with the fire department. He told you there was an evacuation order so he knew when you'd be passing by."

Antonia nodded, grief stricken. "He must have been watching, parked around the turn in the road, waiting for us. I should have known. I never should have left her in the car alone. Oh, Mia, what have I done?"

It was as if Mia was watching it all from a distance, like a dramatic play unfolding on the stage in front of her. She should comfort her sister. Decide on the next step. Find a current picture on her phone to give to the police. Isn't that what the parents of missing children were supposed to do? The faces on milk cartons materialized in her mind. She'd seen the pictures, the sweet little faces printed there, smiling in moments of innocence while the world fractured into a nightmare for the parents who searched desperately for them.

She should take action. Every moment idle meant Gracie was that much farther away.

But she could do nothing but shake, her body vibrating to the rhythm of the shock which her mind could not grasp. The hands in her lap, the hair hanging across her eyes, did not seem to belong to anyone real. Gracie, her heart, the most precious person on the planet, was in the hands of a murdering madman. And Mia was reduced to a mindless zombie.

How could it be real? She was dreaming, in the grip of a nightmare.

The phone in Mia's purse rang. "You should answer it," Dallas prodded gently.

She could not force her fingers into life, so he removed the cell from the outside pocket of her purse and thumbed it awake.

"Hello?"

"I'm glad I thought to get the numbers off your cell phone when you left it in the office. This is Dallas's number, isn't it? The loser? Mia, your choice in men is terrible. Did we learn nothing from the last criminal you became involved with?"

Dallas stiffened. "Elias? Where's Gracie?"

Mia sucked in a breath and forced her teeth to stop chattering. Dallas put the call on speaker phone and the four of them bent their heads together to listen.

"Don't talk to the police," Elias said. "I don't want them involved."

Calm, collected, as if he was orchestrating every terrible moment. "What have you done with Gracie?" Mia tried to shout. Instead it came out as a pathetic whisper.

"She's with me, as you are aware, I'm sure."

"This isn't going to accomplish anything," Dallas snarled. "It's all over. We know the truth about Asa Norton."

He paused. "The truth is relative. I want the photo. I will contact you soon with the location."

"Please," Mia said, her voice breaking. "Don't hurt Gracie."

His tone was slightly offended. "I don't want to hurt her, Mia. I'm a doctor after all." Elias sounded almost as if he was talking to a patient, discussing treatment options or surgical procedures. "This is strictly a matter of self-preservation. Practical. Keep the police out of it, give me the photo, and there won't be any need for me to use violence. She will be returned, in perfect health. I'll call you back soon."

"No," Mia screamed, grabbing for the phone. "I want my daughter. Give me my daughter!"

There was no answer. Dr. Elias had disconnected.

Panic burgeoned through her senses. *Gracie, Gracie, Gracie.*

Dallas was talking, saying something as a police car pulled in behind them.

"Mia." He pressed his mouth to her ear. "Do you

want to involve the police? I think we should, but I don't know if we can trust Stiving."

The words circled slowly in her mind. *Police. Stiving.*

The police car ground to a halt on the shoulder. Stiving got out and walked over to them. "What's this all about?"

Antonia looked at Mia. She gave a slow nod. What choice did she have, especially after Antonia already called them?

"It's Gracie. She's been abducted." Antonia shook her head. "Aren't you here about my call?"

His gaze narrowed. "No, I'm here for Mia. Who's been abducted?"

Antonia stared at Mia. She felt Dallas's weighty gaze on her, also. They were asking what she wanted to do. Should she trust that this officer could rescue Mia from Dr. Elias? What was the alternative? She didn't even know where to start looking for her daughter. Panic constricted her lungs until she feared she was going to pass out.

"I'm here to arrest you," Stiving finished.

The words sizzled through her addled senses. Arrest her?

"What?" Dallas barked.

"The tests came back like we thought. Cora's blood-pressure medicine capsules were emptied out and filled with cocaine. It caused her to fall into a coma and stopped her heart. Fire Captain says she wasn't alert enough to snuff out the candle on her bedside table which started the fire."

"I didn't do anything to her medicine," Mia heard herself say. "I just picked it up from the pharmacy. Dr.

Elias tampered with it. He must have taken it out of my purse at work while I was in the file room."

Stiving raised his eyebrows. "Pretty crazy scenario. A respected doctor in this town murders an elderly volunteer. With a street drug."

"Cocaine is used in nasal surgery all the time. He had easy access," Susan chimed in.

Stiving shot her a look as if he had not noticed her there until that moment. "And why would he do that, exactly? To gain what?"

"Because he's not the man you think he is," Mia said desperately. "He's a murderer, and Cora was onto him. She—"

Stiving held up a hand. "All right. One thing at a time. You'll have a chance to tell me everything when I get you to jail in Pine Grove."

Dallas slammed a hand on the truck. "Listen. She's telling you the truth. He's got her…"

"Enough," Stiving snapped. "There are only two sets of fingerprints on that poisoned medicine, Mia's and Cora's. If the doctor has access to cocaine at the clinic, then chances are Ms. Sandoval did, too, not to mention the fact that she inherited Cora's property. All of that put together gives me more than enough to arrest her. We're going to jail now and if any of you interferes, you can join Ms. Sandoval."

Stiving was an enemy, Mia knew it then. By the time she convinced him that Gracie had been taken, that Dr. Elias was not the man he seemed, Elias might have killed her. The doctor's words came back to her again.

"You're afraid that you can't trust yourself, your choices, your judgments."

He'd seen right down deep into the core of her, the

real essence of her weakness. He was a master manipulator, and he was still in control, still pulling her strings as if she was a helpless marionette.

Mia could not trust herself, nor her ex-husband, or the police officer who stood there with the satisfied half smile on his face. She could not trust in the life she had built for her child, the possessions she'd accumulated, the schooling she was so determined to complete. It was not even a certainty that the town of Spanish Canyon would still be there tomorrow, threatened as it was by the menacing floodwaters set to swallow it whole. There was nothing on this earth that she could count on.

From somewhere deep down in her soul, came snippets that she had heard long ago when she was a child, maybe not any older than Gracie.

Trust in the Lord with all your heart...

Seek His will in all you do...

He will show you which path to take.

Trust God. Could she do something so simple and ultimately so very difficult?

Trust God.

Standing in front of her were two people who had done exactly that.

Dallas let the Lord rescue him from a minefield of sin and come out the other side a changed man. Antonia gave up years of anger and bitterness and the Lord transformed her life and filled it to the brim with love. It was time to trust Him to show Mia the way. There was a reason He had given her life and kept her living and right now, that reason she believed with every tiny atom inside her, was to save Gracie.

Armed with that desperate knowledge, and a faith wild and untamed and new, she closed her eyes and surrendered everything to which she had clung so tightly, pride, independence, fear, anger, hurt. *Lord, I trust You. Help me.*

When she opened her eyes she knew. God was there, right there with her as he had been since the beginning. Even when she'd ignored Him. Even when she'd railed at Him and yes, when she'd hated Him. He would be with her through whatever the next few hours brought.

In a flash, she saw the way. There was one person who knew where Dr. Elias had taken her daughter. Only one.

But Stiving would not let her go there, nor would he follow her leads. He would deliver her to jail before he conducted any search for Gracie. If Mia waited, if she let him take her, she would lose her daughter forever.

Please, Lord.

With cold fingers, she slipped the phone in her pocket and stepped out of the car. "All right, I'll go."

"Mia," Antonia cried out. "There has to be another way."

Mia grabbed her in a tight hug. She saw over Antonia's shoulder the naked anguish on Dallas's face. "It's all right," she whispered to her sister. "Tell Stiving everything. Convince him, if you can."

"What?" Antonia mumbled through her tears. "Where…"

"I'm sorry," Mia said to Antonia and Dallas. She locked onto his wondrous black eyes.

Something in her tone must have told him what she was going to do. He shook his head, hand raised to stop her. With all her strength, she shoved her sister backward, causing her to stumble into Stiving, who toppled against his car door and they both went down in the mud.

Mia ran as fast as she ever had in her life, heading for the rain-soaked forest, running toward the only way she could think of to save her child.

Dallas was thunderstruck. Juno barked and raced after Mia, thinking perhaps that it was some sort of game, until Dallas called him back. He stared as Mia raced over the uneven ground, making for the crowded wall of trees. She ran, fleet as a deer, disappearing between the branches.

Dallas helped Antonia and Stiving to their feet, shock and disbelief rocketed through him in waves. Had Mia really just run from the police? How could she think such a rash move would help find Gracie?

But would he not have done the same thing to find his brother?

Or Mia? He swallowed. Yes, he would.

Stiving barreled toward the trees, making it only a few yards, stumbling and slipping, before he must have come to the conclusion that he had no hope of catching up with her. He turned back to the car, rage suffusing his cheeks with red.

Antonia stood in shock, hands pressed to her mouth, staring in the direction her sister had just taken.

"Bad move." Stiving was on the radio now, calling for assistance in apprehending Mia Verde Sandoval.

The radio exchange seemed to snap Antonia from her inertia, and she started in on him before he could get back in the car. "Her daughter's been kidnapped by Dr. Elias. Whether you want to believe it or not, that's what happened. Dispatch will confirm it. I called it in moments before you arrived."

Stiving's lip curled. "I will confirm it, after I bring your sister in."

Dallas offered up everything he knew about Peter Finnigan's death. Susan reluctantly confirmed the facts until Stiving held up his hands. Was it Dallas's imagination, or did he see the slightest sign of belief on Stiving's face?

"All right. I've got enough to look into. I'll send anyone available to help search for the girl, but you have to know that Mia made an idiotic choice running from the police."

"She wouldn't have done it, except that Gracie's life is in danger," Antonia fired back.

"Seems to me she used that bit before, when she took the kid and went on the run after she served her jail time."

"She knows that was a mistake. She wanted to keep Mia away from her father," Dallas said through clenched teeth.

Stiving ignored him, took pictures of Antonia's car and checked it thoroughly before he ordered her to move it off the road. "They just radioed me that they're ordering evacuations of Spanish Canyon. This road will be jammed. I have to go back to town. You three should head to Pine Grove and wait for me there."

"My sister..." Antonia began.

"Your sister is now a fugitive, and she'll be treated as such." He climbed in the front seat. "If you help her in any way, you're aiding and abetting. Remember that." Tires squelched across the road as he did a sharp U-turn and headed back toward Spanish Canyon.

Dallas considered for a moment, trying to corral the thoughts stampeding through his brain. Mia would not hesitate to sacrifice her own life to save Gracie. Right or wrong, she felt she had no other choice than to run. He had to intercept her. Urgency burned like acid through his veins. "Take Susan and go to Pine Grove."

"What am I supposed to do there?" Antonia demanded. The angry quirk to her lips was so like her sister he almost smiled.

"Convince them to look for Gracie. Get to the chief if you can." He shot Susan a look. "And don't let this lady out of your sight."

"Where do you think he took Gracie?" Susan asked.

"I'm not certain."

"Promise me you won't hand me over to Thomas, even if you do find him," she said, staring at Dallas with those oddly haunted eyes. "You are not that kind of man, I think."

"You're right, and I'm hoping you're not the kind of woman who would walk out on a mother and child. We'll need your testimony to bring Elias down once and for all."

She looked away. "I don't know what kind of woman I am anymore. Before I was just angry, but now…"

"It's time for you to decide." He faced her full-on. "You've been hurt and lost your husband. Now there's a little girl involved." He heard Antonia gulp back a sob. "She needs her mommy, and you can help put things right, but not if you run away. Do you understand?"

She cocked her head. "Yes, I do."

"Then stay with Antonia. When we find Mia, we'll need you to back up her story." He reached out and squeezed Susan's forearm. "This time, the doctor is going to pay for what he's done, I promise."

She nodded slowly.

He started for the truck.

"But where are you going?" Antonia cried. "How can you help Mia?"

"It's my job to protect her, remember?" He opened the truck door.

"You're not just doing a job," she said quietly. "It's something much more than that."

He allowed a moment to acknowledge that she was right. Mia was not a job, she never had been. Not to him. "Juno and I are going to find her."

A freshening wind pulled at Antonia's wet hair as the rain continued to fall. "Do you know where she's headed?"

"I have a pretty good idea."

She came close and gripped his hands. "You have to find her. And Gracie."

"I will," he said, a sense of resolve turning all his fears and uncertainties into hard steel in his gut.

I will.

FIFTEEN

Dallas pulled the truck off the road, crunching across the tall grass, making his own trail to a rocky outcropping behind which he parked. He picked up Mia's purse and offered a sniff to Juno. It was probably completely unnecessary. He had always thought that Juno understood much more than the average member of his species. Juno already knew that he was going to look for the small, determined woman who had crashed through the heavy carpet of grass. Perhaps he thought it was one of their many training exercises where he would be sent to discover a prearranged "victim."

"Find," he commanded anyway.

Dallas watched him run, graceful loping strides over the uneven ground, tail wagging with sheer joy at the prospect of engaging in a search. Mia was no doubt heading for Dr. Elias's house to talk to Catherine. It would be feasible to go there and wait for her to turn up, but he did not want to leave her plunging through a heavily wooded area, wanted by the police and not in her right mind with worry about Gracie. She could fall, break an ankle, sustain a concussion. He shut down the worrisome scenarios.

Juno returned after a short while, alerted with his ear piercing bark, and then disappeared again, scrambling up a twisting road which might have once been a logging trail. Dallas hiked onward, the muddy ground clinging to his boots, rain dripping from his hair. The trail crested the top of a wooded hill and drifted back down toward the highway.

Every now and again, Juno would return and bark, a sign that he had tracked Mia and perhaps even found her already and why didn't Dallas get a move on it and pick up the pace, already? Dallas smiled. They'd cross-trained together, Juno and his awkward human, and the dog was fully capable of both tracking and trailing, and air scenting, but Juno always seemed to relish the opportunity to be off leash and following his impeccable nose toward a rescue. Other dogs could do the tracking on leash.

It never ceased to amaze him. With his paltry sense of smell, he could detect nothing but the odor of rain-washed ground and pine. Juno was easily able to discern the scent left behind by the 40,000 skin cells dropped each minute by his human quarry. Not only that, he could pick that scent from a world awash in odors. Dallas had worked with or known canines that detected everything from cadavers, to explosives, to smuggled fruits and vegetables. And now, his chance to find one small amazing woman lost in a sea of giant trees, all depended on Juno's amazing nose.

Dallas kept himself in high gear. In spite of the aching in his ribs and the pounding rain, he increased his clip until he was at a near jog, avoiding patches of slippery pine needles and puddles as best as he was able. She could not be that far ahead, but her pace was impressive, considering she too had survived a mudslide not many hours before.

Time ticked away, sucking up the minutes until sundown. It was edging toward six o'clock. One more hour of daylight. Juno could track at night, they'd spent enough hours training at it, but Dallas was not as surefooted in the dark, and neither was Mia. She had to be cold and terrified. And what about Gracie? Was she frightened? Had he hurt her? Bound her? The thought haunted him.

The way ahead was overgrown, thick underfoot with soggy debris and crowded overhead by tree limbs, weeping icy droplets down on him. And then, without warning, the trail was gone. They found themselves in a forest that showed no signs that it had ever been penetrated by humans for any reason. He listened to the incessant dripping. Wind played with branches and loosed more water down upon them which Juno blasted away with a vigorous body shake.

Juno stopped and nosed around for Mia's scent. With still victims on fair-weather days, the scent rose in a neat cone, emanating from the search target. Today the rain, shifting winds and highly active target, was making the search more difficult. It seemed likely that Mia would stop at some point, perhaps to try and use the GPS on her phone to locate Catherine's house, or simply to rest, to hide.

His heart was pounding and muscles fatigued after the brisk climb. Falling away to his left was a small hollow of firs, clustered close enough together to protect from the rain. She would head there, to regroup.

"Mia," he called. No answer but a quick darting movement from behind the trees. He charged toward it. Juno stopped him with an impatient bark.

"She's down there," he said as much to himself as the dog, ignoring another louder bark from Juno.

He half ran now, wishing his stiff leg and ribs would work in harmony with the rest of his limbs. He'd spent years, his whole adult life, really, combing through wild corners of the world, quiet forests and ruined buildings, creek beds and mountaintops, searching, searching. Sometimes he and Juno had found the target and he'd celebrated. Sometimes they didn't get there in time and they grieved together. After every mission, the need to search always returned. There would be another some-one to find, another search to be taken on, a restless-ness that told him he had not yet discovered the person he was destined to find.

"Mia," he shouted again, earning another bark from Juno.

He plunged into the clearing, moving so fast he skid-ded a good couple of feet before he stopped his forward momentum. The Stellar's Jays in the shrubs shot out with a deafening screech, taking refuge in the branches and squawking their displeasure. The air was heavy with the scent of wet grass and decaying leaves.

He completed a rough circle of the hollow, sinking up to his ankle in water at one point. Mia wasn't there. Bending low, he peered under the taller bushes, search-ing out any hiding places.

No Mia, nor any sign she had ever been there. Juno stared at him. Recrimination. He'd broken his own rule. Trust the dog. Dallas hadn't.

Early on in his career in search and rescue, a mentor watched him disregard a seemingly impossible positive alert from his dog. That's when Dallas had learned the term "intelligent disobedience."

If you've got a smart dog and you have learned to trust each other, let the dog think for himself. Juno had, and Dallas had disregarded him.

He dropped to a knee in the soggy grass and gave Juno a scratch. "Sorry, boy. I messed up. You're in charge now."

Juno accepted the apology by licking a raindrop off Dallas's chin, before he sprinted back in the other direction. Dallas tried to do the same, stumbling on the uneven earth and slapping aside branches as the slope became steep. He'd lost time with his dumb mistake. He prayed it wasn't too late. As the terrain grew more and more rugged, he had to resort to using his hands to hold on to tree trunks and exposed roots as he hauled himself upward, arriving at the top to find they'd looped back to the road.

Fifty yards ahead a yellow truck was stopped, the passenger door open.

And Mia was just stepping in.

"Mia," he shouted. Juno had almost reached her when she pulled the door closed and the truck rumbled away down the road, leaving Juno and Dallas alone on the rain-soaked highway.

Mia's heart plummeted as she eyed Dallas in the sideview mirror, Juno trotting back over to him as the truck pulled out. He'd come to find her, to help her out of the excruciating mess she'd fallen into. Maybe he'd intended to talk her into going back to the police. Knowing Dallas, he'd more likely determined to help her enact her own desperate plan to find her daughter.

But she could not let him throw his life away on a fugitive. And that's what she was, she reminded herself incredulously.

She realized the woman at the wheel was speaking to her. "Where'd you come from? Popping out of the woods like that, I thought you were Bigfoot, till I realized you're too small and not hairy enough." She laughed, setting her gray curls bouncing. "Name's Fiona. You?"

She smiled, imagining she must look like a deranged hitchhiker. "My name's Mia. I'm trying to get to the Spanish Villa Estates, on the edge of town. Do you know where that is?"

"'Course. Nice digs up there." She eyed Mia more closely, gaze flicking over her jeans and torn windbreaker. "That where you live?"

"No." Mia tried to stick to the truth as much as possible. "My house flooded. I know someone who lives in Spanish Villa. She said she'd help us find a place."

"Us?"

Mia swallowed hard. "My daughter, Gracie. She's four." She could not stop the tears then, hot and fast they rolled down her face. "I'm sorry. We've had a difficult time."

"It's okay, honey," the driver said, patting her hand and offering her a tissue box. "I got three girls myself. All grown now with kids of their own, but I remember how hard it was. Especially when my husband split town." She offered Mia a thermos. "Hot tea. You drink some now."

Mia protested.

"Your teeth are chattering. Drink the tea. I got plenty more."

Mia poured and sipped. The tea delivered warm comfort through her body and it had the added bonus of keeping her busy. Most of all she desperately did not want Fiona to ask her any more questions about Gracie. She could not trust her emotions.

Just get to Catherine and find out where her husband has taken my child.

Fiona kept up a constant commentary about the flooding and the small trucking company that she owned. Mia checked her phone constantly for any message from Dr. Elias. There wasn't any. He was probably enjoying the thought of the agony he'd created.

"Built it myself from the ground up," Fiona was saying. "Got twelve trucks now, out of Pine Grove. That's where I'm headed. Heard they've got the police moved up there during the flooding."

Mia sipped her tea and stared out the window. What else had Fiona heard?

Fiona sighed. "Awww, man. Looks like we got a roadblock."

Mia stared through the water-speckled windshield. Four cars ahead of them were stopped at a set of blockades straddling the road. A police officer, or perhaps a volunteer, swathed in a yellow slicker was making his way down the line, speaking with each of the drivers.

Her hands went icy around the cup. Were they looking for her? Nerves jumping, she darted a glance at the door handle. She could yank it open and jump down. Run away from the road. Right, and broadcast her presence like a signal flare.

The officer finished with the first two cars and made it to the third. It was almost sunset, and he held a flashlight. To search the vehicles for her? The fugitive wanted for murdering Cora Graham?

Fiona shot her a curious glance. "Drink more tea, honey, you're shaking like mad."

She watched the officer straighten and splash along the road, his boots dislodging sprays of water under the rubber soles. As subtly as she could, Mia reached for the door with one hand, fingers gripping the metal catch.

With the other, she kept the cup at her mouth, hoping to help conceal her face.

Her stomach was a lead weight as the cop waited for Fiona to roll down the window.

"Hello, ladies." He peered at Mia. "Where are you headed?"

Don't tell him about Spanish Villa, she begged silently.

"Pine Grove. Shop's up there."

He nodded. "Road's flooded ahead. Going to redirect you east about ten miles and then you can double back."

Fiona sighed. "I should have listened to the weather reports more closely."

"More rain coming. Just evacuating the lower elevations now, but might need to expand that." He looked closer at Mia. "You all right, miss?"

"Yes, I'm okay. I needed a ride, and Fiona was kind enough to stop for me."

"That right?" He took in the bedraggled hair, the scratches on her face from her plunge through the trees. Was there a dawning of recognition on his face? Would there be a request for an ID next? The roar of her own pulse deafened her.

A slow smile spread over his face. "Great to see people helping each other in times of emergency, isn't it?"

"Yes," she said, her sudden movement spilling some of the tea on her lap. She wiped at it with her sleeve.

"You headed to Pine Grove also?" The officer pinned her to the spot with his hard look. Her breath caught and she could not hide the shaking of her hands.

"I…" Mia started.

Fiona broke in. "I'm taking her to see a friend who's gonna help get her and her little daughter fixed up in a new place." Fiona looked at her watch. "When do you think you'll wave us through? I'd sure like to get this old truck in the barn before nightfall."

The officer gave Mia another long look before he consulted his radio. "All clear," he said and began to wave the drivers on to the detour.

She hardly dared breathe. As they rolled by she kept her gaze fastened out the front window, feeling the officer's eyes on her. How could he not hear the slamming of her heart into her ribs? Guilt had to be written all over her face in vivid ink.

Fiona gave the cop a final wave as she eased the truck by. When they were on the road, a good half mile past the roadblock, Fiona sighed.

"You want to tell me about it?"

Mia started. "No, I just can't. I'm sorry."

"It's all right." Fiona sighed. "I knew whatever it was that happened back there, you were anxious to get away from that guy and his dog."

She'd seen Dallas and Juno. And completely misunderstood. "They weren't…"

Fiona held up a hand. "I don't need to hear about it. You're anxious to get to Spanish Villa and just as eager to avoid the police, but you seem like a nice kid and I've got a soft spot for moms and daughters. Here." Fiona removed a plastic-wrapped sandwich from a bag. "We'll split it."

Mia was going to decline but just then her stomach let out a hollow rumble. Humbly, she accepted the sandwich. "Thank you so much, Fiona. How can I ever repay you?"

"You can tell me I make the best ham-and-pickle sandwich you ever ate."

Mia managed a grin. "I think it might be the only ham-and-pickle sandwich I ever ate."

Fiona laughed. "Close enough. We'll be passing Spanish Villa in about a half hour. Sit back and enjoy these luxurious driving conditions."

And Mia did, eating every scrap of the sandwich and clinging to the knowledge that with every mile, she was that much closer to finding Gracie.

Dallas and Juno endured a miserable hike back to the truck. Dallas kicked himself mentally every rugged step along the way. He'd distrusted Juno and lost his chance to catch Mia. Now he was playing catch-up in a big way.

He called Mia's phone again. No surprise when she did not answer. She didn't want to involve him further. *Involved? Mia I'm more than involved now. I couldn't walk away if I wanted to.*

The thought surprised him. He knew she did not want him in her life, nor Gracie's. And he would never force himself into a situation where he wasn't wanted. All true. But also true was the fact that like it or not, he felt deep down in the place where only truth can survive that he was meant to save Mia Verde Sandoval.

He phoned Antonia. She answered before the first ring had died away.

"Dallas? Did you find out anything?"

The Verde women were strong, determined, practical. It would do no good to sugarcoat, nor would he disrespect her by doing so. In the words of his mother, "Every woman's got a spark, Dallas, and adversity turns it to fire." And oh, how he'd fanned his mother's spark into flame. He'd seen it blazing in her eyes when she'd stumbled upon the gun hidden under the seat of his car. He blinked the memory away.

"I didn't catch up to her." Juno gave him the look. Full confession. "Juno found her but I messed up."

Satisfied, Juno set about licking his paws clean.

"I know where she's going, I'll meet her there. I need Susan to tell me where Catherine lives."

There was muffled conversation as Antonia consulted Susan. "She says it's a street in Spanish Villa." Antonia told him the address.

He set the wipers in motion and started the truck. "Are you both all right?"

"We're at a Red Cross shelter in Pine Grove. The chief is supposedly on his way, says a volunteer." She paused. "I'm hearing radio reports about the flooding. It's really bad—road closures all over and a bridge, the Canyon Creek span, is all but underwater."

Dallas let her talk as he headed off. When she ran down, she said what she most needed to get off her chest.

"I feel helpless. I should be searching since I was the one…"

"Antonia, stop right there. We both know who is at fault here and he's going to pay for that."

She let out a soft breath. "What if you're too late, Dallas?"

"I won't be."

"I'll pray for you."

"That's the best thing I could ask for."

The only thing.

SIXTEEN

Fiona let Mia out on a patch of moonlit road at the entrance to the Spanish Villa housing complex. Mia gripped her hand in thanks. "You've done more for me tonight than you know."

Fiona squeezed back. "Take care of yourself, honey. You're strong. You'll make it through whatever it is that's got you in the crosshairs."

One final squeeze and Mia hopped down, avoiding the mud. The sky was leaden with clouds, but the rain had tapered off to a heavy mist. Though she still felt the grit trapped under her jeans and top, her clothes were more or less dry and her belly was not grumbling, thanks to Fiona's gracious gift of a ham-and-pickle sandwich. Had Dr. Elias given Gracie anything to eat? Fear engulfed her in such a tight clutch she had to stop and fight for breath, steadying her shaking legs by locking her knees. One more check of the phone. Still no message and her battery wouldn't last forever.

Go find out where he's got her, and get your daughter back. She set off.

Enormous houses with red tile roofs and white stucco exteriors perched on well-manicured lots. It was a point in her favor that the houses were spaced far apart and the weather kept residents inside, perhaps packing in case evacuations reached even this higher elevation. She had only been to the doctor's house once, for a clinic party which included all the employees.

Fleeting memories trickled across her recollection of the event. White napkins, delicate cheeses and imported olives, plush carpets and a swimming pool in which Gracie had paddled for hours until her button of a nose was sunburned in spite of the cream. Mia's throat ached with unshed tears until a crazy idea flickered into her consciousness. Was it possible he'd brought Gracie here? Catherine had been at Finnigan's for some reason. If she was just as guilty as her husband, this might be the place they were hiding her.

New resolve flooded her with energy. She practically sprinted to the top of the hill, to the last house at the end of a lonely cul-de-sac. Dr. Elias's house.

Knock on the door? It would give them a chance to lock Gracie away or call the police on her. Heart thundering, she moved closer, trying to piece together some sort of plan. A set of arched windows with fancy iron grillwork decorated the side of the house. Most were dark, but golden light glowed from the farthest one. She moved silently to the edge of the neat stepping-stone walk, keeping to the shadows. Did the doctor have a dog? She didn't think so. Too finicky, too controlling. He wasn't the dog-loving type.

You weren't either, until you met Juno.

And Dallas.

Mia realized that she had changed in a lot of ways since encountering Dallas. She had been too far away to see his face, as she got into the truck and left him on the side of the road, but she could imagine the anger and frustration. It stabbed at her. Why were her feelings a jumbled spaghetti mess whenever she thought of him?

Jaw clenched, she pushed the hair out of her face and shored up her strength. *He shouldn't have followed me. His job is done.* It was all on her now.

Her and God.

She drew level with the window now, fingers on the cold metal grillwork. A quick look. She readied herself to move when a hand went around her mouth, muffling whatever scream she might have managed.

She thrashed against the strong arms holding her, iron bands that kept her fastened against a rock-hard chest.

"Quiet" came the hissed whisper in her ear.

Dallas held her there for a moment, captive against him, and then slowly he turned her around, uncovered her mouth and pulled her into the shadows behind a potted shrub.

She couldn't decipher her own rattling emotions. He looked down at her, moisture beading on his tousled hair, a scratch running the length of his cheek, hands on hips, lips hard with anger. "Mia…" he began, then with a sudden rush he pulled her close and kissed her, palms cradling her head.

The warmth rushed through her in a delicious wave and she kissed him back, forgetting for a moment, everything but the elation that swept through her. A tide of warmth, safety and belonging thundered through her, beating back the desperate fear. When they both ran out of breath, he pulled away and put his forehead to hers.

"Sorry. Shouldn't have done that. You're a pain in the neck to keep track of."

She laughed, a quiet, wobbly chuckle that emerged over the sparks still showering through her. "Where's Juno?"

"He's in the truck because he's not good at quiet. And he's massively upset about it. What did you see inside?"

"I didn't get that far."

He started toward the window.

She grabbed his wrist. "Dallas, I've thrown everything away to find my daughter. You shouldn't. You have a future without us. I don't want you going to jail for me."

The moonlight flecked his eyes with an inner glow. "Noted." He continued to the window and looked inside.

"Didn't you hear me?"

"Yes," he said, still peering into the house. "I heard you, but I'm not obeying. There's a difference."

She huffed, uncertain whether to be angry or pleased.

He moved away from the window. "Catherine's in the back of the house. It looks like there's a living room that opens onto the patio. Let's see if we can get in that way."

"What if Dr. Elias is inside?"

"Unlikely. His car isn't in the garage."

Mia sagged. "I was hoping that he brought Gracie here."

"Don't think so, but we'll find out where. Let's go."

"Dallas," she tried again to stop him. This time she put her palms on his chest, feeling the strong beating of his heart. How could she tell him what it meant that he had come to find her? And that she could not allow him to stay? "This is wrong, breaking into someone's house. If you help me do this, there's no going back."

"No, Mia," he said slowly. "This is right, that I'm

here with you now and we're going to get your daughter back."

"It's not worth it for you. I can't repay you in money, or…" She looked at the ground.

He tipped her chin up, his thumb gently tracing the curve of her lower lip. "I know you have a life to build somewhere else. I understand that. This isn't about payment. It's about what's right."

She closed her eyes tight. "Everything's mixed up, Dallas. How can you be sure what's right?"

He waited until she opened her eyes. "You pray and you take your best shot at it."

"I haven't had a good track record figuring out what's right, but…" She faltered. "I've asked His help this time."

Dallas smiled, moonlight illuminating the joy on his face. "Amen to that." He opened his mouth to continue, but instead he pulled her into the shadows. "Security vehicle," he breathed in her ear. "Stay still."

Easy for him to say, she thought, from the circle of his arms. Pressed against his ribs, her chin next to his, her heart was puttering like a motorboat. She was sure it might give out altogether as it ricocheted between comfort at being near him and utter terror about what could be happening to Gracie, to an odd peace that came when she'd given the situation over to God. A mixed up spaghetti jumble to be sure.

When the car passed, she disentangled herself from Dallas and got to her feet, breathing still hitched and unsteady.

"Ready?" he said, infuriatingly handsome in spite of his sodden condition.

"Are you really sure?"

"Mia," he said, cutting her off. "If you ask me that again, you're going to go wait in the car with Juno."

She was not completely sure if he was joking or not, as he headed off toward the patio.

You kissed her? Again? What part of the plan was that, you dope? The woman was running from the law and terrified for her daughter. He had no business kissing her. He willed his gut to stop quivering like jelly at the residual sensation of her lips pressed to his. He felt like Juno when they first worked together and the dog was more interested in rocketing off after enticing birds than engaging in a search and rescue. Impulse had overridden his good sense. Yet he could not deny the irrational happiness that sprang up in his soul that Mia had invited God in.

Still, had he really kissed her? He had. The electricity still tingled through him.

Focus already, would you?

He pulled his mind back to the present. As soon as Catherine caught sight of them, she would call the police or bolt. Since there was no way he wanted to hurt her, that gave them only a few minutes tops to see if they could convince her to rat out her husband or, if she was an accomplice, to bluff her into thinking she and the good doctor were caught.

Not much of a plan, but he couldn't think of anything better.

They reached the patio just as Catherine Elias stepped out. Dallas and Mia watched from behind a screen of bushes as she turned on the propane gas, and a fire pit sprang to life. She watched it burn in silence. The flames danced high in the darkness.

Mia burst out into the circle of light. "Where's my daughter?"

Catherine screamed, hands pressing a file folder to her chest. "What are you doing here?"

Dallas stepped forward so she could see him, too. "Your husband kidnapped Mia's daughter, Gracie. We're here to find out where he took her. Mia said you have a cabin in the mountains. We need to know where."

Catherine's mouth opened in an *O* of surprise. Or was it anger? He couldn't tell. She took a step toward the house, but one step only, eyes shifting in thought.

"Why would he take her?"

She knew something. Maybe everything. "He wants us to hand over the photo that you took to Peter Finnigan that can incriminate him in Asa Norton's murder."

"Asa Norton? The man who drowned all those years ago?" She cocked her head as if listening to the sound of far off music. "Susan's husband."

"Are you helping him?" Mia fired off.

"Helping? You think I helped my husband kill Asa?"

"No, but he also murdered Cora Graham and Peter Finnigan. You might have pitched in for those."

Catherine's mouth went slack. "This is insane. I'm not a murderer."

Dallas could not be sure it was disbelief or lying. Women confounded him. He had no chance of reading her right, but he pressed on anyway. "You went to see Peter Finnigan, just before he was blown up."

"Blown up? What are you talking about? He was perfectly fine when I left him." She sank down on the brick patio wall, heedless of the moisture. "This can't be true."

"It is true," Mia protested. "You know I'm not lying, don't you?"

She chewed on a thumbnail. "I suspected something was going on when that woman Susan showed up, stalking me. He said he'd treated her for a minor injury after her husband drowned and she became fixated with him."

"But you didn't believe him?" Mia pressed.

"Not really. There have been other women," she said wearily. "I suspected Susan was another one of Thomas's flings and he was trying to cover up. But then things started to happen. Cora died. This thug from Miami showed up. And I found Thomas shredding files. These files taken from the clinic." She waved the folder at them. "There's nothing in them now. They're Cora's. Most were destroyed, but I saved one without him knowing. The photo was in it along with a newspaper clipping about Norton's death."

The pieces were beginning to fall into place, Dallas thought. "You recognized your husband in the picture."

"Yes, that's why I went to see Peter Finnigan. I read the paper's account of how Finnigan supposedly tried to save Susan's husband that day. I can't prove it, but I think Thomas was giving Finnigan money, paying him to stay quiet. I found an envelope of cash one time, addressed to P. Finnigan at his Mountain Grove address. Thomas explained it away, but I always wondered about it."

"Did Peter tell you anything?" Mia asked.

"Nothing. As a matter of fact, he snatched the photo and tossed me out, but I didn't do anything to harm him. And now you say he's dead? Are you sure?"

Dallas nodded. He would never lose the memory of how Finnigan lost his life.

"Why kill Peter?" Catherine mused.

"Both were involved in Asa's death," Dallas said. "Peter must have threatened to tell, so Elias killed him."

"After all these years? Why?"

Mia hugged herself. "Something went wrong."

"Susan's no innocent in all this, you realize," Catherine spat. "She kept quiet about Thomas's involvement all these years instead of going to the police, not to mention the fact that she got millions when Asa died."

"But she can bring Dr. Elias down now." Mia shivered. "So he'll need to kill her, too."

"I didn't want to see it." Catherine looked up at the cloud-washed sky. "I mean, I knew about the other women. I'm not so blind that I couldn't figure that out. I didn't want to believe there was anything else."

"Why didn't you go to the police?" Dallas said. "If you're an innocent in all this?"

She turned haggard eyes on him. "I'm leaving him as soon as I can get my things together. He's a manipulator and covering up whatever he did in the past, but the man is the father of my children. Whatever Thomas has done, they don't deserve to live with his sin. Can you understand that?"

Mia clutched Catherine's hands. "Yes, so you can understand why I need to find my daughter. Please, Catherine, you've got to tell me if you know where he might have gone."

"I don't," she said, detaching herself.

"Where's your cabin?" Dallas watched her mouth tighten.

"He wouldn't abduct a child. He's a lot of things, but he has his own children. He wouldn't hurt Gracie."

"But he did," Mia said. "Your husband called me

and told me he had my daughter. You have to face it, just like I had to face the truth about Gracie's father."

"This can't be possible. I would have known I was married to a murderer." Catherine looked away. "What kind of woman wouldn't know?"

"A woman like me," Mia said. "I misjudged my husband, too, Catherine. You feel stupid, vulnerable. And then—" she shot a look at Dallas "—you forgive yourself and you move on."

"I loved him." A tear rolled down Catherine's cheek. "I really did. Maybe I still do."

Mia knelt next to her and took her hand. "Believe me I understand, but your husband has killed and killed again, and now he has my baby." Her voice broke on the last word. Dallas put a hand on her shoulder, trying to squeeze some comfort into her.

"But Thomas is a father himself," Catherine said. "How could he?"

"I think you know deep down that we're right," Dallas said. "That's why you were getting ready to burn this file, isn't it?"

"All the others are shredded. This one only has the clipping left. I... I figured whatever he's been up to, the less evidence the better for my kids."

Mia did not release Catherine's hand. "Even if you can't accept it, would you throw away Gracie's life? A mother couldn't do that to another woman's child."

Her face crumpled. "I'm not a bad person. Really, I'm not."

Dallas sensed they were near to breaking through her defenses. "Then tell her."

Tears cascaded down Catherine's face. "The cabin's near the reservoir, on Sentinel Hill Road."

"Thank you." Mia clutched Catherine in a desperate hug.

"Here," Catherine said, shoving the file folder at Dallas. "Take it. Maybe it will help you prove he's guilty."

Betrayal shone like an exposed wound deep in her eyes.

"I'm sorry," he said.

She waved him away. "I won't be here when you come back. If what you say is true, I'll never come back."

Mia and Dallas left her staring at the fire pit.

SEVENTEEN

Mia was panting hard by the time they made it to Dallas's truck, having had to stop twice to avoid detection by the security people. She still had twigs tangled in her hair from their leafy hiding spots and a new catalogue of scratches. Once Juno was finally convinced to move to the backseat, he could not stop pressing his wet nose to her neck, snuffling her hair until she batted him away.

"Stop, Juno. That tickles."

He responded in doggie fashion by licking her along the hairline which made her laugh.

"I think you blew his mind showing up like this when he was all set to locate you out in the woods."

"Sorry," she said, giving Juno a rub under the chin. "You'll just have to find me some other time." When she'd gotten Juno down to an occasional slurp from the backseat, she called Antonia and put her on speaker phone.

Her big sister alternated between giving her a tongue lashing and expressing heartfelt relief that Mia was now in the company of Dallas and Juno. "I'm still waiting for the chief. Susan's gone to see if she can find a room

somewhere for us, but the town is full of evacuees."
She huffed. "It's driving me crazy. Every minute I'm
thinking about you and Gracie and I want to be doing
something to help."

Mia heard her sister start to sniffle. "Don't cry, sis,
or I'll start, too. We're going to get her, Antonia, we got
some info from Catherine," she explained, giving her
sister the location of the doctor's cabin. Saying it aloud
spread an eagerness inside that she felt would burst out.

"You can't go. This is too dangerous," Antonia said.

"What choice is there? He's got Gracie, and I'm a
fugitive."

"We have to tell the police where you're heading,"
Antonia insisted.

Mia's head spun. "No, I won't risk it. I can't."

She looked to Dallas.

"You know where we're going, Antonia." He checked
the time on the truck's dashboard. "Give us a two-hour
head start, then tell them everything."

If we're not back...if we're too late. Suddenly she
could not get enough oxygen. There was no outcome
possible except that they would find Gracie, unharmed
and get her away from Elias. Forcing a breath in, she
grated out the words. "Tell whoever will listen, but
you and Susan need to stay there where it's safe." She
paused.

"Okay," Antonia said.

"I don't know if Susan is trustworthy," Mia said quietly. "She's unstable, and she benefitted from her husband's death financially."

Antonia lowered her voice. "If she was involved in
the murder, why would she come back and blame it on
Elias?"

"It makes no sense to me, but I wanted to warn you. I can't stand anything happening to you." She scrubbed at a spot of grit on the knee of her jeans. "I wish I could do this by myself and not endanger any more people."

"You've got help now, Mia. You're not alone. Dallas is there, and Reuben's flying here as we speak. He's devastated about Cora and…and Gracie."

Deep breaths. "I'm going to get her back, Antonia." Mia clutched the phone. "I am going to get my daughter back."

"Be careful, sister."

"I'm used to dealing with criminals remember? I used to be married to one." The joke fell flat. She was about to hang up.

"And I wanted to say—" Antonia rushed on "—I'm sorry I didn't tell you about Dallas. Reuben and I…"

"Were trying to protect me." She sighed. "And so was Dallas. I understand." And she did. Though Dallas did not look at her, she knew from his kiss, from his willingness to risk everything, that he was with her because he cared for her. With a stab of anguish, she also knew there could be no future for them. When she found Gracie, she would move back to Florida and be the best possible parent to her child. She would play it safe and humbly accept any help from her sister and brother-in-law. No more striking out on her own. No more independence at all costs.

And Dallas? He would continue to bounce around the country finding the missing, and living the kind of unfettered freedom that was exactly what Mia and Gracie did not need. He found lost souls and returned them home. She would always picture him that way, even when they had separated for the last time.

A branch snapped loose from the trees and cracked into the windshield, shocking her out of her reverie. Find Gracie. That was all that mattered.

"Be careful," Antonia said. "Please, Mia."

She said she would and disconnected.

Dallas kept the truck at a slow speed which maddened her, windshield wipers slapping out their own relaxed rhythm. "Can't we speed up a little?"

"Roads are dangerous right now, and we don't need any cops or security people taking notice of us."

She huffed. "Why do you have to be so…logical?"

He offered a smile which died quickly away.

"What's bothering you? Aside from the insanity which you've gotten yourself into?"

"Finnigan."

"What about him?"

"The way he died. We know Elias killed Asa Norton and Cora. He used drugs in both cases. Neat. No blood. Almost a peaceful way to die. But Finnigan…"

She saw the explosion in her mind's eye, the bright flower of flame that blew away Finnigan's life before the river took his body. "A bomb seems out of place for Dr. Elias?"

"Maybe I'm wrong."

"Could Catherine be lying about everything? Is it possible she killed Peter for some reason and she's trying to hide it by shifting blame to her husband?" The rest remained unspoken. *Could we be driving into a trap right now?*

"That's part of what's bothering me. I don't know if Catherine or Susan can be trusted."

"The only thing I can be certain of is Susan didn't take Gracie and neither did Catherine," Mia said firmly.

"And that's all I care about right now, getting my daughter back."

They ran into two detours which cost them time. It was nearing ten o'clock when Dallas finally started the ascent up Sentinel Hill. Posted signs warned of flooded roads ahead.

The more Dallas slowed, the more frenzy whipped inside Mia. At the top of a winding road, he pulled to the side. "Hang on. Gonna climb up those rocks and check things."

He got out, Juno following. Clouds rolled over the moon, leaving only unreliable patches of light that played across the pile of rocks, marbled with shadows and moisture. Juno sat at the bottom, eyes riveted on Dallas's progress as he climbed.

He'd just scrambled to the top when Mia's phone rang. Dr. Elias.

She scrambled to press the button. "Hello?"

"My apologies for making you wait so long, but we developed car trouble on the way."

She fought for calm. "Where?"

"We're at the cabin, top of Sentinel Hill. Roads are flooded so you'll have to be creative. Bring the photo. If you aren't here by midnight, there will be consequences."

Consequences. Mia's nerves turned to trails of ice. "I want to talk to my daughter right now."

There was a sound of movement.

"Mommy?"

"Gracie." Tears rained down Mia's face, her heart rose up and twined itself with those two precious syllables. "Are you okay? Did he hurt you? Mommy's coming."

Dallas climbed down and joined her. With icy fingers, she held the phone between them.

"We're going on a boat 'cuz…"

The phone was yanked away. "Gracie!" Mia screamed.

"Midnight." The phone clicked off. Mia stared. "She sounds okay, like he hasn't hurt her. Yet."

Dallas pressed her shoulders. "She's all right. Hang on to that. Gracie is all right."

Inside she repeated the mantra. Gracie was all right. Until midnight.

Dallas wanted to reach through the phone line and pummel the man. Mia did not resist when he urged her back into the truck. She clutched the cell as if it was somehow still connecting her with Gracie.

"He's desperate for the photo. He won't do anything to her until we deliver it."

She nodded mechanically, like an automaton. He wondered if she would withstand his next bit of news.

"This area is bisected by a river that feeds into a lake. It's all flooded. There's no way I can drive any farther."

Some flicker of life in her eyes. "Where is the cabin?"

"On the other side of that ridge. The place is flooded, and he can't drive out, either. He's going to try to boat out of here. He's probably booked a flight and has his escape all lined up."

Her eyes were dull, breath coming in harsh gasps. "Mia, are you listening?" Was she going into shock? "We need to hike in and probably swim, there's no other option. Let me go ahead, with Juno. You don't have to…"

She fired back to life, fixing him with a look more

ferocious than some of the gang members he'd tangled with. "I'm going." He was smart enough to know any arguing the point would get him nowhere but left behind. Juno had no complaints either, even though the sky was delivering more rain. The dog would prefer monsoons to the backseat of a truck any day of the week. He didn't want Juno in danger any more than he wanted Mia to be, but there was nothing to be done about that either. He threw up a prayer and let out a sigh. "Text Antonia. Tell her to fill the cops in on the doctor's call. Okay?"

Her fingers flew across the keys. "All right, let's go."

He removed a pack from under his seat and shouldered it, handing her a bottle of water. "Drink."

"I'm not thirsty."

"Humor me and drink anyway." He poured some into his cupped palm for Juno, who lapped it up, tail wagging and ready to begin the adventure, and drained a bottle himself. He wouldn't suggest they eat the snacks he'd stowed in the pack, though his stomach was empty. He had a feeling it was going to be all he could do to keep up with her. From a supply in his stash, he handed her a plastic bag for her phone and two more for the photo which she double-bagged and stowed in his pack.

Juno gave an excited whine.

"It's okay, buddy," Dallas said. "This time we already know where to find her."

The question was, how would they handle it when they did? There was no more time to think about it as they started across the sodden grass toward the top of Sentinel Hill.

The ground had been transformed to a marsh by the relentless rains. Mud sucked at their feet and shins and each step was a struggle, though Juno seemed to have no trouble with it. There was just enough moonlight peering between the clouds to sufficiently light their way. Some half an hour later they made it to the ridge, flopped down on their bellies and scoped out the cabin.

It was what surrounded the neat, wood-sided structure that concerned him most. The lake, which was normally a stone's throw from the cabin, was now engulfing it, clear up to the doorstep. A boat rolled on the rain-speckled surface, tied to the porch support.

Dallas whistled low. "This place will be under water in a matter of hours."

Worse yet, the cabin was on the far shore, a good quarter mile across the lake. He didn't hazard a guess about the depth. Didn't matter. They had no boat and no car. Swimming was the only option.

She read the question in his mind. "I'm a good swimmer."

"A Miami girl? I'd be surprised if you weren't." He emptied the remaining water bottles out of his pack, keeping only the first-aid kit and foil-wrapped food.

She offered the sliver of a smile. "You travel prepared."

"Sometimes it takes a few days to complete a rescue. Conditions are bad more often than not." He felt her watching. "What?"

"I was so mad about how you ended up in my life and just now, I was wondering if God put you here in spite of me, to rescue Gracie."

He reached out a finger and traced the perfect line of her cheek and chin. "Maybe He meant for us to rescue her together."

Moonlight captured the tears gathered in her eyes, jewels that she would not let fall. It made them more precious, somehow, the strength that kept them captive there. Mia was a woman of breathtaking courage, who could not see the best things about herself. If she could see what he saw, only for a moment, it would take her breath away.

"You are an amazing woman, Mia Verde."

She blinked, then blessed him with a smile that would live inside his heart with all the most precious memories he possessed. "Coming from you, I take that as a fine compliment. Thank you, Mr. Dallas Black."

What he wouldn't give to kiss her right then, with the rain covering them in glistening droplets and the moon gilding her hair with a million sparkles. He swallowed hard. "When we get across, try for the east side of the cabin where there's only one window. Okay?"

She nodded, stripped off her jacket and without another word waded into the lake. Juno, who had been busy sniffing, gave him a comical double take.

"Yeah, I know it's a strange time for a swim, but you're up for it aren't you?"

Juno, every bit as silent as Mia, ambled right into the water after her.

EIGHTEEN

Cold. It shivered through her body as she swam into the dark water. Juno paddled ahead, turning once in a while to be sure she was still following along. Dallas kept level at her side. She suspected he could easily outpace her, but he, like Juno, was keeping tabs, ever her faithful guardian.

Her muscles fell into a desperate rhythm. Each stroke, every kick and breath brought her that much closer to Gracie. She would force herself to cross this endless watery barrier between herself and her daughter. Despite her effort, goose bumps prickled her skin. Clearing the water from her eyes, she realized she was still no more than halfway across the expanse. Arms tired, legs leaden and she stopped, treading water.

Dallas was next to her in an instant. "Need a rest?"

She was too winded to respond.

He offered his back. "Hold on. I'll tow you for a while."

Sucking in a breath she shook her head, not wanting to add weight to a man she had already burdened so heavily. "I'm okay." She plunged ahead. More minutes, inching along, the void fighting against her in a strange nocturnal race. There was just the frigid water and her weakened body, battling for each and every stroke. Her heart traveled on ahead, calling Gracie's name into the night.

She remembered Hector and Gracie splashing in the warm Miami waters.

"Blow bubbles, *bebé,* like a little fishy." He'd held Gracie against the foaming sea and laughed at the baby kicks and clumsy wiggles she'd tried. "She's going to be a great swimmer," Hector announced, his face shining with love.

Gracie's soft voice echoed through her memory. *My daddy's a bad man.*

Hector was a man who had done very bad things, but also a man who loved Gracie Louise quite possibly as much as she did. It was a fact she had forgotten, or perhaps, she had not wanted to accept. Maybe someday the Lord could make Hector's path straight, too.

And hers. If she could just get to Gracie. There were so many things she had to tell her, to love her through, comfort her against and lift her over. So many waves to be traversed. *Lord, help me, help me.*

Water broke over her face and she sucked in a mouthful. What if Dr. Elias had hurt her? Or worse? Fatigue and fear started to paralyze her limbs. Her teeth chattered. Wind-driven waves splashed again, sending her into a coughing fit.

His arms twined around her, lifting her head out of the water. "I'll hold you. Rest a minute."

She tried to protest.

"We're in this rescue together, remember?"

"Old habits…"

He kissed the tip of her nose and for a moment, she

thought he might press his lips to hers. Expectation rippled through her body, but then he turned and she clung to his wide shoulders, feeling the muscles moving along his back. Cheek resting against him, she watched the moonlight catch on the surface dappled by the pattering rain. Almost there. What would they find? She pressed her face harder into his back, strong and soothing, a partner in the lowest moment of her life.

Oh Lord, I don't deserve this man who's risking everything to help me. I have been hard-hearted to him and to Hector. Hector was a criminal, yes, and maybe he always would be, but at that moment with the water lapping against them, she prayed he would be redeemed. He was a sinner who could be good with God's help. Just like a small woman in a very big lake whom she now understood was just as much in need of a savior.

"Almost there," Dallas murmured, calling Juno closer as they neared the other side.

"And Lord, thank you for Dallas," she whispered, completing the prayer and giving it to God.

The wall of the cabin facing them had no windows, except a small one cloaked by heavy curtains. They climbed up on what used to be a wraparound porch which was now covered by six inches of water. Juno levered himself out of the water next to them, immediately shaking his sodden coat with such violence both Dallas and Mia threw up their arms for cover.

Dallas peered around the corner, Mia crowding next to him to see.

A motorboat was tied to the porch rail, and a faint band of soft golden light shone from under the drapes in one of the front windows.

"There's a bag and supplies loaded into the boat," he whispered in her ear. "He's ready to get out of here."

The front door was thrown open. Instinctively, Dallas moved Mia behind him.

"Don't be shy," Dr. Elias called. "Come on in."

Mia pictured Gracie inside. What had the monster done to her? She pushed forward but Dallas stopped her.

"If we don't leave with Gracie in a matter of minutes, the police are coming in," Dallas shouted back. "It's all over for you."

"Nice bluff," Elias said. "But it's not going to fly. I've been tracking you with binoculars since you started your swim. Now get in here before I lose my patience."

Mia's heart sank. It was a trap, and there was no choice. What had they expected anyway? To surprise the doctor? Snatch Gracie from under his nose? They splashed along the porch until they reached the door.

Dr. Elias held a small lantern in one hand which added a pool of meager light. He wore jeans and a flannel shirt. His face was marred with stubble and darkened by shadows that added years. He looked nothing like the self-assured doctor, a man respected by the townspeople. He looked, in fact, like a man on the edge of desperation.

He pulled the gun from his pocket. "Inside. Now."

Mia went first, Dallas and Juno following.

It was a small cabin, three rooms, a ratty sofa and an old rocking chair, the only furniture. A fire in the small stone fireplace gave off sooty smoke that burned her throat. "Where's Gracie?" Mia demanded.

"In a minute." Dr. Elias gestured to Dallas. "Put down the pack."

Dallas did so.

"You'd better have the photo I requested."

Mia hurried over, wrenched open the pack and thrust the plastic bag containing the picture. "There. I brought what you asked for, now give me my daughter."

Elias took the bag, flicking a glance inside, while keeping the gun leveled in their direction. "Ancient picture. Old lady was thorough. I wonder where in the world she unearthed it." He tossed it into the flames. "The trouble is, of course, other people could follow the same trail Cora did. Maybe you even made copies before you came."

"We didn't," Dallas said. He wondered if Catherine had, for an extra bit of insurance in case Elias resurfaced in her life someday.

Elias sighed. "In this age of technology, you can't really obliterate anything can you? It's best if I disappear." He shook his head. "Such a waste. I created a good life here, a thriving practice. Raised my kids in Spanish Canyon. I hate to leave it, and them."

"Don't you dare talk to me about your children, after what you did to my child. I want my daughter," Mia shouted. "Where is she?"

Elias laughed. "I have always admired your spunk, Mia Verde Sandoval."

Mia started at a run toward the closed bedroom door which opened abruptly.

"She's here with me," Susan said, stepping over the threshold, holding Gracie's hand.

Mia screamed and ran to Gracie, snatching her from Susan's grasp and sweeping her into a smothering embrace. "Oh, Gracie, my sweet Gracie." Mia cried so hard the tears spilled over onto Gracie's cheeks as Mia planted kiss after kiss on her baby's face.

Gracie looked bewildered, but not physically injured. She wrapped her small arms around her mother and smiled. Dallas's heart tore a bit to see that innocent smile.

"Mommy, you're squishing me," she said. Juno poked a friendly nose at Gracie's leg. "Hiya, Juno."

Mia looked her over. "Are you hurt? Did he hurt you in any way?"

She shook her head. "No, but I want to go home. I don't like it here."

Dallas heaved a sigh. Gracie was safe and his spirit spiraled at the joy of it, but he could not ignore the dread that rose in his stomach as the cost of his error came to light. Somewhere inside, Dallas had known the truth about Susan. Why had he not thought it out before? "You rendezvoused with the doctor when you gave Antonia the slip by pretending to look for a room, I take it."

She nodded. "Easy."

"And you and Dr. Elias killed your husband together, didn't you?"

"That's so heartwarming, like something you'd see on the big screen." Susan was smiling, watching Mia and Gracie as if she was an adoring aunt, not a murderer. "Yes, we plotted to kill Asa together and afterward, I made the biggest mistake of my life. I bolted."

"Leaving me holding the bag," Elias snapped.

"I was young, and I didn't know what I wanted. I apologized for that, Thomas, over and over," Susan said. "I panicked. But I never stopped loving you, not for one moment in all those years."

So it was some twisted form of love that brought her back to Spanish Canyon. The loathing in the doctor's eyes revealed it was purely one-sided. Whatever fondness Dr. Elias had felt for Susan once upon a time, had evaporated when she collected the insurance money and ran.

Elias's nostrils flared. "You should have stopped loving me. You should have gone on and lived your own life and left me to mine. That's what I told you when you came back but you would not listen."

"I couldn't do that. Our love is too deep." A strange guttural noise came from her throat. "Only I came back to find you had married someone else." Her eyes went hard and flat.

"Catherine is a good woman."

"She's a snoop. If she hadn't taken the photo out of Cora's file, things would have been much simpler." Susan considered a moment. "Well, we're all entitled to a mistake now and then."

Elias groaned. "If you'd stayed away, everyone would be better off. You got Cora's suspicions up and filled her head with stories that police were corrupt until she decided to confide in these two."

"And Peter?" Dallas asked. He darted a glance around the dismal room, trying to figure out how to keep Gracie and Mia out of the line of fire. "Did he get scared and threaten to tell?"

"He wouldn't have," Elias said, white-knuckling the gun. "Peter would not have said anything no matter how much these two pried, but you arranged for him to die anyway, didn't you?"

Susan gave him a wide smile, sidling around and putting her hand on his cheek. He flinched away. "It was prudent. When Dallas and Mia are gone, we'll have a clean slate. Peter might have decided to spill the beans someday. That's why we arranged this little kidnapping, remember? To clean up the loose ends, as they say in the TV shows." She laughed.

Dallas bit back a groan. She was the one who had, no doubt, alerted Elias when they'd retrieved the picture from Finnigan's, and who'd called the trailer park to arrange the kidnapping. There had certainly been plenty of time for her to do so while Dallas and Mia dealt with the mudslide.

Water crested the threshold, sending the first gush over the floor. Dallas looked for something he could use as a weapon. He saw nothing within easy reach.

"Floodwater's rising," Elias said. The waves quenched the flames in the fireplace with an angry hiss. "Reservoir's full, and it's dumping into the lake."

Susan's eyes were dreamy, her face soft. "We can go anywhere in the world, Thomas. I've still got plenty of money and we can live the life we were meant to. Finally, after all these years. That's what you want, too, isn't it?"

"Too late to ask me what I want." Elias pointed to a narrow ladder in the corner. "Get up in the attic, Mia. Gracie and your hoodlum friend, too."

"You can't," Mia started.

"The guy with the gun makes the rules," Dr. Elias said, "so that means I can. You get up in that attic and take your chances with the floodwaters, or I can shoot you."

It would not be much of a chance, Dallas knew. Locked in the attic, they would drown. No question about it. Antonia would tell the police what she knew, but by then Elias would be gone. "You're a doctor," Dallas said, edging closer and stepping in front of Mia.

"You took an oath to save lives. Didn't that mean anything to you?"

A flicker of emotion rippled across his face. "I was a good doctor. I helped a lot of people, and they loved me in this town. I just made a mistake a long time ago."

Susan stepped back, frowning. "Our love wasn't a mistake."

He ignored her. He gestured with the gun for Mia and Gracie to start up the ladder. The water was now at shin level and climbing fast. Mia took Gracie's hand, fear strong in her eyes as she helped her little girl. "It's okay, honey. I'm right behind you."

"I'm sorry, Mia," Dr. Elias said.

She turned. "But you're going to murder us anyway?" Mia's chin jutted, her voice low so Gracie would not hear.

"As I said, I'm sorry. I really mean that."

Mia gave the doctor her back and continued up to the attic. Dallas figured he had one chance to turn the tide in their favor, but he had to make sure Mia and Gracie were far enough away.

"Up, Juno," he commanded.

Juno scrambled up the ladder with the ease born of hours of training in every possible situation from planes to boats to escalators. The dog sensed no danger, only another adventure awaiting him.

He heard Gracie giggle from up in the attic. "Good job, Juno."

The tear in his heart widened. They could not die. He could not let them drown.

"Now you," Dr. Elias said, swiveling the gun not to Dallas, but to Susan.

Her mouth fell open. "What? What are you saying?"

"I'm saying," Elias said, fury kindling on his face, "that you ruined me, my career, my marriage, everything. Getting involved with you was the worst day in my life and having you show up in Spanish Canyon was the second. You're going to die along with them, Susan. You should have died a long time ago."

Horror dawned in her expression, creeping up to overtake the love that had been there a moment before. "How can you say this to me? You are the only man I've ever loved. I killed Peter Finnigan and got these people here so we could have a future."

"I never even told Peter you were in on Asa's murder. He didn't even know we hatched that little plot together. He did not have to die."

"Well, he's dead, and that can't be changed," she said. "We have to think about the future."

"We have no future. Can't you understand that?" he said, voice like the last peal of a funeral bell. "You will climb the ladder and die with the rest of them."

The color disappeared from her face. "But I love you. We have a whole life ahead of us."

"I had a future and I threw it away for money and because I thought I cared about you. After I killed your husband, you ran. And you know what? I deserved that because it showed me I never really loved you at all."

"That's not true," she protested. "You did. You did love me."

"You were a means to an end, Susan, a shortcut I never should have taken. That's all." The words dropped like bullets.

With a cry, Susan took out a knife, the one she had stolen from Dallas's kitchen, and sprang at Dr. Elias. He deflected her, dealing a blow to the side of her head that made her cry out and fall backward, grabbing the rocking chair for support.

Dallas used the moment of distraction to launch himself at Dr. Elias.

He threw a fist, aiming for the doctor's face, but an incoming gush of water knocked him off target. His punch connected with Elias's temple, but not hard enough to do the job. Elias fired. Dallas felt a sharp trail of fire shoot through his body as he splashed backward into the water.

NINETEEN

The shot exploded through the cabin, and Mia felt as if the bullet bisected her own body. Instinctively, she shoved Gracie farther into the attic, the floor of which had been covered with plywood to provide a surface for storage.

"Dallas," she screamed, grabbing at the barking Juno to prevent him from going back down the ladder. He whined and looked from her toward his fallen master. She strained to see into the dim space. Had Dallas gone under? Had the bullet passed by him?

"He's not dead," Susan snapped. "You shot him through the shoulder. Terrible aim."

Mia's breath squeezed out in panicked bursts. He was not dead. Dallas was still alive. Her thoughts focused on that one paramount fact.

"I'm a doctor, not a sniper. Help him up the ladder, Susan," Elias commanded.

"I won't."

Juno continued to bark.

"Shut that dog up," Elias shouted, "or I'll shoot him, too. I can't think with all that racket."

Mia stroked Juno's head. "It's okay, Juno," she whispered. "Quiet now."

"Don't cry, doggie," Gracie added, petting his trembling flanks with her tiny hands. The lamplight glinted off the gun as Dr. Elias pointed it at Susan.

"Yes, you will get him up that ladder, because if you don't, I will kill you down here, and I don't think you want to be shot, do you?"

She didn't answer.

"Do you?" he demanded, louder. "You've never liked discomfort, Susan. Always enjoyed the nice things, the easy answers. I don't think a bullet hole would suit you."

Susan splashed over to Dallas and took his arm. His groan of pain shot through Mia.

"Gently," she could not stop herself from saying.

"This is crazy," Elias said with a strangled cry. "The whole thing is insane. How did it come to this?"

"You can stop it," Mia called. "You are an excellent doctor and you've helped lots of people. Catherine said you are a good father, too."

"She said that?" His tone grew soft. "Then I didn't totally destroy everything."

Mia felt a spark of hope. "No, you haven't. You could let us go. Then you would be able to see your children, maybe. Still be a father to them."

He paused. "Thank you, Mia, for saying that, but it will be better for them if I disappear. I'm not going to withstand jail. I don't have that kind of strength. I wish things could have been different. I sincerely do."

"But…" She realized he was no longer listening. He moved aside, water splashing nearly to his waist as Susan staggered with Dallas to the ladder and they crowded up together. Mia reached out and eased Dallas as best she could into the attic space where he knelt, one hand on the wood for support, the other clutching his shoulder. Juno licked Dallas and turned in happy circles.

Mia immediately ripped off the bottom hem of her T-shirt and wadded it up, pressing it to the profusely bleeding wound. "Dallas, I'm so sorry. I'm so, so sorry."

He looked up, gave her a tight, forced grin. "Not your fault. Is Gracie okay?"

"I'm okay," Gracie said. "Didja' get shot?" Her eyes were round as quarters in the darkening attic.

"Yeah. Forgot to duck," he said.

"Silly," she answered.

Susan stood at the attic access, staring down at Elias. "You won't get away from me," she hissed. "You will not go anywhere without me."

He laughed. "Watch me." Then he shut the trapdoor. The sound of scraping wood indicated he'd secured it from the outside.

Susan pounded on the hatch, screaming obscenities. "I knew you were a coward, Thomas. Deep down, I always knew it. That's why I went to Cora's house, to be sure you had the guts to follow through."

Mia drew Gracie away and left the woman to her rant. It was more important to figure out how they were going to escape. Dallas was considering the same thing, eyeing the nailed plywood floor.

He ran his hand over the seams. "Try to find a spot where the boards have warped or broken."

Though she didn't want to tear her attention away from Dallas, she did as he indicated.

Gracie crawled into the low spots near the walls.

Splinters drove into Mia's fingers, but she continued to search feverishly.

"I can hear the water," Gracie announced, her ear to a crack between two boards. Dallas and Mia hastened over. Gracie had found a place where one of the boards had splintered away, leaving an inch gap.

"Good work, Gracie." Dallas shoved his fingers into the gap and began pulling on the weakened board, the effort dappling his face with beads of sweat. When he'd lifted the board enough for her to get her hands in, Mia added her strength, yanking on the old wood until it gave way with a crack and a puff of dust.

"Okay," Dallas panted. "Now we can pull up the other boards."

Susan joined in and soon they had cleared enough boards away to create a small hole. Dallas lowered himself into the opening and kicked away the Sheetrock.

"There's the water," Gracie said. "I see it."

The level was only a few feet below the attic floor. Mia shuddered.

Dallas sat at the edge, feet dangling into the opening. "I'm going to swim through the house and make sure there's an exit."

"Dallas…" But he was already done, dropping down into the water after sucking in a deep breath. Juno dove in with him.

Gracie peered into the water. "When's he gonna come back, Mommy?"

Mia wrapped an arm around her girl's shoulders, holding here there to feel the reassuring rise and fall of her breathing. "Soon."

The seconds ticked into minutes.

"Do you think he drowned?" Susan said.

Mia turned on her. "Don't say that. He's doing his

best to get us out of here in spite of all the damage you and Dr. Elias have done."

Susan broke into a smile. "You love him, don't you?"

Mia turned away from the crazy woman who had her own twisted version of love. Susan's infatuation had turned into an obsession, and Dr. Elias a possession that she had to acquire.

Love wasn't like that. It was an overwhelming desire to see the other person happy, healthy and thriving. She wanted that for Dallas with all the passion inside her. She wanted him to find a reason to put down roots and allow himself to have the family she knew he would treasure, with a woman who wasn't on the wrong side of the law, mother to a child of a drug lord. He deserved more than that.

Susan would never understand. Love wasn't holding on tightly. It was letting go, even when it hurt.

Dallas surfaced, sucking in a mighty breath of air. Juno popped up next to him.

"We have to get to the front door. I wedged it open. Can you do it?"

"Of course," she said, but his eyes were not on her. He was considering Gracie. He reached out a wet hand for hers, wincing only slightly, voice husky with pain.

"Hey, Goldfish girl."

Gracie giggled and took his hand. "You're wet."

"Yep. And it's time for you to get wet, too. I need you to take a big breath and hold it and we're gonna swim to the door down there. Okay?"

Gracie's mouth tightened. "I'm scared to do that."

"Juno will be there with you. You can hold on to his collar. How would that be?"

"Okay, I guess, but what if my breath won't hold in that long?"

Dallas riveted his eyes to hers. "God made you a strong lady, like your mama. You're gonna be okay and that's a promise. We'll get Goldfish after."

"The pizza-flavored kind?"

He laughed. "Any kind you want."

Gracie nodded. She sat on the edge of the plywood and stuck in her feet. "Cold, cold."

Juno paddled over and rested his paws on her lap, which set her to giggling. Dallas switched on a button that made a red light blink on Juno's collar. "Now you can see him. Ready?"

She nodded.

He turned to Mia and Susan. "Straight down and to the right. Give us a couple of minutes then follow."

He held up an open palm, and Mia grasped it, pulling strength and comfort from those long fingers. Then she helped Gracie over the edge, heart pulsing with fear as she watched the water close over her daughter's head.

I must be getting old. Dallas had been a tough guy, once. Recovered from stabbings, alcohol poisoning and even a snakebite, which had been worse than any of it, but now he felt weakened, the pain in his shoulder swelling with every arm stroke. Or maybe it was the added worry about escorting a tiny child through eight feet of water when her eyes were wide and terrified; panic beginning to set in on her face.

She clung to Juno's collar as he swam. They bobbed up, skimming the surface just under the ceiling. Gracie pressed her face so it was nearly touching the plaster, sucking in fearful breaths along with some water that set her to coughing. When they reached the far wall, he called over the surging water.

"We're going under now, Gracie. Only for a minute and then we'll be out the door.

"No, no," she said, choking on a mouthful of water. "I don't wanna."

Dallas was not confident that his calm reasoning skills were enough to counter Gracie's growing fears. What would Mia do? She hadn't yet caught up and there wasn't time. In a moment, the gap would be inundated and Gracie would be breathing in water instead of air. No time, Dallas. What are you going to do?

He flashed on how his mother had handled things when Dallas or his brother had come home bleeding or with some sort of contusion. Quick and efficient, before there was too much time for fear to bloom.

He took Gracie around the shoulders. "All right. Deep breath with me. Ready? Go!" Dallas heaved in a breath in exaggerated fashion and Gracie did the same. Then he pulled her underwater and dove for the door.

It was slow going with one good arm and Gracie wiggling in terror, pressing on his bullet wound. Juno managed the dive ahead of them, and Dallas followed in the dog's wake. He could make out nothing but the red blinking light on Juno's collar.

Gracie's movements became more frantic.

Don't breathe in, he wanted to say.

She grabbed at his neck, then started to push away.

Time was up. She would be sucking in water in a matter of seconds.

He tightened his hold on her and made for the door, kicking as hard as he dared.

They surged through and rocketed out the other

side. He propelled them both to the surface and nearly brained himself on the roof gutter which was inches from the crown of his head. He grabbed the edge with one hand and held Gracie's head above water with the other.

For the longest moment of his life, she didn't make a sound.

Terror balled in his stomach and shot through his nerves. "Gracie," he shouted, giving her a shake.

Her head came up and she started coughing, vomiting up mouthfuls of water in between anguished cries. It was the sweetest sound he'd ever heard.

"Good girl, Gracie. You did great. The scary stuff is over now."

She cried and clung to his neck. "I don't wanna do that again."

He laughed. "Me, neither. I'm going to put you up on the roof now and go get your mama."

She shook her head. "No, I don't want to."

"I heard you could climb up a tree." He gave her a sideways look. "But maybe I remembered that wrong."

"I can climb a tree," she insisted, indignation stiffening her chin.

"Let's see then. Pretend I'm a tree. Climb up on my shoulders and onto the roof."

She did, setting darts of agony zipping through his wound. She got up on the roof and crouched into a little ball. "It's scary up here. I don't want to stay."

"It will just be for a minute, and then your mommy will come."

Dallas removed the blinking collar light and wrangled Juno out of the water and onto the roof. The dog immediately sat down next to Gracie and licked her all over.

"Be right back." He sank back down in the water, hanging the red light to a nail that stuck out of the door-frame. He felt, rather than saw, the two women kicking their way down. He grabbed an arm, Susan's or Mia's he was not sure and dragged that person toward the door before he did the same for the other, orienting himself using the red light. For the second time he emerged, physically spent, just under the eaves of the submerged cabin. It was all he could do to catch his breath.

"Gracie," Mia cried, scanning frantically, as she broke the surface.

He pointed upward, still gasping.

Craning her neck, she must have caught sight of her daughter. Tears began to stream down her face and she closed the distance between them, and kissed all the pain from his body.

Mia was not sure how they would escape from the rooftop, but she simply could not bring her mind to fret about it much. Gracie was there, safe and sound, her skinny knees tucked under her as she threw pine nee-dles into the water below. Juno kept a watchful eye on her. Susan and Dallas scrambled to the peak of the roof.

"There he is," Susan said.

Mia blinked out of her euphoric trance. "Dr. Elias?"

"Out in the lake," Dallas grunted. "Must have had motor trouble because he's rowing."

"He never was much of a sailor," Susan said with disgust.

Dallas peered into the darkness. "After all this. Can't believe he got away."

Susan continued to watch Dr. Elias make his escape. "We could have been together forever."

Mia noted the revulsion that bubbled in Dallas's eyes. "The police will arrest him," he grumbled. "I'll get my phone."

Susan removed a plastic bag with a phone inside.

"No need," she said, voice soft, fingers pressing the buttons. "I knew he was angry with me so I planned ahead." She sighed. "Of course, I thought he would see reason. I thought I could convince him we were meant to be together."

Mia flashed back to Peter Finnigan. "What do you mean you planned ahead?"

Dallas must have come to the same conclusion because he and Mia both lunged for Susan at the same moment. Too late. With a moonlit smile on her dreamy face, she pressed the last button. There was a deafening blast from out on the lake, and Dr. Elias's boat exploded into a shower of golden sparks.

TWENTY

"What was that?" Gracie said, standing up so quickly she nearly toppled off the roof.

Mia closed her mouth, and Dallas was once again amazed at the strength of mothers to make every circumstance all right for their children. "It was a little explosion. It's not going to hurt us."

He could not comprehend Susan, the woman who had just blown up the man she purported to love, the man for whom she had committed multiple murders. Love and murder. How could they go together? There was not much time to mull it over as two Zodiac boats roared up to the flooded cabin.

Mia waved frantically, and he would have helped if his shoulder hadn't been useless. As it was, he struggled to keep upright against the dizziness.

In a moment, one boat had peeled off toward the burning wreckage. The other was captained by Detective Stiving, who grabbed Antonia's arm and forced her to sit.

"You're going to fall out," he snapped.

Antonia stood again anyway and screamed. "Mia, are you all right? Do you have Gracie?"

Mia was crying so hard she could not choke out a response.

"Yes," Dallas called down. "Mia and Gracie are fine. Susan is here, too. She just blew up Dr. Elias's boat."

Stiving held up a pair of handcuffs. "We're ready for her."

With an elaborate combination of coaxing and lifting, Gracie, Mia, Susan and Juno were loaded into the Zodiac. Stiving wasted no time cuffing Susan. Dallas contemplated his useless arm. "I'm gonna jump," he said. "Too hard to climb down."

Stiving shook his head. "You always were a nutcase."

With that endorsement ringing in his ears, Dallas plunged feet first into the frigid water. When he surfaced, Mia and Antonia dragged him into the boat where he collapsed.

Mia pulled a blanket around him.

He tried to protest. "You need it."

She ignored him and opened Stiving's first-aid kit. Antonia sat with Gracie held tight in her arms, crooning some soft endearments meant for the child's ears only.

Susan sat in silence, staring out toward the ruined boat.

Stiving flicked a glance at Dallas. "Took one in the shoulder, huh? Not so agile as you pretend to be."

"Apparently not." He bit back a groan as Mia pressed a cloth to his shoulder. "And you're not as thick-headed as you pretend to be, Stiving. Did Antonia finally convince you we were telling the truth?"

He grinned. "Nah. Actually I did some research, called some colleagues and interviewed Catherine Elias. I even discovered that Susan's poor, drowned husband was a demolitions expert and his wife worked for the company. Interesting, don't you think?"

"It explains her prowess in blowing people up."

"So you see, I really am a good cop after all."

"*Good* is a relative term."

Stiving laughed. "Just be quiet and we'll get you to a hospital, Black."

He did remain silent for a while, the pulsing of the engine shuddering through him. Mia adjusted the blanket, fiddled with the bandages, and mopped his face all the way back to the landing spot where Susan was transferred to Stiving's police car. Gracie, bundled to the ears, was loaded into another official vehicle driven by a volunteer who gave Juno a skeptical look.

"Do I have to take him, too? His paws are muddy."

Juno responded with a massive shake that sprayed the volunteer with water from head to boots.

Gracie laughed. "Come on, Juno. Get out of the cold, quick before you catch germans."

Juno leapt into the car and settled himself on the backseat as the dripping volunteer grumbled his way to the driver's door.

"There's a National Guard rescue crew coming, but they'll be another few minutes," Stiving said. "Most direct routes here are flooded." He raised an eyebrow. "You aren't going to bleed out or anything are you? That would create way too much paperwork for me."

"I'll try to spare you that."

Stiving nodded and went to speak to the captain of the other Zodiac, leaving Dallas propped on a plastic tarp, his back to a boulder, Mia kneeling next to him. She wasn't crying, but her brown eyes were bright, water droplets glittering in her curling strands of hair.

"I can't say the words," she said, taking his hands in hers. "How can I tell you how incredibly thankful I am?"

His heart lurched inside. She was so beautiful, bedraggled, exhausted, bruised and utterly, incomparably beautiful. "We did it together," he managed.

She shook her head. "I've been trying so hard to fashion some sort of life for myself and you know what? I figured out that I already have one."

He stroked the satin of her cheek.

He heard her choke back a sound, the sort of vulnerable tiny peep that a chick might make when confronted with the edge of the nest.

"My whole life," she continued, "is Gracie and…" She stopped, looked away.

Dallas, the man who had never been able to decipher the first thing about women, wondered. Could the tenderness he saw in her face match the love buried deep in his own heart that swelled and undulated like the flood? He took her hand and cleared his throat. Fish or cut bait. Take the chance, or let his heart fly away to Florida. "You and Gracie…" He sucked in a breath and started again. "I hoped that it might be you and Gracie and me."

She jerked, mouth open.

Had he blown it? Scared her right into flight? Misunderstood a woman as he had countless times before? *Do it. Say it,* something deep inside him urged. "Mia, I'm not traditional father material, and you are an amazing mother who doesn't need any help parenting, but all my life I've been waiting for a partner to put down roots with."

She blinked, staring at him.

"You want roots?"

He sighed. *If you're going to bury yourself, might as well go all the way.* "No. I want you. And Gracie. And the life I know we could have together."

Silence.

"I've done bad things, Mia, things I can't sponge away or keep hidden, not from you. You know the good and bad of me and if you feel at all like you could love me, I would like to build a life with you and Gracie." He said it louder than he'd meant to. "I love you."

She gripped his hands. "But I've been to jail."

"Me, too."

"My ex-husband was a drug dealer."

"I know."

"I have control issues and a stubborn daughter and I eat too many sweets and I have terrible handwriting."

"I love you."

Her expression remained frozen somewhere between amusement and something unidentifiable. Fear? Love?

"Dallas, I'm not sure what to say."

"Say we can build a family together as slowly as you need it to happen. I'm not good at following rules, I don't know how to make mac and cheese and I spend most of my time with a dog. But I'm patient. I've got that going for me."

She smiled, lighting a fire in his belly. "Say you love me, too," he choked out.

She leaned closed and stopped, her mouth a tantalizing half inch from his. "I love you, too, Dallas."

Then there was warmth where he was cold, relief for his pain, and the sun triumphing over the floodwaters of his soul as he gathered her close.

Over the crush of joy, he became aware of a high-pitched noise, the squeals and laughter of Antonia and Gracie as they watched the proceedings from the car window. Juno added a robust bark.

He smiled and kissed her again.

Mia turned her face to the sun, relishing the warmth that drove away the last remnants of the storm some two weeks after Gracie's rescue. Spanish Canyon and the entire county was an official disaster area according to the federal government. Efforts were underway for a massive cleanup. Mia was ready to begin her own restoration project.

Dallas looped his good arm around her shoulders and planted a kiss on the top of her head as they stared at the burned wreckage of Cora's house. Gracie poked a stick into the various mudholes she was able to locate with Juno sniffing right along behind. "You sure you want to tackle this?" he said, gesturing to the ruined structure.

She snuggled into his side, careful not to put too much pressure on his shoulder. "I think Cora would have been pleased to see another house built here on the property she loved so much."

"And the matchmaker in her would have appreciated the fact that we're doing this together."

"For our future." Ours. The thought thrilled through her like the spring breeze. If all went well, the house would be built and the beautiful flower beds restored in time for their fall wedding. Closing her eyes, Mia could imagine the details. Gracie with her little basket of flowers, probably followed closely by a four-legged, hairy attendant. Antonia and Reuben would be there to add their heartfelt blessings along with Dallas's friends from the Search and Rescue school where he had signed on to work indefinitely.

"Still," Mia said, an ache in her throat. "I wish Cora was here to see it."

"She'll see it," Dallas said. "And she'll have the best view of all."

"Dallas," she said, turning to face him and marveling once again at the strength and gentleness she saw there. "This place was where I lost my dear friend. I thought I'd never come back."

"And?"

"And now it's the place where I am going to start my life over again. Pain and joy, all in one place."

"Blessings are like that, I think."

She kissed him, pressing him close, her future husband and irreplaceable blessing.

"Hiya," Gracie said, coming over with her muddy stick. "I'm hungry."

Mia laughed. "You're always hungry."

Dallas retrieved a package from the stash in his truck. He handed the pizza-flavored Goldfish crackers to Gracie. "Don't feed too many to Juno," he said, voice stern but eyes twinkling.

"Okay," Gracie agreed.

"And don't fill up before lunch," Dallas said, taking one more item from the truck. He shook the blue box. "We'll go back to the trailer you and your mom rented and I'm going to cook up some mac and cheese. This time, I'm following the directions."

"Hooray," Gracie squealed and Juno barked along with her. "But just in case, can Mommy help?"

Mia and Dallas laughed as Gracie raced off to chase a pair of butterflies.

"I dunno, Mr. Black," Mia teased. "Rebuilding a house is one thing, but tackling mac and cheese?"

"Don't worry," Dallas said, sliding his arms around her again. "Even an old dog can learn new tricks."

"That's what they say." She kissed him. "But I think I'll stick around to help."

His eyes reflected the light as the sun broke through the clouds. "I wouldn't have it any other way."

* * * * *

Margaret Daley, an award-winning author of ninety books (five million sold worldwide), has been married for over forty years and is a firm believer in romance and love. When she isn't traveling, she's writing love stories, often with a suspense thread, and corralling her three cats, who think they rule her household. To find out more about Margaret, visit her website at margaretdaley.com.

Books by Margaret Daley

Love Inspired Suspense

Lone Star Justice

Alaskan Search and Rescue

Visit the Author Profile page
at Harlequin.com for more titles.

TO SAVE HER CHILD

Margaret Daley

If God is for us, who can be against us?
—*Romans* 8:31

To all my readers—thank you for choosing my book

ONE

Ella Jackson looked longingly at the black leather couch against the far wall in her office. If only she could close her eyes for an hour—even half an hour— she would be ready to tackle the rest of the data entry for the upcoming Northern Frontier Search and Rescue training weekend.

She trudged to her desk, staring at the stack of papers she needed to work her way through before picking up her eight-year-old son from day camp, then heading home. She should have been finished by now, but in the middle of the night a search and rescue call had gone out for an elderly gentleman. She had manned the command center for his search, which had ended with the man being found, but her exhaustion from lack of sleep was finally catching up with her.

When she saw her son, Robbie, he would no doubt have a ton of questions about the emergency that had sent him to her neighbor's. This wasn't the first time she'd disturbed her son's sleep in the middle of the night because of a search and rescue, and Robbie was a trooper. Once he'd come with her to the command center when she couldn't find a babysitter. He'd begged to go with her ever since then, but it was impossible to watch over him and fulfill her duties. She'd promised him when he was older, he could.

The sight of the training folder on the desktop screen taunted her to get to work. David Stone, who ran the organization, would return soon and need the list, since the instructional exercises would take place in two days. So much to get done before Saturday. As she sat in her desk chair, she rubbed her blurry eyes, then clicked on the folder. The schedule and list popped up, the cursor blinking hypnotically. When her head started dropping forward, she jerked it up. Not even two pots of coffee were helping her to stay alert.

The door into the hangar opened, and her boss entered. He'd conducted the aerial search for Mr. Otterman, who had finally been found wandering in the middle of a shallow stream two miles from his nursing home.

Her gaze connected with David's. "Mr. Otterman checked out fine, according to your wife, and he's safely back at Aurora Nursing Home."

"Thankfully Josiah and Alex got to him before he made it to the river the stream fed into." He looked as tired as she felt. "Josiah is right behind me. Send him into my office when he comes in."

For a few seconds, Ella was sidetracked by the mention of Josiah. There was something about the man that intrigued her. His short black hair, the bluest eyes she'd ever seen and a slender, athletic build set her heart racing. Although he was handsome, she'd learned to be leery of men with those kinds of looks. No, it was his presence at a search and rescue that drew her to him. Commanding, captivating—and a loner. She knew one when she met one because she was much more comfortable alone, especially after her marriage to an abusive man. For a second, thoughts of her ex-husband threatened to take hold. She wouldn't go there. He'd done enough to her in the past. She wouldn't allow him—even in memories—into her present life.

"Ella, are you all right?"

David pulled her away from her thoughts. "I'm okay. Bree wanted me to tell you to go home and get some sleep since you never went to bed last night."

"My wife worries too much. Josiah and I need to work out some details about the training this weekend." David studied her. "But *you* should definitely go home. You were here before I was this morning."

"But these lists—"

The jarring ring of the phone cut off the rest of Ella's sentence. She snatched it up and said, "Northern Frontier Search and Rescue. How may I help you?"

"Mrs. Jackson?" a female voice asked.

It sounded like one of the counselors at the day camp Robbie went to during the summer. "Yes. Is this Stacy?"

"Yes. I'm so sorry to call you, but your son and two other boys are missing. We've looked everywhere around here and can't find them. We'll continue—"

"What happened?" Stunned, Ella gripped the phone tighter. Surely she'd misheard.

"We don't know. Robbie, Travis and Michael were playing together during free time between activities, but when the counselor rounded up everyone for the Alaskan bear presentation, they were gone."

"I'll be right there with some help to search for them." She didn't know how she managed to speak a coherent sentence, her mouth was as dry as the desert.

Phone still in her trembling hand, Ella rose, glancing around for her purse. Where did she put it?

"I'd hoped you would say that. It's not like them to run off."

"I'll be there as soon as possible." She nearly dropped the phone as she looked around trying to find her leather bag. Beads of perspiration broke out on her forehead. Usually it was on the floor under the desk near her feet.

Where is it? I need my keys. The camp wouldn't call me unless...

Her heartbeat raced. Tears pooled in her eyes. She put the phone in its cradle, and then rummaged through her desk drawers.

David clasped her arms and forced her to stop her search. "What's wrong?"

"It's Robbie. He's missing from Camp Yukon with two other boys."

David released his grasp and reached toward the filing cabinet. "Here's your purse." He put it in her hand.

She hugged her handbag against her chest, then started for the door.

"Wait, Ella. Let me make some calls. We'll get volunteers out to the campsite. Josiah is still out in the hangar with his dog, Buddy. Catch him before his sister leaves. She was heading out to her car when I came in. Have one of them drive you. You shouldn't go by yourself, and it might take me some time to get the search organized and notify the authorities in case the camp hasn't."

As though on autopilot, Ella changed directions and headed to the hangar, scanning the cavernous area for Josiah Witherspoon and his search and rescue German shepherd. They had just been successful in finding Mr. Otterman. But then she thought back to the ones they hadn't found in time. *Not my son. Please, God. Not my son.*

Ella spied Josiah coming into the open hangar from outside, Buddy, a black-and-brown German shepherd on a leash next to him. He walked toward her, his long strides quickly cutting the distance between them.

"What's wrong, Ella?" His tanned forehead scrunched and his dark blue eyes filled with concern. "Another job?"

Words stuck in her throat. She nodded, fighting the tears welling in her. "My son is missing," she finally squeaked out.

"Where? When?" he asked, suddenly all business.

"About an hour ago at Camp Yukon, which is held at Kincaid Park near the outdoor center. They did a preliminary search but couldn't find him or the two boys with him. David said—" She swallowed several times. "I hope you can help look for them."

Josiah was already retrieving his cell phone from his belt clip. "I'll let Alex know to go there. She just left with her dog, Sadie." He connected with his twin sister and gave her the information. "I'll be right behind you. I'm bringing Ella," he told her. Then he hung up.

"You don't have to. I can..." She gripped her purse's straps tighter, the leather digging into her palms. Robbie was all she had. *I can't lose him, Lord.* "Thanks. It's probably wiser if I don't drive."

"Let's go. My truck is outside." Josiah fell into step next to her.

Ella slid a glance toward him, and the sight of Josiah, a former US Marine, calmed her nerves. She knew how good he and his sister were with their dogs at finding people. Robbie would be all right. She had to believe that. The alternative was unthinkable. She shuddered.

On the passenger side he opened the back door for Buddy, then quickly moved to the front door for Ella. "I'll find Robbie. I promise."

The confidence in his voice further eased her anxiety and momentarily held the cold at bay. Ella climbed into the F-150 extended cab with Josiah's hand on her elbow, as if he was letting her know he would be here for her. She appreciated it, but at the moment she felt as though she was barely holding herself together. She couldn't fall apart because Robbie would need her when they found him. He was probably more frightened than she was. Once, when he was five, they had been separated in a department store, and when she'd found him a minute later, he had been sitting on the floor, crying.

As Josiah started the engine, Ella hugged her arms to her and ran her hands up and down them. But the chill had returned and burrowed its way into the marrow of her bones, even though the temperature was sixty-five degrees and the sun streamed through the truck's windshield, heating up the interior.

Josiah glanced at her. "David will get enough people to scour the whole park."

"But so many just came off working Mr. Otterman's disappearance."

"That won't stop us. There are three lost boys. Do you have anything with Robbie's scent on it?"

"I do. In my car."

He backed up to her ten-year-old black Jeep Wrangler. "Where?"

"Front seat. A jacket he didn't take with him to the babysitter last night." Ella grasped the handle. The weatherman had mentioned the temperatures overnight would dip down into the forties, and all Robbie was wearing was a thin shirt.

"I'll get it." Josiah jumped out of the truck before Ella had a chance to even open her door.

She watched him move to her car. She'd only known Josiah and his sister for six months, since they'd begun volunteering for Northern Frontier Search and Rescue, but they'd quickly become invaluable to the organization. Alex had lived here for years, whereas Josiah had only recently left the Marines. They were co-owners of Outdoor Alaska, a company that outfitted search and rescue teams and wilderness enthusiasts.

Although he was a large man, she'd seen Josiah move with an agility that surprised her. He returned with Robbie's brown jacket in his grasp.

He gave it to Ella. "This will help Buddy find your son."

The bright light of a few minutes ago began to fade. Ella leaned forward, staring out the windshield at the sky. Dark clouds drifted over the sun. "Looks like we'll have a storm late this afternoon."

When Josiah flowed into the traffic on Minnesota Drive, an expressway that bisected Anchorage, his strong jawline twitched. "We can still search in the rain, but let's hope we find them beforehand or that the weatherman is wrong."

Ella leaned her head against the headrest and closed her eyes. She had to remain calm and in control. That was one of the things she'd always been able to do in the middle of a search and rescue, but this time it was her son. Now she knew firsthand what the families of the missing people went through. The thundering beat of her heart clamored against her chest, and the rate of her breathing increased. Sweat beaded on her forehead, and she scrubbed her hand across her face.

"Ella, I won't leave the park until we find the boys."

"There are a lot of trees and animals in the park. What if he runs into a bear or even a moose? They could…" She refused to think of what could happen. *Remain calm.* But no matter how much she repeated that to herself, she couldn't.

"How old is your son?"

"Eight."

"Has he had any survival training in the outdoors?"

"A little. One of the reasons I signed him up for the day camp was to start some of that. We've made a few excursions but haven't camped overnight anywhere." Robbie was timid and afraid of everything. If she'd left her ex-husband sooner, her son might not be so scared of loud noises, or the dark. At least Robbie wasn't alone and it was still light outside.

"We'll be there soon."

In the distance Ella glimpsed Ted Stevens Anchorage International Airport, which was north of the park. Maybe the counselors had found Robbie by now. Then she realized that they would have called her if they had. She checked her cell phone to make sure the ringer's volume was up.

Josiah exited the highway, and at an intersection he slanted a look toward her that made Ella feel as though he were sending her some of his strength and calmness. "Thank you for bringing me."

"Remember how successful we were at locating Mr. Otterman? The park is big, but it is surrounded on two sides with water and one with the airport. The area is contained."

"But it's fourteen hundred acres. That's a huge area to cover."

"Can he swim?"

Ella swiped a few stray stands of her blond hair back from her face. "Yes, but why do you ask?"

"I'm just trying to get a sense of what Robbie knows how to do since the park has water and Cook Inlet butts up against it."

"He loves to fish, so I made sure he learned to swim at an early age."

"I love to fish. Nothing beats a fresh-caught salmon."

Ella rubbed her thumb into her palm over and over. "That's how the bears feel, too. What if he runs into one and forgets everything he's been taught?" Her heartbeat raced even more at the thought.

Josiah turned onto Raspberry Road. "If he doesn't run from one and makes noise as he walks, he should be okay. Neither one wants to be surprised. I'm sure the first day the counselors went over how to behave in the wilderness."

"Yes, but…"

Josiah slowed and threw her a look full of understanding. "You've dealt with family members when someone is lost, like Mr. Otterman's son and daughter-in-law earlier today. I've seen you. You always seem to be able to reassure them. Think about the words you tell them and repeat them to yourself."

"I pray with them. I tell them about the people who are looking for their loved one. How good they are at what they do."

"Exactly." Josiah tossed his head toward the backseat of the cab. "Buddy is good at locating people. I know how to track people through a forest. Tell you what—I'll start the prayer. You can add whatever you want."

As Josiah began his prayer for Robbie, something shifted inside Ella. The tight knot in her stomach began to unravel.

"Lord, I know Your power and love. Anything is possible through You. Please help Buddy and me find Robbie and the other two boys safe and unharmed." Josiah's truck entered the park, and he glanced at her.

"And please bless the ones searching for my son and his friends. Comfort the families and friends who are waiting. Amen," Ella finished, seeing Josiah in a new light today. They'd talked casually the past few months, but there was always a barrier there, a look of pain in his blue eyes. She knew that expression because she fought to keep hers hidden since she dealt with so many people who needed someone to listen to them when they were hurting. She could help them, but she wasn't sure anyone could help her.

In the woods, Josiah gave Buddy as much leash as possible and let him dictate where they went. Having insisted she couldn't stay at the command post, Ella trailed behind him as they searched farther away from the base at the day camp. His sister and her dog, Sadie, were following Travis's scent, while another search and rescue worker, Jesse Hunt, had the third boy's backpack, and his dog was tracking that child.

Josiah glanced over at Alex to his right and Jesse to his left, both within ten feet of him. Suddenly the dogs veered away from each other. Buddy went straight while the others made an almost ninety-degree turn.

"They separated?" Ella asked, coming up to his side.

"I believe so." Tearing his gaze away from her fearful eyes, Josiah examined the soft ground. "Someone else has been here recently." He pointed to the ground. "That's Robbie's shoe print and that's someone with a size twelve or thirteen boot."

"A man? Someone else searching for the kids?"

His gut clenched. "Maybe one of the counselors came this way." Or maybe it was someone else who had nothing to do with the day camp. He wouldn't voice that to Ella. She didn't need to worry any more than she already was.

Josiah continued following Buddy, scanning the ground for any signs that would help him find Robbie. He didn't know how Ella could deal with the people who waited to see if their family member or friend was found. While bringing her to Kincaid Park, he'd felt unsure of what to say to help her. He was used to being alone. He was better off working alone with Buddy. He'd learned that the hard way.

Buddy stopped at the base of a spruce tree, sniffing the trunk, then taking off to the left. Josiah inspected the lower branches and found a few of the smaller ones were broken off—recently.

"I believe he climbed this tree." Josiah pointed at the damaged limbs, then headed the direction Buddy went.

"If only he'd stayed here. It's been hours since he disappeared. It's starting to get colder, and he has no jacket on." Falling into step next to Josiah, Ella scanned the dense woods surrounding them.

The quaver in her voice penetrated the hard shell he'd placed his emotions in to put his life back together after being a prisoner of war in the Middle East. "He's walked and even run a long way from where he was last seen. He'll get tired and probably find a place to rest."

Ella's wide brown eyes were riveted to his. "What made them separate? I saw the lengthening of the spaces between the footprints. He was running then, wasn't he?"

Her gaze drew him in, so much pain reflected in it. He gritted his teeth, not wanting to answer her question, not wanting to add to her distress.

"You don't have to say anything. I can see it on your face. Something or someone scared him. The person whose boot prints we found with his. I saw them under the tree, too. He's being stalked." Ella came to stop.

"It could be someone searching for the kids. Don't jump to any conclusions. Speculation can drive you crazy."

"Just the facts, then. We're on point on this search. The rest are spread out and going much slower behind us." Her teeth dug into her lower lip.

Before he realized what he was doing, he touched her shoulder, feeling the tension beneath his fingers. "Let's go. We don't need to stand around speculating." He squeezed her gently before he turned toward Buddy, who was sniffing the ground five yards away.

His dog barked and charged forward, straining against the leash. Five minutes later, Buddy weaved through some trees, yelping several times. Josiah kept pace with his dog, his body screaming in protest at the long hours he'd been awake without much rest. His German shepherd circled a patch of ground.

Josiah came to a halt at the spot with Ella next to him. She stared at the ground, her face pale. Bear prints. Fresh ones.

"A bear is nearby, possibly after Robbie," Ella whispered in a squeaky voice, her eyes huge.

TWO

Ella sucked in a deep breath that she held until pain shot through her chest. Finally she exhaled, then managed to ask, "Is the bear following him?"

"No, but it looks as though Robbie stopped, turned around, then began running this way." Josiah pointed to the right. "The bear is going straight."

"Oh, good." Relief sagged her shoulders until she realized the bear might not be the only one.

After taking his dog off the leash, Josiah signaled to Buddy to continue tracking Robbie. As Josiah followed behind the German shepherd, he said over his shoulder, "I think Robbie is slowing down. His strides are closer together."

Her cell phone rang, and Ella quickly answered it. It was David. "Has anyone been found?"

"Yes, Travis."

Ella said a quick prayer of thanks.

David continued. "Alex located him not far from Little Campbell Lake. She's bringing him in."

"Did he tell Alex anything? What happened? Why did they part?"

"They thought if they split up, one of them could get help."

"How did they get lost?"

"They snuck away from Camp Yukon and were playing in the woods. All I know was a man spooked them."

A man? Were those boot prints they saw *that* man's? If so, the man had not only spooked them but followed them—followed Robbie. What if it was her ex-husband? Could Keith have found them? He'd never cared about his son, but he might kidnap him to get back at her. Her chest suddenly felt constricted. Each breath of air she inhaled burned her throat and lungs.

No. Keith couldn't have found them. *Please, God, it can't be him.* Memories inundated Ella as she fought for a decent breath.

"Ella?" David's concerned voice wrenched her back to the present. "Ella, are you all right?"

No. "We're following Robbie's tracks. We should find him soon." If she said it often enough, it might come true.

"I'll find out more when Travis gets here. I'll call you when I hear something else."

When Ella hung up, she realized she'd slowed her gait to a crawl as she'd talked with David. The space between her and Josiah had doubled. She hurried her pace to catch up with him.

"That was David. Your sister found Travis. That's encouraging." But Robbie and his friend Michael could still be in danger. And there was still a possibility that her ex, Keith, could be the man who had spooked the kids.

"Any info on what happened?" Josiah kept trailing Buddy.

"They were playing in the woods when a man scared them. That's all I know."

Josiah paused and twisted around, his tan face carved in a frown. "I don't see any evidence now that anyone is following Robbie."

"But what about the man? The boot prints we found? He could—"

Suddenly a series of barks echoed through the trees. "Come on. Buddy has something."

Ella ran beside Josiah, who slowed down to allow her to keep up. Buddy sat at the base of a tree, barking occasionally, looking up, then at them.

"Robbie's up in the tree," Josiah said, slightly ahead of her now.

She examined the green foliage and saw Robbie clinging to a branch. He was safe. *Thank You, Lord. Thank You.*

But what about the man? The threat was still out there. The threat that could be Keith.

As she neared, she noticed her son's wide brown eyes glued to Buddy. The fear on his face pierced through her. He might not recognize the German shepherd. "We're here, Robbie," she shouted. "Buddy is a search and rescue dog. He belongs to Josiah Witherspoon. You remember Mr. Witherspoon?"

Robbie barely moved his head in a nod, but he did look toward her. "Mom, I'm stuck."

Standing under the cottonwood, Ella craned her neck and looked up at him. She wasn't even sure how he'd managed to climb so high. He must be thirty feet off the ground. "Don't do anything yet. You'll be all right. Josiah and I will talk about the best way to get you down safely. Okay?" Her heart clenched at the sight of tears in her son's eyes. His grip around the branch seemed to tighten. He was so scared. All she wanted to do was hold her child and tell him she wouldn't let anything hurt him.

Josiah moved closer. "I can get him down. I have a longer reach than you."

"You don't think he can back down, keeping his arms around the limb?"

"Sometimes people freeze once they get into a tree and see how high they are. I have a feeling he was scared when he climbed up, then realized where he was. I did that once when I was a boy, not much younger than Robbie."

"But should I—"

"You should be a mom and keep him calm."

She nodded, relieved Josiah was here because she was afraid of heights. She would have climbed the tree if she had to, but then there might have been two people stuck up there. "Thanks."

Josiah hoisted himself up onto the lowest branch that would hold his weight, then smiled at her. "I once had a tree where I loved to hide from the world, or rather, Alex when she bugged me. She never knew where I went. I used to watch her try to find me from my perch at the top."

For the first time in hours, Ella chuckled. "I won't tell her, in case you ever want to hide from her again."

He began scaling the branches. "Much appreciated."

"I won't, either," Robbie said in a squeaky voice.

"Thanks, partner," Josiah said to her son, halfway up the main trunk of the cottonwood. "Ella, call David and tell him we found Robbie."

Robbie stared down at the German shepherd. "What's his name?"

While her son talked with Josiah about his dog, Ella gave David a call. "He's in a tree, but Josiah is helping him down. We'll return to base soon." She lowered her voice while she continued. "Has Michael been found yet?"

"No, but I'll pull everyone off the other areas to concentrate on the trail Jesse is following."

"Are the police there?"

"Yes, Thomas Caldwell is here. He's talking with Travis and getting a description of the man."

Thomas was a friend of David's and Josiah's as well as a detective on the Anchorage police force. "Good. We'll be there soon."

When Ella disconnected the call, she watched Josiah shimmy toward Robbie as far as it was safe for him to go on the branch. He was probably one hundred and eighty pounds while her son was forty. Josiah paused about seven feet from Robbie.

"I can't come out any farther, Robbie, but I'm here to grab you as you slide backward toward me. Hug the limb and use one hand to move back to me." Josiah's voice was even and calm, as though they were discussing the weather.

"I can't. I'm… I'm scared. What if I fall?" Robbie peered at the ground and shook his head.

"Don't look down. Do you see that squirrel on the branch near you? He's watching you. Keep an eye on him."

"He's probably wondering what we're doing up here." Robbie stared at the animal, its tail twitching back and forth.

Her son scooted a few inches down the limb, which was at a slight incline from the trunk. When the squirrel scurried away, Robbie squeezed his eyes shut and continued to move at a snail's pace. Finally, when he was within a foot of Josiah, her son raised his head and glanced back at Josiah. His gaze drifted downward, and he wobbled on the branch, sliding to the side.

Ella gasped.

Josiah moved fast, latching on to Robbie's ankle. "I've got you. You're okay."

But her son flailed again. "I'm gonna…"

He fell off the limb, screaming. Then suddenly he was hanging upside down, dangling from the end of Josiah's grip. Robbie's fingertips grazed a smaller branch under him, but it wouldn't hold his weight. Ella's legs went weak, but she remained upright.

"Okay, Robbie?" Josiah adjusted his weight to keep balanced.

"Yes," her son barely said.

"You're safe. Nothing is going to happen to you. Hold still. Can you do that?"

"Yes," Robbie said in a little stronger voice.

"I'm lifting you up to me, then we'll climb down together."

Josiah's gaze connected to Ella's, and she had no doubt her son would be safely on the ground in a few minutes. She sank against the tree trunk, its rough bark scraping her arm. She hardly noticed it, though, as Josiah grabbed her son with both hands and brought Robbie to him, the muscles in his arms bunching with the strain.

When Robbie was in the crook of the tree between the trunk and limb, he hugged Josiah. Surprise flitted across the man's face.

He patted her son on the back several times. "Let's get down from here. I don't know about you, but I'm starving for a hamburger and fries."

"Yeah!" Robbie's face brightened with a big grin.

With Josiah's help, her son finally made it to the ground. Robbie threw his arms around Ella, who never wanted to let him go. She kissed the top of his head as he finally wiggled free.

"Can we go eat a burger with Mr. Witherspoon? Can we?"

The eagerness in his voice made it hard to say no, but it wasn't fair to keep Josiah any longer than necessary. "I'm sure he's—"

"I think that's a great idea, Robbie. There's a place not too far from here that's a favorite of mine. After we eat, then I can take you two to the hangar so your mom can pick up her car."

Robbie looked at Buddy. "What about him?"

"He'll be fine while we're inside. I imagine he's pretty tired. He's been working a lot today."

So have you, Ella thought, glimpsing in Josiah the same weariness she felt, but he must have sensed how important doing something normal and nonthreatening was for her son. Usually when Josiah came to a SAR operation, he did his job and went home. He was all business. But not now. The smile he sent her son made her want to join in.

"Can I pet Buddy?" her son asked.

"Sure. He loves the attention." Josiah squatted next to Robbie after he moved to the German shepherd.

"I wish I had a dog like this. No one would bother me."

Josiah peered up at Ella. "You don't need to worry about that man now."

"You know about the man?" Robbie's forehead scrunched.

"Yes." Ella clasped Robbie's shoulder. "Honey, when we get back to camp, you can tell the police what the man looked like. They'll find him."

Robbie ran his hand down Buddy's back, stroking the dog over and over while Josiah stood next to her son. "How's Travis and Michael?"

"Travis is at the command center. They're still looking for Michael. He may even be with Travis by the time we arrive at camp." At least she hoped that was the case. The idea that Michael might still be lost while the man hadn't been found gave her shivers. She rubbed her hands up and down her arms.

The realization it could still be her ex-husband mocked her. Until she found out for certain, she needed to start making plans to leave Anchorage. She'd disappeared once before. She could again. But the thought of leaving the life she had carved out for her and her son in Alaska swelled her throat with emotions she tried not to feel. She loved Anchorage and the people she'd become friends with. She didn't want to leave.

"Let's go. I imagine you've got a camp full of people anxiously waiting to see you." Josiah rose and said to Robbie, "You want to hold Buddy's leash and lead the way?"

Her son's smile grew even more. "Yeah."

Ella fell into step with Josiah while her son took off with Buddy. "Maybe I should think about getting a pet for Robbie."

"I can help you with that. Buddy became a daddy eight weeks ago. My friend will be selling most of the puppies soon, but I can have the pick of the litter free.

I hadn't intended to get another dog, so if Robbie wants one, he can have my free one."

"A mix breed or a German shepherd?"

"A purebred German shepherd. This guy trains dogs for search and rescue. He'll keep two pups to train, then sell them later."

Her pride nudged forward. Ever since escaping her abusive marriage in Georgia and relocating to Anchorage, she hadn't depended on others to help her. It had taken all her courage to seek aid through the New Life Organization and break free of Keith. She was thankful to the Lord that she and Robbie had been able to make it on their own without constantly glancing over their shoulders, looking for Keith, who should have been in prison for years. For four years, she'd been able to live without being scared for her life and now… "I can't accept one. You should take the puppy and sell it."

"I don't need the money. Outdoor Alaska is a successful business. I'd much rather see a child happy with a new pet. I always had one while growing up, and they were important to me."

What if it really was Keith in the woods? A dog would only complicate their lives if they had to move. "I appreciate the offer."

He tilted his head, his gaze slanting down at her. "But?"

Her gaze drifted to Robbie with Buddy. "A German shepherd is a big dog. He'll need to be trained. Any suggestions?"

"I can help when the puppy's old enough."

Again the words *I can't accept* perched on the tip of her tongue, but one look at her son petting Buddy shut that impulse down. Her son was frightened more than most children because of the memories of his abusive father and his temper, all directed at her. Although he'd only been four when she'd finally successfully escaped Keith, a raised voice still shook Robbie, and any man with curly blond hair like his father's scared him to the point that he tried to hide if he could.

She didn't realize she'd stopped walking until Josiah's worried voice said, "Are you all right?"

She blinked, noting her son had paused by a big tree and waited for them to catch up. "Thanks for the offer to help train the dog when we get it." She hoped by the time the puppy was old enough to be separated from its mother, she'd know for sure who the man in the woods was.

The corners of his eyes crinkled as he grinned. "Good. My sister has been teasing me lately. Accusing me of being a hermit when I'm not working."

"When did you leave the Marines?"

"Eighteen months ago. Alex and I grew up in Anchorage. We both left, but she came back when our parents died in a small plane crash and took over the running of the family business, Outdoor Alaska."

"Your store has really grown since I first arrived."

"That's all my sister. She's driven."

"And you aren't?" She started walking again, the darkness of the woods throwing Josiah's face in shadows.

"*Driven?* I'm not sure I would use that word to describe me."

"What word *would* you use to describe yourself, then?"

"I'm just not as driven or singularly focused as I once

was. Except when searching for a lost person—when someone else's life is in the balance."

What was he not telling her? Studying his closed expression, she knew there was so much more he kept to himself—like she did. She couldn't share her past with anyone. That would put her and her son in danger. What happened today had ended well for Robbie, but if Keith ever found them, she knew it wouldn't. The thought sent a shudder down her spine.

When they arrived at the camp, Robbie saw Travis and ran toward him with Buddy trotting alongside.

Ella scanned the area and glimpsed Detective Thomas Caldwell talking with David. "I hope Michael was found," she said to Josiah.

"I'll get Robbie and Buddy and be right there," Josiah said, and then headed toward the two boys, who stood near a couple of camp counselors and Travis's parents.

Both Thomas and David were frowning. That didn't bode well for Michael. Ella's chest constricted at the thought of the boy still out there. Not far from David stood his wife with Michael's mother. Tears ran down the young woman's face while Bree consoled her.

When Ella joined David and Thomas, she asked in a low voice, "Has Michael been found yet?"

David's mouth lifted in a grin. "Yes, just two minutes ago. He hurt himself. Jesse thinks it's a sprained ankle. He's bringing him in."

"Thank God he's safe. Good thing Bree is here. She can check him on-site." Ella spied her son and Josiah making their way toward her.

David peered at his wife with love deep in his eyes.

David had been fortunate last winter to rescue Bree, a doctor who flew to remote villages, from a downed bush plane in the wilderness. That had been the beginning of a beautiful relationship, which had just culminated in their wedding on Valentine's Day. Sometimes Ella wished she had a special man in her life again, but her marriage to Keith had soured her on marriage. But David deserved some happiness.

How about you? a little voice in her head said.

She was happy. She had her son, friends, a good church and a fulfilling job. She didn't need a man to be happy. And yet, when she saw other married couples who obviously loved each other, a twinge stabbed her with the idea of what could have been if she hadn't married Keith.

"Travis's dad told me Michael has been found," Josiah said.

"Yeah, Mom. Can we wait until he arrives before going to dinner?"

Ella slid a look to Josiah, and he answered her son, "Yes, of course."

"Good. Travis is staying, too. I'm gonna sit with him until Michael shows up."

"Ella, I'd like to ask Robbie a few questions," Thomas said.

"Yes, of course."

Thomas smiled at her son. "It's nice to see you again. That picnic David threw on the Fourth of July was great. We'll need to work on him to have one for Labor Day, especially if his father is going to be the chef."

"Yeah. My favorite part was the fireworks." Still clutching Buddy's leash, Robbie stroked the German shepherd as he craned his neck to peer up at Thomas.

"Travis told me what happened, but I'd love to hear it from you, too."

The grin on her son's face vanished. "We were over there." Robbie gestured toward the line of trees near the camp base. "We heard an owl but couldn't see it so we thought we would try to find it." He swung his attention to Ella. "I know we shouldn't have gone away from the camp, but I love birds. I saw a bald eagle earlier today."

"We'll talk about that later. Right now, just tell the detective what you remember."

Pausing for a moment, Robbie tilted his head. "Mom, I think I need to learn how to track. That way I would have known how to get back to camp. We walked for a while, listening to the owl hoot." He closed his eyes for a few seconds, balling his hands. "When I saw a man with a mean face standing by a tree staring at us, I looked around. None of us could really tell which way we'd come from. We were talking and not paying attention. I was gonna inspect the ground for footprints, but the man started heading for us. We ran. Me and Michael followed Travis, thinking he must know the way. He didn't."

"I understand you all split up. Why?" Thomas asked.

"Because the man was still behind us. I've seen it on a TV show. People split up when they are being chased. That way one of us could run back and get help."

"What happened when you did that?" Thomas asked.

"At first, he went after me, but then suddenly he turned and started in the direction Michael went. I decided to climb a tree, but the first one wasn't good. The second one was better." He dropped his head. "Except I couldn't get down. Then Josiah saved me." Robbie's gaze fixed on Josiah.

"What did the man look like?" Thomas wrote on his pad.

"A grizzly bear."

"Robbie, no kidding around. This is serious," Ella scolded him.

"Mom, I know. He was *huge*—" Robbie's arms spread out to indicate not only tall but wide "—and had so much dark brown hair all over him. When I was running and looked back, that was what he reminded me of." Her son trembled. "I don't ever want to see him again. I promise, Mom, I won't ever go off like that."

Relieved that the description didn't fit her ex-husband at all, especially all that dark hair, she released a slow breath. "I'm glad you learned a good lesson." Ella patted his shoulder, realizing the fear Robbie had experienced would be more effective than if she grounded him for a week.

"Anything else about the man that might help me find him?" Thomas scribbled a few more notes on his pad.

Robbie stared at the ground, then slowly shook his head. "Nope. I was running most of the time. I didn't want him to catch me."

"Thanks, Robbie, for helping me. You can go sit with Travis if you want now." While her son handed Buddy's leash to Josiah then left, Thomas gave Ella his card. "Call me if he remembers anything else. I've got police combing the woods right now. Hopefully we'll find the man. We'll work on a composite sketch after I talk with Michael. I'd like to show the boys the picture our artist comes up with and see what they think. Okay?"

"Yes. I want him found. I don't like the idea someone is out there chasing children."

"Neither do I. My partner is checking the database

of criminals who target children in Anchorage to see if one matches the description."

The realization of how close Robbie had come to being taken by a stranger finally took hold of Ella. The campsite spun before her eyes while her legs gave way.

THREE

As Ella began to sink to the ground, Josiah grabbed her and held her up. "When was the last time you ate something?" He looked into her eyes, making sure she hadn't fainted.

"I don't remember," she answered with a shaky laugh. "I was so worried about Robbie, I wasn't thinking about eating."

"Let's go sit on the bench over there." Josiah's arm held her protectively against his side, and he moved toward the wooden seat off to the side.

"Thanks." Ella closed her eyes and breathed deeply.

When David approached, he said, "I'll get something to hold you over until you can eat a real meal." He left for a moment and was back with a granola bar and a bottle of water. "Sorry it's not more, but this should tide you over for the time being."

She took a bite of the granola bar and took a sip of water. "I started thinking about what could have happened if that man had caught Robbie or one of the other boys."

"But he didn't. Keep your focus on that. What-ifs don't matter." The feel of her close to him accelerated his heart rate as if he were running with Buddy. He gently eased her onto the wooden bench, then sat next to her, worried about her pale features.

She dropped her head, her chin nearly touching her chest. Her long blond hair fell forward, hiding her delicate features. What had drawn him to her from the beginning, when he'd met her months ago, were her large brown eyes. One look into them and he'd experienced a kinship with her, as if she'd gone through a nightmare that equaled his. He hoped he was wrong, because being a prisoner of war was intolerable, even for the strongest person.

"Robbie is all I have. I can't let anything happen to him. That man could have hurt him today." Ella finished the granola bar and gulped down some water.

"He could have, but he didn't. The boy is safe. The police will find the man who chased the kids. If he has any kind of record, it'll only be a matter of time before he's found and arrested."

She angled her head to look into his eyes. For a few seconds everything around him faded. His focus homed in on her face. When she smiled, her whole face lit up, and for a moment, he thought he was special to her. Why in the world would he think that? For the past eighteen months, he'd slowly been piecing his life back together, but at the moment he felt as if all he'd been able to do was patch over the wounds.

"Thanks, Josiah. You've gone above and beyond for me. Neither of us got much sleep last night because of Mr. Otterman's search, but I wasn't following a dog on a scent. You were. I hate to impose on you about dinner—"

He covered her hand with his. "I usually have dinner alone after a long day at Outdoor Alaska. Going out with you and your son will be a nice change of pace. Besides, Robbie is expecting me to go. I don't want to let him down. And you are *not* imposing on me."

For the past six months, since returning to Alaska, he'd gone through the same routine every day—wake up, grab breakfast on the run, work long hours at the store, then go home, eat dinner, play with Buddy and then go to bed. Not much else in between. The only time he deviated from the schedule was when he and Buddy helped in a search and rescue. His volunteering had been a lifesaver for him.

Dimples appeared on her cheeks. "All right, then. Dinner it is. And there's more to life than work, you know. I would have thought you would enjoy camping at this time of year."

For a second, all he could do was stare at her smile until he realized she was waiting for him to say something. "I used to camp a lot, but since I left the Marines, I haven't."

"Alaska is a great place to enjoy the outdoors, even in the winter. That's what I love about this state."

"I know what you mean." He wanted to steer the conversation away from him. He glimpsed fellow searcher Jesse coming out of the trees, carrying a boy. Jesse's dog trotted next to him. "There's Jesse and Michael." He pointed in their direction.

Before Ella could say anything, Robbie and Travis raced toward them. "Well, I guess I don't have to tell my son Michael is back."

"We'll give him a few minutes to talk with his friend, then leave. I've worked up quite an appetite."

"It's all that exercising you did today."

"You were right there by my side, looking for Robbie. You must be hungry, too." Josiah rose and offered his hand.

She took it and stood. "Thanks for all your help." When Michael was taken to the first-aid tent, Ella motioned to Robbie to join her.

Her son skidded to a stop. "Let's go. I could eat a bear." Suddenly he swung his head from side to side. "No one has seen a bear, have they?"

"No."

"Good. I really can't eat a bear, but I'm so hungry."

"Then let's go." Josiah indicated where his truck was parked. "Would you like to take Buddy, Robbie?"

"Sure!"

"I need to talk to the camp director first," Ella said, approaching the man.

Josiah watched Ella talk with the guy. From her body language, he could guess what she was saying to the director. It was clear she wasn't happy with what happened today, and Josiah couldn't blame her. She was more restrained than he would have been if Robbie were his son. At one time he'd envisioned having a family, but not after his fiancée, Lori's, betrayal. The thought of her had been what kept him going while he'd been a prisoner of war, but when he'd escaped his three-month captivity, she'd already moved on with her life with another man.

When Ella returned, her expression was blank except for a glint in her brown eyes. "Okay, I'm ready."

"I need to see Thomas for a second." He gave Ella his truck keys. "Go on. I'll be there shortly."

Josiah jogged toward the tent and waited in the entrance while Thomas finished interviewing Michael. He caught the detective's attention, and Thomas walked to him. "I know you're going to let Ella know your progress in finding the man who scared the boys, but I'd appreciate it if you'd call me first."

Thomas's eyebrows shot up. "I didn't realize you two were so close."

"We aren't. Not exactly. But she's a single mother. I don't want her to feel she's all alone in this."

"She isn't. David and Bree asked me to do the same thing." He tried to maintain a tough expression, but his mouth twisted in a slight smile.

Exasperated at Thomas, who he'd known since childhood, Josiah asked, "Does that mean you'll call me first?"

"Yes. Count this as me informing you before Ella. One of my officers at the station just called me. He found a match in the database from the description Travis and Robbie gave me, and I showed Michael the guy's photo. He positively ID'd the guy, so I sent some patrol cars to the last known address of Casey Foster to bring him in for questioning."

"It's probably too much to ask that he'll be home."

"Many criminals do dumb things and get caught." Thomas looked toward Josiah's truck. "I see Ella and Robbie waiting for you."

"Yeah, we're going to grab dinner." Josiah looked up at the clouds as drops of rain began to fall.

"Go on. I'll show Travis the guy's photo. I won't show Robbie until later. I know what a long day you and Ella had, with the earlier search for Mr. Otterman."

"See you later." Josiah turned to leave and nearly collided with his twin sister. They had similar coloring—black hair, blue eyes—but that was as close as they got to being alike. He and Alex were polar opposites in many respects. They were close, though. She was all the family he had left.

"Just got back from helping to search for Michael. I saw Ella and her son in your truck. Is Robbie okay?"

"Shook up but not hurt."

"Travis, too. But I understand Michael sprained his ankle."

"He hurt it while running, I hear."

"At least this one ended well. It's been a good day for us. Will you be home for dinner?"

Alex lived in their large family house with a house-keeper and caretaker while he stayed in a small cabin behind his childhood home. He would sometimes eat dinner with his sister and discuss business. The place was really too big even for the both of them, but they hadn't wanted to sell the house they'd grown up in after their parents died, which was one of the reasons he'd wanted to be involved in search and rescue. It had been the cold, not the plane crash, that had killed them before they could be found. "No, I'm taking Ella and Robbie for a hamburger at Stella's Café."

"I love Stella's. I'd join you, but I'm half-asleep right now."

"See you later, sis." His stomach rumbling, he quickened his pace.

The sight of Ella looking out his windshield—as if she belonged there—spurred his pulse rate. He'd avoided getting too close to others since he'd come home, except for a few he'd known all his life like Thomas, Jesse and his sister. But even with them, he couldn't reveal the horrors he'd endured. His body had healed, but his heart still felt ripped in two. He'd closed part of himself off in order to survive for those three months as a captive.

He climbed into his cab and twisted around to look at Robbie. "You okay back there with Buddy?"

The boy smiled from ear to ear. "Yup."

Josiah started his truck just as the forecasted rain finally started falling. Twenty minutes later, when he pulled into the parking lot of Stella's Café, the small storm was already clearing up. When he switched off his engine, he looked at Ella, her head leaning against the window, her eyes closed. Then he peered in the backseat. Robbie, curled against Buddy, slept, too. He hated to wake them up. But before he could do anything, his dog lifted his head and barked a couple of times.

Ella shot up straight in her seat while Robbie groaned, laid his hand on Buddy and petted him. The sight of both of them shifted something deep inside Josiah.

"That wasn't exactly how I planned to wake you up, but it was effective."

Ella laughed. "That it was."

Robbie stretched and pushed himself up to a sitting position, rubbing his eyes. "We're here?"

"Yes, but if you two want, I can get it to go."

Ella shook her head. "No, burgers are best eaten right away, especially the fries."

Within five minutes, Robbie sat across from Josiah while Ella was in the seat next to him.

Robbie glanced around, his eyes lighting up when he saw a couple of video games lining one wall. "Can I play?"

"Just until our food arrives." Ella dug into her purse and gave her son some quarters.

When he left, Josiah knew this might be the only time Robbie wasn't around to hear the news Thomas had told him about Casey Foster. Dread twisted his gut just thinking Foster had been in the park near the boys. "Thomas has a lead on a man he suspects scared the children."

She clasped her hands tightly together on the table. "Someone with a record?"

"Yes. His name is Casey Foster. The police have been sent to pick him up. Michael identified a photo Thomas showed him."

"Good. I don't want him frightening any other children at the camp."

"Speaking of the camp, how did it go with the director?" The second the question was out of his mouth, he wanted to snatch it back. He didn't usually pry into other people's lives, especially someone who was an acquaintance—well, a little more than an acquaintance, especially after today. Search and rescue operations tended to bring people closer. But when that happened, he felt too vulnerable and often needed to step away.

"I'm pulling Robbie out of the camp. It's no longer a safe environment. Mr. Waters assured me the counselor who failed to watch the boys would be fired, but I can't take that chance again. Of course, I'm going to have to find other arrangements for Robbie until school starts. I'll talk with David tomorrow. I might have to take a few days off while I look."

"That camp has a good reputation."

"I know. I wanted Robbie to learn about Alaska, some survival tips and how to take care of himself. It was a bonus that a couple of his friends were going to the camp, too. I'll call Michael's and Travis's parents to see what they're going to do. Child care is a big issue, especially when I don't have any family here."

"Where are you from?"

Ella averted her gaze for a few seconds before answering, "Back east."

A shutter fell over her expression, and her eyes darkened. He could tell when someone didn't want to continue a thread of conversation, and he was definitely getting vibes on that score. What was she hiding? The question aroused his curiosity, which wasn't a good thing. He needed to step away before she became more than a casual friend, someone he worked with from time to time.

Ella stood. "I see the waitress coming. I'm going to get Robbie."

The older lady placed their burgers and fries on the table as Robbie hurried back to his seat.

"This smells great." The young boy popped a fry into his mouth.

"Where's your mom?"

"She went to the restroom."

As though she needed to step back. *Interesting.* More and more Ella reminded him of himself. He knew why he was reluctant to become emotionally close to a person. What was her reason?

"How long have you had Buddy?" Robbie asked before taking a big bite of his burger.

"Eighteen months, since I left the Marines." Buddy had entered his life as a service dog because he'd been diagnosed with post-traumatic stress disorder. Out of the corner of his eye, Josiah caught sight of Ella returning to the table.

"How long has Buddy been a search and rescue dog?"

"I started training Buddy a year ago." Buddy had

helped him so much, Josiah wanted to help others with his German shepherd.

Ella slipped into her chair, her expression closed. "Is the burger good?" she asked her son.

"Great. Mr. Witherspoon did good choosing this place. We need to come back here."

"Call me Josiah. Mr. Witherspoon makes me sound old."

Finally she looked at him. Again he couldn't tell what she was thinking.

"Is that okay with you?" Josiah drenched his fries with ketchup.

She nodded, then began eating. If it hadn't been for Robbie, the tension at the table could have been cut with a hunting knife. More questions filled Josiah's mind. Did this have to do with the reason she was a single parent? A bad marriage? Did her husband die?

Stop! Don't go there.

"Who was the first person you rescued?" Robbie asked, pulling Josiah away from his thoughts about Ella.

"It was a couple who got lost in Denali National Park." Josiah went on to tell the boy about how Buddy had located them.

By the time the meal was over, Ella's stiff posture had finally relaxed. "I know David appreciates all the time you and your sister give to the organization."

"Alex and I have some freedom in our work because we own the business. We can often leave at a moment's notice. I know others like Jesse can't because he works as a K-9 officer for the Anchorage Police."

His plate empty, Robbie sat back, yawning.

Ella chuckled. "I think that's our cue to go home. It has been a *long* day."

Josiah laid money on the bill the waitress had left and

rose. "Let's go. I need to see if David is at the office. We still need to discuss Saturday's training."

"I forgot all about that." Ella made her way to the exit. "Robbie, I guess you'll be going to work with me tomorrow."

Robbie perked up. "I will? Neat."

"I think you'll find the everyday operations of the Northern Frontier Search and Rescue are boring," Ella said when they were back in the truck.

Robbie sat next to Buddy. The dog opened his eyes to note who was in the cab, then went back to sleep. "Buddy has the right idea." He yawned again.

Ella looked sideways at Josiah. "He'll probably fall asleep on the way home. I would, too, but since I'm driving, I can't."

"I can take you two home and even pick you up and take you to work tomorrow, if you'd like. I wouldn't want you to fall asleep at the wheel."

"No, I'm fine. I'm tired but not that sleepy."

At Northern Frontier's hangar, where the organization's office was located, Josiah parked next to Ella's Jeep at the side of the building. While she and Robbie climbed into her car, he headed into the open hangar since he saw David's SUV inside it.

David emerged from the office and halted when he spied Josiah. "Thanks for the help today."

"I'm glad both situations ended well. I just brought Ella back to pick up her car. She's taking Robbie home right now."

"After you all left the park, Thomas received a report that another boy went missing nearby in a residential area."

"Taken by this Casey Foster?" Anger festered in Josiah. What if he hadn't found Robbie?

"Don't know yet. Thomas promised to let me know. It may turn out to be nothing."

"Let's hope. When he calls, make sure he keeps me informed. Is there going to be a search?"

"Maybe. I won't know until Thomas assesses the situation. If there's reason to believe foul play, the police may use their K-9 unit and not need any extra help."

"I know it's hard to think about this on top of all that's happened, but what about the training on Saturday? That's why I came in here, to see when you and I can meet about it."

"I don't know how effective I would be right now. Let's meet tomorrow morning, say eleven?"

"Sounds good." Weariness finally began to set in as Josiah returned to his truck to drive home.

As he left the airport, his cell rang. When he realized it was Thomas, he pulled to the side of the road to take the call. "David told me there's another boy missing."

"No, he was found, but he ran from a man in a vehicle, who was trying to get him into it. The car had been reported stolen earlier—guess where from? An address a few houses down from where Casey Foster lives. I'm at Foster's house right now. He's not here. I have a BOLO out on him and the car. We'll stake this place out and see if he turns up."

"Have you called Ella yet?"

"No, but I feel like she needs to know Foster hasn't been found."

"I'll swing by her place and tell her. I'd hate for her to hear this over the phone."

"Are you sure? This has been an extralong day for you." There was a hint of curiosity in his friend's voice.

Josiah could imagine the grin on Thomas's face. He and Jesse were longtime friends who knew about his ex-fiancée. Thomas had even tried to fix him up on a date when he had returned to Anchorage. Josiah had declined the offer. "Yes. I want to make sure Robbie is okay."

"Sure. See you at Saturday's training."

If not before hung in the air for a few seconds before Josiah said goodbye and disconnected the call.

Fifteen minutes later he arrived at Ella's house and walked up to her porch with Buddy. If Robbie was still awake, he'd want to see his dog. Before he pushed the doorbell, he steeled himself. He hated telling Ella that the police hadn't found Foster yet, but she needed to know.

When she appeared at the front door, he smiled at the sight of her. She was a beautiful woman who cared about people. And he wanted to know who or what had put that sadness in her eyes.

"Josiah? What brings you by?"

"I heard from Thomas."

"Come in." After she closed the door, she swept her arm toward the living room. "I have a feeling I need to sit down to hear what you have to say."

What was he doing here? Why did he feel he needed to be the one to talk to her? Josiah cleared his throat and proceeded to impart the news concerning the attempt on another boy and the disappearance of Foster.

The color drained from Ella's face. "So he's out there looking for his next victim."

"Everyone is searching for him."

"Then I'll pray the police find him soon before another child is terrorized."

"Where's Robbie?" Josiah sat across from Ella with Buddy at his feet.

"He went right to bed. Fell asleep on the ride home from the airport."

"Good. He needs the rest."

Buddy rose and began growling. Josiah bolted to his feet at the same time Ella did.

She opened her mouth to say something, but a scream reverberated from the back of the house. "It's Robbie."

FOUR

Ella froze at the sound of her son's scream. Josiah and Buddy charged toward the living room doorway. Ella raced after them, overtaking them in the hallway.

"This way." Ella told them, hoping it was only a nightmare caused by today's events.

"Mom! Mom!" Robbie yelled, flying out of his bedroom at the end of the hall.

But the fright on his face belied that hope. He pointed a shaking hand toward his doorway, his eyes wide with fear. "He's…outside my…my window." Robbie swung his attention from her to Josiah then Buddy.

As Ella knelt in front of Robbie and clasped his arms, Josiah said, "I'll take a look outside."

"Use the back door in the kitchen." Ella kept her focus on her son while the sound of Josiah's footsteps faded. "Tell me what happened, honey."

"I woke up. Don't know why. When I sat up, I looked out the window." In the entrance to his bedroom, Robbie lifted his arm and pointed at the closed window at the end of his bed. "I saw…" Robbie began to tremble.

Ella hugged her son as though she could protect him from anything. She wished. "What did you see, honey?"

Robbie hiccupped, then said, "A man staring at me."

Chills flashed through Ella, her heartbeat thumping against her chest like a ticking bomb. "Did you know the man?"

"I don't know. Maybe the guy at the park. It all happened so fast. When I yelled, he ran away."

"Josiah and Buddy will check it out. I see them outside right now." She crossed to the window, watching while Buddy sniffed the ground before she closed the blinds. Her son liked to fall asleep in the summer with the blinds open since he was scared of the dark. From now on, he would have to be satisfied with a night-light. "No one can see you now. You're safe."

Standing in the entrance, Robbie clutched the door frame. "I don't feel safe."

"Tell you what. Why don't you camp out in the living room?"

"By myself?"

Ella pulled the navy blue comforter and pillow off his bed. "There's no way I'm gonna let you have all the fun. I'm camping out, too."

"Can we ask Josiah and Buddy to stay?"

Before today, the question would have been totally rejected. But after everything that had happened, the thought of being alone made her afraid.

Under Robbie's window, Buddy caught a scent and tugged on his leash. Josiah followed him around the side of Ella's house and across the front yard into the street. Buddy headed to the left along the curb past three of Ella's neighbors before his dog stopped and sniffed the road. Buddy stared at Josiah and barked.

He petted Buddy. "It looks like the person left in a car. At least we know he's gone."

He prayed that was the case, but as Josiah walked back to Ella's, his concern for her and Robbie grew. What if it was Foster, and he'd snatched the boy? After what happened earlier today, he would have thought the man would lose himself in the wilderness north of Anchorage rather than stick around and go after one of the kids he'd harassed in the park.

He retrieved his cell phone from his pocket and called Thomas. When his friend came on the line, Josiah said, "I came over to Ella's house to let her know about Foster, and while I was here, Robbie saw a man outside his bedroom window looking in. Buddy and I checked it out and Buddy trailed the scent down the street until it vanished between the third and fourth house to the left of Ella's."

"You think it was Foster and he drove away?"

"Maybe it was Foster. I can't be sure. But how would Foster know where Ella lived?"

"Wish I knew. It could have been someone else, but either way, a man was peeking into Robbie's bedroom. Not good." The controlled anger in Thomas's voice conveyed his concern about the situation. "I'll come out and take a look. Not sure there's much the police can do. I've got everyone out looking for Foster. If he's still in Anchorage, hopefully we'll find him soon. We're notifying the public to be on the lookout. Maybe a citizen will see him and report his location."

Josiah climbed the stairs to Ella's porch. "See you in a while." After disconnecting, he knocked on Ella's door.

When she let him in a minute later, her arms were

full of bedding. "We're camping out in the living room and making sure the blinds are pulled tight. I'm hoping it helps take his mind off the man peeking in the window." She lowered her voice and asked, "Did you find anything?"

He nodded. "I called Thomas. He's on the way."

Ella pressed her lips together, walked into the living room and set the covers on the floor. "I was hoping he was wrong."

"Where's Robbie?"

"The bathroom. He'll be here in a minute."

Josiah quickly told Ella what he and Buddy found, the whole time keeping an eye on the hallway. He didn't want to upset Robbie any more than he already was.

She sighed. "I know Thomas will want to talk to Robbie, but can you explain and show Thomas the window? I don't want Robbie traumatized any more than he already is. My son doesn't know who it was for sure. If he remembers something, I'll call Thomas."

"I'll take care of it. There might not be much he can do, but I wanted Thomas to know about it. When he comes, I'll talk with him out on the porch."

"I've decided it's time we get a dog. Is the offer still good for one of Buddy's puppies?"

"Yes, but it'll be a while before the puppy could be a watchdog."

Ella edged closer, glancing back at the hallway. "Just having a dog in the house would make my son feel safer." Her gaze locked with his. "Me, too."

"Then I'll talk to the breeder and see about arranging a time to see the puppies. Robbie can pick out one, and when the breeder thinks he's ready to come home with you, I can start working with you and Robbie. That is, if you want me to."

A smile spread across her face. "I was hoping you'd say that."

His pulse kicked up a notch. "I said I would, and when I make a promise, I keep it." Josiah caught sight of Robbie coming toward them and turned toward the boy. "I hear you and your mom are going to have a campout in the living room. You could even make a fire in the fireplace and roast marshmallows."

Robbie's eyes grew round. "Mom, can we?"

"Only if Josiah goes out and gets the firewood," she said with a chuckle.

"Will you? We could make s'mores. Isn't that right, Mom?"

"I think I have everything we need."

Josiah remembered having s'mores as a child. He once ate so many he got sick, but that didn't stop him from loving them. "Sounds good to me. Just point me in the right direction."

"On the right side of the house by the garage."

Seconds later the doorbell rang.

"Do you want me to get it?" Josiah watched Ella struggle to contain her concern. He tried to imagine what she was going through. To have a child threatened or hurt had to be a parent's worst nightmare.

"Yes. Robbie and I will be checking to make sure we have enough of everything for the s'mores."

"I'll leave Buddy with you two." Josiah passed the leash to the boy. "You're in charge of him."

"Sure thing. I'll take good care of him. I promise." Robbie petted the top of Buddy's head.

The chimes sounded again.

"I'd better get the door." Josiah walked toward the foyer.

"And we gotta get some wire coat hangers," Robbie said as he and Ella headed to the kitchen.

Josiah waited until they disappeared before he opened the front door. He walked out on the porch to talk with Thomas.

Thomas frowned. "I was beginning to wonder if something else had happened."

"Sorry about that. Ella didn't want Robbie to know you were here. She asked me to talk to you and show you where the guy was."

"But I need to talk with Robbie."

"Can you wait until tomorrow? The kid is pretty shook up, and she's trying to divert his attention from the day's incidents." Josiah descended the steps.

Still on the porch, Thomas nodded. "I understand. I'll take some pictures and check for latent prints on the windowsill. Did Robbie tell you anything about the man?"

"No, he didn't. He might remember something later." Josiah rounded the back of the house and stopped near Robbie's bedroom window. "This is one of those times when I'm glad it's light out till ten-thirty at night."

Thomas took photos of the boot prints in the dirt and then dusted for fingerprints on the ledge. "You didn't touch any of this?"

"No. I think the boot print looks similar in size to the one I followed earlier today in the woods."

Thomas turned toward Josiah. "Let's hope one of these prints on the sill is in the system."

"Will you let me know before you call Ella? If it's

Foster, that means the man discovered where Robbie lives and came after him."

Thomas's forehead wrinkled. "You think he targeted Robbie in the woods?"

"Not exactly, but maybe he's fixated on the boys. After all, they got away from him."

"I'll talk with the parents of the two other boys and alert them, especially if one of these prints ends up being Foster's."

Josiah started for the right side of the house. "Good. I'm going to stay the night. I'd never get any sleep if I left them unprotected."

Thomas grinned. "Does Ella know you're staying?"

Josiah shot him an exasperated look as he bent over and lifted several logs. "Not yet. If I have to, I'll guard them from outside."

"This is the first time I've seen you so invested in a search and rescue case."

"Ella is a friend, and she's alone with an eight-year-old. If you were me, you wouldn't walk away, either." Josiah started for the front of the house.

"No, I wouldn't. I'm glad to see your interest. Since you returned home, you haven't gotten involved in much other than work and volunteering for Northern Frontier. Jesse and I have to practically kidnap you to get you to do anything else."

"Most of my spare time has gone to training Buddy."

Thomas stopped at the bottom of the porch. "Your dog is trained better than most. I think you can relax and enjoy yourself from time to time."

Josiah glanced at his childhood friend. "Look who's talking. When was the last time *you* went out on a date?"

"Okay. I know work has demanded more of my time

lately, so maybe when things settle down you, Jess and I can go camping before winter sets in."

"Sounds good. See you." While Thomas headed for his car, Josiah scanned the neighborhood. Everything appeared peaceful, but as he knew firsthand, that could change in an instant.

He entered Ella's house with the logs, locked the front door and made his way to the fireplace. Robbie, Buddy and Ella came into the living room as he stacked the wood for a fire.

"Do you want me to start it now?" When Josiah peered over his shoulder at Ella, he caught her staring at Robbie kneeling next to Buddy and stroking him.

Her gaze shifted toward Josiah, and a blush tinted her cheeks. "I was telling Robbie in the kitchen about getting a puppy soon."

The boy grinned so big, a gap in his upper teeth showed a missing incisor. "Can we go get it tomorrow? I'm ready. See how good I am with Buddy?"

"I'll have to call the breeder and see what day works for him." Josiah finished setting the logs on the grate, started the fire and stood up.

"Robbie, I know you're excited, but I told you it might be a few days. Besides, I'll be tied up tomorrow at work, then Saturday I'll be working at the training session. All day."

"But, Mom, I *need* a dog."

"You don't need a dog. You want one. And I realize that." She faced Josiah. "So we'll be available anytime after Saturday."

"Okay. I'll let you know what I can arrange." The sight of Robbie's shoulder drooping prompted Josiah to add, "I'll be busy with the training session all day Saturday, too."

Robbie opened his mouth to say something, but Ella interrupted. "No arguing."

The boy pouted. "How did you know I was gonna do that?"

She smiled, her brown eyes sparkling. "Let's just say it's a mom thing."

"Did you have all the ingredients for the s'mores?" Josiah asked. "I can fix the hangers if you want."

"Good. I couldn't find my pliers." She gave him the two wire hangers she held. "We have more than enough supplies, except for hangers. It's getting late, Robbie, so I'll let you fix a couple of s'mores but that's all. We have to go to work early tomorrow."

"Can Buddy—" Robbie glanced at Josiah "—and you stay the night? We're camping out in here. It'll be fun." The boy grinned, but the corners of his mouth quivered as though he was forcing the smile. Trying to be brave.

Josiah could remember he'd done the same thing. Putting on a front for everyone around him when things were wrong. "It's your mother's call." He switched his focus to Ella, whose expression was unreadable.

"Robbie, I think we could use something to drink. Get the milk and three glasses, please."

The boy trudged toward the hallway, his shoulders slumped, his head down. At the doorway, he swiveled toward his mother. "Please, Mom. I know you can take care of me, but you're a girl."

Ella gave her son *the look*.

Robbie hurried away.

"What do you want me to do?" Josiah said when the boy disappeared.

"I…" Her chest rose and fell with a deep inhalation and exhalation.

He closed the space between them and almost clasped her upper arms, but stopped himself and left his hands at his sides. "I think I should stay. I'm not comfortable leaving you alone after what happened at the park and then here today. There's safety in numbers." One corner of his mouth tilted, hoping to coax her into a smile.

"Don't feel obligated to stay. I don't want to be…" She swallowed hard.

"What?" This time he did take one of her hands. "If you're going to say a burden, stop right there."

She grinned. "I was going to say a nuisance. Tonight was probably not connected to the park. I know the Millers down the street were robbed last month. Maybe it was someone casing my house."

"That's not a good thing, either. Let me put it this way. I wouldn't sleep at all if you and Robbie were here by yourselves after this scare." He didn't want to tell her he was pretty sure it was Foster outside Robbie's window. The boot print was too similar. "Do me a favor and let me stay. I need some sleep, especially after last night."

She sighed. "Okay."

"Yippee!" came from the direction of the kitchen.

Ella's cheeks flamed. "Quit eavesdropping, Robbie, and bring the drinks." Then to Josiah, she said, "Sorry about that."

She gently tugged her hand from his, and Josiah instantly missed the contact. He was thankful Robbie entered the living room when he did.

While Ella organized the s'mores production, Josiah

watched her work with Robbie. Ella was a wonderful mother. He and Alex had had good parents who expressed their love all the time. Their deaths had been hard on them, but he'd grown up thinking one day he would have his own family and be a dad like his. Now he didn't know if he could.

His captors hadn't taken just three months away from him, but much more. They'd left him with deep emotional scars he wasn't sure would ever totally heal. Since he'd come home, he'd had only one episode of anxiety when he'd heard a car backfire. Maybe he wasn't the best person to guard Ella and Robbie, but there wasn't anyone else right now.

Early the next morning while Robbie and Josiah slept in the living room, Ella sat at the kitchen table, sipping coffee. She'd opened the blackout blinds in the alcove and stared outside into the backyard, which afforded her a view of her neighbors' homes on each side and behind her. If she got a dog, she would need to fence off the area. Maybe she needed to reconsider. She didn't have a lot of money to spend on something like that.

And yet, having an animal in the house appealed to her. A dog like Buddy would make her feel safer—like an alarm system. After the first two years living here in Anchorage, she should have looked into getting a pet. Robbie had wanted one, but she'd still been worried Keith would find them somehow. And having a pet would make fleeing harder.

Yesterday for a short time, that fear had dominated her as she searched for Robbie. She'd actually been thankful it had been Casey Foster. That meant her ex-husband hadn't discovered their whereabouts.

Thank You, Lord. I don't know what I would have done if Keith had been the one in the woods. It was hard enough fleeing him the first time and giving up my friends and family. At least I have You and Robbie.

"You're an early riser," Josiah said from the doorway into the kitchen.

He'd finger combed his hair, and his clothes were rumpled from staying in the sleeping bag that he kept in the storage container in his truck. But the sight of him soothed any anxiety she felt thinking about her ex-husband.

"Want some coffee? I have a full pot." Ella started to rise.

Josiah waved her down. "I can get it. Do you want a refill?"

She looked at her near-empty mug and nodded. After Josiah poured coffee for them both, he returned the pot to the coffeemaker and settled in the chair across from her.

He peered out the window, his hands cradling his mug. "Five in the morning and it looks like eight or nine anywhere else. I'm still getting used to the long days."

"I thought you were from Alaska."

He took a sip of his coffee. "But I was away for years serving in the Marines and got used to more normal days and nights."

"This winter must have been difficult for you, then. I remember that was the harder adjustment for me than the long days."

"The dark doesn't bother me as much as it being light most of the time." Josiah stared at his coffee, and for a long moment silence descended between them.

His thoughtful look made her wonder if he was

thinking about something in his past. She'd known he'd served in the Marines in combat situations, but he'd never discussed that time in his life. Then again, she wasn't a close friend.

"I appreciate your staying over. I don't think Robbie would have gone to sleep if you hadn't been here. In fact, I'm not sure I would have, either. Then I'd probably be fired when David found me slumped over the computer keyboard at work later today sound asleep."

Josiah lifted his head, his gaze connecting with hers. "I don't think you have to worry. You've got David wrapped around your finger."

For a few seconds his eyes reflected sadness before he masked it. Again she felt a bond with Josiah, and she wasn't sure why. "I hope so. I'm bringing Robbie to work with me today." She drank several swallows of her coffee. "David is a great boss. He's part of the reason I love my job."

"How did you come to work for Northern Frontier?"

"I was working as a waitress at a café not far from the airport. The man who began and oversaw the search and rescue organization was a frequent customer. He'd come in sometimes, exhausted and frazzled. We started talking, and one thing lead to another. He decided he needed an office manager to run the day-to-day operations of Northern Frontier because of its continual growth."

"I understand David took over Northern Frontier not long before I started volunteering."

"Yes. I've been with the organization for over three years and it has grown in the number of searches we're involved in, as well as in reputation." She loved talking about her work because she felt she was assisting people who needed it.

"My sister had read about Northern Frontier, and when she decided to help, she gave me the idea to volunteer with Buddy, as well."

"Alex has been great to work with. She can rearrange her job to help whenever we need her. You, too."

Josiah grinned. "It helps that we own the business we both work for."

The warmth in his smile enveloped her like an embrace. "Robbie loves Outdoor Alaska. We went to the store right before camp started to get some items he needed. I had a tough time getting him to leave."

"It's more than a store. It's a destination if you're interested in the outdoors, hiking, camping or sports related to Alaska."

"Then what's that mini basketball court doing there?"

"Basketball is alive and well in Alaska. It's a sport that can be played indoors or outdoors. Also, the small court is a great place for kids to pass their time while parents are shopping."

"Who came up with the idea?"

"Me. I like basketball, and sometimes it's a great way to let off steam."

"Must be working. I've never seen you angry. Even in the middle of a crisis, you're calm." Contrary to her ex-husband, who flew off the handle at the slightest provocation, to the point she'd been afraid to say or do anything around him.

"Everyone has a breaking point."

Yes, she of all people knew that. Her limit had been when Keith pushed her down the stairs. Unfortunately, it had been a year after that before she and Robbie could escape him safely.

"Mom. Mom, where are you?" Robbie yelled from the living room.

"I'm in the kitchen." She rose and started for the hallway when her son and Buddy appeared at the other end. "I was about ready to fix us breakfast. Are you up for some blueberry pancakes?"

Robbie's furrowed forehead smoothed out. "Yes." He looked beyond Ella. "Can you and Buddy stay for breakfast? Mom makes the bestest pancakes in the whole state."

"How can I say no to that? I love pancakes and blueberries." Josiah moved closer to Ella. "Is that okay with you?"

She shivered from his nearness. "It's the least I can do after all you've done for me and Robbie."

"Yes!" Robbie pumped his fist in the air. He turned and headed toward the living room, saying, "That means you get to stay, Buddy."

"Can Robbie go with me to walk Buddy? It'll give me a chance to check out your neighborhood."

"Sure. That'll give me time to cook breakfast."

While her son and Josiah walked the German shepherd, Ella hurried to her bedroom and changed for work, then returned to start the pancakes. Twenty minutes later, the batter ready, more coffee perking and the orange juice prepared, she made her way toward the porch to see how much longer Robbie and Josiah were going to be. Halfway across the foyer the doorbell rang. Glancing at her watch, she saw it was seven in the morning.

A bit early for visitors, Ella thought as she cautiously peered out the peephole and heaved a sigh of relief. Detective Thomas Caldwell. Then she wondered why he was here so early.

When she swung the door open, she glanced around. "Did you see Josiah and Robbie with Buddy?"

"Yeah, they're heading back here. Josiah got a chance to show me where Buddy lost the scent of the intruder. I thought later I'd check with your neighbors to see if anyone saw a strange car parked there."

She glimpsed Josiah with Robbie and the German shepherd walking across the yard toward the house. "Come in. Would you like to join us for breakfast?"

"Sounds good, but before your son returns, I wanted to let you know about the fingerprints on Robbie's windowsill."

FIVE

Thomas looked over his shoulder at Robbie and Josiah coming up the steps. The detective quickly whispered, "One set of prints isn't in the system, but the other is Foster's."

"So he found out where Robbie lives." Ella clutched the door frame in the foyer.

Her stomach roiled at the confirmation Foster had been watching her son sleeping last night. A sudden thought blindsided her. She whirled around and raced toward her son's bedroom. She yanked the blackout blind up, then examined the window lock. She sagged against the ledge, gripping the sill as she tried to relax. She couldn't. It was locked. But what if it hadn't been?

The sound of footsteps behind her caused her to turn around. She hoped it wasn't Robbie. Josiah stopped a few feet behind her.

"Thomas told you about Foster being outside the window?"

She nodded and stared out the window at the spot where Foster had stood. "Why has this happened?" *On top of all that I've dealt with in the past, now Foster is after Robbie.*

"Thomas told me he'd do everything he could to find this man. Until then, I'd like you to come stay at my family's home."

She faced him again. "I can't—"

He touched his hand to her cheek, setting her heartbeat racing. "All I ask is that you think about it. I know Alex would love to have you. And Robbie will have two dogs to fall in love with. It would just be until Foster is caught."

Tears clogged her throat. She took in his kind expression, full of compassion. She couldn't remember anyone looking at her quite like that. She swallowed several times before saying, "I'll think about it. I still need to make arrangements for someone to care for Robbie while I work."

"Have you taken any vacation time lately?"

She shook her head.

"Then do. Spend time with Robbie at my family estate. When my sister and I are at work, both Sadie and Buddy stay there along with a couple that take care of the place. Harry is an ex-Marine, and his wife, who is the housekeeper, was a police officer."

"A Marine and a police officer? That's quite a combination. And they're caretakers now?"

"Yup. They've been working for my family for twenty-three years. Harry was my hero growing up. Still is. When he retired after twenty years in the US Marines, he married the love of his life, Linda, and they moved to Alaska. I learned so much of what I know about life and the wilderness from him. My parents were busy people, and Harry and Linda basically raised Alex and me."

"Now I understand why you became a Marine."

"He instilled in me a sense of duty to my country."

"How long did you serve?"

Josiah turned away from her and started for the hallway. "Ten years. You have a lot to do today. We better get moving."

What is he not telling me? She knew when someone was shutting down a conversation. She hated secrets. Keith had always kept a lot of them. She didn't want to go down that road with Josiah, also.

After dropping Ella, Robbie and Buddy off at the Northern Frontier hangar at the small airport, Josiah went to his cabin on the grounds of the estate, showered and changed, then headed for work.

"How's Ella doing after yesterday?" Alex asked Josiah when he entered her office at Outdoor Alaska, on the second floor of the main location.

"Foster came to her house and was peeping into Robbie's room last night. Buddy and I stayed the night with them."

"The police haven't found him yet?"

Josiah settled in the chair in front of his sister's large oak desk, which was neat and organized as usual. "No. Thomas came out to the house and looked around last night, then came back this morning. He showed Robbie some photos, and the kid picked Foster out of the lineup."

Alex scowled. "Eight-year-olds shouldn't have to be doing that."

"That's why I'm here. Ella hasn't said yes yet, but I've invited her and Robbie to stay at the estate. I thought they could stay in the main house with you. If not—"

She waved her hand. "Of course they can. It'll be nice to have a child around, and Sadie will love it."

"Yeah, Buddy has taken to Robbie. I'm going to let them have the pick of the litter."

"Where's Buddy now? Sadie missed her playmate last night."

"I left him with Robbie at the hangar. He promised to walk Buddy and play with him."

"But mostly you want Buddy protecting the boy?"

Josiah nodded. "It's hard for me to comprehend people going after children. I also saw that in the war zone. Too many kids being hurt or killed."

"I don't understand how such evil can exist in this world. Look what happened to you. You were tortured and held captive for months in the Middle East. How could God let that happen when you were saving a group of children from a burning building?"

His sister's faith had been shaky after their parents' deaths, but his captivity had caused her to question even more what the Lord's intentions were. He hated that, and nothing he said would change her mind. "At least the children were saved."

"And I'm glad for that, but you shouldn't have had to pay for it like you did." She pushed to her feet. "Let's just agree to disagree about God. He's constantly letting me down."

"But I'm alive and helping others with Buddy." He'd struggled while a prisoner, but his fiancée and his faith had pulled him through. It was hard enough losing Lori and rebuilding his life because of his capture. He was not going to turn away from the Lord, too.

"Will you still be able to go to the Fairbanks store

and meet with the employees and city officials about the expansion on Monday?"

"Yes."

"What about Robbie and Ella?"

"I might take them with me. A change of scenery could be good for both of them."

One of Alex's eyebrows rose. "First you loan Buddy to them, and now you're including them in your life. Is there more going on than simply protecting the child?"

He frowned. "If I'm protecting them, then I need them close by."

"You haven't been apart from Buddy since you got him."

"I don't need him like I did when I first came back to the States."

"But what if you have an anxiety attack or nightmares?"

"I haven't had one in months, and besides, I have other techniques to help me." Having PTSD after his release from captivity had nearly destroyed him until Buddy had come into his life and he'd gotten help for his panic and anxiety attacks.

"Still, it's good to see you forming friendships outside your small circle of close friends."

"Quit worrying about me, big sis."

"I'm only five minutes older than you, little brother," Alex said with a laugh.

The intercom buzzed, and Alex pressed it down. "Your ten o'clock appointment is here."

"I'm leaving." Josiah stood. "See you tonight."

"Let Linda and Harry know if Ella and Robbie come to the estate. You know how they are if they don't have any warning."

At the door, Josiah glanced back. "I'm surrounded by organizational freaks. As soon as I know, they'll be informed."

In the reception area, he passed a young gentleman dressed in a three-piece business suit that mocked Josiah's casual clothing of tan slacks and black polo shirt. Later he would load some equipment into his truck to use at tomorrow's training session, but for now he had reports to write on last month's sale numbers.

As he left his sister's office, he again wondered at the differences between Alex and him. She would fit right in with the man who had an appointment, whereas Josiah would be more comfortable in jeans and a T-shirt, but that would shock his sister. If Alex ever saw how messy he was at the cabin, she would be appalled. On second thought, she probably wouldn't be. They knew each other well—in fact, she was the only person who knew how much his captivity had changed him. He hadn't shared that with anyone but Alex and God, and even his sister didn't know all of it.

Ella finished a chart for the training session tomorrow and printed off the copies she would pass out to the participants. Robbie, Buddy and David were out in the hangar setting up some of the areas concerning search and rescue. She checked the wall clock and noted that it was three-thirty. She almost had everything ready to go, then she could go home, get some rest and—

The phone on her desk rang. She snatched up the receiver. "Northern Frontier Search and Rescue. How can I help you?"

A few seconds' silence, then deep breathing filled the earpiece.

She started to repeat herself when the caller hung up. Ella slowly replaced the phone in its cradle. The second call today. She looked at the caller ID and saw the number was blocked. Since the people who contacted her needed help finding someone, even when she was sure it was a prank call, she stayed on the line in case the person was in trouble.

Was that Foster? If so, why was he calling?

"Mom, what's wrong?" Robbie asked when he came into the office.

"Nothing. Counting down the time until Josiah picks us up."

David appeared in the doorway. "He should be here in an hour with the equipment he's loaning us."

Robbie held on to Buddy's leash. "It's time I take him for a walk. I can do it by myself. I'm only gonna be on the grass near the hangar."

Ella shoved back her chair. "No. I'll come with you. David, I finished the last chart. It's still in the printer. When I get back, I'll put the packets together, and then we should be all ready."

"Great. I want to call it an early evening. Let's pray there aren't any search and rescues tonight or tomorrow." David headed for his office.

"I hope there aren't any the whole weekend. I have some sleep to catch up on." *And how am I going to do that unless I accept Josiah's invitation to stay at his family estate?* He would expect an answer when he came to take her and Robbie home. For the past four years she'd depended only on herself to keep her and Robbie safe. She couldn't tell anyone about her ex-husband. The more people who knew her real past, the greater the risk. The New Life Organization had stressed that to her.

"Mom, Buddy is pacing around. He needs to go outside *bad*." Her son waited by the door that led to the airfield.

"Okay, I'm right behind you."

That was all Robbie needed. He shot out of the office and made a beeline for the patch of grass on the left. At a much more sedate rate Ella followed and gave her son freedom to move in a wide arc with Buddy while she lounged against the building, wondering if it was possible to fall asleep standing up.

Robbie let the dog off the leash to get some exercise. He threw a tennis ball across the grassy area at the side of the hangar to the other end. Buddy barked and raced after it.

Behind Robbie there was a road that was only a few yards from the main street. A black truck, going five or ten miles over the posted speed limit, headed out of the airport. Suddenly the driver swerved the pickup onto the grass, going straight for her son.

"Robbie!" Ella screamed, sprinting as fast as she could toward him. "Run."

Eyes big, Robbie pumped his short legs as fast as she'd ever seen him do. Buddy charged toward the truck, barking. Her son flew into her embrace while Buddy raced after the vehicle.

The driver swerved his pickup back toward the road, the rear tires spinning in the dirt and grass. Even when the black truck bounced onto the pavement, Buddy continued to chase it.

Robbie twisted to watch the German shepherd. "Mom, I can't lose him."

"Cover your ears." Then Ella blew an ear-piercing whistle. "Buddy. Come."

The dog slowed and looked back at her.

"Come!" She shouted the command she'd heard Josiah use with his dog.

Buddy trotted toward her and Robbie. When the animal reached them, her son knelt and buried his face in the black fur on the German shepherd's neck.

Robbie peered up at Ella, tears running down his face. The sight of them confirmed that she would be staying with Josiah and his sister. She needed all the help she could get to keep her son safe.

"Let's go inside."

Her son rose, swiping the back of his hand across his cheeks. "Was that the man from the woods?"

"I couldn't tell. The truck's windows were tinted too dark, and there was no license plate."

"Is...is—" he gulped "—it my—" his chest rose and fell rapidly "—my dad?" The color drained from her son's face, and he continued to breathe fast.

Halfway back to the hangar, Ella stopped and squatted in front of Robbie and clasped his arms. "No. The photo you and the other boys identified looks nothing like your father."

"I'm scared."

So am I. "I won't let anything happen to you. I promise. Josiah has asked us to stay with him and his sister at their house. You remember his twin, Alex. Her dog's name is Sadie. So you'll get to play with two dogs. That should be fun."

He nodded.

Ella fought to suppress her tears. If she broke down, it would upset Robbie. He hated seeing her cry. She'd done enough of that while living with her ex-husband. "I told David earlier that I was going to take at least a week off to spend time with you."

"Can we go camping?"

"Maybe."

"If we leave, the bad man can't get me."

She couldn't tell her son that wasn't always the case. If Keith ever found out where they were, he'd come after them, even though he'd lost his paternal rights because of his criminal activities working for a crime syndicate and his violence against her. "I'll talk with Josiah and the Detective Caldwell to see what's best."

The sound of a vehicle approaching drew Ella's attention. Josiah parked at the side of the hangar. When Robbie saw him climb from the Ford F-150, he snapped the leash on Buddy, then hurried toward Josiah. Ella watched her son run to him, pointing to the area where the black truck had driven off the road.

Even from a distance Ella could feel the anger pouring off the man. As he bridged the distance between them, a frown carved deep lines in his face. A storm greeted her in his blue eyes, but she didn't feel any of the fury was directed at her.

"Robbie, will you let David know I'm here with the supplies?" Josiah asked. "Take Buddy with you."

"Sure."

While her son led the German shepherd toward the hangar, Josiah asked, "Was it Foster?"

"I don't know. Maybe. The license plate was missing from the truck."

"Will you stay with Alex and me?"

"Yes."

"Can you leave now?"

"Right after I put the training session packets together. It shouldn't take me long."

"Good. I'll take you home so you can pack what you'll need. I'll have Robbie help David and me unload the truck while you finish up." He started for the hangar.

"Is this all right with Alex?"

"Are you kidding? She's thrilled to have others in that big old house she lives in."

"You don't live there?"

"I'm out back in the caretaker's cabin. Harry and Linda have a suite of rooms in the main house. They're more like family than employees." As David and Robbie emerged from the office door, Josiah caught her arm to pull her around to face him. "I'll call Thomas while you're packing. He'll want to know about this incident."

Ella nodded. She'd give whatever information she could to the police and pray it would help them find whoever was doing this to her and Robbie.

Later that evening, Josiah sat on the deck at the estate, watching Robbie play with both Buddy and Sadie. The sound of the boy's laughter penetrated the hard shell around Josiah's heart, put there to protect him from further pain after Lori's betrayal. He'd always wanted to be a father but had pushed that dream aside. Having a family meant trusting a woman enough to open up to her. He couldn't do that. If he couldn't give his heart to a woman, how in the world could they ever build a lasting relationship?

When Ella's son finally sank to the thick green grass and stretched out spread eagle, he called Sadie and Buddy to him. One dog lay on his right while the other sat on the left. Robbie stroked each one and stared up at the sky. It was good to see the child lose himself in the moment and forget for a while that someone was after him.

The French doors opened behind him, and he spied Ella coming toward him. Beautiful. Kind. But something was wrong. He could see it in her eyes, even before Robbie had been threatened. Had she been betrayed like him? She never talked about Robbie's father.

He turned his attention back to the boy playing between the dogs. He shouldn't care about Ella's past. But he did care. Why did she always look so sad?

"Well, we're all settled in our rooms." Ella sat in the lounge chair next to him.

"Good. I've decided to stay down the hall, and I want Buddy to sleep in Robbie's room, if that's all right with you."

"I couldn't say no. My son would disown me. He's so attached to Buddy. I need to get him his puppy soon or you'll have a problem when all this is over."

"We can go to the breeder on Tuesday. On Monday I'm driving to Fairbanks to talk with the team at Outdoor Alaska. I hope that you and Robbie will come with me. I'll only have to work a few hours, and then we can spend the rest of the time sightseeing or whatever else you'd like to do."

"Sounds wonderful. Robbie wants to go camping while I'm off. I'm not sure we should."

"If Robbie wants to camp out, we could do it here on the estate. We have woods." Josiah pointed toward the grove of trees along the back and side of his property. "It's not big, but it should give Robbie the sense of camping out in the forest."

"Is it safe?"

"It should be. We live in a gated community and even have private security guards patrolling the area. But the best security will be Buddy and Sadie. Nothing gets by them."

"Thanks. I don't want my son obsessed about the man stalking him. Did you notice on the drive here he didn't say a word?"

Josiah slid his hand over hers on the arm of her chair. "Yes. Young people generally never think anything bad will happen to them, and it is very sobering when that illusion is challenged or broken."

Ella rolled her head and shoulders. "And a challenge for parents to balance letting our children feel safe and really being safe. We want to protect them from every harm that comes their way, but we aren't with them 24/7. I know it was wrong for the boys to leave the camp area, but where were the counselors who were supposed to be keeping an eye on them?"

"It has to be doubly hard being a single parent. What happened to Robbie's father?"

She tensed, withdrawing her hand from his.

She began to rise when Josiah said, "I'm sorry. It's none of my business. I just thought his father might be able to help."

A humorless laugh escaped her lips. "His father is no longer in his life. I'm telling you this so you don't ask about him anymore. It's a subject that distresses my son."

And Ella. Why? It was none of his business, and he usually respected a person's privacy, but he had a hard time letting it go.

"I'm sorry. I didn't mean to upset you."

She took a deep breath and tried to relax in the

lounge chair, but her grasp on its arms indicated the tension still gripping her. "My philosophy is to look forward, not back. I can't change the past so I don't dwell there."

Easier said than done, he thought. He tried not to look backward, but what had happened to him was an intrinsic part of the man he was today. Ella's past was part of her present, too. She didn't have to tell him that Robbie's father was the one who'd hurt her so badly. He curled his hands into tight fists until they ached. Slowly he flexed them and practiced the relaxation techniques his counselor had taught him.

The sound of the French doors opening pulled Josiah's attention toward Thomas coming out on the deck. The fierce expression chiseled into his friend's face meant he was the bearer of bad news.

SIX

Ella saw Thomas heading for her. She straightened in her lounger on the deck at the Witherspoon estate. Not good news.

Thomas grabbed a chair and pulled it over to Ella and Josiah, checking to see where Robbie was.

Her son threw a Frisbee that Buddy caught in midair. "Did you all see that?" he yelled over to them.

"Yeah, both of the dogs love to catch Frisbees," Josiah answered while Thomas settled in his seat next to Ella. "So, Thomas, what happened?"

"A child a year older than Robbie, same hair coloring and height, has been taken by a man that fits Foster's description. A black truck like the one you described was identified near the abduction. We have an Amber Alert out on Seth London."

"Where did Foster get the black truck?" Ella asked, remembering that wasn't the description of the vehicle that his neighbor had reported stolen.

"It was reported stolen. He took the license off it, but we're looking at all black trucks, including those with plates, because we have a report of several license plates missing from a parking lot. We're also immediately investigating any car thefts in case he steals another one. Just like the first car, he probably won't keep the black truck long."

Josiah leaned forward, resting his elbows on his thighs. "What else?"

"We dug into Foster's past and found his record. He went crazy when his girlfriend sent her son to live with her grandparents, and he attacked her. The grandparents moved away from Alaska and disappeared. This month was the anniversary of when that happened."

"Was the child his?" Josiah glanced toward Ella.

Seeing the compassion in Josiah's gaze nearly undid her. Josiah was so different from the type of man Keith was, but then, she'd been fooled by her ex-husband, too.

Numb with all that had happened the past couple of days, Ella averted her head. She didn't want to hear about Foster, and yet she needed to know. The man had come after her son several times and might still try again.

"The girlfriend said no. Foster insisted he was the biological father and should have a say in where the boy lived. I'm joining the manhunt, but wanted you to hear what happened from me."

Finally Ella focused on the conversation. "It sounds as if he's gone crazy again."

"Yes. I'm speculating he saw the boys playing in the woods, and it made him snap. Michael, like Seth, looks similar to Robbie."

After the horror of my marriage, Lord, I don't know if I can do this. Ella lowered her head and twisted her hands in her lap.

"Do you need me to help with the hunt?"

The calm strength in Josiah's question reminded Ella

that she wasn't alone this time. She had people who cared about her.

"We don't have an area narrowed down. Once Seth was taken into the truck, there was no scent for the dogs to follow. I'll let David know if we need Northern Frontier's resources. Right now the police are handling it, but David is on alert."

"I didn't receive a call from him. Did he say the training session tomorrow is still on?" Ella looked toward Josiah, his gaze ensnaring her. "Did he call you, Josiah?"

"No, not yet. I would have said something to you." Josiah's expression softened.

"He told me he's canceling it. He wants everyone ready if there's a need for civilians to search for Seth." Thomas stood.

"But he should have let me know," Ella said. "I usually make the calls when something is cancelled."

Thomas clasped Ella's shoulder and squeezed gently. "He knew I was on my way to talk with you. He wanted me to remind you that you're on vacation and he can handle everything for the next week."

Ella pursed her lips. "There are a lot of people to get in touch with."

"Bree is helping him. I want you to keep your son here. If Foster is fixating on kids like Robbie, he may still try to come after him. Michael and his mother have gone to Nome to visit some relatives." Thomas peered at Josiah. "I'll call with any news."

"I take it Alex knows about the most recent developments." Josiah got to his feet and walked to the railing of the deck.

"She wouldn't let me into the house until I told her."

"Yup, that's my sister. She wants to know what's going on before it happens."

When Thomas left, Ella stood beside Josiah at the railing. "I think if Buddy hadn't been with him, Robbie could have been Seth today."

"I hope someone sees Foster or the truck or something to give the police the break they need, but I am not going to let anything happen to Robbie."

Alex came out on the deck. "Dinner is ready. I would suggest you keep the TV and radio off. The story about Seth is all over the news. Tonight, while Buddy is staying with Robbie, I'm going to let Sadie loose downstairs to prowl. Ella, the alarm system here is top-notch. No one is going to get to Robbie with us around."

"Thanks. It's nice to have friends to turn to for help." Both Josiah and Alex had reassured her that she and Robbie weren't alone. She had to keep reminding herself of that. This wasn't the same as four years ago when she'd fled her husband. When she'd arrived in Alaska, she'd had no friends and a four-year-old to raise by herself.

Ella yelled out, "Robbie, it's time to come in."

Her son stopped before throwing the Frisbee and faced her, a dog on each side of him. "Do I hafta come in? We're having fun."

"Tuesday won't come fast enough. He needs a dog of his own," Ella murmured to Josiah and Alex, then shouted, "Yes. Now. Dinner is ready."

"It's still light out."

She shook her head. "It'll still be light at eleven o'clock when you'll be in bed."

Robbie shrugged his shoulders and plodded toward the steps to the deck with both dogs following closely.

When he arrived in front of Ella, his mouth set in a pout, he said, "We were having so much fun."

"I know, and you'll be able to come out here tomorrow with Buddy and Sadie again, if you want."

"What about the training session? You told me we had to go there early."

"We're not going."

"Why not? You're in charge. David told me you were indi—indispensable."

Ella chewed on her lower lip. She shouldn't have said anything. Robbie didn't need to know about the little boy abducted today. He didn't need to worry. She'd do enough for the both of them. Then she remembered her granny telling her that when she began to worry, she should pray. Give it to God. Easier said than done. "I'm on vacation, remember? David wants me to start right away."

Robbie turned to Josiah. "Are you going?"

"Nope. I'm staying here, too."

A serious expression descended on Robbie's face, his forehead crinkling. "It's because of me and what happened yesterday."

Josiah nodded. "You're my priority and Buddy's."

"Yeah, he and Sadie are great. I can't wait to get my own dog."

"Soon." Ella started for the French doors. "I don't know about you two, but I'm starved. I didn't eat much at lunch."

Robbie peered up at Josiah and fell into step next to him. "That's because she ate while working at her desk."

"I've done that a few times and don't even remember what I ate an hour later. When we sit down for a meal, we should focus on the food and savor it." Josiah cocked a grin. "Or at least that's what my sister keeps telling me."

Robbie giggled. "I don't want a sister, but I'd love to have a brother."

Ella's cheeks flushed with heat. That wasn't going to happen, but at one time she'd wanted three or four children.

"My big sis isn't too bad, but I've always wanted a brother, too."

The laughter in Josiah's voice enticed her to glance toward him. His twinkling blue eyes fixed on her, and he winked.

Her face grew even warmer, and she hurried her pace to walk with Alex toward the dining room. She couldn't deny Josiah's good looks and kindness, but then Keith had been handsome and nice in the beginning. How could she ever let down her guard and trust any man?

Driving toward the Carter Kennels outside Fairbanks on Monday, Josiah took a peek at Robbie in the back-seat, looking out the window. Ever since he'd told him he had something special planned for him, Robbie had kept his attention glued to the scenery as though that would tell him where he was going.

"When are we gonna be there? We've been driving *forever*." Robbie turned forward. "I wonder if Buddy is doing okay."

"Robbie, you need to be patient." Ella shot her son a look that said *knock it off*. "That's the third time you've asked in the past forty minutes."

Josiah saw the mountain, at the base of which the kennel was located. "We're almost there."

"Where?"

"A surprise. After sitting around all morning at Outdoor Alaska, I thought we should do something I think you'll love."

"I miss Buddy."

"He needed a rest."

"He slept all night in my bed."

Josiah smiled and sliced a glance at Ella who rolled her eyes. "Yeah, but he was on guard duty."

"But he was snoring last night."

"Trust me, Robbie. You'll enjoy this."

When the large Carter Kennels sign came into view, Ella twisted toward her son. "This is a kennel for sled dogs. They train them here. One of the owners takes part in the Iditarod Race every year."

"Did he ever win?" The excitement in Robbie's voice infused the atmosphere in the truck.

Josiah chuckled. "He is a she, and Carrie has come in fifth and third. She told me next year she'll definitely win."

"I'd like to do something like that one day. I followed it this year."

"Yeah, your mom mentioned that to me when I asked her about coming here." Josiah pulled into the driveway. "Carrie has tours of the kennels in the summer, but she'll have time this afternoon to give us a private tour."

"She will? Yippee!" Robbie shot his arm into the air. "Will I be able to pet the dogs?"

"Carrie will have to let you know that. She's a trainer and has some great mushers." Josiah parked in front of a small black building where Carrie ran her business while the dogs stayed in a building off to the right.

As Carrie came outside, Josiah, Ella and Robbie climbed from the truck. Carrie was a fellow dog lover as well as a good customer of Outdoor Alaska. "It's nice to see you again." He shook the forty-year-old woman's hand.

"It's been a while since the Iditarod. You need to come out here more often. Great place to relax." Carrie turned her attention to Ella, then Robbie. A smile blossomed on her face as she greeted the boy. "You must be Robbie. I've been looking forward to meeting you today. Josiah said something about how much you love dogs and that you're a big fan of the Iditarod."

Eyes big, Robbie nodded his head. "Yes, ma'am. I was at the starting line this year rooting everyone on. One day I'd like to be at the finish line in Nome."

"Maybe you can drive a team one day."

Robbie grinned from ear to ear. "I hope so. I'm getting a puppy soon."

"An Alaskan husky?"

"No, a German shepherd from Buddy, Josiah's dog."

"Let's go meet my huskies." Carrie began walking toward the kennel area.

"I hope to train my dog to do search and rescue." Robbie's voice drifted back to Josiah, who was trailing them with Ella next to him.

His chest swelled listening to the boy's words. He could remember when he was Robbie's age and thought anything was possible. He was going to conquer the world and save everyone. Then real life had intruded, and he grasped that he didn't need to do it on a grand scale but one person at a time. That realization had helped him deal with the past.

"I think I'm going to stand back and let my son enjoy the special time with Carrie. This is a dream come true for him."

"Good. Hopefully, after the past few days, this will take his mind off someone being after him."

Ella shook her head. "All because he reminds Foster of his ex-girlfriend's little boy. What is this world coming to?"

"Someone once told me that when I wake up in the morning, I should tell myself, 'This is the first day of the rest of my life.'" It was a piece of advice from the chaplain who'd visited him while he was recovering from his captivity.

"Has it helped?"

"When I remember to do it. Changing a mindset isn't always easy."

She looked off toward Robbie. "I know what you mean. I had someone suggest to me to start listing every day what I'm thankful for. To focus on what I have, not what I don't have."

"Has it helped?"

"When I remember to do it," she said with a laugh.

Robbie came running back to Ella. "Mom, I get to feed the dogs, then Carrie is going to show me how to hook up a sled. She is gonna let me go out on a sled run."

"How?"

"She says in the summer and fall she does A…" He scrunched his forehead and thought for a few seconds. "ATV training with her dogs when there isn't enough snow for a sled." Robbie rushed back to Carrie.

Ella released a long breath. "I have a feeling my son quoted her word for word."

"It's good to see him smiling so much."

Ella shifted toward Josiah. "All because of you. I can't tell you how much I appreciate your help. It hasn't been easy for me to accept help, but when your son's life is in jeopardy, you do what you have to do to keep him safe."

"You're a terrific mother."

She blushed.

"And Robbie knows it."

"There were moments this weekend when he wanted to do something I had to nix that I wasn't so sure."

"He shook off his disappointment and each time came up with something else to do." Josiah watched Robbie finish feeding the dogs, then walk toward a shed where he knew Carrie kept the dog sledding equipment. "I guess we'd better join them."

The faint red patches on her cheeks began to fade as she walked beside Josiah. "Thank you for showing Robbie some of Buddy's training. That took his mind off the fact that the activities at Northern Frontier were canceled on Saturday. When I told him last Friday he was going to attend with me, he was so excited. He didn't understand why it was called off, and I couldn't lie so I didn't tell him much of anything."

"It's hard trying to keep him protected from what's going on—Robbie's smart. I think he knows something is up."

"Yes, I'm afraid you're right. I want my dull life back."

As he strolled across the compound, he took her hand and peered down at her. "Dull is good." He'd learned excitement wasn't all it was cracked up to be. He'd joined an elite team in the Marines because he'd wanted more action. Once, when he'd been injured and had desk duty for a month, he'd become so restless he'd tried to get the doctor to clear him for active duty early.

When he and Ella were a couple of yards away, Robbie held up a harness. "I get to put this on a dog, then help set up the tug line and gang line."

"Great," she said to her son, then leaned closer to Josiah. "I know what he's going to be doing the rest of the summer. Reading everything he can find on sled dogs."

"Don't be surprised if he becomes the youngest competitor in the race."

For a few seconds Ella blinked as though surprised. All traces of enthusiasm left her expression as she swallowed hard.

"Is something wrong?"

She angled away from him. "No, nothing's wrong, so long as my son is safe."

Strange. Something didn't fit. He started to ask her about what she'd said, but quickly decided it wasn't his concern. Obviously she didn't want to share it with him, and that bothered him.

Ella opened the garage door to the kitchen, so Josiah could carry Robbie, who was sound asleep, into the house. Buddy and Sadie greeted them at the door when they entered.

Positioned at the sink, Linda glanced at them.

"Where's Alex?" Josiah asked as he crossed the room.

"In the den. She came home right before dinner. I can fix you some leftovers if you want."

"Thanks. We ate in Fairbanks not that long ago." Josiah headed for the hallway.

Ella followed him. "Will you carry him upstairs and put him on his bed? I doubt he'll wake up before morning. He's worn out from today." Josiah had gone out of his way to make the outing to Fairbanks special for Robbie. That was another reason she was attracted to

Josiah when she shouldn't be. He cared about her son, and Robbie hung on to every word Josiah said. Robbie's father had never spent any time with his son.

After he placed Robbie in his room, he backed away. "I'm going to let Alex know how my visit to the store went today."

"I'll be down in a little bit. I'm tired but not ready for bed." Ella removed Robbie's tennis shoes while Buddy settled on the floor next to the bed.

She put a light sheet over her son, then smoothed some of his hair from his face. When she did that when he was awake, he'd act as though he was too old to have his mother fuss over him. In a couple of months he would be nine.

What if I have to leave Alaska?

Ella crossed to the window to pull the shades halfway down but stopped and looked out onto the backyard toward the stand of birch and spruce trees at the rear of the property. It was eleven o'clock at night, and the sun was finally setting but would rise before five. At least she didn't have to worry about a man peeking in at her son sleeping here. Chills shivered up her spine as she thought back to Thursday night, when Foster had done just that. She tugged the blinds another several inches down.

She dug her cell phone out of her jeans pocket and checked to see if David or Thomas had left her a message. Nothing. Still no sign of Foster. People headed into the wilderness all the time to disappear from civilization. What would she do if the police never found Foster?

She'd left Georgia because of Keith. She didn't want to leave Alaska because of Foster.

Her son mumbled something she couldn't understand and rolled over on the bed.

"Robbie," she whispered, checking to see if he was awake.

When she saw his eyes were closed, she released her pent-up breath and headed into the hallway. Her stomach rumbled. She'd worked up an appetite after walking along Chena River at the Fairbanks Downtown Market after visiting the Carter Kennels. She'd enjoyed the music, sampling some of the food and the atmosphere. For a while, she'd felt free, as though they hadn't a care in the world, and she and Robbie were spending the day with a wonderful man under normal circumstances.

Now she wasn't even sure if that would ever be possible. After Keith had been put into the Witness Security Program because he'd turned state's evidence against the crime syndicate he'd worked for, she had no idea where he was. She didn't know if he was in a prison or out there somewhere with a new identity.

Robbie and I are totally in Your hands, Lord. She repeated the prayer as she descended the stairs to the first floor. She'd done everything she could to vanish. She followed the New Life Organization's instructions—as though she and Robbie were in WitSec like Keith—and so far it had worked for four years.

As she neared the den, she heard Josiah ask, "What did David have to say?"

"He's calling everyone about meeting to help with the search now that the state police have found the black truck. What are you going to do?"

Ella paused before entering to hear what Josiah would say to Alex without her around. She didn't want to keep him from doing what he should do. Josiah and Buddy were a great SAR team.

"I'm staying here. My first priority is Ella and Robbie."

"I'm going. You know how I feel about any child that's missing."

"You should. I would go, too, but—"

"Good, because I'm going to be involved," Ella said from the den's entrance.

Josiah looked at Ella. "You can't. What about your son?"

"Robbie will also go. He'll help me at the command center. David will be there, so we'll be fine, but they're going to need all the trained dogs with good handlers if they're going to locate Seth." When Josiah frowned and started to say something, she set her hand on her waist. "And honestly, do you see Foster walking into the command center to take Robbie? We know what the man looks like. With the police crawling around the area, he won't."

Josiah exchanged a glance with Alex. "Okay, but only if David agrees."

She put her other hand on her waist and narrowed her eyes on Josiah. "You're hoping he says no, aren't you?"

He grinned. "Of course. That's why bosses get paid big bucks."

"He volunteers his services just like you."

"But he has the fancy title."

Alex laughed and rose from the couch. "I'm going to let Sadie outside to check the grounds, then I'm off to bed. Four o'clock will be here soon enough."

Ella sat where Alex had been. "So tell me, what have the police found?"

"The black truck used to kidnap Seth was found off Eagle River Road half an hour ago. The area around there is wooded and vast. Although it's going to be dark soon, the K-9 unit is searching the immediate area, but as soon as it's light, they want us in place so we can blanket the vicinity."

"Maybe they'll find Foster and Seth beforehand." Ella shifted to face Josiah at the other end of the couch.

"I hope so, but there are a lot of places to hide, and the Eagle River is nearby. He could try using the water to throw the dogs off."

"Even in July the water is ice-cold."

"There's a chance Foster isn't even there or Seth. But it has to be searched."

"And you need to be there. Robbie and I are going, too. This is why I work for Northern Frontier Search and Rescue. I'm good at running the command center and keeping track of where our volunteers are." She scooted closer to Josiah until they were inches apart. "I'm going, and David can't do anything about it once I'm there."

His blue eyes softened. "Fine. Both Alex and I are dedicated to searching for any child missing, no matter when or where."

Ella wanted to melt under his perusal. "I know. I've seen your dedication."

"Once when we were eleven, a friend went missing. The conditions weren't the best. Only about half the searchers needed arrived. By the time he was found, he'd died. I'll never forget that. That's why I got serious about survival in the wilderness and trained Buddy to be a SAR dog."

"I'm so sorry about your friend."

"The worst part was I couldn't do anything to help him."

The more she got to know Josiah, the more she realized how much integrity he had. But she still felt that he kept a part of himself bottled up and hidden from the world.

She laid her hand over his on the couch. "You were only a kid. Robbie keeps wondering why he can't help search."

His gaze locked with hers, and she felt like she was drowning in those blue depths. "I understand why kids don't join search teams. In Alaska, tragedy can happen quickly. But even knowing the reason doesn't mean it didn't affect me."

The urge to cup the rugged line of his jaw inundated her. She grappled for a subject that would keep her from speculating how it would feel to kiss him. "I wonder how capable Foster is in the backcountry." She relaxed against the cushion, slipping her hand from his. Too dangerous.

"Let's hope he makes a mistake and gets caught."

"That's what I'll be praying for while you all are out searching."

He rose, holding his arm out toward her. "We'd better get some rest. We'll have to leave in less than four hours."

When he pulled her to her feet, she came up close against him. He grasped her, their gazes bound as though ropes held them together. He brushed his fingers through her hair, then cupped her face. He bent toward her, then his mouth claimed hers in a kiss. Suddenly, her legs felt like jelly, so she gripped his arms to keep herself upright.

A series of barks broke them apart as Ella looked toward the door.

"That's Buddy," Josiah said, as he charged from the room.

SEVEN

Could someone have gotten into the house?

Josiah raced for the stairs, taking them two at a time with Ella right behind him. He hit the second-floor landing at a dead run. When he reached Robbie's room and started to open the door, the barking ceased. He slammed into the room, his heart galloping as fast as a polar bear after its prey. Nearly colliding with Robbie a few feet inside, Josiah skidded to a halt.

The boy stood in the center of the room, his arms straight at his sides, a blank expression on his face as he stared into space. Buddy nudged his hand. Nothing. Josiah glanced toward the hallway, not sure what to do.

Ella hurried inside, took one look at her son and relaxed the tensed set of her body. "Occasionally in the past, he has sleepwalked. He used to do it more when he was younger. The doctor thought he'd outgrow it as he got older." She kneaded her neck. "It's been six months since he did it, so I thought he finally had. Usually the age range for sleepwalking in children is between four and eight years old, and he'll be nine in September."

"Then I'm glad Buddy was here. If Robbie had left his room, he could have fallen down the stairs."

"He wanders around his bedroom, and I'd often find

him asleep on the floor the next morning." Ella guided Robbie back to the bed and tucked him in. "He doesn't realize he's done it, even when he wakes up in a different place."

Josiah stood with Ella by the door to make sure Robbie didn't get up. She curled her hand around his and took deep breaths.

"I think he's fine."

"If not, Buddy will let us know."

In the hallway she faced Josiah. "You and your sister have done so much for Robbie and me. I can't thank you enough."

"You don't have to thank me. I do it because it's the right thing to do. You can trust me. I won't do anything to hurt you or Robbie."

"I know."

He studied her for a moment. "Do you really? I'm not sure you do."

"Why do you say that? I wouldn't be here if I didn't."

"Someone has hurt you, made you wary. I certainly understand that. I just wanted you to know where I stand."

She pursed her lips and stared at his shirtfront. "I won't deny that I've been hurt. I divorced a man who didn't love or care about his son." She took several steps to her bedroom door. "Good night. I'll see you in a few hours."

Josiah watched her disappear inside the room, closing the door quietly while her body language screamed tension. It was obvious the man didn't love or care about Ella, either. Under different circumstances, he would pursue Ella, but he didn't have any business getting involved with a woman. The last one had left her mark on his heart.

* * *

By five in the morning the next day, Ella had signed in most of the searchers at Northern Frontier Search and Rescue. She counted only three left in line.

"Mom, why can't I go out with Josiah? I want to learn all I can about having a SAR dog." Robbie whined as he sat next to her at the check-in table for Seth's searchers.

"Because you'll remain glued to my side the whole time." She took the check-in form from another searcher and gave instructions to the next person.

"But I want to help!"

"You are helping. I wouldn't be here if you weren't with me. You'll be able to search when you're older."

Robbie pouted. "I'm always too young. When I get my puppy, I'm gonna start working with him right away. At least I can do that." He slumped against the canvas back of the chair.

"That's a good plan." Ella took the check-in form from the last searcher. It was two minutes until David would brief the search teams on the situation and objectives.

Ella rose and stretched.

Robbie jumped to his feet. "Can I hang out with Josiah until he leaves?"

She nodded, realizing a good part of the day would be boring for her son. Maybe she shouldn't have come, but that would have meant one less team of handlers and dogs. Like Josiah said last night, this was the right thing to do.

She watched her son hurry to the tent and find Josiah standing next to Buddy. A couple of seconds later, he handed her son his dog's leash, and Robbie grinned from ear to ear.

With a deep sigh, she made her way to the tent, wanting to listen to the briefing but still keep an eye on the check-in table. Two searchers had yet to show up—a husband-and-wife team. She hoped nothing had happened to them. They could use everyone to help the state troopers overseeing the search for Seth.

David signaled for quiet. "I've just been updated. We'll be searching this area." He pointed to area south and west of Eagle River Nature Center, where their staging area was. "A trail from the truck Foster used in the abduction of Seth London headed away from the center toward the south. From the tracks the police have found, there's evidence that Foster went into the backcountry with Seth but the boy didn't come out. A vehicle was reported stolen half an hour ago. They believe, based on the footprints, that Foster took the car. There was no evidence the child was with him. Our job is to search that area and pray we find the child alive."

As David continued to fill the searchers in on what they would do, Ella spotted the couple arriving and walked back to the table to check them in.

"We're sorry. We had a flat tire."

"I'm so glad you are here and safe. David is just finishing up with the group now. Talk to him, and he'll give you the spiel and instructions."

They nodded, then rushed to catch the last part of David's briefing. Ella started back toward the tent pitched near the nature center. Her gaze immediately zeroed in on her son, who hadn't left Josiah's side. In the past days, Robbie had followed Josiah around everywhere. They'd bonded almost overnight, and that scared her. What would happen when Foster was found and they went back to their life without Josiah and Buddy?

The thought added a chill to the cool morning air. She zipped up her light parka as though that would warm her. She had a feeling that when Josiah went on with his life, he'd leave a hole in both her life and Robbie's.

Memories of their kiss the night before haunted her again. She'd barely slept because he'd filled her thoughts. She would not fall in love with Josiah. She'd fallen in love with Keith, and her life had become a nightmare not long after the wedding. How could she tell Josiah about her ex-husband?

The searchers began grouping with their team leaders. Josiah knelt in front of Robbie and clasped her son's arm. He said something too quietly for her to hear, but whatever Josiah told Robbie, it turned his frown into a grin.

Robbie hugged Josiah, then gave him Buddy's leash. Josiah rose, and they exchanged high fives. Emotions overflowed her throat. She swallowed hard as Josiah looked around, then caught sight of her. He smiled and waved. Her son had missed out on a male role model. Even when Keith had been around, he hadn't really been a part of Robbie's life. How would she ever be able to make it up to her son for her bad judgment concerning her ex-husband?

"I've noticed you're one of the organizers. Could you answer a few questions?" a woman asked from behind Ella.

When Ella pivoted toward her, she realized a cameraman was standing behind the woman, as well as a photographer snapping pictures as the searchers prepared to leave.

"We just arrived and didn't catch the briefing." The

young lady she recognized from a local television station held a microphone up for Ella to reply.

She froze. She always worked way behind the scenes of a search, and usually kept track of any media covering the rescue. Being fixated on Josiah's relationship with her son had caused her to let down her guard.

Ella pointed toward the tent. "You'll want to talk with David Stone. He can answer your questions."

"Thank you." The woman and her cameraman headed for the tent.

But the photographer stayed behind and continued taking pictures. This rescue would generate a lot more media coverage than usual because of the nature of the story. She quickly put some of the searchers between her and the reporters, grabbed Robbie, then headed around the nature center.

She wasn't worried about the TV reporter, because the station wouldn't air anything that didn't contribute to the story, but she would have to stay away from the photographers. For all she knew, her husband could be dead. He'd certainly angered a lot of people, but she wasn't going to take a chance.

Hours ago after being airlifted to one of the sites where a set of tracks, which the authorities thought were Foster's and Seth's, had been discovered, Josiah gave Buddy a long leash. Josiah kept his gaze trained on his surroundings for any footprints to compare with what he'd seen at the start. He prayed to the Lord to guide his steps and help him find the child. He knew of the dangers in the wilderness—bears, moose, freezing water, falling on the rough trail.

The other searchers were behind the handlers with

their dogs, covering the ground much more slowly, looking for any signs to help them. To Josiah's left, his sister and Sadie were following Eagle River. He hoped the child hadn't fallen into the ice-cold river or the many creeks feeding into it. From what he'd heard in the briefing, Seth didn't swim well.

Buddy reached one creek crossing that branched out over a large area. Josiah and his dog navigated to the other side by using downed logs and stepping-stones.

Buddy was following Seth's scent from an article of clothing while Sadie was following Foster's. So far the two dogs were going the same direction.

Using an SAR satellite phone, Josiah called in to headquarters. "We've come about three miles from the drop-off site. It looks like Foster and Seth crossed a creek here. We'll pick up their scent on the other side."

"The other teams are calling in, too. So far nothing." Ella's voice sounded strained.

"Is everything all right?"

"Yes, just a media circus here. Thankfully David is the spokesperson."

"I'll check in later."

"Be careful. No sightings of Foster or the car he stole at the parking lot in Girdwood, but the police have confirmed from video feeds that Foster took the vehicle. No sign of Seth in the tapes."

He gritted his teeth, hoping the boy was still alive. "How's Robbie?"

"Asleep right now in the tent. Take care and don't worry. David and Bree are keeping a good eye on us."

"Okay. Bye." As he put his phone into his backpack, visions of them kissing last night appeared in his mind.

He was starting to care about her more and more with each day they spent together.

Josiah stepped up to the water. The morning had barely started to warm up. "I'll go first," he said to Alex. "Make sure we can get across."

As he hopped from one rock to another, he slipped and his leg went down into the icy water. He sucked in a deep breath and yanked his foot free. Buddy sat on the other side of the stream, waiting only yards away.

When he reached the other side, Josiah waved to Alex. His sister crossed the creek, learning from his misstep to go another route. As she and Sadie joined him, he said to Buddy, "Search." There weren't too many ways to cross the creek, so he hoped they'd pick up the scent quickly.

His German shepherd sniffed the ground until Josiah finally said, "Looks like Buddy hasn't picked up the scent yet. I'm heading this way."

"I'll go the opposite direction," Alex said.

Josiah only went five yards before Buddy picked up the trail. He gave a loud whistle to indicate that Alex should join him. When she did, Sadie also found Foster's scent.

"What made Foster deviate from the trail?" Josiah looked around at the dense underbrush and forest surrounding the area. "Maybe there was someone he wanted to avoid."

"Whatever the reason, this is the way we go. They're still together."

"This doesn't make sense. Why is Foster even bringing Seth here? This isn't isolated."

"This is pure speculation," Alex said, "but he used

to think of his girlfriend's son as his own. What if he's trying to do stuff he would have done with a son?"

For the next hour, he and Alex went along the trail part of the way then off it then back on the path. When the vegetation thickened, Josiah suddenly veered away from Alex.

"Seth is going this way." He glanced back at his sister.

She took several more steps before Sadie dived into the thicket, as though Foster was chasing after Seth. Off the trail Alex and Josiah came together about forty yards into the thick woods, following the course of a creek upstream.

Josiah let Buddy off the leash so he could go faster through the brush. A couple of minutes later, his German shepherd barked, followed by Sadie. Although Foster had been sighted in Girdwood, Josiah removed his gun. As a soldier he'd learned it was better to be prepared rather than surprised.

He forged through the vegetation, spotting a small green tent nestled among the trees. Alex and he exchanged looks. He motioned for her to stay in case Foster had somehow returned. Taking off his backpack, Josiah left it next to Alex and crept forward, always keeping his eyes open for a bear.

When he reached the tent, he didn't go in through the front but uprooted one of the stakes on the side and lifted the tarp. Inside, Josiah saw Seth, who was terrified. The boy's mouth had duct tape over it, and his feet and hands were bound, but he was alive.

"I'm here to rescue you, Seth. Your parents have been worried sick." Buddy barked again and Josiah added,

"That's my dog. He found you. I'm going to come in through the opening and untie you. Okay?"

The child's eyes were still round as saucers, but he nodded and struggled to sit up.

Josiah called out to Alex, "I found Seth alive. Call base and let them know."

Later that evening, Ella entered the den, tired but so glad that Seth was back with his parents, dehydrated but unharmed. "Where's Alex?"

"She went to bed. She has to get up early for a meeting at the store." With feet propped up on the coffee table in front of the navy blue leather couch, he nursed a tall glass of iced tea while watching TV. He turned the sound down and patted the cushion next to him. "Sit. Relax. It's been a long day."

"Alex is okay that you aren't going into work tomorrow?" She sat at the opposite end of the sofa from Josiah. Getting any closer was just too dangerous. She still couldn't get their kiss out of her thoughts.

Josiah chuckled. "She's fine. Besides, I have a long list of suppliers I'll be contacting tomorrow. I often work from here. That's the beauty of my job. I don't always have to go into the office."

"I was hoping the police would have found Foster by now."

"He'll be found. His photo has been plastered all over town, as well as the description of the car he's driving. Roadblocks have been set up, and all ways to leave the area are under surveillance. He took a child. A lot of people are eager to bring him in. You and Robbie will be home in no time."

Home. The house she lived in now was the first place

she'd called that since she'd left her childhood home and married Keith. Sometimes she prayed that she could go back to Georgia and see her parents, but that wouldn't be smart. "I hope so. I hate being an imposition on you and Alex."

"I've told you a thousand times. You aren't."

She relaxed against the couch and sighed. "I'm bone tired, but I wouldn't have traded seeing Seth reunited with his parents for anything. The other day I had a taste of what it feels like to have your child missing. A parent's worst nightmare."

"If it wasn't for Buddy and Sadie, I'm not sure he would have been found before his dehydration became serious. The Lord was with us today."

"Foster must be crazy. I can't believe he brought Seth all the way out there and then left him. What if a bear had come upon the child?"

"Thankfully one didn't. Thomas thinks that Foster is falling apart, which will probably cause him to make a mistake. After Thomas talked with Seth, he told me that Foster had wanted to share a camping trip with the child. Foster had kept saying how he'd promised him one, and finally they could go. I think Alex had it right that Foster thought of Seth as the son who was taken away from him."

"What if he goes after another child?"

"That's definitely a possibility. That's why the news is making it clear to parents to watch their children, especially young boys." Josiah angled himself on the couch toward Ella. "When Thomas went through Foster's apartment, they found a closet with walls plastered with pictures of his ex-girlfriend's son."

"When did this happen?"

"Right after they identified him, they went through it from top to bottom, trying to find a lead."

She straightened. "That was days ago. Why didn't you tell me this sooner?"

A tic in his jaw jerked. His hand on the couch fisted.

"What are you not telling me?"

Silence.

"I'm not leaving until you tell me. What are you hiding from me?"

"In my defense, I didn't hear this from Thomas until late Sunday night after you had gone to sleep. Thomas called to give me an update on the investigation and told me then about the closet…" He uncurled his hand then balled it again. "He had taken a few photos of Robbie, and they were posted over the other boy."

Ella heard his words, but it took a moment for their meaning to register in her mind. She bolted to her feet and rotated toward him. "You should have woken me up and told me this right away!"

"Sunday was the first time you'd gotten a good night's rest. You had been functioning on minimal sleep for days."

"Then yesterday."

"There was never a right moment. I wasn't going to dampen our outing to Fairbanks, then the truck Foster had stolen was found."

"I can think of a few." Ella began to pace. "How many pictures? Where were they taken?"

"There were four. Taken at the day camp, and his friends were in them, so they could have been shot because of one of them. Remember Michael is similar to Robbie and Seth in size and coloring."

She stopped and faced him, her arms ramrod straight

at her sides. "And yet, Foster came to my house and peeped into Robbie's bedroom. I would say that meant he'd singled out Robbie."

"With all that's been going on with Seth, I didn't want to add to your worry."

"I'm a grown woman who's been on her own for years. I can take care of myself." Had she been lured into a false sense of safety when she of all people should realize no one was ever totally safe? She got up and started pacing, wound too tight to sit and relax.

"You don't always have to do everything by yourself." He rose and blocked her path. "I've learned the hard way there are some things I can't control. In fact, a good part of life is out of my control. But I can control how I react, what I think."

She began to go around Josiah, but suddenly the fight drained out of her. "I know, and I'm working on it, but with all that's happened lately, past fears have a hold on me."

He clasped her hand, threading his fingers through hers. "What fears?"

For a moment she contemplated telling him about Keith, but the words clogged her throat and she couldn't. "One I need to put to rest," she finally murmured, lowering her gaze.

He lifted her chin until she looked in his eyes. "We all have fears we need to put to rest. Easy to say. Hard to do."

What are yours? she wondered. She exhaled and stepped back, her hand slipping from his. "I'm trying not to worry all the time. To give those concerns to the Lord and trust more, but it's a constant battle."

"Faith can be." Josiah took his seat on the couch.

Ella remained standing in front of the fireplace. "Please let me know if you hear something else from Thomas right away. I'm not as fragile as you think I am."

"On the contrary, I think you're a strong woman. You help others. You're raising a wonderful son by yourself. There are many qualities about you that I admire."

The heat of a blush slowly swept over her face. If he only knew about her past. It had taken her years to get away from Keith. She'd kept thinking things would change, and when she realized they wouldn't, she'd discovered how controlling her ex-husband really was.

Needing to turn the conversation away from her, she searched for a topic. When she spied Josiah yawning, she said, "I can't believe you aren't asleep after the day you've had, hiking for miles, carrying Seth to the helicopter pickup site. Why are you still up?"

"I wanted to watch the news. See if anything has happened."

"Doesn't Thomas keep you updated?"

"When he has the time. I didn't know about the pictures right away."

She sat at the other end of the couch. "Probably not a bad idea. I don't know what I'll do if Foster isn't found soon. I can't keep taking time off, and I need my job."

"We'll deal with that when the time comes."

We'll? Like a couple? The idea struck panic in her but also gave her a sense of comfort. For the first time in years she actually didn't feel alone. She'd purposefully held part of herself back from others, and the thought Josiah could break down all her barriers frightened her.

He leaned forward, picked up the remote and turned up the sound. "I figure they'll lead with Seth's story."

But the anchorman cut to a national story first. Ella slid a gaze toward him and found him watching her.

A smile lifted the corners of his mouth. "Maybe we'll see our pictures on the news. Our fifteen seconds of fame."

"Maybe you. I seem to remember a reporter sticking a microphone in your face when you hopped down from that helicopter."

"Earlier today, there was a happy ending to the kidnapping of Seth London. He's been returned home safely to his parents," the anchorman said, the picture on the television switching from him to one of Seth's parents hugging their child.

Then Mr. London made a statement to the press praising the searchers who found Seth.

A video of Josiah as he climbed down from the helicopter came on, followed by him saying, "My dog is the one who found Seth. I was just tagging along."

Ella smiled. "You're about as comfortable as I am in the limelight."

"I'd rather face a grizzly than a reporter."

She laughed, her earlier tension melting away while David came on the screen and told the reporter about his dedicated search and rescue team members. Then a picture of her with Robbie flashed on the TV with a voice saying, "This is one particularly hardworking member, Ella Jackson, with her son, Robbie."

She heard Josiah chuckling. "And there's your fifteen seconds of fame." But it sounded as if he was talking from the end of a long tunnel, his voice echoing off the concrete walls.

Her face—and Robbie's—was on the evening news. For everyone to see. What if the national news picked up the story? And Keith saw it?

EIGHT

Ella's face turned as pale as her white shirt, and her eyes grew as large as saucers.

Josiah moved closer to her on the couch. "Ella? Are you okay?" He didn't understand what was wrong. He laid his hand on her arm and said, "I know you'd rather work behind the scenes, but you are just as important as the people out searching. I'm so glad you got some recognition for your contribution."

She yanked her arm from his grasp. "I didn't know they took that photo of me and Robbie. They shouldn't have."

The frantic ring to her words worried him. Something else was going on here. "Ella, what's really wrong? This is good publicity for Northern Frontier Search and Rescue. I won't be surprised if donations flood the office after this piece."

Her hands began to tremble, and she hugged herself, tucking her fingers under her arms. "This is *not* good." She shot to her feet. "I've got to leave Anchorage. I can't stay. It's not safe."

She ran for the hallway. Josiah hurried after her and caught up with her in the foyer.

He held both her hands in his, and waited until she made eye contact to say, "Foster is *not* going to get to Robbie. You're safe."

"No. You don't understand."

"Make me understand." He wanted to hold her until she calmed down, but she strained away from him.

"I need to go home and pack. Leave. Right now."

"Why, Ella? What are you afraid of? I promise I will never let Foster hurt your son or you."

She shook her head. "It's not just Foster I'm afraid of." Her eyes widened even more. She snapped her mouth closed, swept around and raced up the staircase.

Josiah went after her, taking the steps two at a time. Inside her bedroom, she swung her suitcase up on the bed and hurried toward the closet. He stood in the doorway, watching her, not sure what he should do.

She was worried the piece about Seth's rescue would be on national TV. Why? Her ex-husband? From the one comment she'd made about him, he hadn't been a good father to Robbie. Was there more?

Suddenly Ella came to a halt between the closet and bed, a blouse and sweater in her hand. Her gaze fell on him as the clothes floated to the floor. Tears glistened in her eyes, full of fear.

Whatever it was, she was terrified.

He covered the distance to her and embraced her, tugging her against him as though he could somehow erase the panic by holding her. He would do anything to take away that sense of alarm, but at the moment he felt helpless as he listened to her cry against his shoulder.

He stroked her back, her sobs breaking down the wall he hid behind. He closed his eyes and sent a prayer for help to the Lord.

When her tears stopped, he loosened his hold enough to lean away to look at her. "Ella." He waited until she focused on him. "Tell me what is wrong. If I can help, I will. Please."

Ella blinked and moved back, swiping at her cheeks. "I'm sorry for that."

"Don't be. We all hit a wall at different times in our life." He, more than most, had realized that the hard way.

"That's exactly how I feel. For years I've held my emotions inside, and suddenly they just needed to be released."

He drew her to a love seat nearby, sat and pulled her down next to him. "Maybe it's time you share all these emotions with someone. I get the feeling you haven't."

"Not for four years." She wanted to tell him her story, but she was afraid. And yet, the words *tell him* bounced around her mind. Could she trust him? She was so tired of going it alone.

"You don't have to say anything, but whatever you tell me I'll keep in confidence. I know what it feels like to need to talk, but something holds you back."

She started to ask him about it but realized this wasn't the time. Taking a cleansing breath, she stared at her laced fingers in her lap and murmured, "My ex-husband can't find me. If he does, he'll kill me." Slowly, unsure of his reaction, she peered into his eyes—full of compassion and something else. Anger?

A nerve twitched in his jaw as he covered her clasped hands with his. "Why do you think that?"

"I'm the one who turned him in to the police for his illegal activities. Once he was in jail, I ran from him, taking Robbie with me. Through the New Life Organization, a group that helps abused women leave their husbands, I was able to divorce him and get complete custody of my son. If it hadn't been for them, I don't know what I would have done."

Although Josiah's expression was fierce, his touch against her hands was gentle. "Did he ever hit you or Robbie?"

"Only me, but he'd come close to hitting Robbie toward the end. I'd tried to leave him a couple of times, and he always found me, dragged me back home. I discovered the first time I ran away that his associates were ruthless and would stop at nothing to get what they wanted. That was how Keith was, too."

"Then how were you able to finally get away from him?"

"I arranged through our maid to give the police information I'd discovered about Keith's criminal activities. She was a lifesaver and the reason I'm a Christian. I don't know what I would have done without Rosa. Everyone else who worked for my husband was terrified of him. God sent her to me when I needed her."

"What happened to her?"

Ella could remember so vividly when she'd said goodbye to Rosa. The emotions of that parting inundated her, and the tears welled up in her throat. "I gave her some money, and she went back to her own country. Originally she was going to come with me, but she was homesick. I miss her so much, but for Robbie's sake, I've cut off all ties to my past, including my parents."

"If you turned your ex-husband into the police, why isn't he in prison? Or was he released?"

"He was charged but never went to trial. I found out

that he had turned the state's evidence against the crime organization he was part of."

"Is he in the witness security program now?"

"No one will tell me for sure, but I know he disappeared. I imagine he is, but he has his own problems. The people he worked for won't hesitate to kill him if they find him. I've scoured the internet for any trace of him and never found anything."

"And now you're afraid he might see that photo of you and know where you are?"

She nodded. "I've always been so careful not to have my picture taken. Nowadays one photo can live on the internet forever. TV networks and newspapers all put their photos and videos up on the internet. Now I don't know what to do."

"You think he's still looking for you?"

"I have to think he is. To ignore that possibility could mean tragedy. When Robbie went missing, my first thought was that Keith had found us and he'd kidnapped him. For a few seconds, I was relieved it was Foster. But he's become a problem in his own right." The thumping of her heart made breathing difficult.

"Foster will be found."

"I'm not so sure. He's been eluding the police for a while now. Don't forget, Alaska is a big state."

Josiah frowned. "True, but it seems as though he's losing all sense of reality. He'll make a mistake soon and get caught. I have to believe that."

"Because the alternative is that there might be two people who want to come after Robbie?"

"We have some dedicated people looking for Foster, and now the public is involved."

"I hope we catch him. I love living here, and I don't want to run again. I'm tired of running."

He pulled her toward him, and slipped his arm around her. She nestled against him. "Your ex-husband has his own problems. If he has powerful people coming after him, then I can't see him coming after you. He'll do what he needs to do to protect himself. Drawing attention to himself could alert the criminals he turned against."

"Keith always put himself first, so you're probably right." She laid her head against his shoulder and savored the moment. Right now this was the safest place for her and Robbie. She needed to practice putting herself in the Lord's hands, because the alternative was living a life of fear.

"You'll see. After Foster is captured, everything will return to normal." His hand rubbed up and down her back.

Normal? She wasn't sure she knew what that was. Her life hadn't been normal for years.

"But one thing I promise you. Your past is safe with me. You don't have to do this alone."

She'd always dreamed of someone saying that to her, but Josiah had his own problems that he kept secret. Even though she'd become a very private person out of necessity, she'd never fall in love with someone hiding part of himself. Not after Keith. She couldn't go through that again.

"I think we need to plan something fun to do after Foster is caught. Any suggestions?"

"I think Robbie would like a camping trip."

"What about you?"

"Whatever Robbie wants, I want. But I have to warn

you. I'm a complete novice. I'm not even sure I can put up a tent."

"We can remedy that. I'll make my business calls tomorrow, and then we'll set a tent up in the backyard. You need to know how and so does Robbie, especially if we do go camping."

"That would be great."

"Okay, now, what would you like to do for yourself?"

"Robbie being happy is something for myself."

"What's your heart's desire?"

The fact that Josiah had even bothered to ask her that stunned her. Not once had Keith or anyone else asked her. She couldn't tell him her heart's desire was to be loved unconditionally. "I'd love to go out to dinner at Celeste's. I'd never be able to afford it, though," she said instead.

"Celeste's. Done. I suspect that isn't really what your heart's desire is, but I can understand your reluctance to reveal the truth." He smiled, a gleam in his eyes that made her feel cherished. "I hope one day you'll be able to tell me. It's hard being alone."

The way he said that last sentence held a wealth of loneliness. She wanted to ask him what had happened, but she swallowed the question and pushed to her feet. "Thank you for your help."

A glint of sadness winked at her as he rose, clasped her upper arms and leaned toward her to kiss her forehead. "Good night."

Too good to be true. Remember how Keith had been such a gentleman until you got married? Like Dr. Jekyll and Mr. Hyde.

She squeezed her eyes shut, the click of the door closing indicating he was gone from the room. But not from her thoughts—or her heart.

* * *

Josiah watched Robbie help Ella put up the tent in his backyard. The sight of them working together was beautiful to see. After hearing about Ella's ex-husband, he admired her even more. But he worried that he had too much baggage to be the right man for her. She needed someone who didn't have occasional panic attacks, who didn't wake up soaked in sweat in the middle of the night from a nightmare, who was afraid to ever give his heart to another.

"Mom, you also forgot to tie the poles together at the top. If you don't, it might collapse on you."

After following her son's instruction, Ella moved back from the tent. "Is this what you mean?"

"Yup. Good job." Robbie crawled inside, then poked his head out as Ella made her way to Josiah. "Are we going to your friend's to pick out a puppy?"

"Yes, but he wants to keep the puppies another week before you can take your choice home."

"Aw, I was hoping he could come home with me."

Ella placed her hands on her waist. "Young man, we are not going to get a puppy until we're back in our own home."

For a few seconds Robbie pouted, then his eyes lit up, and he grinned. "But I can choose today, and he won't be sold to someone else?"

"Yes. He'll hold him until you can take him home." Josiah began disassembling the tent.

"Even if it's weeks?"

"Yes. Now help me pack this tent up so we can go."

"I'm going in to get our lunch. We'll have a picnic out here first. I don't know about you two, but I'm starved."

While Ella strolled toward the deck, Josiah glanced

over his shoulder at her. He couldn't stop thinking about Ella's past. How could a man treat his wife like that? What kind of man was he? He thought about the bullies he'd encountered in his life, and anger festered in the pit of his stomach—the same kind he'd endured while held captive.

"Josiah?"

He looked at Robbie. "Yes?"

"Can Buddy go with us? He might want to see his puppies."

"Sure."

"Does your friend have Alaskan huskies, too?"

"No. Only a couple of German shepherds right now. Why?"

"I want to be a musher in the Iditarod Race when I'm old enough."

"Maybe next spring we can see the race end in Nome." Josiah finished stuffing the tent into its bag, spying Ella heading toward them, her arms full with the food hamper, jug and blanket. "Go help your mom while I put this away."

Robbie hopped up and raced toward his mother, taking the jug from her.

"Stay, Buddy," Josiah said.

His dog's ears perked forward, and he remained still while Josiah carried the camping equipment to the storage building. Inside he paused, realizing that in a short time he'd grown accustomed to having Ella and Robbie here. He cared about them—more than he should. It would be quiet when they left.

A bark, then another one, echoed through the air. He poked his head out of the shed and saw Sadie trying to get Buddy to play. But his German shepherd stayed where he was told to. Buddy had been so good for him at a rough time in his life. The puppy would be good for Robbie, too.

"Lunch," Ella said as she spread a blanket over the grass.

Josiah's stomach rumbled, and he hurried from the storage shed. Robbie plopped down on the cover, reaching toward Buddy and scratching him behind his ears.

"Play, Buddy." Josiah sat on the blanket next to the basket.

On the other side of the food hamper, Ella removed the roast-beef sandwiches. "You have to tell him to play?"

"After I give him a working command like stay, saying *play* is my way of telling him he has free time now."

This time when Sadie barked, Buddy ran after her.

Robbie rubbed his hands together. "I can't wait until I teach my dog that."

"It takes a long time and a lot of patience to have a working relationship with a dog, especially if you want one that does search and rescue. The more we work together, the more in tune we are."

"I can do that, too."

After Ella blessed the food, Robbie grabbed a sandwich and began eating. Josiah smiled, watching the boy stuff the food into his mouth and wash it down with gulps of lemonade.

Five minutes later, Robbie jumped up. "I'm gonna play with Sadie and Buddy. I haven't thrown the tennis ball for them today."

Josiah stared at the two dogs and Robbie. "Buddy and Sadie aren't going to know what to do once your son leaves here."

"They've been good for him. Helped take his mind off Foster."

"I was talking with Alex this morning before she left for the store. She suggested camping on one of the islands. She's been wanting to try out some new equipment."

"That sounds great. I haven't gone to any of the islands off Alaska."

"I'm going to check around to see what would be fun and adventurous."

Both of her eyebrows hiked up. "Adventurous?"

"Robbie told me he wants to have an adventure. Hunt animals but not shoot them. He said he has a camera. He wants to take pictures."

"Shooting photographs, not bullets, is fine by me."

"I thought it would be a good time to teach him about being in the wilderness and how to act around the various animals."

"I could learn that, too," she said with a chuckle. "I freaked out when I saw the bear prints in the park. You didn't. I've heard animals can smell fear."

"I'm going to make you into an outdoorswoman before this is over with. That's one of the beautiful things about Alaska. We're the last frontier in the United States." Josiah took a sip of his drink. "Have you talked to David today?"

"No. When I left the search for Seth, he told me he didn't want to hear from me until Sunday. This was my time off. He said he wouldn't answer my call."

"That sounds like him. I haven't heard yet when the postponed training session will be held."

"He wanted to wait and see if Foster is caught. I think he's worried the man will try to take another child."

Ella busied herself putting the trash and bag of chips back into the food hamper. "Has Thomas called with an update?"

"Right before I came out here to demonstrate the camping equipment. And before you say anything, I was going to tell you when Robbie wasn't around." He continued when Ella looked at him, "He dumped the car he took in Girdwood and has stolen another one."

"Where?"

"South Anchorage. The police are tightening the noose, so to speak. Watching traffic cams, keeping a close eye out for any missing vehicles. I don't think it will be long before he's caught."

Ella scanned the yard, her gaze zeroing in on the woods at the back of his property. She shivered. "What if he's back there watching us right now?"

"Not possible without Buddy and Sadie knowing. They guard this property well."

"I knew I should have gotten a big dog when we first came to Anchorage. Foster would never have gotten into my backyard that night, but back then I didn't even know if I would be staying."

"No one should have to live in fear." He could remember each day he was a prisoner, wondering if it was his last one. After a while, he'd become numb to the fear.

"I've forgotten what it's like not to be afraid, but over the years the more I've learned to turn it over to the Lord, the better I've been able to handle it…except last night."

Josiah covered her hand on the food hamper handle. "With good reason. We all have moments of vulnerability."

"Robbie doesn't know most of what I told you last night. In fact, very few people do."

"He won't learn it from me. It's not my story to tell."

"What is *your* story, Josiah?"

"Boring and dull."

"Josiah, can we go now?" Robbie shouted as he tossed the tennis ball for Sadie.

"He lasted longer than I thought he would." Ella picked up the blanket and folded it.

"Let's go." Josiah carried the food hamper toward the house, thankful for Robbie's timely interruption.

Ella's son said goodbye to Sadie and ran toward the deck with Buddy at his side. "I'll get his leash."

Josiah set the basket on the kitchen counter for Linda and walked into the hallway. "I need to get my keys. Meet you two at the truck."

As he climbed the stairs, he glimpsed Robbie leading Buddy toward the kitchen. In a short time, he'd come to feel as though Ella and Robbie belonged here. He'd miss them when they returned to their own house.

More than he realized.

"Okay, David, I'll put the training session on my calendar for that Saturday." Josiah reclined in his desk chair in his home office. "Do you want me to tell Ella, or are you going to?"

"I've been avoiding talking to her. Every time I do, she asks a ton of questions about what's going on with Northern Frontier and when she can return to work." A heavy sigh came through the line. "I'll call her. I think I have an idea how she can work from your house and get most of her duties done, if you're okay with it."

"Sure. She's been talking about work more and more

the past few days and keeps checking the news to see if Foster has been found. That sighting yesterday got her excited, but so far nothing has come of it. I'll keep you informed with what's happening with Ella." Josiah hated seeing disappointment on her face. She tried to hide it, especially for Robbie, but he always saw a glimpse when she didn't think anyone was looking. This was wearing her down.

He swiveled his chair around to stare out the window. Gray sheets of rain fell from the sky. It was a dreary day. Most of the time, when he wasn't working, he, Robbie and Ella were outside enjoying the outdoors. The last thing he'd taught them about camping was how to make a fire without the benefit of a lighter or matches. Robbie learned right away. Ella was a whole different story. They would starve if they depended on her to make the fire.

Suddenly his cell phone rang. He saw that it was Thomas and quickly picked it up. "I hope this is good news."

"It's about Foster."

NINE

Robbie sat in front of the window in the den with his face flat up against the glass. "Mom, it's been raining *all* day. When is it gonna stop? Buddy is bored and wants me to throw the ball for him." He spun around and grinned. "I've got an idea. What if I throw the ball down the upstairs hall? It's long and—"

Ella held her hand up. "You will *not* do that, and if you do, you'll be grounded. You think this is boring. Wait until you're by yourself the rest of the day."

He faced the window again and resumed his staring contest with the rainy day.

She wasn't going to admit to Robbie that she was bored, too. The bleak grayness reflected her mood. The rain had been falling for the past twenty-four hours. Josiah had been working a lot in his home office, which she couldn't begrudge him because he'd rearranged his life to protect her and Robbie. But she missed doing activities with him, and even talking with him. Once she'd opened up about Keith, a deluge had begun. She finally had someone to confide in. She'd felt as though she'd been released from a prison of silence.

Robbie glanced at Buddy. "I'm bored, too."

Ella pressed her lips together. All his toys and books were at their house. Maybe Josiah could take them home so Robbie could get some. She started to say something to her son when her cell phone rang.

"Hi, David. Josiah told me you had an incident you and some of the others helped with a couple of days ago. How did it turn out?"

"Two people died in a plane crash not far from Fairbanks. Pilot error. I'm calling to find out if you'd like to work from home next week or take another vacation week. I think we can set up a temporary office at Josiah and Alex's house. There are some funding reports that are due soon, but if I need to, I can explain they'll be a little late."

"No. I can get them done. You can forward calls to the main number here. It can work. I just need to ask Josiah if it's all right."

"It is. I called him a few minutes ago."

"Good." Ella looked over at what Robbie was doing. He was still at his post at the window.

"I'll come over tomorrow afternoon with what you'll need," David told her.

When Ella disconnected the call, she walked over to her son and settled her hand on his shoulder. "Hon, I think we need to get a few of your toys and games from our house. The forecast is for rain through tomorrow, if not longer."

Robbie hugged her. "That would be great! Do you think Josiah would be okay with it?"

Just then, Josiah came into the den and Buddy greeted him. "Yes, I am. We should have done that in the beginning. Especially for days like this when I'm stuck working and the weather isn't cooperating."

Her son punched the air. "Yes!"

Josiah smiled at Robbie. "We'll leave in a minute. Linda told me she needed a cookie taster. Do you want the job?"

"What kind?"

"Chocolate chip."

"I can do it," Robbie said as he raced from the room with Buddy on his heels.

Ella drew in a deep breath. "Nothing beats that smell. I may have to apply to be Linda's taster, too."

"Before you do, I have something to tell you about Foster."

"You talked with Thomas?"

He nodded. "Last night Foster was spotted at Big Lake by a man who tried to stop him. Foster knocked the guy out, then tied him up. By the time the man was found and reported it, Foster had been gone for twelve hours. They suspect he's heading into the backcountry."

"So he somehow made his way from Girdwood to Big Lake unseen by the authorities."

"The vehicle he was last reported driving has been found. They aren't sure what he's driving now."

She hadn't prepared herself enough for the fact that Foster might never be caught. She couldn't stay at the estate forever. Maybe she would have to leave Alaska and the friends she'd made, not because of her ex-husband, but because of Foster. She didn't want to feel like a prisoner again and certainly didn't want it for her son.

"From the encounter at Big Lake, the police now know Foster has altered his appearance, and has sent out an updated sketch as well as possible variations."

"What does he look like now?"

"Here." Josiah gave her his cell phone.

"Blond hair cut short, no beard, glasses." She could remember when she'd changed her appearance to get away from Keith. It had worked. She prayed Foster's new look didn't work as well for him.

"Mom, can we go now?" Robbie entered the den with a half-eaten chocolate-chip cookie in his hand.

Josiah turned toward her son. "Yes. I'm finished for the day. You'll have to show me your stuff."

"Can I bring it all?"

"Robbie! We are not packing up your room to bring here. You get to pick five or six things you want."

"Mom, that isn't much. It'll be hard to decide."

"But I'm confident you'll be able to do it."

Robbie pouted. "I'm glad you are. I'm not."

Josiah clasped his shoulder. "I'll help. Let's go. Linda said dinner would be ready in an hour."

"And she let Robbie have some cookies?"

"Only one," Robbie said and popped the last bit into his mouth. "She told me I could have more later." He headed toward the garage off the kitchen. "Can Buddy come, too?"

Ella followed her son with Josiah a few steps behind her. "Buddy has been with you every waking moment today. Let's give him time to rest." There was no way the dog had been getting his usual amount of sleep.

Fifteen minutes later, Josiah pulled into her driveway. She hadn't been home for over a week. "Remember, no more than six items. We aren't moving into the estate, just visiting. And we don't have a lot of time."

"Yeah. Alex has a date." Josiah climbed from his truck.

Curious, Ella hopped from the cab and hurried after Josiah. "With who? I didn't know she was dating anyone."

Josiah chuckled. "Neither did I. Honestly, I think

this is a business date." While Robbie ran ahead to the porch, he leaned close to Ella and whispered, "Trust me. She isn't serious. She prefers being single."

"I certainly understand that." Ella dug into her purse and withdrew her key, then opened the front door.

Josiah clasped her arm, stopping her from going inside, while Robbie darted across the threshold. "Not all men are like your ex-husband. Alex was happily married for five years."

"I'm glad," Ella responded, then she turned and called out to Robbie, "Wait up."

Josiah moved past Ella and Robbie. "Let me do a quick walk-through first."

Her son scuffed his tennis shoes against the floor while Josiah checked the house. When the sound of Josiah's footsteps returning to the foyer indicated he'd finished, Robbie ran toward the hallway, leading to the bedrooms.

"He's done. I need all my time to make some serious decisions about what I'm gonna take." Passing Josiah, Robbie disappeared around the corner.

"If I don't supervise, he'll manage somehow to bring his whole toy chest. His school backpack is hanging on a peg in the garage." She heard a slamming sound coming from Robbie's room. "Will you get it while I corral my son?"

"Yeah, sure."

Something else thumped to the floor. She hurried to his bedroom. When she stepped into the entrance, he was looking through a drawer and suddenly plucked a set of action figures out of it then tossed them on the bed.

"That's one." Robbie went to his closet and started to open it.

"That's seven action figures. That's seven items, so…" Something was wrong here. The overhead light was on. She shifted her attention to the window with the blackout shade pulled down. She hadn't left it that way. Quickly she pulled it up. Her gaze widened at the sight of the window ajar a few inches. "Don't open the closet."

Josiah walked through the living room and dining room into the kitchen. He paused at the sink window and looked outside. The rain had let up as they drove here, but now it was starting to come down hard again. He continued his trek to the garage and stepped down into it. Ella's black Jeep Wrangler was parked close to the door, but on the other side was a white Honda.

The hairs on the back of his neck stood up. He pivoted toward the house. Something solid came down on his head. He crumpled to the concrete floor.

As Robbie flung his closet door open, he swiveled around. "Why not? Some of my favorite toys are in there."

Expecting someone to come charging out, Ella frantically searched for something to use as a weapon. When no one came out, with Robbie's baseball bat in hand, she whispered, "Get behind me," then inched forward.

Using the wooden stick, she poked behind the clothes hanging up. "Robbie, did you open your window and forget to close it?" She came out of the closet.

His wide gaze riveted to her. He shook his head, the color washing from his face.

"Stay behind me. Someone might be in the house."

"But Josiah checked each room."

He wouldn't have seen the open window because the

shade was pulled down. Her shaky hand withdrew her cell phone from her pocket. She found Thomas's number and punched it as she crept down the hall to the bathroom. "Thomas, this is Ella. Josiah brought us to our house to get some toys. I think someone has been here. May still be here." Her whispery voice rasped from her throat.

"Where's Josiah?"

"In the garage." Ella checked behind the shower curtain in the bathroom.

"Get him and get out of there. I'm on my way."

As she hung up, a crashing sound came from the garage reverberating through the house. Josiah! If she could get to her purse on the hallway table, she could get her gun.

"Robbie, lock the bathroom door and don't open it unless it's me or Josiah. Okay?"

Fear filled his face. He nodded.

"You'll be all right. The police are on their way."

She waited a couple of heartbeats until her son clicked the lock in place, then she snuck toward the foyer to get her Glock. One of the first things she'd done after she'd left her husband was learn to shoot a gun to protect herself.

A large man, his back to Josiah, headed for the door into the house. Josiah fought to keep conscious. If he didn't, Robbie would be kidnapped. He didn't want him to be taken prisoner. Flashes of his own captivity swamped him for a few seconds. He shut down his emotions and went into combat mode.

He struggled to his feet, steadying himself while looking around for a weapon. There was nothing within reach. With his head pounding, he moved forward as the large man glanced over his shoulder at him.

Foster spun around and came toward him like the grizzly Robbie had called him. Josiah charged the man, ramming his left shoulder into Foster's chest. He slammed back against the wall, the shuddering sound resonating like a shock wave through the garage. The man wound his arm around Josiah and squeezed. His breath leaving his lungs, he kicked Foster, then kneed him as Josiah wrestled to loosen the arms about his torso. Again he struck Foster with the toe of his boot.

The hulking man shoved away from the wall and drove Josiah into Ella's car, swooshing out what little air remained in his lungs. Trapped between the hood and Foster, Josiah pounded his fists into the man's back, gasping for oxygen. Dizziness sapped what strength he had left.

The sounds of fighting coming from the garage sent Ella's heartbeat racing as she neared the open door. With sweaty hands, she held a baseball bat in one hand and her gun in the other. At the threshold she peered around the door frame while preparing to help Josiah. Foster outweighed him by at least fifty pounds from the pictures she'd seen of the man.

Her heartbeat thudded against her rib cage as she spied Foster pinning Josiah against her car. Crushing him.

She had to do something, but she couldn't shoot Foster. She might hit Josiah, too. Fortifying herself with a deep breath, she laid her gun on the counter nearby and gripped the baseball bat with both hands.

The police are on the way. I can do this.

She crept toward the pair and raised the bat.

Foster looked back, his dark eyes boring into her.

He started to turn toward her.

She brought the bat down on his shoulder. The first blow stunned him, but he kept turning. She swung the bat again, connecting with the side of his head. The hulk teetered for a few seconds, then collapsed to the floor.

She hurried to Josiah. Drawing in deep gulps of air, he slid down the side of the car.

He reached toward Foster and felt for a pulse. "He's alive. You need to call the police."

"I already did. How do you feel?"

"I think he cracked a rib. Robbie had it right. He's like a grizzly bear even without all the facial hair he used to have." With each breath, Josiah winced.

Ella gave him the bat. "Hit him if he moves. I left my gun in the kitchen."

She hurried inside, snatched it from the counter and returned to the garage. The sight of the pain on Josiah's face tore at her. "I'm calling an ambulance."

"No. I've had worse injuries. After the police leave, we'll go to the emergency room, but I'm not leaving you and Robbie until Foster is hauled away." Laying the bat on the floor, he held out his hand. "I'll trade you."

"I know how to shoot," she said as she passed him the gun. "But I'm not going to argue with an injured man."

"Where's Robbie?"

"Locked in the bathroom."

The sight of red lights flashing across the walls prompted Ella to push the button to raise the garage door.

"I'll take care of this. Go check on Robbie." Josiah pushed to his feet using the car as support.

Ella spied Thomas walking up the driveway. She hurried into the house to let Robbie know everything was all right and to make sure he didn't see Foster. The man had already traumatized her son enough.

"Robbie, this is Mom. You can come out now."

The lock clicked, and Robbie swung the door wide and rushed into her arms. "I was so scared. I..." Sobs drowned out the rest of his words.

She hugged him to her. When he quieted, she knelt and clasped his arm. "Honey, the police will take Foster away. We're safe. And so is Josiah. We have no reason to be afraid anymore."

Tears ran down his cheeks unchecked. "I didn't know—" he gasped for air "—what was going on."

"Foster attacked Josiah in the garage. He must have been out there waiting. The important part is that he'll be put away for a long time."

"Where Josiah?"

"He's with the police, but you and I are going to sit in the living room and wait until Foster is hauled away. I'm sure the police will want to talk to both of us."

"Foster wasn't in the house?"

"No, the garage." She didn't want him to know that Foster had parked a car in the garage or that in all likelihood he'd been in their house—maybe for hours. She'd have to deal with that, but she didn't want Robbie to.

"But my window was opened?"

She wouldn't lie to her son, but she would try to play down the fact he was inside at some time. "Yes. He might have gotten in that way or another way. We'll let the police figure that out. Let's concentrate on the fact he has finally been caught and we can return home."

"I don't want to," Robbie cried out and ran into the bathroom, locking the door.

"Honey, open up please." She tried turning the knob, hoping she was wrong about the lock. She wasn't.

"Go away. I'm safe in here."

Looking up and down the hallway produced no great ideas of how to get her son out of the bathroom. There was a part of her that wanted to hide in there with him. "Please, sweetie. You're safe now. Come out."

Out of the corner of her eye, she glimpsed movement and reacted. Hands fisted, she rotated as though she would stop anyone from getting to her son. When she saw it was Josiah and Thomas, she sank against the door. The trembling started in her fingers and quickly spread throughout her body.

Josiah strode to her and started to pull her to him. "Okay?"

Remembering his ribs, she sidled away. "I'm okay. You aren't. I need to get you to the hospital."

"Not until I know Robbie is all right. Let me talk to him while Thomas interviews you."

"Thanks." She moved away while Josiah knocked on the door.

"Robbie, this is Josiah. Can I come in and talk to you?"

Ella walked toward Thomas at the end of the hall, praying that Robbie would let Josiah in.

Silence ruled for a long moment.

"Robbie, I'll only stay as long as you want." Josiah's voice softened, conveying concern.

Her son unlocked the door and slowly opened it. Ella stepped out of view. She'd wanted to be the one who comforted her child, but if she couldn't, then she thanked the Lord Josiah was here to help Robbie deal with everything.

Thomas touched her elbow, drawing her attention to him. "Let's go in the living room. This whole situation has been tough for Robbie, but also for you, Ella."

She hugged her arms to her chest and followed Thomas. When she sank onto the couch, the police detective sat in a chair across from her. In the distance she heard a siren. "Is that an ambulance for Foster?"

"Yes. While I was in the garage, he regained consciousness but was groggy. Don't worry. A team of police officers will be guarding him until we get him to the jail. He won't get away from us. I promise." Controlled anger hardened his voice. "He won't terrorize you or any other families again."

As her adrenaline subsided, a chill gave her goose bumps from the top of her head to her toes. "I knew something was wrong when I saw Robbie's blackout shade down and his window cracked open. Now that I think about it, the bed was rumpled." She shivered, picturing Foster lying on it, waiting for her son. "What if he'd been in the closet rather than the garage? Josiah had a hard time fighting him off. I can't imagine me trying."

"You stopped him, though, with quick and calm thinking. Why don't you tell me everything from when you arrived at the house?"

Ella peered toward the hallway, then started from the beginning, but the whole time her thoughts dwelled on Robbie and Josiah in the bathroom.

Robbie sat on the edge of the bathtub while Josiah leaned against the counter across from him, wincing when he moved the wrong way and a stab of pain pierced his chest. The boy stared at the tile floor, his hands gripping the tub edge so tightly his fingertips were red.

"I watched the police take Foster away. He can't hurt you, partner."

Ella's son didn't look up or say a word.

Not sure exactly how to comfort the child, Josiah cleared his throat. He'd had little interaction with kids in the past. He plowed his fingers through his hair, trying to think of something to say that would help Robbie.

"You and your mom are safe now."

The boy lifted his head, his eyes shiny with unshed tears.

"I promise."

"He...he was in my...house." Robbie shuddered.

Josiah squatted in front of the child. "He isn't now and won't be in the future. He'll go to prison for a long time."

"He scared Mom."

"I know, but she's all right. You saw her."

"He scared Mom like my..." Robbie's eyes widened, and he clamped his hand over his mouth.

Dad? Given what Ella had told him about her ex-husband, Robbie had probably been schooled not to say a word about his past. "But you two are all right now. That's what is important."

"But I was so scared. I was a crybaby. I need to be big and strong for Mom."

"There's nothing wrong with being afraid. Fear is an emotion we have to help us deal with certain situations. I've known people who were fearless, and they ended up hurting themselves and others. Fear makes us consider all possible answers to a problem, then hopefully we pick the best solution rather than just reacting."

"Have you ever been afraid?"

"Yes. I was today. I didn't want Foster to hurt you or your mom."

Robbie straightened. "He's a bad man."

"He's done some bad things, and he will pay for that. There are consequences to our actions."

"Like when me and my friends left camp when we weren't supposed to?"

Josiah nodded. "Are you ready to go see your mom now? She's worried about you."

"Yes."

Josiah put his hand on the edge of the counter and struggled to his feet. The sharp pain sliced through his chest. He needed to go to the hospital.

But at least he'd reassured Robbie that he was safe.

TEN

"Mom, is Josiah gonna hafta stay in the hospital tonight?" Robbie looked up from the paper he was drawing on in the waiting room of the emergency room.

"I don't know. We should hear something soon." Ella's gaze strayed to the entrance, as it had so often done in the past hour since Josiah had been taken to see a doctor. The minutes since then had passed agonizingly slowly. He was hurt because of her. She knew how painful a broken or even cracked rib could be.

"How come Alex isn't here?"

"Josiah made me promise not to call her, but if he's admitted, I will."

"You can't break a promise to him."

"Okay, you're right. I'll make sure he calls his sister. She needs to know if he's in the hospital."

"And Buddy."

She smiled. "Yeah, Buddy, too."

Robbie went back to making a picture for Josiah while she kept looking toward the doorway. Worry twisted her stomach into knots.

Ten minutes later, Josiah appeared in the doorway,

looking worn out but relieved. One corner of his mouth lifted. "Ready to get out of here?"

Robbie jumped to his feet, grabbed his work of art and rushed to Josiah. "I made you a picture."

While he looked at the drawing, she bridged the distance between them. "He's been working the past half hour on it."

He tousled her son's hair. "You never told me you could draw like this. Buddy is going to love this."

"I was afraid you'd hafta stay here and you wouldn't get to see Buddy."

"Let me see." Ella stepped next to Josiah. "He wouldn't show me while he was working."

Josiah held a picture of him with Buddy sitting beside him.

"I still have to put in a few more trees. It's a drawing of you at Kincaid Park."

"Tell you what. I'll loan it to you to finish, but I want it back when you're through." Josiah's voice grew huskier as he spoke. "No one has ever made me a gift like that." He swallowed hard. "Let's go. I hate hospitals."

"Me, too." Robbie took Josiah's hand. "I had to visit Mom in the hospital once, and it scared me."

On the other side of Josiah, Ella leaned forward. "Robbie, they fixed me up. Just like they did Josiah. You love visiting Bree at the clinic. Hospitals are just bigger clinics."

Outside Ella stopped. "You two stay here. I'll bring your truck around."

"I can walk—"

She narrowed her gaze on him, halting Josiah's words. "Let me take care of you for once. Keys, please." She held out her palm flat.

"Yes, ma'am." He tossed her the keys to the F-150. "Just remember a man and his truck have a special bond."

She laughed as she left Josiah and Robbie at the entrance to the emergency room. With the capture of Foster, she felt a weight lifted from her shoulders. No more hiding. No more watching over her shoulder.

Twenty minutes later, she drove the truck into the garage at Josiah's estate. She glanced over at him, the side of his head resting against the passenger window, his eyelids half-closed. "Home sweet home."

"Buddy's probably worried. I'll let him know you're okay." Robbie climbed from the backseat and headed for the door into the house.

"Josiah, do you need me to help you inside?"

He perked up. "No, I can make it on my own. They gave me something for the pain, and I believe it's starting to take effect."

"Good. You need rest."

"Will you do me a favor?"

"Yes, of course."

"Don't go home until tomorrow. I think it would be a good thing if Robbie had Buddy with him when he goes back home for the first time after Foster was caught."

"Sure. It's late anyway, and per your request I didn't tell Alex about your being hurt. Before we go inside, tell me what the doctor said about your injuries."

"A couple of bruised ribs and a knot on my head. Time will take care of everything. I'll be fine soon."

"Yeah, you're one tough guy. It's okay to admit it hurts."

"Was Keith the reason you were in the hospital?"

"Oh, no, you don't. Today is about you and your injuries. Not mine. I'm not going to talk about my past right now."

"I respect that." Josiah glanced toward the house. "I think your son is waiting for us to come in."

Sitting next to Robbie, Buddy barked.

"I think your dog needs to make sure you're all right." Ella opened the driver's door, hopped down and started to round the hood to help Josiah whether he wanted it or not. She owed him so much.

But he eased out of the cab before she could get to him, a grimace on his face.

"I think I remember someone I know telling me it's okay to accept help." Ella closed the space between them.

"I'm putting up a brave front for Robbie and Buddy."

"Sure." She walked next to Josiah and watched as he put on a brave front—no doubt for Robbie. She'd done that herself in the past.

At the door, Robbie stepped to the side to let them into the house. "Buddy missed me badly. So did Sadie."

"Let's go upstairs. You need to rest," Ella said to Josiah, proceeding through the kitchen toward the foyer. "Now that you're home, can I tell Alex, Linda and Harry what happened to you?"

"Yes, I can't hide much from Alex. The twin thing."

"Is there really something to that?"

"Yup, at least with me and Alex there is."

Robbie and Buddy followed behind them to the second floor.

At his bedroom door, Josiah turned toward them. "I'm okay. I'm going to bed. I don't need a nurse."

Ella frowned. He didn't see his face each time a certain movement caused him pain.

Josiah's eyes softened. "I'll be fine. Promise." He opened his door and started inside.

"Wait," Robbie said. "You need Buddy tonight. I don't. Foster has been caught." Robbie waved his hand toward the room. "Go, Buddy."

When Buddy didn't follow the command, Josiah ruffled Robbie's hair. "Thanks." Then to his German shepherd, he said, "Come."

When the bedroom door shut, Ella placed her hand on her son's shoulder. "That must have been hard for you."

"Yup, but Buddy is his dog." He stood up taller. "I'm fine. Josiah isn't."

"It's past your bedtime. You need to get your sleep, too. Tomorrow we go back home and get our normal lives back."

"But I don't want to leave."

"You'll get your own dog soon and be busy taking care of him."

Robbie's face brightened. "And training him. When can I go get him?"

"Maybe sometime next week. I'll be in to say goodnight in a few moments."

Ella slipped inside her bedroom and sank onto the bed, the day's events flooding her mind finally. She'd managed to hold them at bay while talking to the police and making sure Josiah was all right, but now the implications of what had occurred earlier deluged her. Her body shook. She hugged herself trying to control the tremors rocking her, but it didn't stop them.

Today could have ended so badly.

Thank You, Lord. Without You, I couldn't have done half the things I've had to do these past four years.

* * *

While watching Robbie play with Buddy and Sadie in the backyard, Ella sipped her coffee on Josiah and Alex's deck. Earlier she'd called David and let him know she was returning to work the next day. He'd already heard from Thomas about what had happened at her house. She was glad she didn't have to go into details. She just wanted to put Foster behind her and move on. Today she'd need to find a place for Robbie to stay while she was at the Northern Frontier office.

The sound of footsteps invaded her thoughts.

Alex sat in the chair next to her. "I really need this coffee. Thanks for putting a note on my bedroom door about Josiah. I should wring his neck for keeping the fact he went to the hospital from me."

"I tried to convince him I should call you. But he wanted you to enjoy yourself since there really wasn't anything you could do."

"Sometimes my brother exasperates me."

"Just sometimes?"

Alex laughed. "He keeps hoping I'll meet another man and marry again. That isn't going to happen. I had a beautiful marriage and five glorious years. I don't see anyone taking my husband's place. He may be gone, but he still lives in my heart."

Ella had wanted that so much and had thought Keith was the man for her. Now she felt the same way Alex did about marrying again, but for the opposite reason. "You don't get lonely?"

"No. I have friends and my business. Those keep me busy. I don't have time for a man. How about you?"

"I have all those things and my son. I have a fulfilling life." But as Ella said that, something was different than before. She hadn't gotten to know Josiah until recently. Even if he could make her forget the nightmare of her marriage, she didn't plan to make the same mistake twice. She hoped Josiah and her could be good friends. He was wonderful for Robbie. But anything beyond that wasn't possible.

"I'm going to miss you two after today. I've enjoyed getting to know you. And I know Josiah has. You've made him laugh and smile more than I've seen in a long time."

"Did something happen to him?" Ella stopped herself from asking anything further. If she ever learned about his past, he should be the one to tell her. She knew little about him other than that he grew up in Alaska. There were too many years unaccounted for before and after he was a US Marine.

"He doesn't talk about it."

"I can understand. The past is the past."

"I like you a lot. I hope one day he'll share his past with you."

Her curiosity was aroused. Just because she'd shared her past completely with him didn't mean he had to do so, but she'd hoped he would trust her enough to confide in her.

"I hope you two aren't conspiring." Josiah, dressed in jeans and a long-sleeved T-shirt, joined them and took the seat on the other side of Ella.

"Yes, because you've been a bad brother. Next time you go to the emergency room, you better call me or have someone else let me know. If you don't, you're going to rue the day you made that decision." Her voice was calm and quiet, yet as Alex sipped her coffee, her gaze drilled into Josiah.

"I tried to tell him yesterday." Ella shot him a look of satisfaction.

"I see. You are ganging up on me. I'm injured. I need your sympathy." A twinkle danced in his eyes as he carefully leaned back in the lounger, his legs stretched out in front of him.

Robbie raced toward the deck with the two dogs close by. "You're up. How are you?"

Josiah threw Ella and Alex an irritated glance. "At least Robbie cares. Yes, I'm okay."

"Great. Then you can come show me some more commands. I'm getting my puppy this week."

"That's good. I'll be out there in a sec."

Robbie ran back to the middle of the yard and flung the Frisbee for Buddy while Josiah struggled out of his lounger. He winced.

"It's okay to admit you're in pain." Ella hated seeing him like that.

"Nope. I'm not letting it get the best of me. Life goes on."

Slowly Josiah made his way toward her son.

"That's his motto. Mind over matter."

"Has he been injured a lot?"

Alex's forehead scrunched. "Yes, but he doesn't talk about it."

Ella watched him interact with Robbie. She and Josiah were similar in a lot of ways—even about keeping secrets.

"Are you sure you don't want me to leave Buddy here tonight?" Josiah sat on Ella's couch with his German shepherd at his feet later that evening.

She settled next to Josiah. "Robbie slept without him

last night at your house. He should be okay. We're going after work on Wednesday to get the puppy he picked out."

"Does he have a name for him yet?"

"Sam."

"Where did that name come from?"

"He didn't know. It just popped into his head when he saw him at the breeder's house last week."

"Is everything set for you going back to work tomorrow?"

"Yes. My neighbor will watch him for me. I loved staying at your place and we both know Robbie did, but it feels good to be home and back to my normal life."

"The vacation is over," Josiah said with a chuckle.

"If the past week was a vacation, I never want to go on another one. Loved the company but not the reason for being there."

Josiah sobered. "Yeah, a normal life is good, but I still owe Robbie a camping trip."

"That would be nice. Now, that would be a real vacation without a lunatic coming after us."

"That's what I was thinking. I already have one of the islands picked out."

She clasped his hand and cupped it between hers. "You don't have to. Robbie and I have taken up too much of your time." She needed to put some distance between them before she fell in love with him. *I have to listen to my head, not my heart.*

"First, I want to. Second, I promised Robbie and third, I enjoy camping and sharing the experience with others. I've even persuaded Alex to take some time off from work, which is a feat in itself, to join us."

Ella rubbed her fingers across the back of his hand. "What about your injuries?"

"We'll wait until they're better. Thankfully my threshold for pain is high."

"I'm just glad you were here when Foster decided to hide out in my house." She refused to think what would have happened if he hadn't been there.

"So is Thomas. He called today to tell me we've made his life a little easier with the capture of Foster."

"It's always nice to accommodate the police. Although I can't believe Foster had the nerve to use my home as a hideout."

"He figured you weren't coming back as long as he was loose."

"How do you know that?"

"He told Thomas." Josiah rose slowly and carefully. "I'd better go. You have to get up early. You've been a woman of leisure for the past week, and it may take you a while to get used to your work routine again. Do you have someone to watch Robbie beyond tomorrow?"

"Yes, my neighbor insisted she would since she and her husband are back from their three-week trek through Alaska. Both of my neighbors on each side have been a good support system for me."

"Good." He headed for the front door.

Ella went out on the porch with him as the sun was starting to go down. "Thank you again for your help. With everything."

He turned toward her, a smile dimpling his cheeks. "My pleasure. We'll talk before you go to pick up Sam. I'd like to go with you." He inched closer.

"I'd like that." She tilted up her chin, so close to Josiah she could smell mint on his breath. She lifted her hand and cradled his cheek, wanting him to kiss her and yet hesitating to make the first move.

He bent toward her, his lips softly capturing hers. Then he pulled back. "I'd better leave."

No, don't. But she wouldn't say it out loud because he was right. It was better that he left now. She didn't know what to do about the feelings swirling around in her head concerning Josiah. She needed some space between them until she figured out how to be a friend and nothing more.

"Yes, you're right. Talk to you this week."

She waited on the porch until he drove away, thinking back to all that had occurred recently. Josiah had always been there in the center of the action. In that short time she'd become dependent on him. She'd vowed she would never feel that way about a man again. She wasn't a risk taker, although everything in her shouted that Josiah wasn't a risk.

She shook her head, trying to empty her thoughts of him. But she wasn't successful.

With a deep sigh, she pushed open the front door.

To find her son standing in the foyer looking into the living room, fear on his face.

He whirled around and flew at her. "I thought you'd left me alone or something."

"No, honey. I was saying goodbye to Josiah on the porch. Is something wrong?"

"I can't sleep. I tried really hard, Mom." His eyes filled with tears, and he bit his lower lip.

"That's okay. Sometimes it takes a while to fall asleep."

A tear ran down his face. "I'm scared. What if Foster escapes from jail?"

She smoothed his hair off his forehead. "He won't."

"He was in my bedroom."

"We don't know that for sure." Although she thought he had been, she didn't want to confirm it for Robbie.

"He must have opened my window. I didn't. You didn't."

"Well, he can't now. He has police officers guarding him, and he's behind bars."

"I miss Buddy. He made me feel safe."

"He wasn't with you last night."

"That's because Josiah needed him more, and I felt safe at his house."

"You love this house, and your room."

"I want to move to the other bedroom."

"It's smaller."

"I don't care. That man ruined my room for me."

Sadness enveloped Ella, and she wished she could turn back time. *Lord, please help Robbie. He shouldn't have to feel this fear at his age.*

"Will you sit with me while I fall asleep?"

"Of course."

He hugged her. "You're the best."

A few minutes later, Ella sat against the headboard in Robbie's room with her son cuddled up against her. For the first half hour, his eyes kept popping open to check she was still there. Then the next thirty minutes, they stayed closed, but her son twisted and turned. By the second hour, he finally calmed, and soon he fell asleep.

But Ella was wide-awake with no hope of going to bed anytime soon. Darkness shrouded her, and if it wouldn't have awakened her son, she would have turned on a light. She didn't want to take that chance. Like her son, she'd slept well at Josiah's. Now every sound outside spiked her heartbeat. Even staring at the window, she imagined Foster crawling through it and snatching Robbie from her arms.

With thoughts of Keith, it had taken her over a year in Anchorage before she'd gotten a good night's sleep. She was determined Foster wouldn't invade her peace— her son's. She searched her mind for something to think about that brought a feeling of safety, calm.

Josiah.

No doubt about it. She'd never met someone quite like him. She could talk to him about things she didn't with others. That still amazed her.

But a big part of his life was a mystery to her. He held a large part of himself back. She could never allow her heart to become involved. Could she?

Josiah sat at his desk in his home office. "I'll bring Buddy over this evening. He can stay the next two nights until you take Sam home. Do you think that will help Robbie sleep?"

"Thank you, Josiah. Are you sure?"

Hearing the relief in Ella's voice confirmed his decision, even though he'd awakened last night in a cold sweat. "Yes. It's only for a couple of nights. I'll be fine. Remember, you two had Buddy before." If he wasn't, he'd deal with it. He didn't want Robbie becoming so scared he couldn't sleep.

"You're a lifesaver, and I know Robbie will be thrilled. At least let me treat you to a dinner. I hope you'll be able to stay when you drop Buddy off."

"I'll make time in my busy schedule," Josiah said with a chuckle. "Since the doctor told me to rest and take it easy for two or three days, I've been working from home."

"Good thing you have an understanding boss. See you later."

After he hung up, Josiah leaned back in his chair and stared out the window at his backyard. Serene. Peaceful. And yet inside, he couldn't shake the memories of Foster's heavy weight pressing down on him, squeezing all the air from his lungs. The sensation of not being able to breathe had thrown him back to his time as a POW. The past two nights, his nightmares had returned, and Buddy had been there to wake him from the horrors he relived.

A tightness in his chest that had nothing to do with his bruised ribs spread. Before he could call Buddy, his German shepherd was in front of him, nudging his hand. Taking breaths as deep as was possible, he stroked his dog, thinking of his present life. Ella. Robbie. Slowly his panic subsided.

But would it tonight, without Buddy?

ELEVEN

Thursday evening, Ella inhaled a deep breath of the outdoorsy scent of the Russian Jack Springs Park. "It was a good idea to walk Buddy and Sam together. Sam is already responding to Buddy, and he's a great role model for our puppy."

"How was your first night with Sam?" Josiah walked beside her on the trail while Robbie held both leashes.

"Robbie insisted on Sam sleeping in his bed, and somehow there wasn't one accident—at least last night."

"So Robbie slept all right without Buddy?"

"Yes and thanks for the use of Buddy for a couple of nights." She slanted her head and assessed Josiah. He didn't look as tired today. Yesterday she'd wondered if he'd been getting the rest the doctor recommended. "How have you been sleeping with the bruised ribs?"

"When the doc told me to sleep on the side that's bruised, I thought he was crazy. But believe it or not, it actually is much better."

He didn't exactly answer her question, so she said, "I'm glad you're getting the rest he said would help you get better, because my son has already started bugging me about the camping trip."

"I'm adjusting, and over-the-counter pain meds are all I have to take now. I think we could look at the first weekend in August. That's only a couple of weeks away. I know how it is when you're a child and want to do something badly, but Sam should take his focus away. I'll come over after work and help him with the puppy."

"That'll be great. I appreciate it, and so does Robbie. You and Buddy are all he talks about." But what would happen to Josiah and Robbie's relationship if another woman entered his life? He deserved to be married and be a father. He was fantastic with her son.

"Is he going to be at the training session this weekend or staying with your neighbor?"

"He wants to be at the session, but this Saturday is all business for Northern Frontier. Now that it's safe, I need to focus on my job or David might fire me."

Josiah tossed his head back and laughed. "Are you kidding? He knows a great office manager when he sees one. You should hear him rave about you."

A blush heated her cheeks. "Enough, or I might get a big head and grow right out of my ball cap."

Josiah stopped on the path while Robbie let the dogs sniff a tree off the trail. "That's just it. You don't realize how good you are. Efficient. Caring. More organized than most people. Great with people. You remind me a lot of my sister."

She was growing uncomfortable with all his compliments and needed to change the subject fast. "Is she able to come camping with us?"

"Yes, I'm sure."

"Good, because I like her a lot, and it'll give us more time to get to know each other."

"She's looking forward to it. Our love of camping

as children is the reason we didn't sell Outdoor Alaska when our parents died. So it'll be good to get back to our roots. This camping trip will help us to see what new products work or don't."

"So this is a business trip?" The corners of her mouth twitched with the grin she was trying to contain.

"Not really. Not even for Alex. As much as she's a workaholic, she still sees the value in taking some time off."

"But you're not a workaholic?"

"Not like Alex. She's a diehard."

"I'm glad you aren't. There's more to life than just work."

"Believe me. I discovered that the hard…" His voice faded into silence. "We better catch up with Robbie. Sometimes it's hard to control two dogs at the same time."

Frustrated, she chewed on her bottom lip. She wanted to shout at Josiah, *Let me in!* Finally she stopped and blocked him on the path. "Why didn't you finish what you were saying?"

"Because I don't share my life with anyone. Some things are best left in the past." He skirted around her and increased his pace to catch up with Robbie.

At that moment, she realized he'd never really share his life with her. If it weren't for Robbie, she would put some distance between her and Josiah right away before she became even more invested in him. But it would break her son's heart. He'd never had a good male role model, and Josiah was quickly taking that position in Robbie's life.

That realization made her decide that after the camping trip she would have to find other role models for her son. Maybe through the Big Brothers program. She was afraid when Josiah moved on in his life, it would devastate Robbie.

"Mom, what's keeping you? I want to play on the playground before we leave."

There was no easy solution to her dilemma concerning Josiah and Robbie. She exhaled slowly. "I'm coming."

Ella came into the kitchen from her backyard and noticed Robbie hanging the phone up. "Who was that?"

He shrugged. "Wrong number, I guess."

"Josiah will be here soon. After Sam's training, we're going to Outdoor Alaska to get the camping equipment we need, so remember not to get dirty."

"Hurray! We leave in two days, and I need to practice putting up our tent."

"Only when I'm watching." She couldn't afford to buy a second tent if he ruined the first one.

"Sure, Mom. I wish you'd quit babying me. I know what I'm doing. Josiah taught me, remember?"

"True, but that was a couple of weeks ago." She'd tried to stay away from Josiah as much as possible when he came to help Robbie, but it wasn't easy when she saw him being more of a father than Keith had ever been.

"Mom, why can't Sam go with us?"

"We aren't taking the dogs. Linda and Harry will watch Sam. He'll have fun with Buddy and Sadie. I don't want to have to worry about your puppy when what we're doing is new to us."

"We're gonna be on an island. Sam couldn't go too far without meeting the Gulf of Alaska."

"What if we run into a bear? Do you want to worry about Sam doing something to get himself hurt?"

"Bears? I hadn't thought of that. Are there going to be many?"

"It's Alaska. The possibility of a bear encounter is part of living here. Remember that time the moose came down into our yard during the winter and ate our bushes? We live in a big city. That didn't stop the moose."

Robbie giggled. "I doubt much could stop a moose or a bear."

"It would take a lot. That's why you never confront one."

The doorbell chimes resonated through the house.

"That's Josiah. I'll get it," Robbie said as he rushed from the kitchen.

"Check before you open the door," she called after her son, but she doubted he heard her because two seconds later he admitted Josiah into the house, then began telling him about his day.

Ella smiled. Poor Josiah. Sometimes he couldn't get two words in.

When Josiah entered the kitchen with Robbie, he smiled at her, which sent goose bumps up and down her arms. "How was your day?"

"Fine. Just wrapping up the information about the search and rescue of a tourist in Katmai National Park."

"From what I heard, you all did good yesterday."

Robbie looked at Josiah. "Why didn't you go with Buddy?"

"The area where the tourist disappeared has a lot of bears. In the summer they are all over Brooks Camp and the surrounding area. Dogs and bears don't mix, and they prefer that K-9s not be used in the search, at least initially. The personnel working SAR missions will vary depending on where the person went missing and who the person is."

"Sam and I are ready." Robbie started for the kitchen door.

"Good. I'll be out back in a second." When her son left, Josiah moved to her. "Are we still on for the camping trip this weekend? I know Northern Frontier has been extra busy lately."

"That's normal for a summer with so many tourists around. Robbie is counting down the hours until we leave. David has insisted I go and not to worry about Northern Frontier. There are a lot of people who can step in temporarily. Do you still want to go?" Most of the searches were outside of Anchorage, and when that happened, she manned the phones at the office, coordinating and supporting David and the searchers. With her gone a lot because of her job, she hadn't seen Josiah as much as Robbie had. Josiah had ended up helping Robbie with the puppy at her neighbor's a few times.

Josiah stared out the window at her son playing with Sam. "Most definitely. Robbie is like a sponge. So eager to learn everything. His enthusiasm is contagious. It's good to be around him."

"Then it's still a go. Friday we leave."

Josiah went out to the backyard to start the puppy training. She stood at the sink and watched him and Robbie training Sam to obey simple commands. Her heart swelled at the sight. Robbie should have a father who cared about him.

Toward the end of the lesson, Ella went outside to remind them they still needed to go shopping at Outdoor Alaska.

* * *

As Josiah wrapped things up, he caught sight of Ella on the patio and waved. He'd tried to stay away from her after Foster's capture, but he kept being drawn back to her. And Robbie. The boy reminded him of how he'd been growing up. Eager to learn. Curious about everything. Robbie loved Alaska as much as he did. It was one big outdoor park with so much to offer.

"Are you guys ready to leave?" Ella asked as she crossed the yard to them.

"Yes. I can't wait to get my own tent." Robbie grinned from ear to ear, excitement bubbling out of him.

Josiah needed that. To find the joy in life that had been beaten out of him. To truly reconnect with God. "Let's take my truck. Your gear will easily fit in the back."

Rush-hour traffic had subsided, and he drove to the main store in less than fifteen minutes. The moment he entered, an employee approached to help them.

Josiah waved the man away. "Thanks, but I'll take care of this. I know where everything is." He'd been spending more time in the corporate offices and had lost touch with some of the day-to-day activities of the stores. Maybe he needed to become more involved.

"First we need to pick out a tent."

Robbie immediately went to an orange, brown and white dome tent. "I like this one."

Josiah smiled. "That's a good choice. Big enough for up to four people but not too big."

Ella's son beamed. "What's next?"

An hour later, Josiah pushed a cart toward the front while Ella had a second one. He got in line behind a woman with two kids. A large man, similar in build to Foster, came up behind Ella.

With Robbie next to him, Josiah put his hand on his shoulder. The boy had said little about Foster since the day they'd talked in the bathroom, but from the nightmares he'd had at first, Robbie still needed to talk about it. He, of all people, knew that took time. He wanted to be there for the boy when he did.

When Robbie glanced back at Ella, he stiffened.

Josiah squeezed his shoulder gently. "All right?"

"For a second I thought that man was Foster. He isn't." The child took a deep breath. "I'm okay."

"If you ever need to talk, I'm here."

Robbie slanted a look up at Josiah. "Thanks."

"Remember the other day I gave you my cell phone number in case something happens to Sam or you're having a problem with him? Well, you can use it for yourself, too."

The bright light returned to the boy's eyes. He thrust out his chest and moved up to the clerk to check out.

After the woman rang up the merchandise, he started to pay for the purchases, but Ella quickly moved forward and handed the woman her credit card.

"I wanted to do this for you and Robbie."

"No way. I appreciate the thought, but I'm taking care of it."

"At least let me use my employee discount."

She peered at him for a few seconds, and he wasn't sure if she would even accept that, but then she nodded. He gave the clerk his employee discount information.

When the woman realized who he was, she blushed. "I didn't realize you were Josiah Witherspoon. So sorry, sir." She hurried to finish the transaction.

As they were leaving, Josiah paused and looked at her nametag. "Pam, thank you for doing such a good job."

As he left the store, pushing one of the carts full of items, he said to Ella, "I need to become more involved with my employees. Make sure they feel important. We're growing, and I don't know the new people working for me like I should."

"How many are there?"

"Three hundred and two."

"That's a lot of faces."

"I know their names on paper, but I've only dealt with the employee representatives."

Ella started unloading her cart and putting the supplies in the back of the truck. "You could always do what David does and have a big shindig once a year."

"Yeah, I love that picnic. The softball game is so much fun." Robbie tossed the ground cloth into the pickup's bed.

"It's a good suggestion, and one of the many parks in Anchorage would be a great place to host it."

The idea of having an annual celebration at the end of the summer season felt right. Since returning to Alaska, he'd held himself back from connecting with others, only stepping out of his comfort zone to help with Northern Frontier Search and Rescue, and even then, he often searched with just Buddy.

It was time to reconnect with the world again.

Ella stared out the window of David's plane at the forest-covered island with mountains jutting up in the middle of it. It was green everywhere she looked. Beautiful. Although she hadn't camped since she was a child, she was getting excited about it.

"We're gonna stay here?" Robbie asked Josiah, her son's eyes big as he took in the eastern shore. "Do people live here?"

"Some. Not many. Hunters and visitors come in the summer, though, so we may run into a few people. But essentially, we're bringing in what we need and will take it back out, even our trash."

David landed on the water of the gulf and steered the floatplane to shore. "I'm going to be back here on Sunday evening to take you all home. Six o'clock. Have fun."

"Yippee, we've got two and a half days of camping." Robbie pumped his fist into the air while Alex exited the seaplane, then Josiah.

Her son hopped down, splashing in the few inches of water David landed in. Robbie hurried toward Josiah.

"Are you ready for this?" David asked with a laugh.

"I'm relying on the others to know what to do. Robbie needs this time away, and I'm glad we know people who have camped a lot. See you on Sunday evening, and thanks for dropping us off." Ella climbed out of the airplane as Josiah came back, minus his gear, to get the rest from the back of the plane.

Josiah placed his arms under her and carried her toward shore. "No sense in your boots getting wet. There'll be enough times when we cross a stream."

"Is that why you told me to bring more than three pairs of socks?"

"Smart woman." He set her on the small beach, then returned to the plane to grab the inflatable boat packed in a duffel bag. When Josiah had retrieved all their provisions, he waved to David. "Last chance to go back to civilization." Josiah planted himself next to her and watched as their friend took off.

"Is that what the boat is for? If we have an emergency, we can leave by paddling to the mainland." Ella pointed to the left and in the distance, only miles away, she saw the outline of the Alaskan coast.

"I'm stashing the boat bag in the bushes. Since this isn't Grand Central Station, I don't think a thief will be walking around and stumble upon it, but I like to be prepared for emergencies."

"We could have brought one of David's SAR satellite phones."

Josiah leaned close and placed his forefinger over his mouth. "Shh. I didn't want Alex getting distracted with business. This is for her as much as Robbie. Besides, if someone goes missing, David would need the few he has for a search and rescue operation." He dragged the duffel bag to the thick brush at the edge of the spruce forest lining the beach. "This will be a perfect place for the boat."

"So no rivers to go down?" Ella asked, anxious but excited about this new experience.

"Nope." He arranged the branches to hide the green bag. "Only a few streams. I have a place in mind to set up camp, and then we can explore from there."

"Mom, are you ready? Alex has been here before, and she's going to be the leader."

"I'll be right behind you." Ella adjusted her backpack, glad the temperature was quickly nearing sixty degrees. Perfect hiking weather.

"And I'll take up the rear," Josiah whispered into her ear.

A shiver streaked down her neck and spine. The idea he was right behind her sent her heart beating faster.

Ella followed her son into the woods off the shore, the light dimming from the dense foliage surrounding her. As she hiked, the scent of the trees and vegetation infused the air, and the sounds of the birds calling echoed through the forest. As she inhaled the fresh smells and drank in her peaceful surroundings, serenity flowed through her. She hadn't felt this in years, not since she was a child. She might not be a good camper, but she was glad she'd come. She needed this.

Two hours later, in an open area at the base of a mountain, Josiah stopped, sliding his backpack off his shoulders. "This will be home for the next couple of days." He pointed toward the rock face behind him. "On the other side of the ridge is a waterfall that feeds a pond. Farther down the south side is a lighthouse on the cliff."

As her son listened to Josiah talk about the island and what to expect to see, especially the animals, Alex said, "He should be a guide leading groups into the backcountry. I'm surprised he ever left Alaska. It's in his blood."

"It's home. I can understand that, even though I've only been here four years."

"I don't know if I could ever leave here."

"What made Josiah?"

"He wanted to serve his country. Harry was a big influence on him as he grew up, so after he finished college, he enlisted in the military. But the man who came back to Alaska was a changed person," Alex whispered almost to herself, surprise flittering across her expression. She turned, wide-eyed, to Ella. "I shouldn't have said anything. He doesn't talk about his time in the Marines much. All our lives we've been close except for those ten years he was gone. Please don't say anything to him."

"I won't," Ella said. "If he doesn't want to talk about his past, that's his prerogative." But that didn't mean she had to stay around, waiting for something that wasn't going to happen.

Forcing someone to do something would never work in the long run. Keith had used force with her all the time, and finally she'd managed to escape. She knew the situations were different, but after the camping trip, she had to find a way to look at Josiah as only a friend. If not, she'd need to cut her ties completely. She was falling in love with him in spite of trying not to. The very thought sent a bolt of fear through her as all the peace she'd been feeling fled under the memories of her first marriage, based on secrets and lies from the beginning.

"Let's give them some time to bond. Let's put up our tent, then I want to show you a place I loved when I last came."

"I'm glad we decided the guys should share a tent and we girls bunk together. Two tents to carry in are better than three."

"I heard Josiah had to curtail what you were bringing."

As she and Alex worked, Ella said, "I packed my backpack and still had half of the items scattered around me on the floor. Necessary things like a flashlight, insect repellant that I didn't have room for in the bag. I quickly got a lesson on what was essential and what wasn't. I finally convinced him that my moisturizer was important because it was also a sunblock."

"One of the hardest things for me to leave behind was my cell phone. I feel lost without a connection to the outside world. Josiah insisted I not even bring it in the car, so it's sitting on the dresser in my bedroom." Alex chuckled. "I have it bad. But in my defense I run a big business and have a lot of employees."

Ella wished she'd had a sister like Alex, but she'd grown up an only child. She didn't want Robbie growing up like that.

As Alex and she finished erecting the tent, Robbie came over to her. "You did good, Mom. Josiah is gonna let me put up ours and only help if I need it."

Ella ruffled her son's hair. "Ask for help if you need it. That's what you're here for—to learn, so when we go by ourselves we'll know what to do."

He looked at her in all seriousness. "I'm here to have fun. That's what Josiah said."

"Then have fun putting up the tent. Alex and I are going to do some exploring. We'll be back in a little while."

Josiah approached. "Where are you two going?"

Ella nodded her head toward Alex, who was laying the canvas floor down and crawling out of the tent. "She knows. I'm just tagging along."

Alex rose, dusted off her jeans and glanced at her brother. "Overlooking the stream. You know where. Join us when you're through if you all want."

As Robbie went to retrieve the tent, Josiah said in a low voice, "Don't forget to take your gun."

Alex grinned. "Have I ever?"

"Should I bring my revolver, too? It's in my backpack." Ella glanced at her belongings.

"I thought you were leaving that at your house. Alex

and I have our rifles. That should be enough. There haven't been any problems with the bears on this island. The weapons are more a precaution."

"Just so you two know, I'm capable of using a weapon. I learned after I divorced my husband."

With her binoculars hanging around her neck, Alex slung her rifle over her shoulder, plopped her hat on her head and said, "Let's go. Bring your camera instead. You should get some great wildlife pictures."

Ella grabbed her camera and water and quickly followed Alex. "We'll see you all in a while."

Forty minutes later, after hiking up a trail that led to an overhang that overlooked a stream, Ella collapsed on a rock perch. "I thought it was a short walk."

"By distance it is. It's the terrain that makes it longer."

"Yeah, climbing up a small mountain for a gal who sits behind a desk most days is a bit of a challenge. How do you keep in shape? You have a desk job, too."

"I work out when I can, and in the winter cross-country skiing keeps me fit. I sometimes ski to work."

"That's something I could do, but not to work. Twice this winter I had to pick up Robbie unexpectedly from school because he was sick."

"You have a terrific kid, Ella. Having him in the house a couple of weeks ago made me realize I'd love to be a mother one day. I suppose I could look at adopting."

"Or marrying again."

Alex stared at the treetops of the forest across the stream. "No, my husband was my high school sweetheart. Since I was a sophomore, I knew I would marry him. I had five fabulous years with Cade. I can't see myself finding anyone to fill his shoes in my life."

"You never know."

Alex slanted a look at Ella. "How about you? You're a great mother to Robbie. Don't you want more children?"

"I'd love to, but for different reasons I don't see myself marrying again, either."

Alex opened her mouth, but instead of saying anything snapped it closed.

A noise behind Ella drew her around. Robbie appeared on the trail with Josiah right behind him. "What took you all so long?"

"We got some wood for a fire after setting up our tent. So now all you two have to do is fix dinner. Both of us—" Josiah pointed at Robbie then himself "—are hungry. We worked up an appetite."

"First, I'm going to take some photos." Ella lifted her camera to her face. "I'll cook if you agree to clean up."

A black-tailed deer came down to the water about ten yards upstream. She took several pictures as two more joined the first one.

She gestured toward the animals when a fawn moved out of the foliage. "Robbie, a baby deer. Do you see it?"

Robbie sat near her. "It's so cute. I hope no bears are around."

"So do I." Josiah stood behind her son.

Alex passed the binoculars to Robbie. "Take a look through these. You can see the black tails better and the spots on the fawn."

Ella rose to move closer to the ledge. As long as she wasn't at the very edge, she was all right with the height. She wanted to see if anything was on this side of the water. Suddenly all the deer looked up, then raced back into the forest. *What scared them? A bear?* She scanned up and down the stream. The sunlight glinted off something for a second, then disappeared.

"Can I have the binoculars, Robbie, for a minute?"

Her son held them up for her. She took them, then swung around to locate the dense vegetation across the water downstream where she thought she'd seen something—some*one*. It couldn't have been a bear. Then, in the midst of the thick undergrowth, she spied an individual, almost totally camouflaged, with binoculars directed toward them.

"We have company."

TWELVE

When Ella moved nearer to the ledge, keeping the binoculars fixed on the same spot, Josiah closed the space between them. "Found something interesting?"

She turned her head toward him, sliding a glance toward Robbie, then passing the binoculars to Josiah. "I saw someone in that brush down there." She pointed downstream about fifty feet.

He followed the direction she indicated, but he didn't see anyone. "Whoever it was is gone now. Although not many people live on this island, it does get some campers, hunters and hikers. We'll probably run into some while hiking tomorrow. Could be someone looking for deer. It's hunting season."

Suddenly the noise of a gunshot split the air. Ella jerked back, brushing up against Josiah, her hand splaying across her chest.

Josiah clasped her upper arms. "You okay?"

"That stopped my heart. I hope the guy missed, if he's a hunter."

"Mom, Alex and I are heading to camp, but you should stay and take a few more pictures. Maybe you'll get one of a bear."

Ella's eyes narrowed. "I get the feeling those two are conspiring."

Josiah laughed. "When I moved over here to see what you were looking at, they kept exchanging glances, so I'd say you're right."

Another shot rang out. Ella tensed. "You'd think I'd be used to hearing gunfire since I practice at the shooting range. But coming out of the blue like that…"

He leaned close to her ear and lowered his voice. "We'll hear that occasionally this weekend. You'll learn to tune it out."

"Never. Even on the shooting range, I'm aware of every shot fired. When my ex took me there, Keith liked to demonstrate his 'gift,' as he put it. But what it was really was another intimidation technique."

Josiah squeezed her arm gently. "Don't think about him. He's not here, so don't let him ruin your vacation."

She looked back at him. "I know, but no matter how much I try to put him out of my mind, at odd moments he intrudes."

"Don't let him win. You lived in fear for four years. You don't have to now."

She rotated toward him. "How about you? Something has happened to you. By all accounts, I've heard you aren't the same person you were when you went into the Marines. I know you served several tours of duty in the war zone. I also know you don't like to talk about it. I was like that, too. Confiding in you was one of the best things I've ever done. Of course, I can't go around telling the world, since I'm in hiding, but having one person know is enough. I felt a burden lifted from my shoulders. Let me help you, Josiah. And if not me, at least talk to Alex."

"She knows some of it." He stepped away.

"But not all?"

He pursed his lips and averted his gaze. "I can't. I…" He felt as though he was on the side of a cliff, ready to rappel down the rock face, and yet he couldn't make that first move and step off. He wanted to, but something held him back. The memories were buried deep, where he wanted to keep them, and yet…

She started for the path down the mountain.

"Ella."

She turned to him, expectation on her face.

"Wait up. I'll hike down with you."

A mask fell over her features, but not before he saw the hurt in her gaze. She'd given him a part of herself when she'd told him about her husband, but the words inside him were dammed up behind a protective wall.

"That's okay. I'd rather be alone." An impregnable expression met his appraisal. "We're friends, but that's all. I know that, but as a friend, I wanted to help. Now I know my boundaries."

Although her look didn't reveal much, her voice cracked on the last sentence. She swung around and marched down the trail. He'd give her a minute and follow her, staying back a hundred yards. But he wanted to keep an eye on her. He had a rifle; she didn't.

As she descended the mountain, she called over her shoulder, "What part of *alone* do you not understand? I figured you knew that definition well."

He sucked in a breath and slowed his pace, catching sight of her every minute or so on the winding path.

Lord, why can't I talk about it?

As he came into camp, he knew the answer. If he acknowledged out loud the brutality he'd endured, it would be real. It was bad enough that the memories dwelled in his mind. All he wanted to do was swipe them clean from his thoughts. Hatred toward his captors jammed his throat, and when his sister asked him a question about dinner, he couldn't answer.

A fist rose above Ella's head and came crashing down on her, pounding her over and over while Josiah watched, his arms held behind him by an unseen force. He screamed out to her to hold on and struggled with his invisible bonds.

Ella tried to bolt up, but something trapped her to the ground. She clawed at it. Her eyes flew open, a faint light streaming through the tent flaps, as she wrestled with her sleeping bag. Her breath came out in short pants, her chest rising and falling rapidly. Slowly she orientated herself to her surroundings.

Alex still slept soundly two feet away from her. She was camping with Robbie. Josiah. The thought of him broke her heart. He was unreachable. She couldn't fall in love with a man who kept his life hidden from her. She'd shared her dark past and felt better that she finally had because she'd trusted Josiah with her secret.

But he didn't trust her.

She slid her eyes closed for a long moment, trying to compose herself before getting up. After her dream, she wasn't going back to sleep even if the time was only—she glanced at her watch—5:15 a.m. At least it was daylight. She could check the food supplies and plan what she would make for breakfast. Put on a pot of coffee. She needed it to stay awake.

She walked to the edge of the campsite and yanked on the rope that held their food in a tarp off the ground.

It wasn't nearly as heavy as she thought it would be. She brought it to the ground and moved to pick the items she would need. When she flipped the canvas top away, she gasped. All she found were rocks.

All the food was gone.

For a long moment, she knelt on the tarp, stunned.

She heard a movement behind her. She swiveled around, wishing she had her gun with her.

Yawning, Josiah approached. "What's wrong?"

"Our food has been stolen, and not by bears." She leaned to the side so he could see.

His eyes grew huge, and a thunderous expression chased all sleepiness from his face. "Is this how you found it? On the ground?"

She pushed the cover totally off the rocks. "No, it was hanging in the air with these in it. Someone deliberately stole our food and left us rocks."

"This has got to be a joke. Alex has played some on me in the past."

"Like this?"

"Well, not exactly." He strode to her tent and stuck his head inside.

Not a minute later, Alex emerged and charged over to the tarp to inspect what happened. "I'd never do this. I love my food more than you do."

"I wish Buddy was here. I'd like to track down who did this." His scowl evened out a little, and he pulled the tarp off the ground. "I might be able to follow the tracks." He looked at the forest around them and headed back to his tent.

When he came out with a flashlight, probably to use in the dimly lit forest, Robbie was right behind him, rubbing his eyes. Josiah grabbed his rifle and held it in one hand as if he were ready to use it at a second's notice.

"I'll be back."

"Can I come with you?" Robbie asked, starting to follow Josiah.

He turned to her son, clasping his shoulder. "You need to stay here. Help your mom and Alex. I'll be back in a little while. Okay?"

Robbie nodded.

As he left, Alex put one hand on her waist. "We need to start looking for something to eat. I saw some berries not far up the trail. Let's start there, then we can pull out our poles and try to catch some fish when Josiah comes back."

"That'll be a healthy breakfast."

"But, Mom, I hate fish."

Josiah found boot prints that led to the stream, but as he stood on the edge of the flowing water, he was afraid the trail had ended. In many places, the stream wasn't deeper than his thighs, so someone could go ashore in countless places. The freezing water numbed his legs as he started downstream first, not even sure if the thief had crossed to the other side or only used the water as a means to throw him off his trail. Finally, an hour later, he made his way back to the camp, not wanting to be gone any longer.

Ella saw him first and hurried over. "Did you find anything?"

"He used the stream to cover his tracks. I didn't see where he came out, but there were places he could have found stones. I saw footprints but not like the ones I found going away from our camp. To be honest, the guy could have taken his boots off. I figure we should forget about him and enjoy ourselves. He didn't get our bottled water at least."

"We found some berries, and Alex is ready to go fishing. Robbie is all excited. He feels as if he's living off the land like a survivalist."

"Leave it to a child to turn our thinking around. It's a challenge, but one we can deal with. We had a big dinner last night. We have clean water and a stream with fish in it. And to top it off, we can have dessert—berries."

"And we have each other—*friends* enjoying a weekend away from the rat race."

The emphasis on *friends* didn't miss the mark with Josiah. After last night at the bluff, he knew he would always remain broken, and there was no way he would ever enter into a relationship with a woman, especially one with a child, when part of him couldn't shake the hate that kept him locked in a prison of his own making. He wanted to see all of his captors rot in a cell until they breathed their last breath. That realization stunned him. He hadn't known how deep his anger went until now.

"Josiah, are you all right?" Ella touched his arm.

The feel of her fingers on his skin shocked him from his thoughts. He blinked, trying to tamp down the emotions reeling through him. He'd never have a full life without finding a way to forgive his captors. He didn't know what to say to Ella.

She looked long and hard at him, then went to Alex and Robbie to help them with the fishing equipment.

For a moment he watched them, unable to move, to think beyond what he'd discovered about himself. Had

Ella forgiven her ex-husband? Or was she stuck in limbo like him? Unable to move forward with his life?

"Josiah, we're ready," Robbie called out.

"I'm coming," he finally said, shutting his past back into the dark recesses of his mind. He was going to have fun right now, and examine his life later when he was back in Anchorage. "I'm hungry. Let's go get some breakfast."

Later, Ella stuck the trash in a plastic bag to take with them when they left the island. "Robbie, did you get enough food?"

Her son swiped the back of his hand across his mouth. "I'm stuffed. Josiah, the salmon was great."

"This from a boy who less than twenty-four hours ago declared he hated fish. Obviously when you're starving, you'll eat anything." Ella finished cleaning up their used paper products. "Who wants to walk with me to the stream to wash our pan out?"

"I will," Josiah said before anyone else. "Alex and Robbie can get more firewood."

"I think we got the raw end of this deal." Alex stood. "C'mon, Robbie, let's get it so we can sit around relaxing. I promised to tell you about my first search and rescue with Sadie."

Ella had purposefully stayed away from Josiah all day while they'd fished, hiked and gathered a few edible items to complement the salmon. Now she was stuck walking with him. She started toward the stream. He snatched his rifle and hurried after her.

"Wait up. I'm supposed to be your guard."

"In case the thief comes back to steal our skillet?"

"He could. Or a bear could be fishing for salmon.

A better place for fishing is farther upstream, but you never know."

"Sheesh, thanks. Now I'm going to be on pins and needles the whole time."

"Right now, the bears are focused on eating all the salmon they can before winter."

Ella kept walking, concentrating on each step she took rather than the man to the left and slightly behind her. The sound of the water rushing over the rocks lured her closer and closer to the stream. She'd wash the pan and quickly return to camp.

If there had been a way to leave the island, she would have. But she had less than a day before David picked them up. She'd have to deal with being in close confines with Josiah until then, but once she returned to Anchorage, she would keep her distance. She realized she was falling in love with Josiah, but this morning, when she'd tried once more to reach out to him, he'd rejected her. She'd seen that look of pain and vulnerability on his face right before going fishing. But all she'd met was a wall of silence.

"Ella, could you slow down? We don't have to jog to the stream." Josiah's request cut through her thoughts.

"Why? I want to wash this—" she waved the skillet "—and get back to camp. It's been a long day, and I'm ready to sleep."

"It's not even eight o'clock and still bright outside."

She came to an abrupt halt and swirled around. "What do you want from me? You've been sending me mixed messages all day. I can't keep doing this." The words exploded from her as if she'd released the built-up pressure in a carbonated drink.

"To talk."

"Now?" Her gaze drilled into him. She tried desperately to read in his expression what was behind that request. But he was too good at hiding his emotions.

"Yes. I've angered you, and I think we should talk about it."

"Just go back to camp. Leave me alone."

She charged toward the stream at a fast clip. She wasn't going to argue with him. At the creek, she knelt by the edge, dipped her skillet in the water and swished it around, letting the rapid current wash the bits of food away.

Josiah squatted next to her and covered his hand over hers, grasping the pan. He took it and placed it on the ground, then drew her around. "Please hear me out."

The soft plea in his eyes was her undoing. She nodded.

He rose and tugged her away from the rushing stream to a pile of smooth stones. Taking a seat on one, he patted the rock next to him. When she sat, he clasped her hand and turned toward her. Her heartbeat sped like the flowing water.

He inhaled a deep breath and let it out slowly. "I'm not even sure where to begin. I've only shared part of what I'm going to tell you with two people—my sister and the counselor I saw for a year. It isn't common knowledge that I was a prisoner of war for months because my mission was a secret one behind enemy lines. I can't talk about it even now."

"You were a POW?" She'd known he must have gone through some horrific situations while in the Marines, but not that.

"Yes. I was captured and beaten for the details of my mission. When I finally broke, I was thrown into a cell only three feet by three feet. I hated myself for breaking down and tried to console myself with the fact that, by that time, the information I'd given them didn't mean anything. All I wanted at first was for them to kill me. End my pain."

Ella had once thought that herself, after her husband had pushed her down the stairs and she'd broken both arms. Then she'd remembered Robbie, who'd only been three at that time, and knew she had to protect him. She'd begun fighting back then and making secret plans to get away. She cupped her other hand on top of their clasped ones.

"I can tell you every gory detail of captivity if you really want to know."

Tears filling her eyes, she shook her head. "No, there's no need. The fact that you would is all I care about. My relationship with Keith was full of secrets and lies. I care so much for you, Josiah. I didn't want anything to stand between us, or I would never have told you about my ex-husband."

He captured her chin and caressed the tears away with his thumb. "After a while I turned to the Lord, begging Him to end my suffering. He didn't. Instead, slowly I felt my fighting spirit return. I thought of Alex. I thought of my fiancée, Lori, who I was going to marry when I returned from the mission. Suddenly what they did to me didn't mean anything anymore. I had a goal—to escape. To return home. And the Lord would help me."

Like I did. The power of God overwhelmed her. She couldn't stop the flow of tears running down her face, splashing onto their entwined fingers.

"The Lord was with me in that cell. Lately I've forgotten that. I was letting the traumatic past haunt me, letting it drive a wedge between me and God. But not anymore. I know what I have to do. I have to forgive my captors."

She wanted to hold him, but she was afraid that would be a distraction. His greatest need at the moment was to talk about his past. "How did you escape?"

"I could tell something was going on in the camp. A flurry of activity. Many days went by when I never saw my jailer. On the day I made my escape, a young boy brought me water and food." He stared off into space as though he was seeing it all again in his mind.

She stroked her thumb over the curve of his hand. "What happened next?"

His gaze returned to hers, awe in the depths of his crystal-blue eyes. "There was a commotion outside the cave. The boy hurriedly left, and I guess he didn't lock the door correctly. After I ate, I went to the door to see if I could hear anything. That's when I discovered it was unlocked. Without a second thought, I left my prison and managed to sneak away."

"How long did it take before you made it to safety?"

"Just hours. The commotion was a force of our men drawing near their cave hideout. The terrorists were trying to get away."

"Did they?"

"Some did. Others were killed or captured. At least that's what I heard. Our troops called for help when they found me at the bottom of the mountain. A helicopter took me back to the base. Then my journey to healing began."

"And look where you are now. Helping others. Me." She tugged him toward her and wrapped her arms around him. "I'm so sorry for what happened to you. I wish I could erase that part of your past."

He pulled slightly away and framed her face. "And I wish I could erase parts of yours. Have you been able to forgive Keith? Because I don't know how to take that step. If I don't forgive my captors, I'll never be whole again."

She closed her eyes, wishing she could help him. "I haven't forgiven Keith yet. I've prayed to God to help me, but so far I'm still as angry as I was after I managed to get away from him."

"Do you think we have a chance to be more than friends?" The feel of his thumb as it whispered across her cheek tempted her. But she couldn't. "I don't know. I'm afraid our pasts will always be there as a barrier to the true, loving relationship we deserve. I don't know if I can ever let go of the fear and mistrust I have because of Keith."

His hands slipped away from her face. He clenched them, and the strong, tense set to his jawline shouted he felt that way about his situation, too. "The reason I have Buddy is because he was—really still is—a service dog for a person with post-traumatic stress disorder. I still occasionally have nightmares and panic attacks. Not often, but enough to remind me I'm still far from healed. When I came home, I desperately wanted what happened to me to go away as if it had never occurred. When I got out of the hospital, I went to see Lori. I didn't want anyone to tell her I was home until I could see her myself. I didn't want her to see me in the hospital."

"When you love someone, that shouldn't matter."

He looked into her eyes, his stiff posture relaxing

slightly, but tension still poured off him. "I know. In the end it didn't really matter. She'd already moved on and was in love with another man. Thoughts of a life with her were one of the ways I kept myself going while a prisoner, but I realize I've forgiven Lori. I wasn't in any shape to be in a relationship when I returned to the States anyway."

Her throat swelled with emotions. Ella fought the tears rising inside. She couldn't stop them.

He took her into his embrace and pressed her against his chest. The pounding of his heart beneath her ear finally calmed the tears to a whimper. "We are quite a pair," she murmured. "What are we going to do?"

"Maybe when we get back to Anchorage, we should spend some time apart. We both need to figure out what we really want for ourselves and find a way to make it happen."

She leaned away and stared into his eyes, realizing these past weeks she had been fighting the feelings that had developed in spite of her trying to avoid an emotional involvement. In spite of her fear, she'd make the same mistake as she had with Keith. "I love you, Josiah, but I'm not sure that's enough. I can't make a mistake about this because it doesn't just affect me. I have Robbie to consider, too."

Josiah bent forward and kissed her lightly, but before he could deepen it, he put some space between them. "I agree. I never want him to be hurt."

"Then what do we tell him when you suddenly stop coming around?"

"I'll think of something, but for the time being let's just enjoy each other's company for the rest of this trip. Going camping was important to Robbie."

"I can do that." On overload with all that had transpired, Ella rose from the rock. "Are you ready to go back? They're probably wondering what's keeping us."

"Yes." He stood, taking her hand.

When she glanced upstream, she gasped and froze. Three brown bears were in the water catching salmon. "Have they been there the whole time?"

"Yes, but I was keeping an eye on them."

She'd been so focused on Josiah she hadn't even been aware of the huge animals only a football field away. Josiah did that to her. And yet, he also protected her.

As Ella strolled back to camp, she kept glancing over her shoulder. Although she'd lived here four years, it wasn't a common occurrence for her to see three brown bears at one time. But she saw no sign of them being bothered by her and Josiah. As she neared their campsite, she began to relax.

"What are we going to do tomorrow?" she asked, finally breaking the silence between them.

"There's a place we can sit on the shore and watch for whales. I can't guarantee we'll see them, but we can try. I think Robbie will get a big kick out of that."

"He certainly was excited about seeing the bald eagle in the tree today."

"That excited me. A majestic bird. Being around Robbie has renewed the awe I used to have while growing up here. You have a special son."

Suddenly a gunshot reverberated through the woods. Coming to a sudden stop, Ella tensed. "That was close."

Another blast rang out.

"It's coming from the direction of our campsite," Josiah said, grasping his rifle with both of his hands as he set out in a jog.

THIRTEEN

The pounding of Ella's footsteps matched his as Josiah raced toward the camp. As he came closer, he slowed, the beating of his heart thundering in his ears.

On the outskirts, he crept forward, Ella mirroring him. Alex stood with Robbie in front of a rocky facade, a piece of paper stuck on a small tree limb. She was demonstrating how to handle a rifle. A look of deep concentration was on the boy's face.

Ella moved around him, headed toward the pair across the campsite and said with a laugh, "You should warn me before you start target practice."

Robbie whirled toward her. "Alex was showing me how good she is. I drew a bull's-eye on the paper. She hit it twice. I want to learn. Can I, Mom?"

Alex faced Ella and Josiah. "We got bored waiting for you two to come back. Robbie wanted to know about my gun. I was pointing out how it worked and why we carry it when we go into the backcountry."

Ella turned to Robbie, a solemn expression on her face. "When you're older. Until then, you aren't to handle one. I imagine from Alex's demonstration you see how dangerous a weapon can be in the wrong hands or with someone who doesn't know what he's doing. Okay?"

With an equally somber expression, Robbie nodded.

"If we had our food, right about now, we'd be roasting marshmallows and making s'mores," Josiah said to lighten the moment of seriousness. "But we have some berries left instead. Anybody up for finishing them off with me?"

Robbie giggled. "What about breakfast tomorrow morning?"

"We'll need much more than berries tomorrow." Josiah drew the boy toward the fire ring. "We have over an hour's hike to a place I want to show you. We'll need to leave early, so I'm going to get up at the crack of dawn and go fishing. Want to come with me?"

"If you're gonna tell me where we're going to hike."

"Hopefully to see whales."

As Robbie sat near the dying fire, his eyes grew huge. "Really?"

"Maybe seals, some more eagles, too."

Robbie clapped. "Yes!"

Ella joined Josiah and Robbie, taking a seat next to her son. "I gather you're going fishing, then."

Robbie twisted toward her with his solemn expression on his face. "If we're gonna have breakfast, I have to. I'm the one who caught the most fish today."

"I think you threw down the gauntlet, Robbie." Ella's eyes twinkled.

"Gauntlet? What's that?" her son asked.

"A glove. In olden times when someone did that, it meant they were challenging another person to something." Ella glanced toward Josiah.

He smiled. "And I take up that challenge. I'm going

to catch more fish than you by seven o'clock. Deal?" Josiah held out his hand.

Her son shook it. "Deal."

"While you two battle it out at the stream, Alex and I will sleep in and have a blazing fire going by the time you come back in anticipation of all the fish you're going to catch. Now, I wonder who can top me in telling the tallest tale."

Josiah lounged back on his elbows as first his sister and then Robbie took up the dare. Around the fire, with the sun going down, the leaves rustling in the cool breeze and the sound of insects and birds filling the air, he thought about what he had told Ella at the stream. As he'd gone through the details of his ordeal, he'd always thought it would send him into a panic attack. It had when he'd first talked with his counselor. It had when he'd shared some of it with Alex. Would his nightmare return tonight with Buddy at home?

Josiah caught Ella staring at him, her warm brown eyes probing, as though trying to reach into his mind. He averted his gaze. He didn't want to let her go, but he didn't think he was good for her.

The next morning Ella woke up, snuggled comfortably in her sleeping bag. She'd gotten a good night's rest and was ready for the day of hiking before David came at six to pick them up. This weekend had been a revelation—from Josiah, but also inside her. Somewhere deep within her, she needed to find a way to let go of her anger toward Keith and move on completely. Josiah was right. She could never truly embrace the rest of her life if she didn't.

Sitting up, Ella stretched the kinks out of her body,

which wasn't used to sleeping on the hard ground. Even as she crawled from the tent, she continued to work out the stiffness from her muscles. She spied Alex sitting on the ground, her eyes closed, her body relaxed. She'd learned when living at the estate that Alex always meditated first thing in the morning if possible. It was her special time with God. Ella liked that idea, but she found the end of the day worked best for her.

When Ella stood, Alex opened her eyes. Ella quickly said, "I'm gathering the firewood we need. Go back to what you're doing."

Ella hurried into the wooded area near the campsite as Alex slid her eyelids closed again. She'd slept so well she hadn't heard Josiah or Robbie leaving at sunrise to fish. Glancing at her watch, she knew the guys would be back in about twenty minutes, ready to cook the fish. Bending over, she began picking up stray tree limbs until her arms were loaded with firewood.

She heard an owl in an upper branch of one of the trees and stopped, trying to determine where he was perched. Another hoot echoed through the woods. Suddenly she thought about what had started all of this—falling in love with a man who wasn't ready for a relationship. It had been weeks ago when Robbie and his friends went in search of an owl. Something good had come out of the incident with Foster. Maybe sometime later, Josiah and she would have a chance.

I hope so.

All she had to do was let go of the hold Keith had on her. Somehow she would do that because she and Robbie deserved more. She leaned over to grab one more piece of wood before heading back to camp. She straightened and swung around to retrace her steps when she saw him.

The collected firewood tumbled to the ground about her feet.

Keith.

With a rifle pointed at her.

"I won. I won." Robbie danced around in circles at the stream.

Josiah laughed at the glee on the boy's face. "You're a natural outdoorsman. The skills will come as you get older. That doesn't have anything to do with being a natural."

Robbie puffed out his chest. "Can I learn how to cook these salmon you filleted?"

"Sure. Let's go." Josiah washed his hands in the stream, grabbed the fish he'd prepared and headed toward the campsite.

"Thanks, Josiah, for showing me all these things this weekend. Mom isn't too big on camping, but when I get older, I'll be able to go with friends."

"Until then, you can go with me again, if you like," Josiah said, before he realized Ella probably wouldn't want that. Yesterday evening, they had agreed to put some distance between them.

"I'd love that."

They walked through the woods in silence for a while, then Robbie asked, "Do you like my mom?"

Josiah could answer many questions about Alaska, dogs and camping, but that question left him speechless. He couldn't lie to the boy, but he didn't want to give him false hope concerning him and Ella. "I think your mom is very special," he finally said, praying that would satisfy Robbie.

"Would you ever consider being my dad?"

Stunned, Josiah came to a halt. He opened his mouth to say something, but couldn't think of a reply.

The child stopped, too. "I know you two haven't dated long—"

"We haven't really dated at all."

"Well, you have my permission to date my mom." Robbie started again for the campsite.

It took a moment for Josiah to gather his wits. What was he going to say to Ella about this? Then the thought of being the child's father began to worm its way into his mind. He finally trailed a few feet behind the boy, thinking of the prospect of having a child—children. Yesterday that thought would have scared him, but now it didn't sound quite as far-fetched.

When they entered the camp, Alex had her gun in hand and was starting for the forest on the left.

"Where are you going?"

"Ella has been gone too long. She left to collect the firewood we needed. That was over half an hour ago."

Josiah walked to her and gave her the fillets. "Get these ready. I'll track her and bring her back."

As he headed into the trees, he stamped down the gut feeling something had happened. She might have gotten turned around in the woods, especially if she'd wandered too far away.

Ella is all right.

He kept repeating that as he followed her tracks.

Shocked and frozen, Ella stared into the diamond-hard eyes of her ex-husband, boring into hers with such hatred. No words came to mind. Her heartbeat began to hammer against her rib cage at such a rapid pace she thought it would burst from her chest.

"I've been searching for you for four years." His gaze raked down her length. "Finally I get to pay you back for turning me in."

How had he found her? Fear choked her throat, making it impossible to say anything. All her past nightmares came crashing down on her.

"I'm going to kill you slowly, then take *my son* and raise him to be a man."

Robbie. No, he can't. She tamped down the terror threatening to make her useless. Her son's life was at stake. *Lord, I can't do this without You.*

"What? You have nothing to say to your husband?"

"No." It wouldn't do any good.

He tossed her a set of handcuffs. "Put these on. And make it fast."

They fell at her feet. She glared at him.

"If you don't cooperate with me, I'll make Robbie's life worse than you could ever imagine."

Begrudgingly she bent over and snatched the handcuffs, then snapped them on.

"That's a good little wife. No piece of paper will change that fact." Keith slung the rifle over his shoulder and took out a handgun. "Let's go. I have a nice secluded spot for a special celebration between us."

She shuddered at the sneer in his voice, the evil on his face. How had she ever thought she was in love with this man? Because he had been a master at putting up just the right facade for people—at least for a short time. Then his true nature always came out.

He approached her, gripped her arm and dragged her

in front of him. He leaned close to her ear and whispered, "I've been thinking for years about what I would do with you when I finally found you. When you were splashed across the news, you made it so easy for me. You might look different, but Robbie looks just like me." He yanked her long hair tied in a ponytail. "I like this blond color much better than that mousy brown you had. Let's go."

The glee in his voice left her stone-cold. He had to shove her to get her to move. He rammed the barrel into her back and kept prodding her forward through the undergrowth until he came to an animal trail. She knew that Josiah could track, but she wanted to make it as easy as possible. The only thing she had access to was a beaded bracelet Robbie had made her at camp.

As she trudged before Keith, she managed to slip the piece of jewelry off her wrist. She pulled it apart until she held a handful of small beads. Were they large enough for Josiah to see?

Following the set of tracks from the area Alex had indicated, Josiah reached a small clearing and homed in on some scattered branches lying on the ground near a set of her footprints. What had happened here? Why had she dropped the firewood? Had an animal scared her?

He studied the surroundings, taking in the boot prints—similar to the ones he'd tracked after their food had been taken. The tracks stopped right in front of hers. Then they both moved off to the northeast.

His gut twisted and knotted. Ella had been taken. It didn't matter why. He just had to get her back and protect the others. She wouldn't have gone off willingly without letting Alex know.

He raced to the campsite and motioned for Alex to come to him. When she did, he lowered his voice, keeping an eye on Robbie so he wouldn't hear, and said, "Someone took Ella. A large man, by the size of the boot print. I think it's the same man who stole our food. Leave everything, take Robbie and use the inflatable boat to get help on the mainland. The man is taking her northeast."

When she nodded, Josiah snatched up his backpack with binoculars, rope and a flashlight, waved to Robbie, then whirled around and hurried after Ella and her kidnapper. When he reached the small clearing, he began the slow tracking process until he found a yellow bead in the dirt. About twenty yards away, he saw another one—blue.

Ella's legs protested with each step she took. Sweat rolled down her face. Her eyes stung from the saltiness. The constant poking of the gun into her back had become an irritant that made her want to scream out in frustration and fear.

Ahead, a rocky path started to slant upward. She craned her neck at the direction Keith was taking her. She didn't know if she had the energy to go twenty feet up the slope, let alone climb a mountain. But the worst part was how scared she was of heights.

Lord, what do I do?

She slowed her pace at the bottom of the incline. Keith plowed into her.

She fell forward, her knees taking the brunt of the fall onto the stones. Pain shot up her body, and she bit her lower lip to keep from crying out.

"If I have to, I'll drag you up there. Get up. Now."

She placed her fists, one that still clenched the few remaining beads, on the hard surface and pushed herself to her shaky legs. God was with her. She could do this.

"This is for every day I've feared for my life. For my lousy life in the witness security program trying to live on a measly amount of money. But I'm taking my life back. I'm gonna take care of you. Then I'm getting Robbie and leaving the country."

Taunting words filled her mind, but she gritted her teeth to keep them to herself. He'd never be free of the organization he'd worked for because he'd betrayed them. She could only imagine the horrors of what they'd do to a traitor. Even halfway around the world. Somehow she had to find a way to prevent him from getting her son. She wouldn't let Robbie live a life on the run from men bent on murdering Keith.

He shoved her forward, but she managed to keep her balance and tramped up the rocks.

Please, Lord, protect Robbie from Keith. Get him to safety.

She prayed with each step she took up the mountain, her body shaking. She kept her gaze focused on the ground in front of her, not on how far she had come up the incline. She dropped the few beads she had left at the halfway mark of the sixty-degree slope. Part of their ascent was hidden by trees, and she knew they were on the other side of the range from where they had camped.

I'm in Your hands, Lord.

About a hundred yards from the top, Keith propelled her around a large boulder and into a cave in the stone facade. Dark and musky with only one way out, and Keith blocked it, towering over her with a fierce countenance.

His eyes became black pinpoints. "Now we're

far enough away from anybody else that even if you screamed no one would hear." He waved his revolver at her. "I have a little place set up just for you. Get up and get moving." Keith gestured toward the black hole that led deeper into the cave.

The last bead Josiah found was a fourth of the way up the side of a mountain. But nothing since. Had he missed the direction Ella and her kidnapper had gone? On a small ledge, he used the binoculars and scanned above him then to the left and right before he surveyed the area below him. Either Ella and her kidnapper had already made it to the top, or they were hiding somewhere on this face of the mountain.

Sweat drenched him. At the moment the only choice he had was to continue straight up and pray the Lord showed him where Ella was. He hoped Alex had gotten Robbie off the island by now. At least Ella's son would be safe.

Since he didn't want to miss Ella and the man who'd taken her, he stopped periodically and panned his surroundings. For the third time he came up empty-handed, and frustration ate at him.

On the fourth survey from the small outcropping where he stood, he sidled carefully to the right, wanting to check out a boulder on a ledge a hundred feet away. Was that an opening? Creeping as far as he could, he held on to a small bush growing out of the side of the mountain to lean as far away from the rock wall as he could.

The second he figured out that the hole in the stone wasn't just a crevice but a cave, the brush pulled away from the rocks. He teetered on the edge, flapping his arms to get his balance.

* * *

Deeper in the cave, Ella spied a faint glow up ahead of her; the only light guiding her way was the one Keith wore strapped to his head.

"We aren't far from the cavern I've prepared for us."

They turned a corner, and the faint glow was gone. She couldn't hold her arms out to feel the side of the cave as he did. She took another cautious step, and her foot twisted as it came down between two rocks.

She cried out as she went down, her left arm colliding with a jutting piece of the wall. She fought the tears that welled into her eyes, making what little she could see blurry, and she averted her head before he saw. He'd loved to see her cry and beg. She wouldn't give him the satisfaction.

"Get up." Keith kicked her leg, now pinned between two stones.

Rising anger vied with her fear as she finally yanked her foot free.

"Now."

"I am! If you'd give me a light, I could see where I'm going" were the first words she spoke since he'd asked her if she had anything to say to him.

"Ah, she finally speaks." Mockery laced each of his words.

She struggled to stand, keeping her back to him while she blinked the last of her tears. Her fury was taking over. She wouldn't give up the fight until she drew her last breath.

"As usual, you think you're a big man because you *think* you can cow a woman a foot shorter than you."

He snorted. "I haven't even begun toying with you. To even the playing field a little, I'll give you a head start. I'll count to one hundred while you try to get away from me. I suppose it's possible you could find a hiding place. Who knows? But the only way you can escape is into the mountain."

She finally glanced over her shoulder. The bright light nearly blinded her. The only thing she could see was him holding the gun aimed at her.

"One, two, three. You better get going."

She started forward.

"Four, five, six."

She brought her left arm across her chest so she could run her hands along the side of the wet, cold cave. She tried to block his counting from her mind.

But she couldn't.

"Twenty, twenty-one, twenty-two."

Using the wall as a guide wasn't working well. She gave it up and lifted her arms out in front, then increased her pace. The cave curved to the right, and the glare of his headlamp no longer lit her way, even vaguely. Darkness shrouded her, but she kept going. She needed to find somewhere to hide.

"One hundred. Here I come."

FOURTEEN

Josiah lost his balance and slipped from the ledge. He began to fall down the slope, his arms flailing for a handhold. A stone jutting out from the outcropping grazed his fingers, and he grasped it, stopping his descent down the side of the mountain. He swung his other hand around the rock while his legs dangled in the air. Willing all his strength into his arms, he slowly pulled himself back up to the shelf, his muscles twitching with the strain.

He lay on the rough surface and dragged oxygen into his lungs. He couldn't stay here. He needed to get to that cave and see if Ella was in there. Otherwise she and her kidnapper were already on the ridge, and it would take him a while to pick up their trail. Cautiously he made his way to the right and up.

When he reached the cave's entrance, he checked the ground for any sign Ella was in there. In the dirt just inside the opening, he glimpsed footprints like the ones he'd been tracking. He took a step toward them and halted. Sweat popped out on his forehead. His heartbeat thumped against his chest, and his pulse raced.

Suddenly he was thrust back into the past when he

was kept prisoner in a cage in a cave. His legs refused to move forward into the waiting darkness, as though he'd been flash frozen.

Ella groped around another turn, moving away from the glow she'd spied earlier. She wouldn't put it past Keith to have set it up as a lure, knowing he was going to do something like this. The longer she kept Keith away from Robbie, the better the chance her son would get away. Alex and Josiah would know something was wrong by now and go for help.

You're not alone in this. She felt those words deep in her heart. This wasn't the same as before with Keith when she'd become so cut off from friends and family. When Keith found her, he would discover she wasn't the same docile woman he'd terrorized. If she didn't leave this cave, neither would he.

She glanced back and noticed a light coming closer to the turnoff she'd taken. Twisting forward again, she picked up speed, going several yards when her left foot slammed against a rock. Even in her boots, pain zipped up her leg. She stumbled and went down, using her arms to break her fall. At the same time the collision with the wall knocked the breath from her. She labored to sit up and tried to stand. She crumpled to the rock surface, back against the side of the tunnel.

Before trying to rise again, she patted the area around her. She had to hide. Watching the light growing brighter as Keith stalked her, she hoisted herself to her knees and checked the evenness of the floor in front of her. She encountered another rocky obstacle. She crawled forward to see if there were more. For the next twenty feet she painstakingly made her way from one stone obstruction to another. The path ahead grew narrower.

Until she came to a drop-off. Trapped.

Josiah lifted his foot and moved forward into the cave's entrance. His body shook. His past captors were not going to control him. The anger he always experienced when thinking about them flooded him, making the next step even more difficult.

Lord, help me. Please. Ella needs me.

But the panic threatened to immobilize him. He quaked even more. His breathing became shallow inhalations that left his lungs starving for oxygen-rich air.

Let it go. Forgive.

The conversation he had with Ella took over his thoughts. *As long as I hate them, what they did to me will influence all aspects of my life. Will dominate my actions.*

No! I won't let them.

Time was running out. Every second could be Ella's last. He gritted his teeth and focused on eradicating his hatred, on washing his mind clean, as though he'd been baptized again.

He raised another foot and put it down in front of him. Then another. A faint light ahead drew him in a little farther. Sweat stung his eyes. He swiped the back of his hand across his forehead and pictured Ella's smiling face, her eyes bright with the gleam of mischief.

Then the illumination drawing him into the cave vanished. He halted.

Ella lay flat on the cave floor, inched forward and felt to see if she could figure out how deep the drop-off was. Reaching down as far as she could, she couldn't touch the bottom.

"I will find you, Ella. You won't escape me this time. Never again."

Keith's words echoed through the cavern, chilling her to the bone.

With a quick glance back, she watched the brightness grow nearer. Although it lit that last bend she'd taken, it wasn't enough to illuminate her surroundings. She began exploring them with her hands, searching for anywhere to conceal herself from Keith. To the side was a large stone. Maybe she could hide behind it and pray he didn't know she'd gone this way.

She crawled behind the rock and curled into the smallest ball she could, sending up her prayers to be saved.

His headlamp washed the area in brightness as though a spotlight was pointing to her hiding place. Her heartbeat pounded against her skull. Her body ached all over, and she couldn't seem to breathe enough.

"Come out. Come out. Wherever you are."

She couldn't even cover her ears to keep from hearing Keith's taunting words. They bombarded her as though he was hammering his fists into her body.

The light came closer. The sound of his breathing seemed to resonate against the rocky walls, drowning out her own thundering heartbeat.

"Gotcha."

Claws grabbed her upper arms and yanked her from her hiding place, which in the glow barely blocked her from his view. He hoisted her into the air, his bright light glaring in her eyes. Squinting, she peered down.

Her legs dangled a few feet off the stone ground. He edged toward the dark drop-off.

"I wonder what's down there, how deep it is."

He held her over the hole. She refused to look and instead stared at his waist.

"Mmm. I can't see the bottom."

He'd put his rifle down and had stuffed his revolver in his belt because his two hands were busy gripping her. As he finally stepped back from the ledge, Ella decided it was now or never.

She shrieked and swung her legs toward him.

A high-pitched blood-curdling cry vibrated through the tunnel. Josiah's grasp on his flashlight tightened. The sound chilled him. He increased his pace. In his gut he knew that was Ella, and she was in trouble.

He rushed around the bend in the cave where the glow had disappeared to a faint then nonexistent illumination. He stumbled over the uneven surface and caught himself before going down. Noises drifted to him. A fight? Although the ground was rugged, with large cracks, he accelerated even more.

"I'm gonna kill you," a gruff masculine voice shouted.

Then the blast of a gunshot, the sound ricocheting off the stone walls in deafening waves. Then another gun went off—different, though. A revolver?

Click. Click. Click, followed by an explosion of words that scorched Josiah's ears. Had the gun stopped working?

He flew over the rough terrain, readying his rifle the best he could one-handed since he held the flashlight in the other. As he neared another curve in the tunnel, he slowed because light shone as though it came from somewhere nearby. He flattened himself against the wall and peeked around the wall into the corridor.

The first thing he saw was Ella racing toward him, a revolver clasped in her handcuffed hands. Then he glimpsed a large, muscular man with blond hair charging Ella, holding a rifle like a club, his face red with rage.

Ella rounded the curve. She spied him and slowed her pace. When she was safe behind him, Josiah thrust the flashlight into her hand, then stepped out into the corridor.

"Stop! Drop your gun," Josiah said, and raised his rifle.

But before he could line up a shot, the tall man kept coming, swinging his gun toward Josiah's head. He crouched and barreled into the blond giant, driving both of them deeper into the tunnel. The man's rifle came down on Josiah's back. Josiah rammed him into the wall. Once. Twice. Until the rifle clattered to the ground.

The giant wrapped his arms around Josiah's torso instead and squeezed so tight that pain stabbed into his chest as if his bruised rib hadn't healed. Josiah brought his hands up and hit the man's ears, hoping to throw him off balance so he would loosen his grip. His arms slackened enough that Josiah broke his hold. Then quickly he moved in and punched one fist into the man's nose and the other into his throat.

The guy staggered back, gasping for air while blood ran down his face. His left foot came down on the edge of a drop-off. He flapped his arms, trying to regain his balance, but before Josiah could reach him, he fell backward. The giant's scream echoed through the cave, followed by a thumping sound.

Panting, Josiah peered down into the hole. The man's light still shone, illuminating his broken body at the bottom of a deep pit.

"Is he dead?" Ella's voice quavered behind him.

Josiah swung around, took one glance at her pale features and wide eyes and drew her away from the drop-off. Then he retrieved the flashlight from her and checked the bottom of the pit again to reassure her that it was over.

When he returned to her, he tugged her against him, trying to absorb the tremors that racked her body. "Yes, he's dead. You're safe now."

"That was Keith. He was going to kill me," she murmured against his chest in a monotone as though she was going into shock.

"Let's get out of here. Into the sunshine. He can't hurt you ever again."

"Are you sure?" A sob tore through her.

"He fell sixty or seventy feet onto a rocky surface, and by the pool of blood around his head, I'm positive."

"Is Robbie all right? He was going to take him." She shuddered.

"He's safe. My sister is guarding him."

When he brought Ella into the sunlight, he sat her down on the ledge and pulled her into the crook of his arm. "When you're ready, we'll hike to the beach to be picked up. Alex and Robbie left in the boat to get help. Then when Keith's body is recovered, you'll have to ID him, and the medical examiner can confirm he's dead."

Ella stood at her living room window as Alex parked her car, hopped out and walked toward her house. For the past two days, since returning from the island, Ella had gone through the motions of living, but a part of her was numb as though she was still in the cave with Keith, listening to him telling her how he was going to kill her.

Earlier she'd talked with her minister, but didn't really think she was free from her ex-husband. She'd thought she was before and he'd found her.

He's dead. Everyone has told me that.

She'd repeated that so many times in the past forty-eight hours she would have thought it would finally sink in. But for so long she had lived in terror, and it wasn't that easy to shake it off.

Maybe when she finally identified his body, she'd be free. No more nightmares for her or Robbie. Was that even possible?

Then her minister's words repeated themselves in her mind. *You won't be free until you forgive Keith. You can't let go while holding on to that kind of hatred.*

Alex rang the doorbell. Ella headed to the foyer to answer it, knowing she had to find the power to forgive.

She forced a smile on her face and greeted Alex. "I'm glad you could take Robbie while I go to ID Keith."

"Sadie is waiting for him to come visit. We'll have fun. Don't hurry to come pick him up. You and Josiah should talk. You haven't had much of a chance since all this happened."

"Do you know if they found Keith's campsite?"

"Yes, I got a call when Josiah landed at the airport. They found it and a stash of firepower that could wipe out a lot of people. Josiah said it looked as though he was planning a small war."

Ella hugged her arms. "A US Marshal came to see me this morning to find out what happened. Apparently my husband left their protection and in the process killed a man. He obviously was very determined to get to me."

"He can't anymore."

"I'm trying to realize that, but he's been such a big part of my life for so long. It's hard to think I'm really free." *Am I really until I finally say that I've forgiven Keith and mean it?*

"Sam and I are ready to go, Alex," Robbie said behind Ella.

"That's great. Sadie's in the car waiting." To Ella she added, "We're going to the park before going to my house. Don't worry about the time you pick him up." Alex looked pointedly at her. "Take care of *all* your business."

"I will."

Robbie threw his arms around Ella. "I love you, Mom."

She ruffled his hair. "I love you, too."

Ella stood in the entrance and watched her son lead his twelve-week-old puppy to Alex's car. She was right about talking with Josiah. She needed to. Once they'd walked out of the woods onto the beach, they hadn't been alone in the midst of Josiah helping with the recovery of Keith's body and the search for his campsite. She'd had her hands full with reassuring Robbie they would be all right and then being interviewed by the authorities about what had happened. A whirlwind forty-eight hours. She desperately wanted her life to return to normal, or rather settle into a new normal. She knew where she would go before she went to ID Keith and see Josiah.

Emotionally and physically drained, Josiah entered the State Medical Examiner's building. He didn't see

Ella's Jeep out in the parking lot, so he would wait for her in the lobby. Thomas would be here soon, too.

As he stared out the double glass doors, he realized that now that he'd had time to think, he wanted to move on in his life. Seeing what Ella had gone through for years, all he wanted to do was be there for her and give her a life that would erase her ex-husband from her memories. He'd seen firsthand what anger could do to a person if left to fester and grow. He didn't want that for his life.

As he'd accompanied Thomas and trudged all over the island with Buddy looking for the campsite, they had talked. He'd finally shared his captivity with his best friend. Through Thomas's guidance, he'd given his rage at his captors to the Lord. He never wanted to hate someone so much that he ended up consumed like Keith.

He caught sight of Ella. He held one of the doors open for her, and she entered the building. When she turned toward him, he sucked in a deep breath. She was beautiful inside and out. She gave him hope for the future.

"Are you ready to ID him?" he asked, clasping her hand.

She nodded. "Let's get this over with."

When she saw Keith's face, all she said to the ME was "Yes."

Thomas came into the room as she turned away.

"Thomas, you look as tired as Josiah."

"I've hiked miles the past two days, and I'm ready for a rest. Sorry I'm late. I was turning in the evidence we found at Keith's campsite."

"All Keith said to me was I should have realized I

would never escape him completely. He mentioned the story about Seth's rescue at Eagle River and said that I should quit worrying about people besides myself."

"We found a copy of the story written in the newspaper with a photo where you appeared in the background. Not the same one that was on the TV channel. But that had to be how he discovered where you were." Josiah settled his arm on her shoulders.

Thomas frowned. "He bribed an airport employee for David's flight plan that day you all left for the island."

Ella tensed. "Is the employee still alive?"

Thomas's eyes hardened. "Barely. He was left for dead."

Beneath Josiah's arm, she relaxed the tightness in her shoulders. "I'll pray he makes it. Keith liked to tie up loose ends, and I'm glad he didn't succeed here."

"Your ex-husband's death has been ruled an accident. He'll be buried tomorrow. Everything is over, Ella." Thomas smiled. "Now you two can get on with your lives."

His best friend zeroed in on Josiah's face, his look practically shouting what he meant, especially when he looked back and forth between Ella and Josiah.

"We're leaving," Josiah said. With Ella beside him, he walked into the hallway.

Out in the parking lot, he grasped both of Ella's hands to stop her from getting into her Jeep. "You're a sight for sore eyes, and I really mean sore. I didn't sleep an hour last night. I couldn't rest until any danger of Keith's weapons being found by someone and being used illegally was taken care of." He inched closer. "Now you and I need to talk about our future."

He half expected her to say, "What future?" but she

grinned, her eyes bright. She cupped his cheek. "I like the sound of that. I was a little late because I went to church to pray and ask God to help me let go of my anger toward Keith. By the time I left, I felt it lifted from me. He paid the price for his evil. I won't give him the satisfaction of influencing my life for one more second. I want to spend that life with you. I love you."

He brushed his lips over hers and whispered against them, "I love you, too, with all my heart."

Ella wound her arms around him and deepened the kiss. When she finally pulled away, she said, "I'm here for you. I know with help you can move on—"

He pressed his fingers over her lips. "I came to that conclusion when I saw the extremes a person can go to for revenge. It takes over your life and destroys it as much as you want to destroy the other person."

"No matter what, you would never turn into Keith. You aren't capable of that. You want to help others. He wanted to harm them. You two are worlds apart, and I know that now. For a long time I doubted my ability to really know a person. I thought I did with Keith, and look what happened."

He kissed the tip of her nose. "I want to marry you. We can wait as long as you need, though."

"I don't want to wait any longer. I've been waiting a lifetime for someone like you."

He lifted her against him and swung her around, laughter pouring from him. "Then we aren't waiting anymore. Let's go let Alex and Robbie know to prepare for a wedding soon."

EPILOGUE

Two months later

Josiah put his arm around Ella and approached the elegant restaurant. "We're finally having that special dinner I promised you at Celeste's."

She looked at him, a smile deep in her eyes. "*Special* is the right word. This was the perfect place to have our wedding reception, but you didn't have to buy out the whole place for the night."

"Yes, I did. We have a lot of people who care about us."

When they entered, a sea of familiar faces greeted them with a round of applause and a few loud whistles.

Robbie broke away from Ella's parents, who had come to Alaska for the wedding, and hurried to his mom and hugged her. Then Robbie threw his arms around Josiah. "What took you all so long?"

"You couldn't have been here long. You left the church with your grandparents ten minutes before us." Josiah clasped his shoulder. "Are you going to be all right for a week with your grandparents while your mom and I are away on our honeymoon?"

Robbie grinned. "Yes, I'm going with them to show them the sights of Alaska. I warned them about seeing bears and moose. It didn't seem to bother Grandpa, but Nana isn't so sure about the trip now. Grandpa said that she'd change her mind."

"It's hard to come to Alaska and not see the wonders. I think she'll come around, too."

Robbie signaled for Josiah to lean down, then whispered in a serious voice, "Can I call you Dad now?"

The question stunned Josiah. He'd hoped Robbie would want to one day, but he hadn't expected it so soon. "I'd be honored if you would."

"Thanks, Dad."

"Josiah, we need to greet our guests." Ella touched his arm, the elated look on her face indicating she'd heard what her son had said.

In front of two hundred people, Josiah couldn't resist kissing his wife of an hour. He drew her into his arms and kissed his bride for a second time that night before an audience.

* * * * *